FATHER COMPLEX

HAZARD AND SOMERSET: ARROWS IN THE HAND

BOOK 4

GREGORY ASHE

H&B

Father Complex
Copyright © 2022 Gregory Ashe

Published by Hodgkin & Blount
https://www.hodgkinandblount.com/
contact@hodgkinandblount.com

Published 2022
Printed in the United States of America

Version 1.03

Trade Paperback ISBN: 978-1-63621-033-9
eBook ISBN: 978-1-63621-032-2

CHAPTER ONE
APRIL 10
FRIDAY
7:26 PM

"ARE YOU BLIND?" Hazard shouted. He was halfway out of his seat, and his husband, John-Henry Somerset, was trying to pull him back down. "Come on!"

"Ree," Somers said, pulling harder this time.

Hazard sat, but he waved at the baseball field. He directed his words at the umpire, who was pretending he couldn't hear him. "That pitch was wide!"

"You're being that parent."

"I'm not being anything, John. I'm asking a simple question."

Somers sighed. He was blond and beautiful, still in his uniform as chief of police but with the coat over one knee and his tie and top button undone. The spring night was mild, almost warm. The air smelled like clay and new grass and hot dogs kept warm in disposable trays. A few insects drifted in the beams from the halide lights. The ballast buzzed, providing a background to the sounds from the bleachers: the hub of voices, the shift of bodies, the aluminum planks chiming under children's running footsteps, the whisky-voiced murmur and scratch of a pencil from Susan Jinks, who had scored every home Wahredua Wildcat baseball game since 1979, including, according to local legend, the time they'd had to move a game up, and she'd rushed straight over from getting a permanent and worn a plastic bag over her head to protect it from the rain.

"I just want to know," Hazard said—loudly enough, to judge by the increased tension in the umpire's shoulders, to be heard—"why he can't see what's right in front of him?"

"It was only his first strike," Noah, their neighbor and newly drafted member of the Colt Kimble Ballantyne Baseball Fanatics, said. The members of their group shifted from game to game, but there were recurring appearances: Noah, his wife, Rebeca, and their kids; Somers's former partner, Dulac, and his boyfriend, Darnell; Hazard's ex-boyfriend and current administrative assistant, Nico; Somers's ex-wife, Cora; and Auggie, whose partner, Theo, was one of the assistant coaches. That was a recent development, since the previous coaching staff had been removed after Nico had turned up some details about them in an investigation months before. Tonight, the Fanatics had all turned out, probably because it was the first perfect spring night of the year.

"It wasn't a strike," Hazard said. He turned to face Noah. "It was a ball."

"Right, but the ump—"

"It was outside the strike zone."

"I know; I saw it too. But the ump—"

"Therefore, Noah, it was a ball."

"Emery, stop bullying Noah," Rebeca said. "You're going to miss it."

Hazard turned his attention forward. His foster-son, Colt, was readying himself for the next pitch. He was tall and lean; he'd come to them half-starved, but he was adding on weight and muscle at the expense of Hazard's grocery budget. Good stance, Hazard thought. Loose, but with a little anger wired through him now because of that first strike. That was good too. The next pitch spun through the air.

"Strike two!" the umpire called.

Hazard shot up from his seat, knocking aside his husband's attempt to restrain him. "Are you kidding me?"

In the next section of bleachers, a man called down toward home plate, "Who let the whiffer on the team?"

Hazard started to shrug off his jacket.

"No, no, no," Somers said. His fingers locked tight around Hazard's wrist. "Do not make me get out the handcuffs."

"I'm not going to say anything," Hazard said, still trying to work Somers's grip loose. "I'm just going to show him all the possibilities of a baseball bat."

"Ree!"

The urgency made Hazard turn back to the game. That anger was steel now, stiffening Colt's spine. The boy still had his gaze locked on the pitcher.

"Wait for it," Hazard called down. "You're swinging too early. Let it come to you."

"Whiffer," the man in the next section called.

Hazard opted, in that moment, for compartmentalization. One part of him would stay fully focused on the game. The other part would enjoy vividly estimating how far he could get a baseball bat down that asshole's esophagus before it ruptured.

As the pitcher wound up, Colt tensed. The ball blurred through the air.

"Strike three! You're out!"

"Good swing, Colt!" Hazard shouted. Then he dropped back into his seat. Shoulders slumped, Colt made his way to the dugout. He passed his best friend, Ashley, on the way, and they traded fist bumps. Under the helmet, Ashley wore a mixture of commiseration and excitement; after all, it was his turn now. Ashley's parents, Brendon and Anais Boone, sat a few rows down from the Colt Kimble Ballantyne Baseball Fanatics; they didn't turn around to offer Hazard and Somers any show of sympathy or understanding, the way many of the team parents did. They were focused on their son, which was part of the reason. The rest, Hazard knew, was his own fault.

As Ashley took his place at the plate, Hazard asked, "What kind of hitting practice are they doing?"

"You know what they're doing," Somers said. "You've been email-blasting the whole coaching team with those YouTube videos. That last one was when I was trying to do my supervisor training course, remember?"

Hazard did, in fact, remember; the supervisor training course had been an important first step in helping his husband learn how to manage his new responsibilities. He opted, however, to focus on what was important in the moment: "I meant, what kind of hitting practice are they doing now? Based on the new information I provided."

Somers rubbed that spot in the center of his forehead. "I don't know. I don't care. You should know; you cornered Coach Herrera last week after a game, and then you showed up at Theo's house uninvited."

"He had diagrams," Auggie stage-whispered from his seat next to Rebeca. Young, strikingly handsome—his dark hair and dark eyes complemented his smooth brown skin—he had a magnetic kind of attraction that Hazard found annoying as fuck. Auggie wore a wicked grin. "One of them was about deceleration, I think."

"Oh my God," Noah groaned.

Rebeca smirked.

"So many parabolas," Auggie said.

This time, Somers groaned.

"Bro," Dulac said, leaning in behind Hazard to clap him on the shoulder, "you're totally right: that ump is a fucking piece of shit."

7

Hazard grimaced and nodded. But, for form's sake, he said, "Language."

As though on cue, half of Noah and Rebeca's passel of children thundered across the bleachers, the aluminum planks shivering under them.

"I'm serious," Dulac said. The detective was young, handsome, and had a bewilderingly innocent appearance completely at odds with what was underneath—Hazard blamed it on the freckles. He'd looked better the last couple of months; in February, he'd hit some sort of rough patch with Darnell, and he'd spiraled into drinking and depression. Tonight, though, his eyes were clear, and his color was good. "I'm going to talk to that ass— that guy after. I'm going to let him know he needs to get his eyes checked."

"All right, honey." That was Darnell. He was a big man with a big beard, in flannel and jeans and boots that didn't fit his remote-Silicon Valley career, which was probably the whole point. He put his hand on Dulac's knee. "Let it go now."

Dulac nodded, and he waited almost long enough for most people to turn away. Hazard only saw by chance, glancing back, when Dulac's expression flattened and he moved Darnell's hand away.

"You're being too hard on him," Nico said. The younger man, with his shaggy-but-somehow-more-adult-now dark hair and flawless copper skin, looked surprisingly mature in a sweater and jeans and white kicks. He spoke without looking up from a sketchpad where he and Cora were studying something. "I dated this guy whose kid played Little League—"

"Oh, did you?" Hazard asked. "Because you've only mentioned it every time you've come to one of Colt's games. So I wasn't sure."

"—and trust me, kids hate when their parents yell stuff at them. Especially when they're at bat."

"So, you just kind of power through it?" Cora murmured. "When he yells at you like that?"

"God, yes, otherwise I'd never get any work done."

"Ha ha, mother—" Hazard cut himself off.

"One time it was something about the electric bill—I have no idea what—and his face got red, and we had a client invoice that had to go out that day, certified mail—"

"You have no idea what I was yelling about? You left the lights on, Nico. All of them. Do you think electricity is free? Do you think I'm looking for ways to throw away my hard-earned money?"

"—and so I put in these concert ear plugs, and voila, it's like magic. I was actually more productive than usual. I told him he should teach a class."

Somers lifted his head. His face was horrified.

"Do not," Hazard growled at him.

"That's why there were, like, eight variations in your search history of, 'Is there already a course on motivating by yelling?'"

"I said do not!"

Auggie and Noah and Rebeca burst into laughter; a smile tugged at Nico's lips, but he pretended to be focused on the sketchpad. Cora leaned past him to squeeze Hazard's arm. He couldn't exactly bare his teeth and snarl, so he let her get away with it.

"We all love you, Emery," she said. "You're just too much fun to tease."

"I'll show you how much fun I am—"

The pop of wood connecting with rawhide cut him off, and a cheer went up through the crowd. Ashley sprinted toward first base. Brendon and Anais were out of their seats, screaming with excitement. Hazard's eyes cut away from the crowd to find his son in the dugout. Colt was shouting too, pumping an arm, but Hazard knew him well enough to see the envy there, the wish.

Somers wrapped his hand around Hazard's knee and squeezed. When Hazard looked over, Somers wore a small, tight smile.

"He'll be fine," Somers said, barely loud enough for Hazard to hear him over the excitement. "Don't worry so much."

Sure, Hazard thought, but his eyes drifted back to his son. The halide lights left the dugout under a skein of shadow. Colt's short hair—no longer quite as short as it had been—stuck up in tufts from sweat and the helmet. Dirt stained his uniform; he'd jumped for a fly ball and taken a dive. He had one hand wrapped around the chain-link fence that ran along one side of the dugout, and Hazard had the strangely disorienting realization that his hand was a man's hand, and that his son, whom he'd had less than a year, was in his own kind of sprint toward adulthood, that it was happening when Hazard wasn't looking, that one day he'd blink and the boy would be gone.

"Ree?" Somers asked. "Hey, what—"

Hazard shook his head, and Dulac leaned between them to shout something, and the moment was lost—the universe kicking it like a tin can down an alley.

When the game ended, the Wildcats won. The celebration was splintered, though, because two of Noah and Rebeca's kids—Rafe and Roman—tumbled up the bleachers crying, their faces smudged with dirt and tears, the heel of Roman's hand scraped raw.

"This is why I said we shouldn't come on a school night," Rebeca said between breaths as she blew on Roman's hand.

"You said the kids would be tired the next day," Noah said. He spoke in that low, taut tone of a couple not-fighting in public.

"Which is why we shouldn't have come."

"If you didn't want to come, that's what you should have said, not that the kids would be tired the next day."

"We'll see you later," Rebeca said, looking up into the middle distance of the group—not meeting anyone's eyes was part of the polite fiction of the moment.

"I'll help you," Auggie said. He already had Rocio riding piggyback, and he caught Roman's uninjured hand and pretended to get electrocuted. That made Roman giggle and forget about the near-life-ending scrape on his palm. "Come on, Theo's going to be forever."

"And I've got to get Evie from my mother's," Cora said. "Don't tell her Colt had a game; she'd die if she knew she had to spend time with Grandma instead, but Grandma wasn't going to take no for an answer. She's practically swooning at the thought of Evie being a flower girl."

Hazard opened his mouth and stopped when Somers not so gently stepped on his foot. The question of Evie being a flower girl had become, over the last couple of weeks, a hotly contested topic around their house. Cora's sister, Naomi, was getting married to a man named Landon Maas, one of the rising stars of the neo-Nazi-lite Ozark Volunteers. The announcement had taken the county by surprise, including the Hazard and Somerset family. Somers's position was that Evie was Cora's daughter too, and Cora had a right to include her in her family's events. Hazard's admittedly less solid ground could be summed up as *No fucking way*.

"Do you want to finish this tonight?" Nico asked, gesturing at the now-closed sketchbook.

"I'd better not," Cora said. She bussed cheeks and headed down the bleachers with a final wave over her shoulder.

"Do you guys want to go to St. Taffy's?" Dulac asked.

"Gray—" Darnell began.

"Right, right." Dulac wore a hard smile. "Never mind. God forbid we have any fun."

Darnell turned and headed down the steps, the aluminum frame ringing out under his hammer-blow steps. Dulac rolled his eyes, shook his head, tossed them a smile like they were all in on the joke, and trailed after him.

"That," Nico said, chafing his arms even though the night was still pleasant, "is why I keep telling you I'm fine with not being in a relationship."

Hazard snorted.

"I'm serious, Em. John-Henry, tell him."

Somers frowned. "Ree, you don't have to be in a relationship to have a happy, fulfilling life. I'm surprised you're not the one making that point to Nico."

"Who's talking about happy?" Hazard said. "He came to work this week with his sweater on inside out."

"Ok, but—"

"Twice."

"Oh my God, Em, I told you: the second time I did it on purpose. It was a fashion statement."

Hazard snorted again.

The bleachers were emptying rapidly, and on the field, the coaches had finished their after-game bitchings. The players from both teams were grabbing gear and lugging it toward the school.

"I guess I should get home," Nico said.

When Hazard didn't respond, Somers gave him a curious look and, in a carefully neutral voice, said, "It's getting late."

"I've got to be up early tomorrow. Even though it's Saturday, I've got work. And I've already got 7.14 demerits this month, so I can't be late."

"How do you get 0.14 demerits?"

"I think it was a relative clause."

"Ok, but—actually, back up. You have demerits?"

"They're not called demerits," Hazard said. "They're called infractions."

"Dear Lord."

"They're part of a new incentive system."

"Nico, go home." Somers rubbed his eyes. "Get some rest. And Godspeed."

Nico nodded. He stood there another moment, shifting his weight, hands rubbing his arms. Then he gave a little wave, low, from the hip, and his shoulders hitched up as he started down the steps.

"And the 0.14 was orthographic," Hazard said. "We've talked about that."

Nico glanced over his shoulder. His mouth moved in an Etch-a-Sketch smile, and then it dissolved like someone had given him a good shake.

"Well," Somers said, "do you want to pick a fight with Colt's coaches now, or is that more of a weekend-ambush type of thing?"

"You act like it's a criminal offense to have a passing conversation on someone's doorstep."

"Is that what they call it at eight in the morning?"

Hazard could sense the trapdoor in that question, so instead of answering, he scoured the field. The boys from the Wildcats formed a straggly line of twos and threes that snaked up to the school's main building. Even in the gloom, Hazard could pick out Colt; he and Ashley were lugging a pitching net between them. Ashley said something, and Colt shook his head. Hazard had seen it enough times to recognize the gesture as annoyed but unwillingly amused. Ashley said something else, and Colt tried to kick him in the ass—playfully wide and telegraphed. Ashley laughed so loudly Hazard could hear him from the bleachers. The whole thing looked like something from one of Somers's stupid *Three Stooges*, with the boys trying to keep the pitching net from falling while Ashley dodged and Colt tried to nail him.

"God, they are definitely teenagers," Somers said.

They followed the stragglers up the hill to the parking lot. Some of the parents mingled and chatted, but most of them piled into family vehicles— minivans, crossovers, mammoth SUVs—and drove away, their headlights cutting arcs through the night. Somers was watching one group of parents who lingered. They were clearly the popular set: expensive clothes, expensive cars, and, for the women, expensive hair and nails.

"You can go talk to them if you want," Hazard said. "I'll wait here."

Somers shook his head. He wore a crooked smile. "I don't think they'd appreciate the chief of police popping in to say hi."

"Please. You'd have them eating out of your hand in five minutes. Go talk to them; I know you want to. It won't bother me."

"That's not exactly my crowd anymore, Ree. Or your crowd, I don't think."

"John, I'm not—"

"They're part of that gang that held up the last school board meeting."

Hazard frowned and looked more closely. Nothing immediately gave the parents away—no devil's horns, no swastika patches, no visible tails. But then, that didn't necessarily mean anything. A few weeks before, a group of parents had shut down a school board meeting. They had thronged the school gym, where the meeting was being held, chanting things like SAVE OUR KIDS and STOP THE SHAME. It had escalated, in spite of efforts by the school board president to bring the meeting under control, until the board had finally withdrawn. Or, as they'd put it in the next day's Wahredua *Courier*, until the board had run for their lives.

When Hazard glanced at his husband, Somers shrugged. "Like I said, not exactly my crowd."

The conversation between the parents was too quiet to overhear, but they were animated, and Hazard doubted they were talking about the tepid baseball game they'd watched. One of them, a square-headed guy with a patchy beard, said something, and then heads swiveled to stare at Hazard and Somers.

"Good game, right?" Somers called across the asphalt.

"Smooth," Hazard muttered.

"I don't care if they know I'm watching them. Maybe they'll be a little better behaved."

No one answered, and the moment stretched. Then the double doors to the gym banged open, and boys spilled out into the night, laughing and shouting over each other, still flushed with the thrill of victory. Colt and Ashley reached Hazard and Somers a few minutes later. Both boys had changed into shorts and tees. Both boys also obviously needed showers.

"Good game," Somers said.

"Can I spend the night at Ash's?"

"Did you hear John?"

"Yeah, thanks. Can I?"

"Well—" Somers began.

"No," Hazard said. "You've got a volunteer shift at the shelter in the morning."

Colt shook his head. "They texted me and said I didn't need to come in because they've got something else going on."

"Then you can pick up an extra shift at work. Or you can get in some study time; you've only got six weeks before the ACT."

"I don't need to pick up an extra shift. J-H doesn't need me, and I paid you guys back."

"Great. Sounds like you'll be studying."

"Ash can take me home first thing in the morning."

"No. Get in the van."

"Oh my God, why can't I—"

"Because I'm telling you no. You've barely been home this week. When you're there, it's only long enough to inhale food and go to sleep. You're coming home, you're getting a good night's sleep, and tomorrow, you're going to catch up on all the stuff you should have been doing that got pushed to the side so you could play five games this week. That includes chores."

Somers was making a barely audible groaning noise.

Ashley was staring at his slides.

The muscles in Colt's jaw were visible, straining. Then he managed one word: "Fine."

"How about tomorrow, Bubs?" Somers asked with a questioning look at Hazard. "After the game tomorrow."

"Yeah," Ashley said, looking up and pushing back jaw-length auburn hair. His voice had a slight huskiness to it and a twang. "That'd be fire."

"Whatever," Colt said. "Sorry, Ash."

"No, bruh, it's—"

"Sorry my pops is being a dick for absolutely zero fucking reason."

"Ok," Somers said. "There must be a full moon or something because everybody is having a night."

"Get in the van," Hazard said.

"Fine." But Colt didn't move.

"Get in the van right now!"

"I said fine! Are you going to move, or do I have to walk around?"

The parking lot had grown silent except for the faint, whiskering brush of tires from the next street. Hazard kept his gaze locked on an empty patch of air between Colt and Ashley; he could feel eyes on him. He yanked open the driver's door and got into the Odyssey.

"Goodnight, Ashley," Somers said. "Drive safe, please."

"Yes, sir, Chief Somerset."

Colt grabbed the passenger door handle. He pulled, but the door was locked. Then he pulled again. And again. And again.

"Cut it the fuck out," Hazard snapped as he jammed the unlock button.

The door slid open, and Colt climbed inside.

"Night, bruh," Ashley said, sounding decidedly miserable.

In the rearview mirror, Hazard caught Colt's expression: a mixture of fury and embarrassment and indignation.

Then Somers got in the car, and they shut their doors, and Hazard backed out of the parking stall. The stereo picked up the Bluetooth from Somers's phone, and Gillian Welch—along with someone else—was halfway through telling them her big plans about flying away. Away from these prison walls. Away from these iron shackles. Somers reached over and turned the music off.

It wasn't a long drive, but it felt long. Every red blinker. Every stop sign. Hazard hadn't kept up to date on the best practices for transporting dangerous goods, but he understood, at that moment, why some truck drivers and railroad operators did stupid things sometimes. If you kept driving, if you didn't slow down or speed up, if you didn't change anything at all, maybe shit wouldn't explode.

"That was an amazing catch in the second inning," Somers said. "I couldn't believe you made that one."

Behind Hazard, Colt must have moved slightly; he could hear the whisper of fabric against the upholstery, the plastic click of something adjusting in the seat's base. When Colt spoke, his voice was coiled. "I still can't get a fucking hit nine times out of ten."

"You're working on it, bubba. You're getting better."

"That wasn't your fault," Hazard said. "That umpire was a joke. Half of those strikes should have been balls."

Colt made a disgusted noise.

"If you'd had a couple more swings—"

"Don't," Colt said. "Jesus."

Hazard's whole face was hot. He was aware of his hands. His vision tunneled, and he focused on the road ahead of them, looking for their street. They rolled through the next stop, and Hazard ignored Somers's raised eyebrow. Dangerous goods, motherfucker. Can't stop, won't stop.

He forced his voice to normalcy and tried again. "Did you finish your poetry project?"

The silence dragged on for five seconds, then ten. Then Colt bit out, "Yes."

"Have you been studying for the driving test?"

"Yes."

"Tomorrow, in the test prep book, I want you to do another chapter on algebra—"

"What is it with you and that stupid test?"

"That stupid test—" Hazard started to say, his volume already slipping.

"Uh uh," Somers said, and he said it low, barely loud enough for Hazard to hear, but firmly.

Hazard blew out a breath.

But Colt pressed on. "Maybe I don't even want to take it."

Somers shook his head, but Hazard ignored him. "You have to take it."

"I don't have to."

"You do if you want to go to college."

"Maybe I don't want to go to college."

"What the fuck gave you the idea that college was negotiable?"

"You can't tell me—"

"I absolutely fucking can!"

"Ok," Somers said. "That's it. That's time. Everybody's going to stop talking for the rest of the night."

"Do you have any idea what your life—"

"Emery!"

Hazard managed to close his mouth. The skin of his knuckles was so tight it felt like it might split.

In the rearview mirror, Colt was staring out the window, wiping his cheeks.

When Hazard parked in the garage, Colt shot out of the van and into the house. Somers popped his door open, but when Hazard didn't move, he leaned back in the seat. After a moment, Hazard let his head fall against the glass. He stared out at the pegboard: the rakes, the pruning shears, the hand trowel. All neatly outlined in black marker where they should go. Everything fitting. Everything in the right place.

"Ok," Hazard said. "What did I do wrong this time?"

Somers's intake of breath was a qualifier. But all he said was, "You didn't let him do what he wanted to do. That's not a crime, Ree; he'll get over it."

"Come on."

"It got out of hand," Somers said. "That happens to everyone. Don't beat yourself up about it."

Does it, Hazard wanted to ask. Does it happen to everyone? Does everyone feel like they open their mouth and someone else is speaking for them? Does everyone feel like they're in the back seat, watching a stranger drive them into a brick wall?

The automatic headlights blinked off.

"Yeah," he said and unbuckled himself.

They'd been gone all day, both of them, so Hazard headed down the driveway. He was aware of his husband behind him, a question mark in the mouth of the garage, waiting for an answer. But Hazard didn't know the answer. He wasn't even sure he knew the question. Why, maybe. Somers would want to know why. Why did you say no when he wanted a sleepover? Not the bullshit reason you gave him, but the real one, the deep down one. Why did you keep pushing? Why did you keep making it worse?

Hell, Hazard thought. Fuck me if I know. Ask the midnight fucking driver.

"Ree?"

"Grabbing the mail."

The mailbox door stuck; Hazard had to pull harder on his second try, maybe too hard, because the mailbox and the post it was mounted on rocked forward. He grabbed the mail, closed the mailbox—it stuck again, but he wasn't willing to give it another go, not with Somers standing there, not with that low-pressure silence trying to vacuum something out of him.

They went inside, Hazard first, Somers a step behind him. There'd been a bad guy in one of those action movies when Hazard had been a kid. His leotard—or whatever you called a villain's spandex suit—had been covered in question marks. Well, fuck, Hazard thought as he flipped on the lights in the kitchen, here we are. Everything comes around again.

He flipped through bills, a Pendleton catalog, a postcard from a local dentist advertising a cheap cleaning for new customers. Then he stopped at a small envelope. The handwriting was crabbed, a cobbled-together penmanship of upper- and lower-case letters. The return address was for the Jefferson City Correctional Center.

"One of us needs to go to the store tomorrow," Somers was saying as he opened the refrigerator, "because I don't know if we'll have a chance before Colt's birthday—" He stopped when he turned around. The door swayed slightly, betraying the involuntary motion of his hand. "What?"

"Danny Lee," Hazard said. His tongue felt fuzzy, too thick, like he'd had a bad trip to the dentist and gotten sloppy with Novocain. Maybe the new one. Maybe the one who'll clean your teeth for $49.95.

Too late, he sensed the presence in the opening to the living room.

Colt's face was bloodless. "Is that from my dad?"

CHAPTER TWO
APRIL 11
SATURDAY
8:36 AM

SOMERS WAS GETTING HOME from a run when his smartwatch chimed and showed an incoming call. He slowed to a walk, stretching his back, as Dulac's name flashed on the screen.

"Morning, Gray."

"Bro, I mean, Chief, uh, I think you should come down here."

"Look, if it's about Carmichael, I told her she couldn't keep putting up those posters at work, and I told her to keep that kind of talk out of the station. But I can't control what she says or does when she's off duty."

"No, dude, it's not that, although she does have more of that Bright Lights, neo-Nazi propaganda taped to her desk again; I saw it this morning. Something about America for Americans, and she doesn't mean Native Americans. I'm talking about this murder we caught."

Somers stopped on the porch. He'd gotten the call about the bodies, which was standard procedure because it was a small town and because he didn't like to get caught unaware, but he'd let the detectives on duty respond—part of a relatively new project that he called *Trying to have some sort of work-life balance and not burn out and lose my goddamn mind.*

One of the things his supervisor training manual drove home again and again was that the supervisor wasn't supposed to do everything himself— even if less than a year ago, for the sake of example, the supervisor had been the department's star detective. The manual also had something to say about employees who called their supervisor bro and dude, but Somers had dog-eared those pages for later. He'd already had two hard conversations with Dulac: the first about Dulac's drinking and his unprofessional appearance at work, and the second about Dulac's partnership with Palomo. If he tried to take away bro and dude—right now, anyway—Dulac might implode. To be fair, Somers had also had a hard conversation with Palomo—they had agreed to start over, both of them. After all, Somers had hired her because she was an excellent detective, and he recognized his own failure to support her when she first started.

One step at a time, Somers told himself as he adjusted the phone against his ear. "Gray, I'll come down there if you ask me to. But I'm not a detective anymore, and I'm not your partner. If this is about you not wanting to work with Palomo—"

"Bro, Chief, no. It was her idea. Hold on."

The phone changed hands, and a woman's voice, perfectly neutral, perfectly modulated, came on the call. "Chief Somerset, good morning."

"Good morning, Detective Palomo. What's the situation?"

"Well, sir, it's clearly a double homicide. Dr. Boyer has already come, and we're waiting for her to make it official. But I thought you might want to see the scene before she moves the bodies. And, frankly, sir, I thought you might want to stick your oar in on this one. It's complicated."

A couple of months before, Yolanda Palomo wouldn't have made that remark—not unless she was trying to save her own hide. She was a climber, as Dulac put it, and she had a keen sense of when to press her advantage and when to cover her ass. Now, Somers wasn't sure what her motive was, but another thing the manual had reinforced was his responsibility to be a leader and a team-builder, even when it was hard. "How so?"

"One of the victims is Landon Maas."

He saw, again, Cora's face in the zebra-stripe of the baseball field's halide lights, her comment about Naomi's wedding. "Christ, are you sure?"

"Yes, sir. He's well known; the responding officers and Detective Dulac recognized him on sight."

"Great. Exactly what this town needs—for the Ozark Volunteers' Prince Charming to get murdered." Somers regretted the words; Palomo might not be recording this conversation, not on Dulac's phone, but he had no doubt she was filing the words away. "And the other victim?"

"According to personal effects in the room, sir, he's Zachary Renner."

"I don't know that name."

"He's not local, Chief." Palomo hesitated. Then she said, "His family is prominent in Missouri politics, sir. They're located in St. Louis, but they have reach."

Of course, Somers thought. Of course Palomo knew that. Hell, she was half politician already. "What was he doing here? For that matter, what were they doing in the same room?"

"That's not clear, sir."

Somers swore under his breath. So much for breakfast. So much for replacing the siding on the back of the garage. So much for a nap.

From inside the house came Hazard's bellow: "I don't care if it's Saturday. Get your ass out of bed; it's time to get up."

At least, Somers thought as he let himself into the house, he wouldn't have to be a one-man bomb squad. "I'll clean up and be there as soon as I can; ask Dr. Boyer to wait on moving the bodies."

They disconnected, and Somers jogged upstairs. He passed Colt in the hall; the boy, in nothing but his sleep shorts, was stumbling toward the bathroom. Somers opened his mouth for a "Morning, bubs," but before he could, Colt gave him a sleepy, dead-eyed look that was the silent equivalent of a snarl. Somers decided to keep his mouth shut. Sometimes, he was smart like that.

He rinsed off quickly in the shower and dressed in jeans and a polo with the Wahredua Police Department's seal on the breast. He was pulling on socks and shoes when Hazard walked into the room.

"Double homicide," Somers said, snugging up the heel of one sneaker.

"That's why you pay detectives."

Somers grinned. "Funny, I said something like that." He stood and kissed Hazard on the cheek. "I'm going to take a look because apparently they're both big deals."

"Anyone's death is a big deal, John. If we don't start with that premise, the justice system is already flawed."

"You know what I mean. What happened? You're already on a tear."

"Nothing." When Somers studied him, though, Hazard's cheeks colored, and he cleared his throat and looked slightly off. "Colt threw the pancakes I made him in the trash. He's, quote, 'not hungry.'"

"Uh huh. Which means in an hour, he's going to be chewing the sheet rock." Somers grimaced. "What's the plan this morning?"

"I was going to get the main floor straightened—"

"No, with him."

"He's got his homework. And his ACT practice."

"How about you let him have the morning off? He'll be grumpy and stomp around, but eventually, he'll eat something, and maybe by then I'll be home."

"What's that supposed to mean?"

20

"You know what it means." Somers kissed his cheek. "Don't let him ruin your day either."

Hazard rolled his eyes. Then he studied Somers. His gaze became predatory. "You just got back from a run."

"Yeah, so?"

"What time did you tell them you'd be there?"

Laughing, Somers shook his head and skirted his husband toward the door. "No way, mister. Not a chance."

Hazard folded his arms. His amber eyes glittered.

"Absolutely not," Somers said, pulling the door shut. He hesitated. Then he said, more firmly than necessary, "No. I'm serious, Ree. No."

The silence on the other side of the door hooked him in the gut. Somers hurried toward the stairs because his willpower was fading fast.

He found Colt downstairs. The boy was curled up on the sofa, shrouded in a blanket, spooning milk and Lucky Charms into his mouth, his eyes fixed on the TV. Some sort of show about paranormal hunters. Someone was making high-pitched noises that sounded like they were experiencing intestinal distress. Apparently that meant a case for the ghost hunter and not Gas-X because a man with complicated headgear— presumably some sort of technology that would help him sense ghosts—got excited and continued to talk over the moaning.

"—when the departed come back, they often choose to remind us that they're very much still with us, no matter what we want to believe—"

"Not hungry, huh?" Somers said.

Colt shoveled more Lucky Charms into his mouth.

"Be nice to him, ok? Please?"

The next bite sounded particularly chompy.

Somers bent and kissed the crown of Colt's head. The boy jerked away, making an angry noise. "Love you, bubba."

"He's an asshole."

"Sometimes. But he's our asshole, and he loves us, and he has so many good qualities, so we're nice to him and we put up with it, right?"

"It's my life. I can do whatever I want."

Somers sighed. "How about this? We'll talk about it when I get back, you and I, and we'll see where we get. How's that sound?"

"He can't tell me what to do."

"Right, well, let's talk about it when I get back. We want what's best for you, that's all." This apparently didn't merit any kind of reply, so Somers decided to try his favorite game of stick-the-fork-in-the-outlet. "Did you open that letter from your dad?"

There was that noise again—that cocktail of disgust and irritation. "He's not my dad."

Sure, Somers thought. Sure. Never mind last night. Never mind the look on your face, or the fact that I could hear you up all night, hear you on the phone, hear you talking to Ashley, hear you pacing. And Hazard had been doing pretty much the same thing in their bedroom: wearing a hole in the floor, winding himself up, spitting out predictions and guesses and curses and threats.

What Somers said was "Well, if you want my opinion—"

"I don't."

In spite of himself, Somers grinned. And then Colt smiled too—a tiny, hurting thing that barely curled the corner of his mouth. He rubbed his eyes and shook his head, and Somers figured in that moment, it was as close to an apology as Colt could get.

"If you want to open it, that's ok. And if you don't want to open it, that's ok too."

Colt offered a one-shouldered shrug. The Lucky Charms were gone; the remaining milk was tinged bluish green. The spoon scraped the bowl as he dragged it crisscross, again and again. In a low voice, he said, "I should throw it away."

"Whatever you want."

The shrill sound of the stainless steel against the tempered glass filled the room for another moment. Then Colt set the bowl down, pulled the blanket over his head, and lay down on the sofa. The guy on the TV was telling a woman—presumably the one with the bad cramps—that her estranged—and presumably dead—father wanted to speak to her. Get in line, Somers thought with a wild laugh building in him that didn't feel like a laugh at all. He scrubbed Colt's hair through the blanket, smiling at the outraged grumble, and headed out through the garage.

He drove across Wahredua in the Mustang with the windows down. The April day was still cool, and the air tasted wet and full of the smells of a world coming back to life. The dogwoods were flowering, pink-and-white confetti fluttering in the morning breeze. The grass was vibrantly green; it made him think of the Emerald Isle. Their neighbor, Horace Tomlinson, was wearing a paisley nightgown as he knelt in a raised flowerbed, bony shanks exposed to queen and country. Maybe they all needed to get outside, Somers thought. Maybe they could go on a family hike. And then he thought how that would go, Hazard and Colt butting heads every step of the way, both of them refusing to back down. They'd end up going seventeen miles in a circle because neither one would quit. Maybe just Evie, Somers thought. He dropped back against the headrest at a red light, tired now. Maybe I'll just take Evie, and the two of them can string up barbed wire in the house.

The Presidential was located in one of those gray areas that blighted every city—a section of town that had once been middle class and had slowly lost jobs and residents, so that now it consisted of tract housing rentals and strip malls with tattoo parlors and CBD shops. The motel itself was a slapdash attempt at a colonial look: two stories of red brick and white columns, possibly intended to make you think of George Washington—if Washington had picked out a matching red asphalt-shingle roof. The sign at the front spelled it out pretty clearly: *Romantic Whirlpool and Fantasy Suites - Weekly and Short Naps.* If anyone stayed weekly, Somers was pretty sure it was to eat a shotgun by Saturday night.

He recognized the department-issued Impala that Palomo and Dulac used, and two black-and-white cruisers also sat in front of the motel. The medical examiner's van was parked across two handicap spaces where the sidewalk sloped down to the parking lot's broken asphalt. At a door on the second-floor exterior corridor, a uniformed officer was standing guard; the mussed black hair looked familiar even from a distance, and Somers tried not to groan as he worked the keys out of the ignition.

When Somers got to the second-floor corridor, Sam Yarmark straightened his posture. The boy kept looking straight ahead, pretending he hadn't noticed Somers yet. Somers wondered if he'd been this bad when he'd been green. Probably, albeit not in the same way. He'd had his own problems.

"Morning, Officer Yarmark," Somers said.

Yarmark snapped a salute. He was still baby faced, although otherwise, he didn't look much like the kid who'd been hired the year before—the minefield of blackheads was gone, and he'd given up on the waxed spikes and was doing something messy with his hair that looked, Somers thought with what might have been a touch of paranoia, an awful lot like what he saw in the mirror most days. "Morning, Chief."

"Were you the responding officer?"

"Officer McGraw and I, sir."

"And where's Officer McGraw?"

"With the clerk, sir. The one who found the body."

"And everybody else?"

"Detectives Dulac and Palomo are inside with Dr. Boyer, Chief. Officers Norman and Gross are in there as well."

"Got the whole gang. Do you have booties?"

Yarmark passed him a box, and Somers put on a pair of disposable shoe covers. He accepted disposable gloves next. Yarmark was trying so hard not to say anything that he was practically vibrating, and Somers finally took pity on him.

"How's the book, Sam?"

"Finished, sir."

"And?"

"Uh, I liked it." It was half question.

"Yeah, it's a good one. We're still on for lunch next Saturday?"

"Yes, sir."

"Good. I want you to bring a list of ten things you learned from the book. They don't have to be things you're going to change or start doing yourself; they might be things you're not going to do, mistakes you're not going to make. And we're going to talk about your continuing education plans. I've got some money to send officers out for training, and if you're interested, there are a couple of workshops I want you to attend."

The smile on Yarmark's face was so big that it must have hurt. "Yes, sir."

"You and McGraw already knocked doors?"

"Yes, sir."

"Good work."

Somers had, up until this point in his career, never had an officer die out of sheer happiness at receiving praise, but he figured Yarmark was in the running, and hell, it was only Somers's first year as chief.

Inside, the smell of death met him—loose bowels and urine and bodies torn open by violence. It was a sewer smell, but worse because something in the animal part of his brain recognized the violation and responded to it. The motel room looked like it had once been painted the same red as the exterior, but unlike the exterior, it had never been touched up, and the years had faded the paint to the color of cooked shrimp. Overhead, fluorescents hummed behind plastic panels; they gave everything in Somers's peripheral vision fluttering rainbow shadows.

The first thing he noticed were the bodies. One lay a few feet from the door. Somers recognized Landon Maas—the Ozark Volunteer darling and his ex-sister-in-law's fiancé. He was a big, blond man, ruddy cheeked in life and now waxy in death. He lay on his back, his Wahredua Wildcats sweatshirt soaked in blood and torn open in at least two places where, Somers guessed, he'd been shot. Around him, the wine-colored shag carpeting was matted with blood. The gallows-humor defense of every cop who's worked homicide said, *At least you can't see the stain.*

The second man lay on the far side of the room, and Somers had a harder time making out details in the weak flicker of the fluorescents. He looked like he was average height, thin, with dark, curly hair long enough to fall over his ears. His features were what Somers would have thought of as somehow European—in this case, slightly aquiline, like something he'd once seen in an oil painting. He lay on his side, facing the door, eyes blank and open in death. More blood soaked the carpet around him. He wore a white bathrobe—and not, Somers guessed, one that the Presidential had provided. It, too, was soaked in blood. It had fallen open enough to show where Renner had been shot in the chest; it also told Somers that the man had possessed that lucky combination of good genes and regular visits to the gym.

Somers took in the rest of the room. The only possible sign of an altercation was an overturned suitcase. The shrimp-colored walls had taken the blood spatter clearly, and Somers wondered if Norman and Gross would be able to make anything of it—the two uniformed officers were the closest thing Wahredua had to a forensics team. Somers could always try calling in the Highway Patrol's specialists, but God only knew when they'd actually get here. The same went for the shoe prints in the shag carpet; he hoped his officers had been smart enough to document everything before adding their own tracks to the mess. Dulac and Palomo stood inside the room, and next to Landon Maas, Dr. Boyer was making notes on a clipboard. Norman and Gross must have been in the bathroom; the light was on, and their low voices carried indistinctly into the main room.

"Well," Somers said, "what have we got?"

Dulac looked at Palomo; his partner was a dark-haired woman, thick across the shoulders and hips, face locked into neutral—as usual. When she spoke, her voice was like a bald tire, nothing to grab on to. "We discussed the victims' identities on the phone. As you can see, the door was not forced, but there are some signs that might indicate a struggle. Considering the identities of our victims, our first thought was either a murder-suicide or that they killed each other, but that doesn't seem to be the case."

Somers's eyebrows went up. "What do you mean, considering the identities of our victims?"

Palomo made a moue, but behind the microexpression lay a familiar smugness. We're starting over, Somers had to remind himself. A fresh start for everybody. And things with Palomo were getting better. Really.

"Chief," Dulac said, "you know Landon."

"Not really," Somers said. "He was ahead of me in school—he was the same grade as Bing." Then he looked at his detectives and the medical examiner and added, "Not that any of you know who he is."

"What are we?" Norman called from the bathroom.

"Chopped liver?" Gross bellowed.

"He was a few years older," Somers said, "so I knew the legend more than I knew the guy. Good athlete. Huge ego. I've run into him around town, but his family was always deep in the Volunteers, and it's not like we had much to chat about."

"Well," Dulac said, "Detective Palomo is referring to his connection to the Volunteers. That's half of the problem we're looking at."

"And I'm guessing the other half is Mr. Renner?"

Palomo cleared her throat; even that sounded self-satisfied. "Mr. Renner and his family are well known for giving to progressive causes throughout the state. That includes progressive politicians, but a lot of it has to do with Mr. Renner himself."

Somers reconsidered the dead man: the fluffy white robe, the precisely cut tangle of curls, the absence of wrinkles. "He was a rich boy turned activist."

"I don't know about turned," Dulac said drily. "I don't think he gave up the money; more like rich boy moonlighting as activist."

"Why was he in Wahredua?"

Dulac made a weird coughing noise; Somers turned and saw the younger detective covering his mouth. In a strained voice, Dulac said, "Detective Palomo?"

Palomo glared at him. Then with a barb in her voice, she said, "Cocks for Glocks."

Somers had to take that one in for a moment.

Dulac burst out laughing. He smothered it almost immediately, but it danced in his eyes, and he was still keeping one hand over his mouth.

"Dear Lord," Somers said. "Run that by me a little more slowly."

"He's the head of a gun safety program called Cocks for Glocks." Palomo's voice was still peeled of any emotion, but a hint of color rose in her cheeks. "From what we could find online, it operates like gun buyback programs—people can surrender firearms, no questions asked, and in return they receive a free sex toy."

"A dildo," Dulac said, dropping his hand to expose a huge grin. "Bro, a legit dildo."

"Not exclusively dildos," Palomo said. The color in her face deepened when Somers looked at her, and she added, "From what I understand, sir."

The bizarreness of the whole thing buzzed at the front of Somers's brain, but in the background, two of the pieces clicked into place. "He was here to protest the gun show."

"Well, not to protest," Dulac said, fighting laughter again. "More like, you know, provide a public service. A lot of those gun nuts are definitely compensating for something."

"Jesus," Somers muttered.

"They might be too shy to ask for help on their own."

"Gray, grow up."

Dulac offered a huge smirk.

"Ok, the Dore County Knife and Gun Show started Wednesday, right?" Somers ticked off days in his head. "Do we have a check-in for Mr. Renner?"

"Wednesday," Palomo said.

"So you think maybe the crazy liberal and the crazy conservative ended up in the same motel room and killed each other," Somers said, considering the room again. "Is this Mr. Renner's room? Can't the son of a rich family afford somewhere nicer than a place that rents rooms for 'naps'?"

Palomo nodded. "It's Mr. Renner's room. We're not sure why he's staying here, but the room is booked through the end of next week. We're also not sure why Mr. Maas is here. But yes, sir, that was our initial theory."

"Let me guess: no murder weapon."

"Bingo," Dulac said.

Dr. Boyer, the medical examiner, spoke up now. She was tall and thin— a look that on a man would have been called gaunt, especially with her hair silvering steadily. "Both men appear to have died from gunshot wounds, although I won't know more until I'm able to conduct the autopsies. As you can see, Mr. Maas was shot twice, once in the abdomen and once in the chest. Mr. Renner was shot once in the chest. The bullets didn't leave exit wounds, so I have hopes of recovering them, or at least the fragments, to give you a better idea of the ballistics involved in this case."

Somers's gaze swept the room. "But you didn't find a gun."

A hint of frustration crept into Palomo's voice. "No, sir."

"If there's a gun in this room—" Gross yelled from the bathroom.

Norman finished for him: "—the dream team will find it."

"Good Christ," Somers said in an underbreath, "why did I ever put them back together?" In a louder voice, he said, "Walk me through what you have so far."

Dulac spoke, looking at Palomo for verification as he ran through the points of the case so far. "The body was discovered a few minutes before six this morning. The Presidential runs on a tight staff, as you can imagine, and overnight, they only have one person working—Kristie Zander. She goes home at six, when Lori Workman comes on. Ms. Zander had gotten several complaints from motel guests about Mr. Renner's alarm; apparently, it had been going off for over an hour, which puts it somewhere around five, and that lines up with what we found when we got here. The clock radio was still going off, and the alarm was set to five AM."

"Let me guess: the overnight clerk took advantage of having somebody else here for a minute to run upstairs and pound on the door."

"That's her story. She says she doesn't leave the motel office at night for anything. They've had robberies, and the clientele doesn't exactly inspire trust. But the sun was coming up, and her coworker was here. She went upstairs to see if the room was occupied and, if not, if she could turn off the alarm. She says she'd tried calling after the first few complaints, but nobody answered. When nobody came to the door, she used her passkey, and that's how she found them. She says she puked, which looks like the truth—you can see for yourself if you look over the railing—and then she called us. She's downstairs with McGraw."

"Have you talked to the other guests?"

"McGraw and Yarmark dragged them all out of bed. There aren't a lot of them at this hour; my guess is that most of the guests come here for a 'nap' and then go home. Palomo and I are going to talk to them again, but McGraw and Yarmark say they all told them the same thing: they didn't hear anything."

"Except the alarm," Somers said drily.

Mouth tight, Dulac nodded.

"Anybody registered in the rooms on either side?"

"No, sir," Palomo said.

"So, nobody wants to help the police." Somers sighed; it was not an uncommon problem in places like this, where resentment toward the force combined with an unofficial code of silence kept people from talking. "Well, like you said, you'll have to talk to them again."

"They don't have security cameras, of course," Dulac said. "But if you can lend us some more uniformed officers, I want to do a sweep today, a big one, and try to find businesses with their own security systems, ATMs with cameras, even check the traffic cameras. A lot of those places have a quick turnover for the recordings, even the digital ones, so the faster we can check them, the better."

"I'll see what I can do. Dr. Boyer, does this line up with what you're seeing so far?"

"As I said, I won't know until I've got them back at my office, but livor is fixed, and rigor is at its peak. There are other factors to consider, but on average, that means the time of death is somewhere between eight and twelve hours ago. I did check their body temperatures when I arrived, and assuming that the room temperature has been consistent and that there are no other unusual conditions, the change in temperature suggests approximately ten hours since death. That was around eight this morning, which puts the window for time of death sometime between eight PM last night and midnight, although it was probably closer to sometime between ten PM and midnight."

Somers nodded; he wondered if that had been Yarmark's first time seeing how body temperature was most frequently taken at crime scenes. If the young officer had never seen a rectal thermometer before, then his education was being completed in all sorts of interesting ways.

"As you can see," Dr. Boyer said, "both men appear to have died close to where they were shot. Mr. Maas was shot twice, which accounts for some of the more extensive blood spatter that you're seeing, but the real reason for that is arterial spray. One of the bullets must have nicked an artery. Mr. Renner's wound was fatal as well, but with less spatter."

Somers squatted to examine the carpet more closely. It was difficult to make out the pattern of droplets against the wine-colored shag, but he could see the difference in quantity, and it was clear that Landon Maas's injuries had left significantly more blood at the scene. More droplets marked the wall near the door. There was a relatively clear space, and then more spatter appeared on the wall, thinning out until it was pretty much gone by the time it reached the door to the bathroom. That, he knew from Hazard's extensive reading about blood spatter analysis—and his even more thorough rehashing of his reading material in bed, no matter how many times Somers plumped his pillow or yawned or reached for the lamp—was called a void pattern, a gap where something blocked the spray.

Indicating the relatively clear spot, Somers said, "The shooter was standing here."

"I saw that first." Norman poked his head out of the bathroom. The balding uniformed officer stabbed a finger at the detectives. "Tell him."

"Don't listen to him," Gross called. "He's grumpy because his gout is acting up again."

"Motherfucker, what did I tell you about talking about my medical conditions?"

"Medical conditions. He's got a padded toilet seat for his hemorrhoids. How's that for a medical condition?"

The two uniformed officers went back to bitching at each other as Somers stood.

"That's our belief as well," Palomo said. "The killer appears to have been standing near the door, perhaps to leave, when he shot Mr. Maas and Mr. Renner."

Somers picked a path across the room, careful to avoid the shoe prints that he'd spotted in the carpeting, and crouched next to Zachary Renner. The front of the robe was soaked in blood, but as Dr. Boyer had explained, the spatter itself seemed to be significantly less than what Somers had seen around Landon's body. In fact, as far as he could tell, there was no visible spatter. That wasn't actually the case, of course; Luminol would probably show a spray of fine, mist-like particles in front of where Renner had been standing. But with smaller caliber gunshot wounds, and particularly the entry wound, the spray was often extremely fine—sometimes invisible without tools or other ways of detecting it.

"Anything in his pockets?"

"What appear to be edibles," Dr. Boyer said. "They'll have to be tested to be sure."

"All right," Somers said. He was starting to rise again when he stopped. He leaned closer to inspect the back of Renner's robe, but the angle was wrong, so he crabbed around the body to get a better look. "How did he get blood on the back of his robe?"

"What?" Palomo asked sharply.

"There are a few droplets here. They're tiny, but they're here."

"On his back?" Dulac asked.

"Stay there," Dr. Boyer said when the detectives started to move. "I don't need everyone clumping up around my bodies." She picked her own path across the room and bent over Renner. Then she made a disgusted noise. "I'd like to say I would have seen this back at the lab, and that's true, but it sounds too much like an excuse. I'm sorry I missed that, Chief Somerset."

"You didn't miss it," Somers said. "You're right; you would have seen it."

"What does that mean?" Dulac drew an invisible line between the bodies. "He had his back turned when Landon got shot?"

"He was turned away," Boyer said. "Perhaps in the process of turning."

"Maybe it's from his injury," Palomo said.

"No," Boyer said.

"They're not the right shape," Somers said. "These aren't droplets that soaked into the robe. You can see the trajectory and the force of impact when they connected; they're elongated."

"Potentially, this gives us the sequence of events. Currently, Mr. Renner is facing the door; it would have been impossible for him to get blood spatter on his back if he'd been killed first. Therefore, it seems most likely that Mr. Maas was killed first, while Mr. Renner was facing the suitcase. A small amount of the spatter made contact with the back of his robe. Then Mr. Renner turned around, and he was killed himself."

"God damn it," Dulac said. "How the fuck did you miss that, you old fucking goats?"

"Watch your fucking mouth," Gross shouted back.

"Go fuck your mother," Norman shouted over him.

"What was he doing?" Palomo asked. "Going through his luggage?"

The suggestion seemed strange until Somers turned and saw the luggage stand behind him and the overturned suitcase. He hesitated. Then, as carefully as he could, he righted the suitcase. Clothing lay in a heap where it had fallen, and he picked through it carefully — there was no telling what might be hidden in there, and Somers didn't want to find out the hard way. He stopped after moving two shirts, cursed himself, and called for Gross and Norman to come photograph the mound of clothes. When they'd finished, he began transferring the pieces to the suitcase again, doing his best to preserve their order. It didn't seem like it would be important, but the whole point of an investigation was that you never knew what was important, sometimes until it was too late. Best practice was to treat everything as though it were significant, document all of it, and hope some of it paid off.

The last articles of clothing, the ones at the bottom of the pile, were a pair of white Calvin Klein briefs. Somers turned them over and swore.

Tiny red stains marked the front.

"Is it spatter?" Palomo asked from her spot near the door. Her voice was strained, and Somers guessed it was killing her to have to watch them pick apart her crime scene.

"I don't think so," Somers said. The stains were round and infinitesimal. On something else — the wine-colored carpet, for example — they'd have been invisible.

Dr. Boyer shook her head. "The shape isn't right. It looks like the suitcase fell or was knocked over shortly after Mr. Renner was shot; the blood spatter, as fine as it was, transferred to the underwear when it landed on the floor."

Somers considered the distance between the body and the luggage rack. "He didn't knock it over when he fell."

"The killer might have dumped it out," Dulac said. "Maybe this was a robbery of some sort."

"Maybe," Somers said. He indicated the set of shoe prints that led from the door. "Someone was clearly in here, and judging from those prints, it was a man, and he walked around. They might belong to Renner or Maas; we'll have to check their footwear. But the fact that the prints are clear and aren't overlapped by additional prints suggest that they belong to the last person who was in this room alive."

"See?" Dulac said. "See? This is why I called you. This is a fucking mess."

"We reached out to Mr. Maas's fiancée after we found the body," Palomo said like a woman tiptoeing over dynamite. "And she said she would arrange for Mr. Maas's son to be cared for. But he still needs to be officially informed of his father's death. The Renner family also needs to be informed. The parents, I mean; Mr. Renner's Facebook profile says he's single. We should contact the local police in St. Louis, right? A personal visit by local police would probably be best."

"That sounds like a good start. You'll need to speak to them eventually, though. They might know something about this."

Palomo glanced at Dulac, and Somers had an idea of which one of them would be making that particular phone call. He rose, and together he and Dr. Boyer moved back across the room. As he passed the door to the bathroom, he paused. It was like any budget motel bathroom anywhere: the worn fiberglass shower pan, the blackened grout, tile running up the walls because it was easier to clean. It was a small room, but standing there, Somers now had an idea of why Norman and Gross had been in there for so long. Zachary Renner apparently traveled with a personal pharmacy — prescription vials covered the countertop, and more filled a dopp kit on the toilet tank. One by one, Norman and Gross were photographing each vial and its contents and then bagging and tagging and logging them. That was pretty much how all police work ended up: a grind of procedure, making sure every box got ticked.

"Anything interesting?"

"Uppers and downers," Gross said. With the exception of a brief split that Somers had engineered, he'd been partnered with Norman for the better part of their careers, and like a lot of married couples, the men had an uncanny resemblance: pot bellies, thinning hair, stretched and sagging polyester, even their mannerisms.

"Mostly uppers," Norman said. "This guy wanted to go, go, go. I've bagged three different scrips of Adderall so far."

"They're all legal," Gross said. "So far, anyway. But I'm telling you, I think this guy could have taken a horse tranquilizer without getting knocked down. He'd be right back up there, doing the Lindy Hop, before you could sneeze."

"The Lindy Hop?" Somers said.

"Go fuck yourself," Gross said with a grin.

"Go fuck yourself, Chief," Norman corrected with a matching smile.

Somers might have followed up on that, but his phone buzzed. He stripped off his gloves, checked the screen, and answered the call, trying not to sigh.

"Hello, Father," he said as he pushed out of the motel room into an oblong of warm April sunlight.

"I want you to get over to the Presidential right now. Now, John-Henry. This minute. It's a little hot-sheet place—"

"I'm at the Presidential, Father. And yes, I'm fine. Thank you for asking."

As usual, the words glanced off Glennworth Somerset's impenetrable armor. "You're already there? Good. I just got off the phone from having the lieutenant governor eviscerate me."

"The lieutenant governor? We haven't even informed the Renners—"

Glenn Somerset's voice sharpened. "The Renners? Edward and Rosemary?"

"I don't know those names, but one of the victims is Zachary Renner."

Dead silence dropped on the other end of the call. When his father spoke again, his voice was tight. "Do you know who the Renners are?"

"I'm starting to get an idea. How much money do they have?"

"Don't be vulgar." A few deep breaths rasped against the receiver. "The Renners did not call the lieutenant governor. The Renners, I'm sure, will have the governor on speed dial, and most likely at least one senator."

"Well, if the Renners didn't send the lieutenant governor after you, who did?" The penny dropped, and Somers swore. "Are you kidding me? Naomi? I know she's got some sway with the Volunteers, but this is too much."

"She doesn't have 'some sway,'" Glenn laid scorn on the words, "with the Volunteers, John-Henry. She owns the Volunteers. Whatever influence she lost after the election, she's more than made up with her performance protecting Dunkie Newcomer." He was referring to a recent killing that Somers and Hazard had investigated—one in which, in fact, Naomi had hired Hazard to prove an Ozark Volunteer was innocent. "Add to that her engagement to Landon Maas, and, as of today, her status as his widow."

"They weren't actually married, Father."

"I'm well aware," Glenn said. "I'm also aware that a little thing like reality won't keep Naomi from using this new development to her own advantage." Another of those deadfall silences came, and then, his voice laid bare in a way Somers had heard only a few times in his life, Glenn muttered, "Good God, this is going to cost me the election."

The silence seesawed. Somers tried, "Father—"

"You'll need to start by finding out why in the hell those two were even in the same room," Glenn said, his voice rough at the beginning but smoothing out as he spoke. "Use whatever resources you need. I have contacts in the Highway Patrol, and, of course, I can speak to Judge Platter if there are issues with obtaining a warrant. Whatever you do, I want you to resolve this, and I don't want anyone to be able to come back and question your decision. Is that clear? Speedy, thorough, and bulletproof, John-Henry."

"It's my department, Father."

"I'm sure you'll find that to be a great comfort when we're both out of a job. Use whatever resources you need and handle this."

The call disconnected.

Yarmark was trying to look like he hadn't heard anything.

"Dads, huh?" Somers said.

"Uh, yes, sir."

Somers slapped the phone against the palm of his free hand a few times. Then he placed the call.

"The avocados have gone bad again."

Somers looked at his watch.

"We needed one for tacos on Tuesday. You bought three. The other two went bad."

"Hi, Ree."

"They're a dollar and change each, John. That's the same thing as throwing money in the trash. Do you realize that our monthly avocado overspending in, let's say, a high-interest savings account—"

"Hey, how do you feel about solving a double murder?"

The caesura was a question back at him.

"I'll tell you about it when I pick you up," Somers said. "See you in a few."

When Somers pocketed his phone, Yarmark's face was carefully neutral.

"Husbands, huh?"

"Yes, sir." Yarmark cleared his throat. "Chief, they've got these little things that you can strap an avocado in, and it stays good a whole lot longer. They look kind of like an avocado themselves. My mom swears by them."

Somers rubbed the center of his forehead.

"Or you can buy chunks of frozen avocado. That's what my Nana does."

"Samuel Yarmark, I cannot handle another smartass in my life."

"No, sir."

Somers tried not to rub that spot on his forehead as he went back into the motel room to give Dulac and Palomo the good news.

CHAPTER THREE

APRIL 11
SATURDAY
10:08 AM

WHILE THE OFFICERS PROCESSED Zachary Renner's motel room, Hazard and Somers headed out to notify Landon Maas's family of his death. After the notification, they would search the house for anything that might help them understand what had happened the night before. As they drove, Hazard listened as Somers explained what they'd learned in the preliminary stages of the investigation. He made a few notes, mostly follow-ups about the forensics—they'd need an expert to confirm what the blood spatter, in particular, had suggested—but mostly he listened.

They drove out of town, and the world opened up around them. Spring was bringing rural Missouri back to life. On the windbreaks, white blossoms weighed down the lines of hawthorn, and when they passed the turnoff to the Butts' place, their tulip tree, early this year, dangled the cup-shaped flowers that gave it its name. Cockspur bristled with white like bits of bone. On either side of the state highway, furrowed fields were freshly planted. Snap beans, maybe. Or corn—corn was a good bet. But it could have been endive or beets; it was too early for Hazard to tell what was going to come up. His mind caught that up, turned it over. He was starting to get his own sense of that. You did what you could, which felt like fuck-all sometimes, and then all you could do was wait and watch and hope.

"Earth to Ree."

The world came into focus again: a rusted body grip trap pitched up against a culvert, a tuft of gray fur caught in the jaws. And then they were past it, the Mustang eating up the miles.

"Ree?"

"I'm listening."

"Great. So you heard that part about organizing your coupons by expiration date instead of first by redemption value and then by cash value?"

Hazard's head swiveled. "Are you out of your mind?"

"It'd be nice to know when I needed to use them." Somers flashed a smile. "What are you thinking about?"

"That I'd be a fucking terrible farmer."

That blunted the smile, and Hazard had the feeling he'd done that a lot to John-Henry Somerset over the few years they'd been together—knocked the edges off grins, pulled the shade down on happy moments. Somers's voice was even as he asked, "Do you want to talk about it?"

Hazard dropped back in the seat and looked forward. Trees crowded together ahead of them, where the road curved around another of the rumpled folds of the landscape. The leaves were new, still small. A late freeze, a hard wind—just about anything could happen.

"Ok," Somers said. "How was Colt after I left?"

"He was fine, John. He was wonderful. We had a reasonable conversation about what happened last night, and then we had another reasonable conversation about college and the lifelong benefits weighed against a relatively minimal initial cost, and then we had yet another, even more reasonable conversation about grades, extracurricular activities, his job, and his personal interests that might turn into stable, rewarding careers." Hazard let his head fall back. He stared at the headliner. "Isn't that great?"

The tires thrummed. They passed under the trees, and the yaw of light and shadow was like falling.

"So, it wasn't great?"

The old urge was there: to attack, to hurt, to be first so it didn't happen to him. Instead, Hazard rubbed his eyes. Then he looked out the windshield, into a tunnel of latticed branches. "We had a huge fight about the ACT practice he was supposed to be doing. I sent him to his room. When I went up there to check, he was dicking around on his phone. When I told him to get to work, he said he didn't know where the book was."

"Please tell me you didn't—"

"I found it stuffed under the floor register. Things went downhill from there."

Somers took a sharp, unhappy breath. Then, with the sound of a man bracing himself, he said, "Ok. That's not the end of the world."

"No." Hazard laughed; the sound felt curdled. "No, I guess it's not."

"Come on, don't beat yourself up. He knows how to push your buttons."

"Yes, well, I'm the adult, so I don't think that's exactly an excuse." Hazard ran his fingers along the Mustang's door. "I understand, at a rational level, that he's a teenager, that his brain isn't fully developed, that he's an amazing kid and that I love him. But sometimes, when we go at it, it's like my brain shuts down. I can't hear what he's saying. I can't even really see him. It's like it's not even me." He gave another of those sour half-laughs. "I knew I had a temper, but I had no idea—" And then helplessness tore the words from him: "I mean, why can't he see that I want what's best for him?"

They drove through the dappled light; it washed over them like a river. Somers reached over and took Hazard's hand. When Hazard trusted himself, when some of the ache of holding himself together had passed, he squeezed his husband's fingers.

"First of all, congratulations," Somers said with a tiny smile. "Saying those words is the final rite of passage for the 'parents of teenagers' club. I think you get a jacket."

In spite of himself, Hazard's lips twitched.

"Second of all, yes, you have a temper, but most of the time, you and Colt get along like a house on fire. He's going through some sort of rough patch, and that's all right; everybody does. It's not exactly a surprise considering—" He stopped the words like he was slamming on the brakes.

"I'm not an amnesiac," Hazard said drily. "I do happen to remember that he got a letter from his piece-of-shit father last night."

"I know, but I wasn't going to bring it up until, well, you know. Until you were ready to talk about it."

"What's that supposed to mean? It happened, John. The letter came in the mail. Colt has it. Those are facts. In what sense would I need to be ready to talk about it?"

Somers shook his head. "How's Colt doing with it?"

"I don't know. Unfortunately, between screaming at me that I'm ruining his life and screaming at me that he hates me and somehow finding time to tell me, in detail, every fucking flaw I have, Colt didn't get the chance to tell me how he's feeling about that fucking letter."

"Could you take it down a notch? I'm on your side, remember?"

Hazard didn't trust himself to answer; he looked out the window, into the darkness of green things.

"What about you?" Somers asked evenly. "How are you?"

The disgusted noise rose in Hazard's throat before he could stop it.

"I mean, what are you thinking?"

"Nothing. Danny Lee is his biological father; there was bound to be some sort of communication. How do you feel about it? You're the one he beat the shit out of."

The words landed a beat after Hazard heard them in his head, too late to call them back. Somers was motionless for a moment. Then he twisted his hand free of Hazard's and wrapped it around the steering wheel. They'd gone a hundred yards before Somers shook his head and said, "Wow."

The next mile was silent except for the tires, the pocked asphalt, the hiss of the vents.

Hazard's phone buzzed, and he checked the screen. He let the call ring its way to voicemail, and then he pocketed it. He rubbed his eyes and, like a footbridge, said, "My mom."

Somers nodded.

"And I'm sorry."

The lines of Somers's shoulders and arms softened. He nodded again.

"Maybe I'm not...ready," Hazard said. "To talk about this. Maybe you were right."

"Huh," Somers said. "Maybe."

Hazard's face heated. Then Somers rolled his eyes, and a small smile tugged at the corner of his mouth.

"I am sorry, John."

"It's all right. I know it's a lot. It's a lot for all of us. But Colt loves you, and whatever happens with Danny Lee, that's not going to change."

Hazard nodded. He watched the woods stream around them, oak giving way to oak, phyllotaxis and venation and morphology. Different, sure, but also the same. Over and over again, the same. That's not going to change, sure, but then again, it might. Everything falls apart. That was the real bitch about thermodynamics: entropy was always increasing. Relentlessly. He closed his eyes. The ripple of light and shadows against his eyelids was a familiar comfort. He had ridden like this, eyes closed, sometimes half asleep or on the cusp of waking, in his father's truck. The hour-long drives to this lake or that one. Fishing. But that had been a long time ago, and that, too, had been different.

Somers, in that way he had, must have known to be silent, because they drove the rest of the way without talking.

When the sound of asphalt under the tires changed to gravel, Hazard opened his eyes. Somers had turned off the state highway, and now they were following a smaller road between the trees and up a low hill. Then they cleared the trees, and April sunlight fell over them again, and Hazard found himself looking down on a fallow field, an enormous house, and bluffs scraggily stitched with oak and ash and walnut.

"Jesus God," Hazard said, sitting up straight. "What did Landon Maas do for a living?"

"Apparently hate-mongering pays better than I thought."

The house was a million easy, maybe a million and a half, with its slate roof and mix of fieldstone and brick. The attached garage had a carriage house design on the doors. Riding the bluffs, on who knew how many acres of land, with river frontage, it was the kind of spot that the hillbilly elite dreamed of. Hazard heard that last thought and decided he might, just possibly, need to reconsider some of his prejudices.

The driveway looped in front of the house, and Somers parked. On the porch, Hazard waited while Somers rang the bell. He couldn't hear the chime, but that didn't necessarily mean anything; the house looked new and well constructed. The soundproofing might be first rate. Sure enough, when the door opened, it was his first sign that someone was coming to answer the bell.

Hazard had known Landon Maas the way people knew about the asteroid that had wiped out the dinosaurs—leaving aside, for a moment, his qualms about the oversimplification of that comparison. Landon had been that kind of disaster in high school: cataclysmic, life-ending annihilation for anyone different from him. And this man, standing in the doorway, might have been a blood relation: he had the same ruddy blond coloring, and he was the right age to be a cousin or a brother, although he was smaller than Landon. But he wore a Dunder Mifflin t-shirt, flannel pajama pants, and Birkenstocks with black socks. It was the footwear that made Hazard decide this was probably not a blood relation of Landon Maas.

"May I help you?"

"Hello, I'm Chief Somerset with the Wahredua Police Department. I'm sorry to bother you, but may I come in?"

"Kurt Kuhn. Yeah, I guess you'd better." The look on the man's face was like newsprint: he already knew, of course. They all already knew. He stepped back, opening the door farther, and beckoned them inside. Then he shut the door, threw the deadbolt, and padded down the hall in his Birkenstocks.

Inside, April light like beeswax filled the high-ceilinged room where he stopped. It was clearly some sort of living room, and the wall at the back of the house was all windows, looking out on the bluffs and, a muddy, glinting smear, the Grand Rivere. The carpet was white. The wood accents were dark. The furniture—a massive sofa, a console, armchairs, built-in cabinets for, presumably, the television—were all the kind of thing that looked like they had come out of Grandpa's barn but that had really cost you four figures a pop, everything oversized, everything with raw wood and textured upholstery, everything in what magazines would call earth tones.

A woman and a teenager were sitting on opposite sides of the sofa, and it wasn't clear to Hazard what, if anything, they'd been doing before he and Somers had arrived. He had the sense that they might have been sitting there, like flies caught in this amber light, the silence ticking away the minutes worse than any clock could. The woman was probably the same age as Kurt, although she'd made herself look younger. Her lip gloss and makeup suggested too many TikTok videos about how to get a dewy finish, and her dark, sleek hair reminded Hazard of a mink. She wore black scrubs, nurse's clogs, and a ring with a diamond the size of a piece of Bazooka Joe gum.

But it was the boy who held Hazard's attention. He was clearly Landon's son; he had his father's complexion and build, although he had that toned, cut look that only teenagers were capable of. His face was softer than Landon's, though, and Hazard wondered if that were genetics—he only vaguely remembered Landon's out-of-state wife, who had divorced him years ago—or if Landon, too, had looked gentler before adulthood. It took Hazard a moment to identify the little differences: long lashes that were a darker blond than the hair on his head; pink, full lips; startled doe eyes, although that might have been only the day's fresh grief. He wore baggy joggers and a sweatshirt, although the house was warm and the day was mild.

"My wife, Angela," Kurt said. "And this is Carson."

Carson raised his head, like a dog hearing his name, but his face stayed blank. Angela said something—a string of hellos and pleased-to-meet-yous that dissolved into meaninglessness.

"Carson," Somers said, "I'm here with bad news. I'm sorry to have to tell you this, but your father was killed last night. We're not entirely sure what happened; he and another man were shot in a motel in Wahredua."

Angela let out a short scream. She clapped her hands over her mouth. It didn't seem staged, but it did have a kind of canned, sound bite quality that made Hazard think she'd seen too much TV. Kurt let out a breath and nodded. Carson stared. The beeswax light left part of his face in shadow, and for a moment, Hazard thought he traced the hint of a smile.

"Carson," Somers said, "do you understand what I said?"

The boy nodded. He started to speak and then stopped to clear his throat. "My dad's dead."

"Yes."

Hazard had the rare, and in this case, surprisingly unsatisfying opportunity of seeing his husband flatfooted, as Somers opened his mouth and then closed it again. Hazard understood; he felt some of the same disorientation. Death notifications had a pattern, almost a rhythm. This was the time when the bereaved would ask questions: how are you sure it's him? what happened to him? when did this happen? where is he now? It didn't matter that Somers had answered these questions, or most of them, already. What mattered was the questions as stays and supports—handholds as they stepped out over the abyss of grief.

Carson, however, sat there, his eyes liquid and unfocused, his cheeks almost as pink as his lips, his breathing slow and even.

"Is there anything you want to ask us?" Somers finally prompted.

Carson shook his head, dream-like.

"You're sure it's him?" Kurt asked, his voice rocky. He stood behind his wife, hands on her shoulders. She was still pressing her expensive nails to her mouth. She was the only one crying, but after that one, short scream, she'd been silent. The question broke the strange, stuttered tempo of the notification, and the world surged forward again.

"Yes," Somers said. "I knew Landon, and several of the other officers at the scene knew him as well. The medical examiner has his wallet, including his driver's license. One of you will need to make an official identification, but it's definitely him."

"It's him," Carson said. "I knew he was dead."

"He's in shock," Angela said. "Honey, do you need to lie down?"

Somers returned his attention to the boy, but it was Hazard who asked the question: "How did you know your father was dead?"

"They came this morning." His gesture took in Kurt and Angela. "They told me Naomi called them, and that's when I knew. I just knew."

"When Ms. Malsho called you," Somers asked, "did she say why she wanted you to come over?"

Kurt nodded. "But we didn't say anything to Carson. She told us to be quiet until the police were certain. She said they'd come talk to Carson and tell him."

"Which one of you is related to Landon?" Hazard asked.

Angela raised her hand like they were in school. "He's my brother."

"Do you have any idea why he might have gone to that motel last night?"

She shook her head and glanced up at her husband. When she looked back, she said, "We weren't close. I didn't even know—" She cut off.

"You didn't know what?"

"A lot of things."

"That's not helpful. What specifically did you not know?"

Patting her mink-like hair, Angela stared at the carpet and shrugged.

Hazard opened his mouth, but Somers spoke first. "We thought Ms. Malsho would be here. Is she coming over?"

Carson gave a splintered laugh.

When the boy fell silent again, Kurt said, "She didn't say anything about coming over."

"Why was that funny?" Hazard asked.

Carson looked at him. His eyes were still a washed-out sky, but for the first time, Hazard had the feeling that the boy was seeing him. "She won't come over."

"I understood that she and your dad were going to be married."

"She won't come over," he repeated.

"Why?"

A dreamy half-smile slipped out. It looked like he was on the verge of laughing again.

"How did you feel about your dad's relationship with Ms. Malsho?"

"Is that important?" Angela said. "He's in shock. Can't you see he's in shock?"

"She's all right." Carson tugged on his sleeve, pulling it down to his wrist. "She keeps him busy; that's nice."

There was a lot to work with in the last few comments, but the ground felt marshy to Hazard, and he glanced at Somers. His husband's eyes showed some of the same hesitation. When Somers spoke, it was with the professional detachment of the chief of police again. "Carson, we want to find whoever did this to your dad. We need all the help you can give us. Can you do that?"

The boy shrugged. Then he nodded.

"Last night, were you and your father home?"

"No."

"Where were you?"

"I was here. He was with Naomi."

"How do you know that?" Hazard asked.

"He's always with her. When he's not working, I mean."

"But he might have been somewhere else."

Carson frowned as though that had been a curveball. "No, he was with her." He must have sensed the silent question because he added, "At the gun show."

"Had he gone to the gun show?"

Again, Carson looked confused by the question. When he answered, he had the tone of someone stating the obvious: "It's his responsibility, you know? The gun show. He had to be there."

"Your dad was one of the organizers?" Somers asked. "Of the gun show?"

"Yeah, with Naomi. They planned it together."

"Of course they did," Hazard muttered. More loudly, he said, "What time was your father going to be home?"

Carson shrugged. "They have friends. Visitors. Important people. They always have important people coming around. So they go to dinner. My bedtime is nine, and they usually aren't home by then."

Hazard had the brief, aneurysm-inducing vision of telling Colt he had a bedtime.

"Do you know who those important people are?"

A half-shrug. A shake of his head.

"Did your dad tell you where he might have been going yesterday? Besides the gun show, I mean?"

Another negative.

"Do you know why he might have wanted to go meet someone at a motel last night?"

Carson hesitated and shook his head.

"Carson?"

"No. I don't know."

"Did your dad own a lot of guns?"

"Well, yeah." It was the same tone Colt used when he thought Hazard—and occasionally Somers—was being too stupid to be believed.

"Why?"

"He's a salesman." He paused and added, "Kaiser Arms?"

"They make guns," Kurt put in. When Hazard looked at him, he cowered down behind his wife.

"Are they all accounted for?"

A furrow appeared between Carson's eyebrows.

"Are any of the guns missing?" Somers asked.

"I don't know."

"We'll have to check," Kurt said.

"Carson, has anything strange happened lately? Anything that stood out to you?"

After a moment, the boy shook his head.

"Maybe your dad was in a bad mood one day? Or you overheard an argument? Or you saw something strange, something that didn't make any sense?"

"No."

"What about new people around the house? Or new people your dad talked about?"

"No."

"Think about it," Somers said. "Something might come to you later."

Carson shrugged and nodded again.

"Can any of you think of someone who might have wanted to hurt Landon?" Hazard asked. "Old grudges? Disagreements about money?"

Kurt shook his head first, with Angela only a moment behind. When Carson shook his head, his expression was turned inward, as though he were answering a different question—one he'd asked himself.

"If you could all provide statements about your whereabouts last night," Hazard said, "that would be helpful."

"We were in Columbia," Angela said. "We live in Columbia. We had dinner with friends, and we went to a movie and—and then she called us this morning." The last was delivered in a rush, dissolving into a wail at the end. Kurt nodded and pulled her against him.

"I was here," Carson said.

"By yourself?" Hazard asked.

Carson nodded.

"At what time?"

"Uh, nine. I come straight home after the baseball game."

"And the rest of the night you were, what? On your phone?"

He shrugged. "I ate dinner. I watched our game from Thursday. One of the parents always records it. Then I went to bed."

"Our son plays baseball too," Somers said, relaxing into that familiar, easy smile. "Do you know Colt?"

Carson nodded. "He's nice."

"That's hard to believe," Hazard said under his breath.

"Carson," Somers said, "what was your dad like? I knew him to recognize him around town, but I didn't know him, if you get what I mean."

"He's my dad," Carson said. "He wants what's best for me."

When it became clear that nothing more was coming, Somers nodded. "Do you want to call your mom? She needs to know, but if you'd rather, your aunt or uncle can do it. Or I'd be happy to."

The boy turned a confused look on Kurt and Angela.

"We don't know where she is," Kurt said. "We don't have any contact information."

"She ran off," Angela said bitterly. "Carson was a baby."

"I wasn't a baby." Carson's words had the hurt defensiveness of teenage pride. "She didn't have what it takes to be a mom. We were better off without her."

Somers nodded and handed out business cards. "If you think of anything, please contact me. You can also call the station at any time, night or day."

All three of them accepted the cards—Kurt like it was an under-the-table deal, wrapping his hand around it and sliding it in his pocket; Angela like she'd gotten a gag gift, turning it over as though it might do a trick; and Carson like Somers had pulled a fast one, his gaze strangely suspicious as he studied the card.

"I'm going to get him settled," Angela said, putting an arm around Carson's shoulders. "He's in shock."

Kurt gave an awkward roll of his shoulders and said, "I'll walk you out."

"Actually," Somers said, "we'd like to take a look around. If we could see Landon's room, his gun collection, anything that might—"

"You can't," Carson blurted. His face was colorless, and he looked like his knees had gone soft, but he shook off his aunt's arm. "It's not—you can't—he didn't do anything wrong, so you can't!"

"Carson, it's not about your dad doing something wrong. He was the victim of a terrible crime. We want to find whoever did it. There might be something—"

"There isn't! He just—whatever it was, you're not going to find anything here."

Somers smiled. Your buddy. Your pal. "I understand, but it's not that simple. Part of the investigation—"

It was the first time the boy had raised his voice, and the ragged shout rang out in the high-ceilinged room: "You can't!"

Hazard studied Carson: wide eyes, rapid breathing, a sickly, greenish cast to his face.

"Naomi told us to ask you to get a warrant," Kurt said apologetically as Angela took Carson under her arm again. "I'm sorry, but she thinks that, well, you know about Landon and his, uh, politics, and she thinks it would be better if you have an official warrant."

"Landon's dead," Hazard said. "Whatever happens now makes absolutely no difference to him, trust me."

Kurt's expression hardened. "I don't know about that. I'm telling you what Naomi told me. We'd like you to come back with a warrant."

"Mr. Kuhn, it's not quite that simple." Somers still had the smile in place, but it had its own gravity now, the weight of the chief of police behind it. "The need for a warrant arises from Fourth Amendment protection against unreasonable search and seizure, basically a citizen's right to privacy. But the expectation of privacy ends with death, and courts have consistently upheld that the presumption is that victims would want their killers found. We're getting into a gray area with Carson's bedroom, I suppose. If he doesn't want us going in there, I'm not willing to press the issue right now. But we are going to take a look around the house. And we are going to take a look around the property. And then I'm going to have a team of officers join us, and they're going to do it all over again, even more thoroughly. Am I making myself clear?"

"Naomi—"

"Ms. Malsho is a lawyer; she knows everything I told you."

Kurt's jaw tightened. He looked at Angela, and she offered only a helpless look in return. Finally, he nodded.

"I'm going to ask the three of you to wait outside," Somers said. "Carson, if you want to shut your bedroom door, now's the time to do it."

Still white-faced, the boy sprinted toward the stairs in the entry hall. A moment later came the crash of a door from the second floor. When he came back, his steps were slower, and he glared at them.

"I apologize for the inconvenience," Somers said. "Let's walk outside together."

The Kuhn-and-Maas clan followed him outside and gave him identical dirty looks. Hazard waited at the door, watching. The day was pleasant, and the sky was clear. They'd be fine for however long it took them to go through the house. When Somers stepped inside again, Hazard shut the door and asked, "What the fuck was that about?"

Somers shook his head.

"Is Naomi trying to fuck with us?" Hazard asked.

"That's my first guess, but she had to know it wouldn't work."

"What about Carson?"

"No clue. Maybe he's got some pot under his bed."

"Or maybe he killed his dad."

Somers sighed and nodded.

"That kid is giving me the creeps, John."

"No argument here. Do you want to split up?"

"No fucking way. Not with the three of them right outside."

After Somers called for officers to secure the house, he and Hazard started on the main floor. They found Landon's bedroom quickly enough. Like the rest of the house, it was done in dark woods and stark whites, with a set of rustic furniture that had clearly come as a set. Aside from needing a thorough cleaning, it didn't look different from most of the bedrooms Hazard had seen, and it had the usual accumulation of bedroom junk: loose change, charger cables, a full hamper, a half-full glass of water. They worked their way through the room and the attached bathroom. Aside from a bevy of hair-loss treatment products—minoxidil, finasteride, and then sprays and creams and ointments, all over-the-counter shit that would do as much to prevent hair loss as a tube of toothpaste—they found nothing. In the walk-in closet, two massive gun safes were bolted to the floor. Both were locked.

"No drugs, no cash, no signs of a search before ours," Hazard said.

"No sign that Naomi spends any time here, either," Somers said. When Hazard blinked, he grinned. "This is bachelor living at its finest. He got this bedroom furniture as a set, and it's got some seriously masculine energy."

"I'm sorry, the furniture has energy?"

"Besides, nobody is straightening up. The pillows all over the place like that. The junk on top of the dresser. Don't tell me you didn't notice the dust."

"This is sounding surprisingly sexist for a man who is married to another man."

"I didn't say this is how guys live, I said this is how bachelors live. Specifically, straight bachelors."

"That feels like a sophistical distinction."

"What about the toothbrush? There's only one in the bathroom."

Hazard frowned. "She might have one that she carries with her."

"No feminine products of any kind."

"That doesn't mean anything, John. She could keep it all in an overnight bag."

"I was married to her sister; I've seen what a bathroom looks like when Naomi takes up residence, even as a guest. If she ever comes over here, she's learned to clean up after herself a lot better than she did before."

"So, what? You think they're not sleeping together?"

"I don't know. I don't think she's spending much time here, though. You saw how Carson reacted when we asked if she was coming over."

Hazard nodded slowly.

"Want to give it another go?" Somers asked.

"Leave it for Norman and Gross; they'll have fun picking the place apart."

They moved through the main floor, checking the hall bathroom, the enormous living room, the kitchen, the mudroom. They found all the usual things—signs of daily living and of cleaning at less-than-recommended intervals. The built-in cabinets in the living room were stocked on one side with DVDs and flash drives labeled with the names of regional high schools and dates running back eight years. The other side of the built-ins held VHS tapes, labeled with masking tape. Like the DVDs and the flash drives, these held the names of schools and dates, although these were twenty years older. Hazard gave a silent thank-you to the universe that he'd never played sports.

Everywhere he turned, he found more signs that Carson's athletics had dominated the father's and son's lives. In the mudroom, pairs of football cleats were piled near the door like some sort of primitive shrine, filling the room with foot funk. In the kitchen, the refrigerator held two gallons of whole milk, several containers of unflavored Greek yogurt, and prepared, high-protein meals stacked on every shelf. The Maas men apparently weren't doing their own cooking. In the unfinished basement, they found a pitching net and a weight set, as well as a tackling dummy, a punching bag, an agility ladder, and other items that Hazard had no idea what they were for.

"That's to help you with your catching," Somers said when Hazard nudged a piece of plastic with three handles sticking out of it. "Hand-eye coordination, that kind of thing."

Hazard grunted and looked at the tangled fabric in Somers's hand. "Is that a parachute?"

"Well, I wouldn't recommend jumping out of a plane with it, but yeah. It's for speed training."

"Jesus."

"Yeah, this is all…kind of intense."

"It's nauseating. This is an unbelievable amount of pressure to put on a child."

"Says the man who told Colt, quote, 'anything less than a thirty-four on the ACT means you're retaking it.'"

"He's getting thirties regularly, John. He can get a thirty-four if he practices."

Somers smiled, but it looked hard worn. His gaze roved the equipment. Hazard looked again, trying to see it all through his husband's eyes. The gear. The chill of the cement slabs. The faint after-smell of sweat—a kind of locker room mustiness that felt out of place in a home.

"He might like it," Somers said.

"What? Who?"

"Carson. He might like the attention. Sometimes—sometimes, with a dad like that, it's the only attention you get. So you like it. Not the pressure, but what the pressure means. Or what you tell yourself it means."

"John, I'm sorry. I didn't think—"

Somers waved him to silence. "It's fine. I hadn't thought about it in a long time, actually. And I only said it because—well, you look at all this, and you might think he resents his dad. But it might be the opposite."

Maybe, Hazard thought. And he thought of his husband at family dinners, his husband at holidays, his husband smiling and nodding and shrinking so his parents could take up more room, his beautiful, smart, hardworking husband squeezing himself into smaller and smaller boxes for this party or that fundraiser or the photo on the door-hanger, until he was nothing but a smile and a badge and, if you were lucky, a handshake. And Hazard thought maybe. He thought maybe the resentment comes later, and by then it's part of you, and you don't even know it's there, let alone how to get out of all those boxes.

All he trusted himself to say was "Upstairs?"

They went upstairs.

They stopped in the bathroom first: acne-treatment face wash, Brut deodorant, a scale pulled out from the wall, what looked like hand-drawn football plays taped to the corner of the mirror, the Scotch tape yellowing, frayed ends peeling up. The medicine cabinet held a tub of IcyHot, a bottle of ibuprofen, a prescription vial for fluoxetine, the date current, still half full.

"Prozac," Hazard said.

Somers nodded.

The next room was a guest bedroom: an unmade bed, an empty dresser, dusty blinds. He realized that he'd been wondering if Naomi stayed in the guest room when she came over, and now he tossed that theory out.

There were two doors left, and both doors were shut.

Somers frowned, considering them.

"He only has one bedroom," Hazard said.

"We don't know that."

"I only heard him shut one door."

Somers nodded.

"You could go practice your hand-eye coordination downstairs," Hazard said, resting one hand on the doorknob.

Eyebrow raised, Somers turned to look at his husband. "We talked about this."

"It doesn't hurt to ask."

"Not in my town."

"We both grew up here, so I don't see why —"

"Not in my town, Ree."

"You've become very possessive since your promotion."

Somers gave the doors another considering look.

"It's not only the town, John. You steal the blankets. That seems inconsistent with your professional duties as chief of police."

"Let's pull him back in here. We'll ask him which room is his."

"And give him a chance to tell us why we can't look in the other room?" Hazard snorted and turned the doorknob.

"Ree!"

"Whoops."

He shoved, and the door wobbled open. On the other side, he saw a bedroom. It was clearly Carson's. It fit with the rest of the house: the bed perfectly made, the floor empty of clothes and shoes and backpacks and homework, a few books on the desk squared up in the corner. On the walls hung Mizzou basketball posters; a Rams helmet, scrawled with what might have been Kurt Warner's signature, mounted on a plaque; a framed jersey. But then Hazard's brain caught up with his eyes, and he recognized the design of the jersey, the Wahredua Wildcats. It was grungy and showed the signs of hard wear. It wasn't the current design; this one was twenty years old, which Hazard recognized because he'd spent a lot of time watching his husband wear a similar jersey on the football field. MAAS was printed on the back of the jersey.

"This is fucking psycho."

Somers shrugged. "Again, you're over-interpreting. It might be the only thing they have that they can talk about. It might be the only point of contact. We don't have enough information yet."

"His son has to sleep under his dad's framed high school jersey. That's enough information for me."

"Close the door, Ree. We're not going in there."

Hazard yanked the door shut.

The last room was empty, although it must have been intended as a bedroom. The carpet still showed vacuum tracks. The blinds were dust free. Only a little of the beeswax light made it into this room, and it smelled shut up, like the door was always kept closed. Hazard crossed the room and opened the closet.

Women's clothes hung on hangers: dresses, skirts, blouses, a winter coat with a faux-fur trim around the hood. The styles were dated; Hazard glanced at Somers.

"They look fifteen or twenty years old to me," Somers said with a shrug and snapped several photographs. "But I'll show these to Cora."

"This doesn't up your psycho factor?"

"It's the closet of an empty room, Ree."

"Yeah. Why is he hanging on to his ex-wife's clothes, over a decade later?"

"I don't know. Sentimental."

Hazard snorted and shoved the hangers along the rod. Metal shrieked on metal. The musty smell of old fabric floated up. He pressed into the opening, examining the shelf and the back of the closet for anything hidden, but he found nothing.

"Maybe he holds on to things," Somers said, "like, oh, say, a Death Cab for Cutie t-shirt that is literally disintegrating from being washed so many times, and he won't explain why it can't go to Goodwill. Or to the trash."

"I told you why," Hazard said, shutting the closet door. "Because it's mine."

Somers rolled his eyes.

When they joined Carson and his aunt and uncle outside, the wind had shifted, and it carried a stockyard smell that made Hazard cover his nose. Angela had pulled up her scrubs to breathe through the fabric, and Kurt was making a face. Carson, however, just stood there, hands at his side, face empty.

"Can we go back inside now?" Kurt asked.

"No," Somers said. He opened his mouth to say more, but a patrol car crested the hill at the edge of the property, and he pointed. "Actually, yes. You can wait inside with these officers. They're going to keep the house secure until I can have a team come over to process it thoroughly."

"But—" Kurt's eyes went to Carson. "That could take hours."

"It could take days," Hazard said flatly.

"Let's hope that's not the case," Somers said. "Mr. Kuhn, the best thing is to have a responsible adult on the premises to keep a record of anything that the officers need to take as part of the investigation. You could send your wife and Carson to get something to eat, or they could spend time at a friend's house. There's no need for all of you to stay here."

"Angela—" Kurt began.

"No," Carson said.

"This has been a hard day—"

"No! They'll go in my room if I'm not here. They aren't allowed in my room."

Kurt and Angela stepped aside to confer; Carson folded his arms, staring fixedly at the house.

"Carson," Somers said quietly, "if it's something you're worried or embarrassed about, that's not what we're looking for. We just want to know who might have wanted to hurt your dad."

"In other words," Hazard said, "we don't care if you've got weed in a shoebox or a jerkoff rag under your bed."

The boy's cheeks colored. His gaze stayed locked on the house. "It's my room, and you can't go in there."

Somers sighed and nodded; when Hazard opened his mouth, Somers shook his head and pulled Hazard by the arm to stand a few yards off.

When the patrol car parked behind the Mustang, Nickels and Carlson got out. Somers gave brief instructions on keeping the family together and making sure none of them had time alone in any of the searchable areas of the house. Then the officers took Carson, Angela, and Kurt inside.

"Garage?" Somers asked.

Hazard led the way. They went through the house; inside the garage, the light switch next to the door turned on a single incandescent bulb that gave off a weak, yellow light. Hazard hit the control, and the garage door rumbled up, daylight rushing in. A Jeep Wrangler occupied one side of the two-car. The other side was empty except for a bump-out where what looked like a reloading bench was installed.

Hazard started with the Jeep. The Wrangler had to be new—a 2018, 2019, he guessed—and it was an olive green close enough to pass for camo. Hazard walked around the Jeep. The doors were locked, which seemed strange for a vehicle parked in a secure garage. Through the windows, he could see the spotless leather interior.

"No coins," Hazard said. "No straw wrappers in the cup holders. No leaves tracked onto the floor mats."

Somers nodded.

"I take Colt out to practice driving for an hour, and by the time we get back, it looks like a band of hippies has been living in the back of the van. This kid has a Jeep that looks like nobody's ever driven it before."

"Well, he obviously drives it," Somers said. "He got home last night in it."

Hazard shook his head.

He walked the perimeter of the garage, passing a bag of kitty litter, a bag of ice melt, a snowblower snugged up against the wall, a steel shelving unit painted yellow and black—DeWalt, Hazard guessed, which was pretty easy after God only knew how many hours with Somers in the power tool aisle. He examined the reloading bench, which he realized upon inspection, was more of a condensed gunsmithing station: pin punches, hammers, bench blocks, canisters of various cleaning solutions, files hanging from the bench's pegboard back. The air smelled like cold concrete and, faintly, motor oil and solvent.

"He doesn't have any tools at all except the gunsmithing and reloading stuff on the bench," Hazard said.

"I guess he doesn't spend his Saturday nights replacing the wax seal on the hall toilet."

"It was one time, and you got some good thank-you sex after. Get off the cross."

Somers flashed him a massive grin that disappeared just as suddenly. He held up a finger, displaying a brown smudge.

"What's that? Mud?"

"From the tires. It's still damp."

"He said he came straight home after baseball."

"Yup."

"So where'd he hit a patch of mud between Wahredua High and here?"

"Kind of what I was wondering."

They went out onto the driveway and followed the side of the house toward the bluff and the river. The house blocked the wind, cutting the stockyard smell, and the sun glinted on the water: a shimmer of trapezoids and parallelograms and shark-toothed triangles. The trees, still leafing out, whispered and trembled. He watched his husband in profile. The breeze stirred some of the mussed hair above Somers's ear.

"Knock it off," Somers said with a smile, still looking straight ahead.

Hazard turned to look forward. He realized he was smiling too.

A massive deck was attached to the back of the house, but a quick perusal of the patio furniture yielded nothing. Beyond the deck, at the edge of the bluff, a firepit looked down on the water. They followed the path from the deck. When they got closer, sunlight glinted on glass.

"Watch your step," Hazard said.

Somers slowed, and they closed the last ten feet picking a path between broken bottles. A lot of the bottles were Budweiser Select, brown glass glittering like dog's eyes, the black paper furred at the torn edges. But some of the bottles were Grey Goose, the bottle's familiar skinny neck, the broken wing of a blue seal. Hazard crouched beside a particularly dense cluster of glass shards. Out of the corner of his eye, he was aware of Somers bending over the fire pit.

"This paper, the labels on the bottles, it's in good condition," Hazard said. "It hasn't been outside for long; hell, it practically looks new."

Somers made an affirmative noise. When Hazard glanced over, Somers was leaning into the fire pit, one hand moving as though he were stirring the ashes—or fishing something out.

A moment later, Somers straightened; he'd donned disposable gloves, and now he held something out at arm's length. It was a scrap of paper, charred and blackened, and he brought it closer slowly. Then he said, "Ree?"

Hazard straightened and stepped over to his husband. The smell of smoke and something else, a chemical sharpness that he guessed was left over from some kind of accelerant, met him. What remained on the singed paper was an image that was difficult to make out.

"Horse's ass," Hazard said.

"Come on, I was proud of finding this."

"No, John. I think that's a horse's ass. That curve, that's the tail."

"Oh."

"What did you think it was?"

"Uh, not that."

"What?"

"I don't know. I thought maybe it was the background. Like, part of a curtain."

"No, that's wrong."

Somers let out a slow breath. "Do you want to try again?"

"Well, if it's not a horse's ass, I suppose any other equine, possibly—"

"Not that."

It took a moment. "Oh. That."

"Yes, that."

"Everyone makes mistakes, John. You're right about so many things; it shouldn't be an issue that in this case, you're clearly wrong—"

"Ree, baby, stop talking."

They spent some time, both of them gloved now, digging through the ashes in the pit, but none of the fragments they recovered were any easier to identify. They bagged and labeled the pieces they'd found. Then, after a sweep of the yard that yielded nothing, they returned to the front of the house.

Nickels was waiting on the front step with Angela Kuhn. The front door stood open.

"She said she needed to talk to you," the officer said, gesturing to the woman beside her. "She was insistent. The other two didn't like it at all."

Before Somers could ask, Nickels said, "Carlson's with them, and I've got a line of sight to the living room from here."

"All right," Somers said. "Mrs. Kuhn, what can I help you with?"

"Kurt said I'm—I'm getting myself in trouble. He said this isn't any of our business, and there's a reason I left Wahredua in the first place, and he's not wrong. He's not wrong." She was trembling as she pulled out her phone. The Bazooka Joe diamond scattered light across the porch, across her scrubs, across the pallor of her face. "I didn't want anything to do with my parents anymore, not after college. And Landon—Landon is like them. Worse. And Kurt's such a good man, and he's not wrong. It's trouble, and it's not even my trouble, but it's not Carson's fault either, and that boy has no idea—" She cut off.

"What doesn't Carson have any idea about?"

She shook her head. The phone in her hand shook as she held it out. On the screen, a video was ready to play.

"They kept coming this morning. Watching us. Waiting. Mr. Murphy scared them off, I think, only he's gone now."

"Who?" Hazard asked. "Who's Murphy? What are you talking about?"

"Mr. Murphy is the man my father sent over to keep us safe." Hazard wanted to follow up on that, but she played the video before he could. It had been taken from inside the Maas' house, he realized, looking out at the driveway. As he watched, a black SUV crested the hill at the edge of the property. It rolled down the driveway and circled in front of the house. Hazard's brain kicked into gear, noting facts: no license plate, probably an American make, tinted windows, driver likely male, at least one passenger, also likely male.

Then the SUV passed the house, directly in front of the window where Angela had been recording, and Hazard saw that the man in the passenger seat had his arm up, resting against the window, like he wanted them to see. And then Hazard realized that yes, of course he wanted them to see. He was holding a pistol.

CHAPTER FOUR
APRIL 11
SATURDAY
11:54 AM

THE DORE COUNTY KNIFE & Gun Show was set up a good half hour outside of Wahredua. It was the next logical step; they could place both victims at the gun show on the day they died, and it was the most likely explanation for whatever had brought the two men together the night they were killed. They drove the miles without talking; Somers was on the phone, getting updates from Dulac and Palomo and filling them in on what they had learned, including the strange video of the SUV that Angela had shown them. Hazard spent the miles thinking.

"Well," Somers said when he finally disconnected, "they're on their way to talk to Naomi right now. The short version is that they didn't get anything useful from the motel room. It's full of Zachary Renner's stuff, but it's all what you'd expect: nice clothes, an expensive watch, a laptop, promotional materials for his nonprofit."

"Cocks for Glocks," Hazard said drily.

Somers smirked, but the expression faded quickly. "And aside from that video Angela showed us, I'm not sure we found anything useful at Landon's house either."

But Hazard pictured Carson's face, the porousness of his expression, everything seeming to run right through him. "We need to look at that kid's room."

"Why? Because he doesn't want us to?"

"Because his father was murdered, his reaction was abnormal, and that home felt like a custom-built father-son mindfuck."

"Is that what you want me to write on the affidavit?"

"Don't be a smartass."

"I'm serious, Ree. What am I supposed to put when I apply for the warrant? 'The kid didn't cry, but, yeah, it's entirely possible he was in shock, and there's no such thing as a normal reaction to grief, oh, and he didn't want us in his room, but that could be because he's got steroids or weed or Natty Lights or, I don't know, his favorite jack-off toy in there.'"

Hazard gritted his teeth. He looked out the window. Some dickwad had planted sweetgums along a fence line. A big old bird was messing around near the top of one of them. Hazard thought it was a jay—the assholes of the avian world. He tried to control his voice when he said, "You told me your dad said any available resources."

"Sure, but I don't want him pulling strings with Judge Platter. That's the wrong way to do this—and he'd know it if he weren't in such a panic. What we need is an airtight case; what we don't need is a floppy warrant for a kid's bedroom that Naomi and the Ozark Volunteers could shred like a tissue."

The jay took flight, swooping. Driving off a smaller bird—a chickadee, maybe, although they were too far now, and the bird was nothing more than a dark spot disappearing behind them.

"A floppy warrant?" Hazard asked.

"You know what I mean," Somers snapped. Then, taking a breath, he rubbed his jaw. A little smile slipped out. "God, all right, I hear it now."

Hazard reached over and squeezed his neck, and Somers pressed into his touch.

"I'm sorry," Hazard said.

"You're getting so much better at that," Somers murmured.

Hazard squeezed a little more tightly, and Somers laughed.

"We'll do it, Ree. And we'll do it the right way. We trace their movements. We figure out who else is involved. We keep digging and prying and looking until it all comes out."

Hazard didn't trust himself to answer that. But he did think, just to himself, that Landon Maas's house was technically outside the city limits, and the deal he'd brokered with his husband had been about not breaking the law inside Wahredua proper. He squeezed Somers's neck again, the pad of his thumb following the bumps of his spine, and they drove the rest of the way in silence.

The Dore County Knife & Gun Show had been set up on several acres of pasture, and the smell of cow shit as they pulled into the parking lot—which was nothing more than a mowed section, the ground torn up and muddy from fresh rain and too many trucks—made Hazard think someone would regret wearing new boots to this little wet dream. The show itself appeared to be taking place inside several massive white tents, the sidewalls opened in places by vinyl windows. People streamed in and out of the tents—more men than women, yes, but not exactly what Hazard had expected. Not everyone was white, for starters. He saw some black men. He saw a Latinx pair that had to be father and son. And not everyone fit his mental pattern for the Ozark Volunteers-slash-white trash cultural niche. The guy with the Mercedes and the wool jacket. The woman with a Jonathan Sacks book. Her arm was covering the title, but if it was *The Dignity of Difference*, Hazard was afraid his head might explode.

Somers made a noise and cocked his head, and Hazard glanced out the window. On the other side of the state highway, a much smaller white tent, this one approximately the size of a mall kiosk, sat on the shoulder. At that distance, Hazard could read the sign that said COCKS FOR GLOCKS, but all he could make out of the figure inside the tent was that it might, possibly, be a woman.

"They're not getting much traffic," Somers said.

Hazard unbuckled himself and got out of the car. "Big surprise."

When they approached the closest tent, Hazard saw that chicken wire had been staked out around the tents. It was the kind of fence that relied on good social conditioning; installed that way, the chicken wire wouldn't keep out a fox or a coyote or even a chicken, much less a grown-ass man trying to solve a murder. But the fence did funnel all the new arrivals to a checkpoint, and the men and women ahead of them pulled out their phones and pieces of paper. A few of them glanced more than once at Hazard and Somers; some of them Hazard recognized, either from growing up here or from the years since he'd moved back, but he was surprised yet again to realize many of these people weren't familiar to him.

"Nobody seems particularly worried to see you," Hazard murmured as they joined the line.

"Why would they be?"

"Oh, I don't know, John."

Somers laughed. "They don't know why we're here, and I'm not in uniform. It's not like they're all going to a panel: *How I Got Away With Murder And You Can Too!* It's not even an Ozark Volunteers event. It's a county gun show. There are a lot of people in the area who like guns who aren't tied up with the Volunteers."

"That must be a nice thing they can tell themselves after pawing through Nazi memorabilia."

"Ok, that seems like a stereotype."

"Really? All right. If there are fewer than, let's say, eight swastikas inside, I'll do the dishes for a month."

Somers opened his mouth; then he shook his head. "No deal. You'll bully Colt into doing them."

"Nope. I'll do them myself."

"Ok. Fine. If there are more than eight, I'll do the dishes for a month."

"Are you sure? You hate doing dishes."

He offered one of those smug smiles Hazard had been seeing—and dreaming about—since childhood. "I'm not worried about it."

"You're always so tired when you get home. You just want to watch TV. Why don't you make this easy and tell me, right now, that you know I'm right?"

"I'll have plenty of time to watch TV while you're doing the dishes."

Hazard would have responded to that, but the line moved quickly, and they found themselves stepping forward to face a man blocking their path. He was older, his hair gray and long, and he had a billy goat beard. Chaw stained the topmost whiskers yellow brown. His t-shirt, tucked in and belted, was printed with the outline of a card and the words MY GUN PERMIT - THE 2ND AMENDMENT - ISSUED 12/15/1791 - EXPIRATION NEVER.

"Ticket," he said.

Somers produced his badge and said, "I'm Chief Somerset with the Wahredua Police. I'd like to talk to whoever is in charge."

"Ticket," the man said again. This close, Hazard could see the flecks of tobacco between his teeth.

"This is regarding a murder investigation."

The man made a chewing movement with his jaw, as though it were automatic at this point. Then he said, "Ticket, or get out of line."

"Did you hear what he said?" Hazard asked. "He's the fucking chief of police. Either get whoever's in charge or get out of the way."

He stared at them again, chewing absently, and then he turned and shouted over his shoulder, "Mir!"

A moment later, the tent flaps parted, and Miranda Carmichael stepped outside. She was a small woman, well-muscled for her size, with her short hair already graying. She wore a camo vest over a tank top and leggings, and for a moment, it was unreal, seeing her out of uniform, seeing her here, and Hazard had to back up and try to process it again.

Next to him, Somers seemed to be having the same problem.

She gave them a cool look, as though she didn't know them, as though she hadn't worked with them for years, and then asked the ticket taker, "What's the problem?"

"No tickets."

She turned to face them.

"Miranda, what—" Somers bit off the question. He was silent for a moment, and then he said, "I'm here as part of an official investigation. Are you in charge here?"

"What do you need, Chief?"

"Well, I'd like to look around, talk to people—including you, if you were here yesterday. We're following up on a double homicide, and we believe both of our victims were at the show yesterday."

Carmichael's face was blank. "If you don't have a ticket, I'll have to clear it with someone higher up."

"Are you fucking kidding me?" Hazard asked. "What the fuck is going on? Is this some fucking *Candid Camera* bullshit? Miranda, it's us. It's a murder investigation. Tell this fucko to get out of my way; we need to talk to these people."

"Do you have a warrant?"

"What?"

"Warrant. Got one?"

"Miranda, we're not talking about a search here," Somers said. "We want to talk—"

"This is a safe space. It's a place for like-minded people to get together and feel comfortable, feel like they can be themselves."

"This is a fucking joke," Hazard said. "It's space camp for middle-aged men who can't get it up anymore, so they get brain boners from rubbing on guns and thinking about all the shit they'd never do in real life."

That cut through the murmur of the crowd behind them. There was still sound: the hub of voices from inside the tents, canvas flapping, the breeze in the grass. But the crowd outside had gone still, and Hazard could feel the weight of their eyes on his back.

The man in the Second Amendment t-shirt leaned forward and spat; it struck Hazard's boot and glistened there.

"This is a private event," Carmichael said, and although her voice was even, a kind of restrained glee flickered in her eyes. "And it's on private property. If you've got a ticket, you can come in. If you've got a warrant, you can come in. But if you don't have either of those, you can fuck off." She smirked, a razor-edged little thing, and added, "It's called the Fourth Amendment, sir."

"You have no idea—" Hazard began.

Somers took his arm. "Come on."

Hazard wanted to yank his arm away, but after a moment, he mastered himself and let Somers lead him back to the mud-churned lot. They stood there a moment, silent. Several of the men and women in line had turned, following them with their eyes. Hazard gave them the finger. Some were recording on their phones, so he upped his game: double birds. Then everyone seemed to realize the drama was over, and they shuffled forward in line, turning their backs on Hazard and Somers.

"This is fucking bullshit," Hazard said.

Somers was breathing mechanically—slow and deep and wholly artificial. He was rubbing that spot at the center of his forehead.

A semi whipped past, a wall of air flattening the weeds along the shoulder.

"John?"

Somers held up one finger.

Seconds trickled away. Hazard cleared his throat. "I realize that I may have acted injudiciously. Slightly."

"Nope. Not yet."

"Uh, right."

It was almost a full minute before Somers shook his head and looked up. "Brain boner?"

Heat rushed into Hazard's face. "I might have gotten carried away."

"Ree, Jesus Christ."

"I'm sorry." It was getting easier, but it was still so hard. Worth it, though, to see some of the starched anger in Somers's face yield. "I was off-balance after seeing Carmichael, and then to have her turn on you—"

"She didn't turn on me, Ree. She's right. This is a private event. I'm not invited, I don't have a warrant, and I don't have exigent circumstances to force entry. Hell, it's not even in my jurisdiction."

That, Hazard recognized, was an opening to another conversation, but he tucked it away for the moment.

"Carmichael..." Hazard hung the name out there.

Somers shook his head. "I know. What the fuck was that?"

"Well, it's not good. Did you know she was part of the Ozark Volunteers?"

"She's not a Volunteer!" Somers drew a breath. "Christ, I hope she's not, anyway."

"It's one thing for someone to attend a gun show, not knowing— possibly, anyway—who's sponsoring it or who they're affiliating with. It's another thing to be so involved in the operation that in an emergency, you become the de facto authority."

Somers scrubbed his hair, mussing it worse than usual. He made a face. "Moraes told me—he said she's been talking a lot of that shit lately. He said she's been angry. One time, she about bit my head off; that was something to do with Dulac—"

"Then she probably wasn't wrong," Hazard murmured.

"—but, God, I didn't know it was like this." He was silent a moment. Somebody had turned on music, and a country rock anthem was blaring from inside the tents, a twangy voice singing about America. "I guess it's too optimistic to hope that she just really loves guns."

Hazard kept his silence.

"God damn it," Somers muttered. "All right. I guess I've got to figure out what to do about that."

"Would Judge Platter—"

"And give them something to drag my ass through court? No thanks. Not until we've got a legitimate reason to get a warrant."

Hazard glanced across the two-lane at the COCKS FOR GLOCKS stand. "Then let's see what the other batch of fucknuts has to tell us."

They jogged across the asphalt. The sun was heavy and warm on Hazard's shoulders. He could smell the dust of broken stone from the shoulder of the road, the trampled thistles, the faint hint of new vinyl—that last one, he guessed, was from the COCKS FOR GLOCKS tent. As they got closer, he could make out the woman at the table inside.

She was young, black, and dark, with her hair straightened and pulled back into a ponytail complete with headband. She wore a red-and-white gingham blouse and buff-colored slacks. She might have looked like a good girl from Riverdale until she stood up and Hazard saw the massive silicone cock bouncing between her legs.

"Good…God," he said in an underbreath.

"Yeah," Somers said. "That would be, uh, a stretch."

"Hello." The girl offered a cracked smile, and her voice wobbled as she said, "I'm Jalisa with Cocks for Glocks. Can I tell you a little about what we do?"

Somers introduced himself and then, studying her, asked, "Have you heard about Mr. Renner?"

A sob slipped free, and Jalisa wiped her eyes. "Yeah. Benji told Courtney, and Courtney told the rest of us. Everybody knows. It's awful."

"Well, Jalisa, that's why we're here. We're hoping you can help us try to figure out what happened yesterday."

"Yeah, ok."

"Why don't you start by telling us about the nonprofit?"

Jalisa blinked. "Cocks for Glocks? Oh, um. Ok. Well, we give away sex toys in exchange for guns. Mostly dildos, but we've got other stuff." She gestured behind her, where on a display rack hung cock rings, nipple clamps, fuzzy handcuffs, a Fleshlight, and a disturbingly featureless male sex doll. "It's kind of like a buyback program, you know?"

"Why?" Hazard asked.

"We're gun safety activists."

"It sounds like you're gun reduction activists," Hazard said. "But I meant, why dildos?"

"Well, you know. It's ironic."

Hazard must have made a noise because Somers gave him a look that Hazard had learned to interpret as *leave it*. Instead, he glanced in the plastic tote next to the table. Several handguns—three pistols, one revolver—lay there. "Four guns have been surrendered?"

"Well, not exactly." When Hazard looked at Jalisa, she pulled on the neck of her blouse. "Those are, uh—Zach put them there."

Somers nodded slowly. "To make it look like other people had already participated, is that it?"

"For fuck's sake," Hazard said. "He's salting his own buyback program?"

"Well, yeah. I mean, otherwise nobody would ever surrender a gun. They've got to think other people are participating, you know? Group think. The bandwagon approach."

"Don't tell me that actually works. Does anyone ever give you a gun?"

"Yes! There was a guy in Farmington!" She faltered, and her voice took on a dubious note. "He was super gay, though."

Somers looked like he was trying not to laugh, and his voice sounded like a strained effort at normalcy as he asked, "Have you been with them for a while?"

"Only since January. I needed something good for my Vassar essay; they've wait-listed me twice. I'm at Mizzou now, but it's, like, way too conservative. I mean, not compared to this town. Ugh." She seemed to realize what she'd said and offered, "Sorry."

"That's all right. What do you do?"

"Oh, they mostly have me on the booth. I don't mind talking to people, and Benji says I'm almost as good as he is. Courtney doesn't like to do it; she gives all these speeches about sexual liberation or whatever, but give her a strap-on and she's ready to die, she's so embarrassed. I think it's fun." She gave a few hops to demonstrate, and the dildo wagged up and down.

"Imagine how much fun it would be getting split open by that thing," Hazard said.

"Oh, I had a boyfriend who liked it. You just have to use lots and lots of lube. It's a head game, really. If you think you can, you can."

"Uh huh," Somers said with a sidelong glance at Hazard that, for some reason, made a flash fire start in his face. "And Benji and Courtney are..."

"Benji is Zach's brother, duh. Oh my God. You didn't know that?"

"No," Somers said. "We didn't know that."

"They look like twins. Well, I mean, except Benji's younger. But you know what I mean, right?"

Somers made a noncommittal noise. "And where is Benji?"

"Dealing with stuff. You know, Zach's stuff. Benji was already overwhelmed; he does all the finances because Zach can't keep the numbers straight, and now he's going to have to do everything. He can't count on his parents to help, you know?"

"And Courtney?" Hazard asked.

"Oh, yeah. Courtney is, like, operations. She buys all the dildos and harnesses and other toys we want to give away. When we get guns, she's in charge of figuring out how to get them to the police. She makes sure we have signs and a tent and, you know, stuff like that."

"Does she pick where you're going to protest?"

"Uh, no. That's Zach."

"What about your accommodations?" Somers asked.

"No, that's Zach too."

"Where are you staying?"

"I don't know—it's a La Quinta, I think. I can show you on my phone."

"Not at the Presidential?"

Jalisa shook her head.

"You don't stay together?" Hazard asked.

"Of course not," Jalisa said. "That's how they get you."

"That's how who gets you?"

Waving a hand at the milling people across the two-lane, Jalisa said, "Them."

Behind them, a horn blared. Hazard glanced over his shoulder; a truck swung out onto the state highway, rednecks sticking their heads out the window, jeering and shouting as they passed the Cocks for Glocks stand. The insults weren't anything original—certainly nothing Hazard wanted to keep in his back pocket—but it was slightly satisfying to see one of the dumbasses hit his head when he tried to pull it back through the window.

"See?" Jalisa asked.

"Someone screaming 'faggot cocksuckers' isn't exactly reason to hide," Hazard said drily. "If it were, I'd be living in my mother's basement."

"They could make a TV show out of that," Somers said.

When Hazard rolled a scowl toward his husband, Jalisa grinned.

"You have no idea," Somers told her. "They'd go antiquing, and she'd want to buy what she thought was a table runner, and he'd ruin it by telling her it was some sort of Victorian mourning garb and giving her a forty-minute explanation of funeral customs."

"That was one time!" Hazard snapped. "And this is why I never tell you stories about high school!" He straightened his shirt and fixed Jalisa with a glare. "Answer my question."

"You didn't ask me a question."

"It was implied. Have you been threatened, clearly and directly, in a way that suggests a specific danger? Or are these precautions based on the general hostility you experience at these events?"

"I mean—" Jalisa cast about, but Somers was looking at her expectantly too. "I don't know! I'm just a volunteer. That's the way we always do it. Zach likes it that way."

"So there was no specific reason Zach might have been afraid for his safety?"

"No, I didn't say that. He got attacked yesterday."

"What do you mean?"

"He got attacked! Some guys in there tried to beat him up!"

"Zach went inside the gun show yesterday?" Somers asked.

"Yeah, of course. I mean, nobody wants to come over here. Whenever we go to a show like this, he buys a ticket and goes in, you know, undercover. Then he puts on his equipment and starts sharing our message."

Hazard snorted. "And promptly gets kicked the fuck out."

Jalisa nodded.

"Do you know who these men were?" Somers asked.

Jalisa shook her head. "Zach was mad, though. He kept calling them fuckers." In a wounded tone, she added, "They tore his cock off. Well, not his real one."

"But you don't know what happened? What started it? How far it escalated?"

"No, sorry."

Somers sighed. "Would you be willing to make an affidavit—"

"Actually, John," Hazard said, "if I could suggest something else."

Somers raised an eyebrow.

"As has been pointed out, this technically isn't your jurisdiction," Hazard said. "And also technically, my promise was about certain behaviors within your jurisdiction."

"Oh my God, Ree."

"If you're able to get a warrant, how effective do you think that will be? I have a hard time believing you'll find any physical evidence of the fight, and you'll alienate everybody inside those tents. Nobody will talk to us."

Rubbing that spot in the center of his forehead, Somers sounded like a man trying to keep calm. "Or?"

"Or we try a different approach."

"I can't believe I'm asking this, but what is this alternate approach?"

Hazard looked at the featureless sex doll and asked Jalisa, "Do you have a marker?"

She nodded.

"How would you feel about the possibility of being arrested? The charges wouldn't be anything serious; most likely they'd be dropped. I suggest using the argument that you're protected by your right to freedom of expression."

"Yeah, I don't know—I mean, my mom—"

"Think about the Vassar essay you could write about this."

Her face brightened. "Oh my God!"

"It's too bad," Hazard said, mostly to himself, "we don't have time to get it a spray tan."

He explained his idea, and while Jalisa locked up the guns in a safe in her Malibu, they stopped at the Mustang, where Somers pulled on a gray Under Armour windbreaker. He was too attractive, and Dore County was too small, for his face not to be well known, but Hazard was counting on dealers and buyers from outside the area—and regardless, the seal of the Wahredua PD on Somers's polo wasn't helping matters. Then they left Jalisa at the Cocks for Glocks stand and hiked fifty yards down the state highway. An older man in an ancient F-150 passed in the opposite direction, and he stopped, something rattling under the hood of the truck, to shout an offer of a ride. Somers leaned through the window and said something that made the old guy laugh, and he rolled on down the highway.

When Somers looked over, he asked, "What?"

Hazard shook his head. "Last chance?"

"Oh, fuck that," Somers said with surprising heat. "Not after Carmichael gave me my balls in a doggy bag."

They reached the end of the pasture where the gun show was set up, and Hazard turned to face the Cocks for Glocks stand. He waved. A moment later, Jalisa trotted across the highway, her strap-on wobbling, the sex doll compressed under one arm.

Two minutes later, the shouts started. A minute after that, people began to stream toward the front of the gun show — toward the parking lot, more specifically, and Jalisa's diversion.

"Show time," Somers said, tugging on Hazard's hand to jog across the highway.

"For her," Hazard said, "literally. Fortunately, there's no concern about performance anxieties with a marital aid."

For some reason, that made Somers laugh. He was still laughing when they trampled a section of chicken wire and approached the back of the gun show.

"It wasn't that funny," Hazard growled as they approached the closest tent. "It was an observation contrasting physiology and the resilience of silicone."

"The fact that you called it a marital aid is just the cherry on top," Somers said. "God, Dulac is going to die when I tell him he missed this."

"Don't you fucking dare," Hazard growled as he snatched the tent flap and held it open for Somers to pass through.

Inside, they were met by the smell of sweaty men and wood smoke, cigarettes and leather, and, of course, the metal-and-solvent combination that Hazard's brain decoded automatically as guns. The tent had fluorescent lighting panels overhead, but it was still dim compared to the sunny April day, and it took a moment for his eyes to adjust. When they did, he blinked.

He'd never been to a gun show before, and he was starting to realize he had absolutely no idea how genuinely batshit they were.

The crowd was thinner than he'd expected, but then, a significant portion had probably been drawn away to witness — and share in the outrage — about Jalisa's modern art installation. But if the people Hazard had seen in the parking lot were at least somewhat more diverse than he'd assumed, these here more than exceeded his expectations. Most of them were white, most of them older, most of them heavyset, most of them with unruly beards. Then there were the ones who veered the other direction: country-boy skinny, clean-shaven, kitchen-chair haircuts. Some of them were talkers, shouting over each other to make themselves heard; others were taciturn, answering questions with nods and grunts. One man passed them; he was wearing a biker's cut, and on the back, he'd taped a sheet of college-ruled paper that said, REVOLVER FOR SALE.

"So much for fucking background checks," Hazard muttered.

"The licensed dealers have to run background checks," Somers said, but even he sounded a little doubtful.

"Well, I'm sure that man wearing a piece of paper is equally thorough in vetting potential customers."

"God, you know, I think I actually like it when you get this grumpy. It's like I turned this corner, and now I want more and more of it."

"You are a moron," Hazard said and strode off.

The more he saw of the gun show, the more he felt like he'd crossed over into some other world. There were, of course, the anticipated items: the Confederate flags, the MAGA hats and shirts, the wire display units with assault rifles and pistols and shotguns. In addition to guns and knives, people were selling clothing—military-style fatigues and lots of camo, of course—and reloading supplies and military surplus. Two women were arguing over a stack of MREs—they both wanted the chili mac. But then there were the...unexpected elements. Behind one dealer's table, an enormous banner showed Trump's face pasted onto Rambo's body, carrying a rocket launcher—Hazard was pretty sure it was an M72 LAW, which in some ways made it even more impressive since production of that model had stopped in 1983. At another dealer's table, a sign read INVEST IN PRECIOUS METALS: BUY LEAD. There were life-size cardboard cutouts of Trump and Pence dressed like secret agents, some kind of James Bond knockoff with none of the cool, none of the flash—at least, that was the only thing Hazard could figure they were supposed to be.

"Good fucking Christ," Hazard said when Somers caught up.

"Yeah, this is something." Somers considered the women who were struggling, now, over the beef ravioli meals. "It's kind of like a swap meet."

"Why is there so much fucking beef jerky?"

A huge grin broke out across Somers's face. When Hazard glowered at him, Somers fought it down—with obvious difficulty.

"All right," Somers said. "Let's see what we can find."

The problem was not, as Hazard had feared, that people would recognize Somers—or Hazard—and refuse to cooperate. No, the real problem was two-fold: first, they were outsiders in a highly protective and self-aware community; and second, the people inside that community hated outsiders.

The first man they tried to talk to wore a leather vest over a t-shirt that said IN GOD WE TRUST. Somers got as far as "Hey, we were looking for—" when a conversation at the next table drew the dealer's attention.

"Don't listen to him," he shouted, turning away from Somers. "He's got no damn idea what he's talking about. You got to fill out Form 4 as a trust. You want the government crawling up your ass?"

The dealer at the next table was red-faced behind a Santa Claus beard, and he got as far as "Loren, shut your gob—" before things got worse.

On their next attempt, Somers was buttering up a woman with severe white hair and enormous eyeglasses on a MAGA chain when a twentysomething kid stumbled up to the table. He pointed to a rifle—some sort of Ruger, although Hazard didn't know the model—and said, "Oh my God, that's the one I was talking about. Dad! Dad! It's over here!" To the lady, he said, "Hey, how well does that gun work?"

Somers nudged Hazard to back away as all hell broke loose.

Some of the dealers wouldn't talk to them. Others wanted to talk too much, but no matter how Somers, with all his intuition and social graces, steered them toward Cocks for Glocks, they had nothing to say about Zach or a fight the day before. A few followed a familiar model of social engagement that Hazard had seen men—primarily older, aggrieved white men—use before: explanation as argument.

"Did you know that there's a bunch of the Democrats that keep kids in cages—"

"Did you know that the thing with the Russians was because George Soros—"

"Did you know that—"

"Did you know that—"

"Did you know that—"

"No," Hazard growled as Somers dragged him away from a conversational gambit about Pizzagate. "No, I did not fucking know that—"

"Cut it out," Somers whispered.

And then they struck gold.

She had a table loaded with camo gear for babies—infants, primarily, with a variety of onesies and coveralls and rompers, stitched with various patriotic designs. *Don't Tread on Me* and the old Ben Franklin cartoon, *Join, or Die*. She was middle-aged, with the middle-age sprawl, her hair long and chemically blond and obviously the victim of too many passes through a curling iron. Her black t-shirt read, *Home of the Free – Because of the Brave*, which, Hazard had to admit, was actually not wrong.

She couldn't wait to tell them.

"He was prancing around in here with, you know, a thing hanging out there. Like a man's thing. I swear to God, I said a prayer right then. I said, 'Lord, don't let Satan take me now.' And he didn't, praise Jesus."

"Yes," Hazard said. "I'm sure that an omnipotent being had nothing better to do than intervene to preserve you from the soteriological threat of a dildo—"

He had more, but it was hard to finish after your husband elbowed you in the gut.

"What did he want?" Somers asked. "He sounds crazy."

"Oh, yes, sir, he was crazy. One of those sex fiends, I suspect. My friend Martha got caught up with them. She was so pretty, but you know how that can go to your head, and then one day I saw her dancing at The Tap, and she had on this little skirt, and I said, 'Martha, if Tommy dips you like that one more time, God and the angels are going to see your hoo-haw,' and Martha said, 'Well, if God ain't seen my hoo-haw yet, He's been walking around with His eyes closed,' and I said, 'That's about the kind of language I'd expect from a woman letting Tommy Dunn escort her to a place like The Tap,' and Martha said, 'You're in here too, aren't you?' and I said—"

Some of the existential blackout Hazard was experiencing must have translated into a noise because Somers elbowed him again. Harder.

"And that's all," Somers asked, cutting in smoothly. "They let him walk around in here like that?"

"Oh no. Do you know Mr. Landon?" Her voice caught, and her eyes filled with tears. "I heard he—I heard he's dancing with the angels now."

"If you can't stop making that noise," Somers whispered furiously in Hazard's ear, "go away." Then, to the woman, Somers said, "What did he do?"

She wiped her eyes. "He was so brave. He went right up to that sex fiend and he said he had to get out of here. Well, that man didn't care what Landon said. He was trying to ruin the gun show with his—his sexual devilry. And he had no legal right to be here, did you know that?"

There were those magic words again.

"That's what Mr. Landon told him," she continued. "He didn't have any right to be here. He was breaking the law. And Mr. Landon was going to throw him out, only—" She cut off. Color worked its way under her powdered cheeks.

"Only what?" Somers asked.

"He stuck it in his mouth."

Hazard couldn't help himself; the word broke free. "What?"

"That man, the sex fiend. He stuck that—that thing in Mr. Landon's mouth. And he said—" More color rushed into her face, pushing her into tomato territory. "He said something like 'choke on it.' I think that was it. 'Choke on it, fascist.'"

"And then?" Somers prompted.

"And then they started brawling. A couple of the guys pulled them apart. The sex fiend was going crazy. Mr. Landon said he was going to kill him, and the sex fiend said, oh, you know, something about his motel—he was telling him where he was staying, you know, daring him to show up. And then Miss Naomi, you know her I guess, she was there, and it was like—it was like somebody flipped a switch. That sex fiend stopped and stared at her. And then he started to laugh. They were dragging him away, and he was laughing, and he said something to her—I didn't hear what because I was so worried about Mr. Landon—and she started screaming that she was going to kill him." She paused and then, as though unable to hold the comment back, said, "It was very unladylike."

"You didn't hear any of what he said to Naomi—" Hazard began.

Before he could finish, though, a voice interrupted him from behind.

"Well, well, well." It was a knock-off version of a preacher's voice, with a televangelist's rise and fall, and Hazard recognized it immediately. He turned to face Brother Gary and, alongside him, Red Alvin—the Dore County Sheriff's Department fuck-wonder detectives. Brother Gary was smirking as he glanced at Miranda Carmichael and said, "Looks like you were right. Looks like we've got ourselves a couple of trespassers."

CHAPTER FIVE
APRIL 11
SATURDAY
5:42 PM

THE SUN WAS SETTING by the time they got out of the sheriff's office.

The afternoon had been one of those professional humiliations on par with college stress dreams—the one about showing up for class naked seemed pretty close. Somers, as chief of police, had been forced to ride to the sheriff's office in the back seat of Brother Gary and Red Alvin's department-issued Charger. And that wasn't the worst part; he'd been jammed back there with Hazard and with Jalisa and—because, of course—with the sex doll. The doll was still wearing the red MAGA hat Jalisa had found for it, and some of the messages she'd written on it in big black marker were a breath of fresh air. Fuck the Patriarchy was old, but Make Anal Great Again was a nice change.

But it hadn't just been the ride back to the station. And it hadn't just been the professional ass-chewing that Dennis Engles had given him. The sheriff was about as good a man as you could find, in Somers's opinion, but he had a job to do, and he wasn't wrong about what he said. About any of it, actually. It wasn't even the impending phone call from his father that Somers could feel homing in on him like an ICBM. None of that bothered Somers because he'd gambled, and it had paid off; the information was worth the embarrassment.

No, what made his gut clench and his head throb was Naomi Malsho, his former sister-in-law, current unofficial leader of the Ozark Volunteers, and perpetual pain in Somers's ass. She was involved. Beyond her engagement to Landon, beyond her role as the head of the Volunteers, she was now a person of interest. Because she had threatened to kill Zach Renner. And because Zach Renner was dead less than twelve hours after their public confrontation.

The April day was dying slowly; the horizon was sooty orange, huge tongues of color licking the sky. Exhaust and the smell of rubber came on the hard slap of air from passing cars on Jefferson. Dulac, in his department Impala, was waiting at the curb for them.

"Bro," he said when Somers opened the door.

"Gray, don't start."

The car rocked when Hazard got into the back seat. The door slammed shut.

"Did you guys seriously—"

"I said, don't start."

"But, like, a sex doll?"

"What the fuck did you not understand," Hazard asked, "about don't start?" He slapped the back of Dulac's headrest. "Drive, fuckwad."

Dulac gave Somers a sidelong look and whispered, "Dude, it gets you right in the balls when he's like this, doesn't it? It's like a fucking tingle."

Somers covered his eyes and sank down in the seat.

Dulac drove them out to the gun show. The crowd was gone; only a few vehicles remained, all parked well away from the Mustang. No one had defaced it, which seemed like a small miracle—Somers was still paying off the paint job from a couple of months before. The Cocks for Glocks tent still stood on the other side of the road, but Jalisa's Malibu was gone; the sheriff had released her without charging her, which felt like a small win in a long, shitty day.

When they got into the Mustang, Hazard said, "We need to talk to her right now. We've already lost hours."

Somers nodded. He started the car, and they headed into the dusk.

Naomi Malsho lived in a house that was much like Naomi herself—or how she must have imagined herself. It was hidden behind acres of cornfields, where the first green blades broke the soil, and sat on top of a hill. It wasn't a farmhouse or a colonial or even a McMansion. It was modern, maybe too modern, mostly glass and steel. The sunset combed fire along the walls of windows. Out of place was one way of saying it, but Somers guessed that Naomi looked at it and saw a hidden gem.

In front of the house, the gravel drive spread out into a kind of miniature parking lot. A green Scion xD, the bumper's plastic scratched, was parked in front of Naomi's house. A sticker in the rear window said SCIENCE FLIES YOU TO THE MOON – RELIGION FLIES YOU INTO BUILDINGS.

Farther down the lot, parked facing the gravel drive, was a Dodge Ram. It looked new, the blue they sometimes called cobalt to make it more appealing, and it had been lifted so high that Somers wondered if the driver needed a stepstool to get in and out. The driver—or, at least, the man he figured was the driver—leaned against the truck, watching the house.

Somers drove the length of the lot and circled around, slowing as they passed the man by the truck. He figured it was pretty obvious they were inspecting him, but Somers was recently out of fucks to give, and the man didn't seem particularly bothered by it. He was white, average height, and thin. He wore a stringy mullet, an orange sleeveless tee grimy with stains, and western boots, the kind with a cowboy heel that made them impractical for any substantial amount of walking. On one sinewy arm, he had a tattoo.

"Fucking Tasmanian Devil," Hazard said, shaking his head.

Somers tried for something light, something to shake off the afternoon they'd had. "It was that or Tweety Bird."

They parked near the house. Voices met them as they approached, audible even through the closed door.

"I know who you are!" a man was shouting. A young man, Somers guessed. "I don't care!"

Someone answered, the words indistinct.

The door flew open, and the next shout rang into the evening: "You can't tell me what to do! I worked too hard for this, and I'm not going to let you ruin—"

The man stopped when he saw them. He was young, white, dressed in the kind of tee and jeans and sneakers that screamed dollar signs. His dark hair was cut in a skin fade on the sides and back, long on the top—long enough, in fact, that he'd styled it to bring out the waves that were almost curls. And he was handsome, handsome in a way that went beyond what people called hot. The kind of face and build people wanted to paint and sculpt. The kind people wanted to own however they could.

"If you think you can—"

That voice belonged to Naomi. She stopped at the door, the words drying up as she took in first Somers and then Hazard. There was always a moment, after Somers hadn't seen her in some time, when he forgot how much she looked like her sister, and the experience was disorienting. But the similarities were in the bone structure, the bird's-wing shoulders, the nose. Where Cora had cut her hair short and kept it dark, in keeping with her relative pallor, Naomi had highlights that went with her perpetual tan. She was dressed in jeans and a sweater—cashmere, Somers guessed from the look of it. Simple jewelry: a gold bangle, gold stud earrings, a small gold cross on a chain around her neck. And, as always, the mask of reserve she always wore around him—the thin crackle of ice that overlay her hatred.

"Is there some kind of problem?" Somers asked.

"No," Naomi said.

"You'd better believe there's a problem," the young man said. "Who are you?"

Somers identified himself.

"Thank God," the young man said. "I'm Benji Renner. And she—" He jerked a thumb at Naomi. "—is trying to suppress free speech."

"You're Benji Renner?" Hazard asked. "Zach's brother?"

Benji nodded. Now that the rush of the argument was fading, Somers was surprised he hadn't figured out the connection himself; the resemblance was striking—almost uncanny.

"Mr. Renner, I'm not sure if you've been officially notified," Somers said. "I have some bad news about your brother."

"I know he's dead. That's why I'm here." He studied them for a moment and apparently decided to say more. "She says their friend owns the land on the other side of the highway, so we can't be there. But the highway's shoulder is common ground. We have a First Amendment right—"

"Why are you here, John-Henry?" Naomi cut in. Her lips curved, and she glanced at Hazard. "Do you need a dog sitter?"

Hazard didn't even glance at her. His eyes were still locked on Benji.

Somers kept his voice level. "Naomi, we need to talk to you."

Her eyes slid to the truck and Taz.

"No need to bring your bodyguard into this," Somers said.

Something flickered in her eyes, something that might have been confusion. He waited for the refusal, the denial, *talk to my lawyer*, but instead, Naomi gave a crisp nod. "Come in. I've been waiting all day, and I want to get this over with."

"I want to talk to them too," Benji said.

"Find a public toilet," she said pleasantly, "or a patch of bushes in Truman Park. I'm sure the faggots will end up there eventually."

"Really, Naomi?" Somers asked. "I'd like to keep this professional."

"I imagine that's the first time you've had to say that without bending over. Come inside, John-Henry. I don't have all night."

"Jesus Christ," Hazard muttered as he followed Somers inside.

"I want to talk to them," Benji said again, more loudly.

But when he took a step forward, Naomi shut the door in his face. She offered each of them a curl of her lip and then led the way deeper into the house.

The inside matched the outside: the high ceilings, the slate tiles, the minimalist décor—here and there, a few abstract pieces of art and metalwork. It didn't look like the home of a white supremacist. It looked more like a museum than anything else, and it felt like one too: sterile, cold, chrome-and-ivory furnishings.

She led them into a large living room, where a wall of windows looked out on the sunset. The last light of day gave the tops of the trees an ember flicker, while everything else sank into a morass of shadow. When she gestured to a chrome-and-ivory sofa, Somers sat, and she took a white rattan chair opposite him. Hazard stood by the window, the sunset tiger-striping him.

"Can't sit?" Naomi asked in that same tea-and-bridge hostess voice. "I suppose some discomfort must be part of your way of life."

Hazard bared his teeth in a parody of a smile. "He's a little young for you, don't you think, Naomi?"

Naomi's face reddened under her golden tan. Somers blinked in surprise. It was a measure of how much Naomi had unbalanced him that he hadn't sensed what Hazard had picked up—some sort of undercurrent to Benji and Naomi's interaction, something that went beyond an argument about a dildo buyback program.

But a heartbeat later, Naomi recovered. "It certainly didn't stop you with that...boy you've got your claws into."

"For God's sake, Naomi," Somers said. "Both of you, actually. Cut it out."

"What do you want, John-Henry? I'm tired, and I'm grieving, and I would like some time to myself. I've spent all day dealing with—with fallout."

"First," Somers said, bracing himself with a breath, "I want to tell you I'm sorry for your loss."

Naomi laughed. "Don't give me that. It was a marriage of convenience; you know that. Landon offered me a way to cement my position." Her voice became dry. "You may find it hard to believe, but there are elements of the Ozark Volunteers who do not like listening to a woman. Landon was established in the area. People looked up to him. He had a certain amount of money and influence. And, of course, he had a penis. That made him an ideal partner."

"And you?" Hazard asked from the window.

"What do you mean?"

"What did you offer Landon?"

The lie was so smooth that if Somers hadn't known this woman, grown up with her, married her sister, he would have missed it. "My own sway with the Volunteers."

No, Somers thought, trying to catch the truth in her face. No, that wasn't it at all.

"I was in St. Louis last night," she said. "The whole night. I left Wahredua shortly after four, and I didn't come back until I got the phone call this morning. Incidentally, that was why I had to ask Kurt and Angela to check in on Carson; otherwise I would have handled the boy myself."

"That's your alibi?" Hazard asked.

"I had dinner with a pair of wealthy donors. We were at their house until almost ten. I imagine you can place me—and my car—in that area if you do a little work. Then I went to my hotel."

"That's convenient."

Somers knew what his husband meant; if she'd been at dinner until ten, she couldn't have been back to Wahredua before midnight—the travel time was around two hours. And while it was possible that she could have shaved off time by speeding, the window was too tight for Somers's comfort. If nothing else, it would be impossible to convince a jury beyond a reasonable doubt that she could have returned to Wahredua within the window of Landon and Zach's time of death. He nodded and said, "We'll need their names and a way to contact them. And the hotel's information."

Naomi smiled and made a flicking-away gesture with one hand.

"We understood that you had an encounter with Mr. Renner at the gun show yesterday," Hazard said.

For a moment, something flickered under the ice caps—like a signal switch being thrown, or a traffic light changing. Somers saw the microexpression, caught it, but he didn't understand it. And then it was gone.

She said, "Yes."

"Do you want to tell us about that?"

"To borrow his words, he said I had a cunt like an infected sewer and that I was the Volunteers' designated ball-drainer."

"And because of that, you said you were going to kill him?"

Naomi shrugged one delicate shoulder. "I don't remember what I said, to be honest. I was so angry that I was beside myself."

"That's convenient," Hazard said. "Again."

She offered him a smile.

"Did Landon tell you that he was going to the Presidential last night?" Somers asked.

"No."

"Did he tell you that he was planning on confronting Zach Renner, or that he intended to continue their argument from earlier, or anything of the sort?"

"No."

"Do you have any idea why your fiancé was in Mr. Renner's motel room last night?"

"No, although I imagine it's because Landon was a bully and a combative asshole." She watched them and then laughed. "Don't tell me you don't feel the same way; you have to remember how he was when we were in high school. Trust me, he's not gotten better. If anything, he's worse. Being an adult has a way of inoculating thugs like Landon against many of the social controls for that kind of behavior."

"Not what I'd expect from a woman planning on marrying him."

"As I said," Naomi said with another shrug. "He was useful."

"That kind of behavior often leaves hard feelings," Somers said. "Grudges. Can you think of anyone who would have wanted to hurt Landon?"

"Many people. But no one who would have done what you saw last night."

"You're sure?"

"He was a bully. A victim might snap, of course. Might turn on the bully. But from what I understand, that's not what happened last night. Someone shot Landon, correct? And then shot and killed Zach Renner? That doesn't sound like someone who snapped and came after the man who'd been torturing them."

"That's some bullshit armchair psychology."

"Then I'll put it more simply: no, I can't think of anyone who would have done that to Landon last night."

"What about recent trouble?" Somers asked. "Has Landon had anything seriously bad happen lately? Financially? Professionally? In his personal life?"

"I am his personal life. Or I was."

"And let me guess," Hazard said. "Everything was aces?"

"No, John-Henry. No recent trouble."

Somers nodded. "Has anything strange happened lately? Phone calls that Landon wouldn't explain? New people in his life? Times when Landon went missing or you couldn't reach him? Did he seem disturbed, afraid, worried, upset?"

Naomi shook her head. An arid smile dusted her single word: "No."

"What kind of interactions have you had with Zach Renner and his organization?" Hazard asked.

"Only the one. He showed up the first day of the gun show and put up that ridiculous stand. Some of the more enthusiastic volunteers went over to convince him to leave, but we made sure they understood not to cause any trouble. The Volunteers are a law-abiding organization, and we had legal recourse to remove them from the area. Of course, when he infiltrated the show and made a spectacle, things escalated. You already know about his argument with Landon and me."

"You'd never interacted with Zach Renner or his organization before that?"

"No."

"Or since?"

"Not unless you count that boy showing up at my house and threatening me. He wanted to scare me into backing down. He's not from here, of course, so he doesn't know me. I tried to help him understand. I think the sheriff's department will see that the land they want to use is private property, and that using the shoulder of a state highway poses a public danger. I'm sure that they'll be asked to move to another location before the end of the day."

Hazard swore under his breath.

"Is there anything else you can tell us?" Somers asked. "Anything about Landon, or about what happened to him?"

A single shake of her head.

The sun had dropped below the trees. The last light of day glimmered through the canopy in pyrite flecks.

"If that's all—" Naomi began.

"What about Landon's son?" Hazard asked. "What was their relationship like?"

Naomi sank back into her seat and examined him for a moment. "Landon wanted the best for him, of course."

"I've heard that before."

"I don't feel like I can say more than that. I didn't have much to do with Carson. My interest was in Landon, and I'm not exactly the maternal type."

"Don't be too hard on yourself," Hazard said, baring his teeth in another flash. "Plenty of animals eat their young."

Naomi blanched, and then color rushed into her face. One hand wrapped around the arm of the chair, and the rattan creaked and crackled. When she spoke, her voice was a strained attempt at the tea-and-bridge tone she'd used before, and her smile had a peeling, leprous quality. "Tell me, Emery, what does little Colt think of Danny Lee's offer?"

"What offer—" Hazard cut himself off. Somers watched as the walls came up, and Hazard's face became stone.

"Really, he hasn't told his beloved Pops?" Naomi's hand tightened on the rattan again. "Pity."

"Leave it alone, Naomi," Somers said. "Whatever your little white supremacist information network told you, drop it."

"I'm surprised is all."

"Leave it."

"Such an important decision. And affecting all of you. It's hard to believe he wouldn't at least ask you what you think."

"You fucking bitch—" Hazard shouted, and he lunged two steps before Somers got in his path.

"Stop it," Somers said, pushing him back. Hazard retreated, lunged again, and fell back when Somers shoved him. "I said stop!"

"I'm sorry," Naomi said. "I had no idea."

"Don't talk about my son," Hazard shouted over Somers's shoulder. "I don't want to hear his name in your fucking mouth."

"But then, Emery, that's the whole problem, isn't it? You're a faggot." She broke the syllables crisply. "You don't have a son. He's not your son. He's Danny Lee's son. He has a real dad."

Growling, Hazard tried to get past Somers, but Somers grappled with him until he got a good hold on Hazard's arm. He spun him around and steered him toward the door.

"We're done here," he said back to Naomi.

"Goodbye, John-Henry. Kisses to Evie."

It was a struggle, but Somers got his husband to the front door. That was when Hazard tore free.

"Emery Francis Hazard!"

"No, John. I'm going to find out how she knows what was in that letter, and then I'm going to explain to her why she's never going to so much as think about Colt again—"

A shout from outside interrupted him, followed by a cry of pain. Indecision waffled in Hazard's face, and then Somers reached past him and yanked the door open.

On the far side of the gravel stretch, the guy with the tattoo—Taz, Somers's brain supplied—was kneeling astride Benji Renner, pounding his face into the ground.

CHAPTER SIX

APRIL 11
SATURDAY
6:28 PM

SOMERS SHOT THROUGH THE doorway first, and gravel crunched underfoot as he sprinted across the open ground.

Near the Ram, Taz—or whatever the hell his real name was—was straddling Benji, punching the young man in the face. The blows came fast and frenzied, without any hint of control or finesse. Taz wasn't looking for style points. He was going straight for a redneck TKO. Or, Somers thought, watching Taz spray spittle, maybe straight for the kill.

"Hey!" Somers shouted as he ran. "Get off him!"

Taz never looked up.

When Somers reached him, a combination of things happened: he grabbed Taz by the sleeveless tee, shoved him backward, and tried to slow his own forward momentum. Instead, the loose gravel slid underfoot and threatened to topple him. Somers lost his grip on Taz as he skidded and tried to stay upright. Taz landed on his back and released a short cry of surprise.

Somers straightened and took another step—he wanted to get a pair of handcuffs on Taz before this escalated any further. Taz, however, had different ideas. The man kicked, and his western boots sent up a sheet of loose stones. Somers drew back, shielding his face with one arm, wincing as chunks of gravel struck him.

The delay only lasted a handful of seconds, but by the time Somers was moving forward again, he'd lost his advantage. Taz was hauling himself into the lifted Ram, and a moment later, the door slammed shut. The engine roared to life; lights sprang on. The truck lurched forward.

Somers grabbed Benji under the arms because he had the vague idea that Taz was going to try to run them down. But the truck shot straight toward the drive that led back to the state highway, and a moment later, the taillights winked out behind the swell of the next hill. The engine's rumble faded too, and Somers became aware of his own labored breathing, heavy with the weight of the adrenaline still running through him, and of the silence that seemed strangely loud after the percussion of blows.

"Motherfucker," Hazard said, sliding to a stop. He glanced at Somers, swiveled toward the Mustang, and asked, "Do you want me to—"

"No," Somers said, dropping into a squat by Benji.

"No plate," Hazard said.

The adrenaline still had Somers doing a few loop-the-loops, and a laugh tumbled out. "God, thank you. I should have seen that."

"You were focused on other things."

Other things, in this case, was a young man who looked like he'd gone ten rounds. His nose and eyes were swollen, and one of the blows had lacerated the skin along his cheekbones. All in all, the damage could have been a lot worse.

"Can you hear me?" Somers said. "You still with us?"

Benji groaned.

"He needs to be examined for a concussion," Hazard said. "And maybe stitches."

"My head," Benji moaned.

"Really?" Hazard said. "Is that where it hurts?"

Somers flashed him a look, and Hazard had the good grace to turn slightly pink.

"Want to try sitting up?" Somers asked. "We need to get you to the hospital."

"No," Benji said. "No hospital."

"Yes, hospital. Come on, up we go."

Somers got an arm around Benji and helped him sit. The younger man's neck looked a little noodly, but his eyes were clear, and he seemed to be aware of where he was. Gravel crunched as Hazard went to the Mustang and came back with the first aid kit. While Somers kept Benji upright, Hazard went to work, cleaning the cut with an antiseptic wipe and then taping a bandage in place.

Benji winced and flinched and made little noises through the whole process.

"Stop being such a baby," Hazard said. He took Benji's hand and placed it against the bandage. "Apply pressure."

"It hurts," Benji said.

"Well, of course it fucking hurts. Someone tried to knock your block off." Hazard sat back on his heels and then snapped, "What the fuck did I say about applying pressure?"

Benji's eyes widened, and he pressed more firmly against the bandage.

As Hazard returned the first aid kit to the trunk, Benji whispered, "Holy God."

"No, just my husband, unfortunately." Somers said with a slanted smile. "All right, Benji. Let's get you up."

"No—" He shook his head and winced again. "No, please. I do not want to go to the hospital. I've got so much to do, and I'm fine, honestly."

Somers traded looks with Hazard as he came back from the car. The big man shrugged. "We can give him a few minutes and see how the bleeding looks. The concussion is the real worry."

"Yeah, that—let's do that. You'll see in a few minutes. I'm fine, really."

"Uh huh," Somers said. "Let's get you to your car, then. No point sitting on the ground."

Helping Benji to his feet, Somers was struck by two things. First, by how young the man seemed—barely older than Colt. Benji had a little more of an adult's build to him, but he still had that supple leanness to him that suggested adolescence. True, some men carried that look into their twenties. But also true, some high school seniors looked as much like an adult as Benji. The second impression that Somers couldn't shake was how much Benji looked like Zach—true, the aquiline features were softened and filled out, even more attractive on Benji with the rough edges hammered out, but the resemblance was uncanny.

"I know," Benji said, catching Somers's eye and then looking away with an uncomfortable laugh. "People say we look like twins."

"I wouldn't say that," Hazard said. "He's substantially older than you."

"Well, yeah." Benji fished his keys out and passed them to Somers, who unlocked the xD's rear door. Benji grunted as Somers eased him down onto the bench seat. "I meant twins if we were the same age."

"Let me guess: you were a happy little surprise."

Benji's face colored. "Unhappy little surprise is more like it." Then, with what looked like an effort, he offered a smile. "I get the impression my mom was not happy when she found out she was having a kid at forty-three."

"That would definitely be a surprise," Somers said.

"In what way would it be a surprise?" Hazard asked. "Was she still not sure how women get pregnant? Was she under some sort of misunderstanding about the basic steps of the human reproductive process?"

"Ignore him."

Benji laughed and let his head fall back. "She thought she couldn't get pregnant. That's what she tells everyone, anyway. And then bang, here I am."

"Bang is right," Hazard muttered.

Somers kicked him in the ankle; when Hazard glowered at him, Somers flashed him a smile. Turning to Benji, Somers asked, "Want to tell us what that was all about?"

"He's a hoosier asshole." Benji's voice held a note of outraged self-satisfaction. "That's what it's all about."

"You're in Dore County," Hazard said. "You'll have to be more specific."

"Well, I don't know what you want me to say. I was waiting for you; I told you, I wanted to talk to you. He didn't like that. He told me to leave. I told him no. He said I had to leave right then. I told him to fuck off. He got in my face, and when I wouldn't back down, he started hitting me."

"That seems stupid."

"Most of these guys, they're bullies. If you stand up to them, eventually they'll go away."

"I guess this was an exception."

"Yeah," Benji said sourly, adjusting his hand on the bandage. "I guess so."

"But when I said that seems stupid, I was referring to him. Why would he attack you? He knew a law-enforcement officer was in the house. He had to know that we'd intervene and that he was risking arrest."

Benji stared at him, slack-jawed for a moment. "I don't know what he was thinking. I mean, do you think he drew me a game plan before he started trying to break my nose?"

"Had he given you any trouble before?" Somers asked. "When you got here to talk to Naomi, I mean?"

"What? No, he wasn't here then."

Somers nodded and considered the young man. He let the silence gape, and Benji shifted on the seat, looking away and then back.

"So, like—" Benji tried.

"So," Somers said over him. "You're Benji Renner."

Benji nodded. "Do you need my ID or something?"

His ID was written all over his face, but Somers nodded, and Benji shifted his weight to work his wallet out of his pocket. He passed it over, and Somers examined the Missouri driver's license: Benjamin Renner, address in St. Louis, born May 5, 2001. That made him eighteen, almost nineteen. Somers passed the wallet to Hazard and resumed his consideration of Benji.

"All right, Benji," Somers said. "You wanted to talk to us."

Benji nodded. He was trying to keep his eyes on Somers's face, but they kept sliding to Hazard, who was making no effort to hide his inspection of the wallet's contents. "Uh, can he, like, do that—"

"Yes," Hazard said as he pulled out another credit card.

"What did you want to talk to us about?" Somers asked.

"Well, my brother got murdered, right?"

Somers nodded. "Yes, I'm afraid that's true. How did you hear about that? This morning, we had no idea you were in town."

"My parents. My mom, actually. You can't count on my dad to do anything." His voice trembled. "He's like Zach. They talk big, and then—" He shook his head, and then he wiped his eyes. Voice thick, he continued, "Anyway, my mom called after the police told her about Zach. So, then I had to tell everybody, you know? We're all here because of Zach, and they needed to know. And everybody believes in what we're doing—"

"Who's everybody?"

"Well, Courtney and Jalisa and me. And we all believe in this, in Zach's mission, so we decided we needed to stay until the gun show ended. I guess you met Jalisa; she called me from the sheriff's office."

"Shouldn't you be in school?" Hazard asked.

"Can I have my wallet back?"

His tone was sharp, and Hazard raised his eyebrows, but he handed it back.

Benji wedged it between his legs. It looked like he was fighting hard not to check the wallet to make sure everything was still there. "I graduated last year, for your information. Principia."

Hazard's eyebrows arched more sharply. "I meant college."

"Oh. Uh, I guess. I mean, this is my gap year." When they didn't answer, he rushed to fill the silence. "I didn't want to go to school. I thought maybe I'd do something with the family business, you know? And I never knew Zach, not, like, really. I mean, he's twenty years older than me. So when he asked if I wanted to do this with him, I was like, hell yeah."

"Tell us a little bit about working with Zach. What's that like?"

"Pretty good. Courtney is uptight, but Jalisa is cool, and Zach is—well, you never met him, right?"

Somers shook his head.

"He's awesome. He was awesome. I mean, he could talk to anybody, and they'd be best friends by the time they walked away."

Except Landon Maas, Somers thought; he didn't like having a dildo shoved in his mouth. Except Naomi, after whatever Zach had said to her.

"That's why he's so good at this stuff," Benji said. "Causes and activism and stuff. He's a good person; he genuinely cares about this kind of thing. And he's got this charisma, I mean, you wouldn't believe it." He had to stop again, and his voice was wiry when he added, "I wish you could have met him."

"Benji, there are some questions we need to ask you," Somers said. "You understand that they're routine, right?"

Benji nodded doubtfully.

"Let's start with where you were last night."

"What are you—"

"Routine, Benji. Routine questions."

"My motel. It's—I don't know. Something Bridal. They call it a motor court."

"All right," Somers said, "we know the place. Were you there all night?"

"Yes."

"What time did you get to your room?"

"I don't know. Eight, maybe. We had dinner as a team, and then I went back."

"Alone?"

Benji blushed, but his voice was scathing. "Yes, alone."

"All right. Did you have any contact with Zach last night?"

"No, of course not."

"Why 'of course not'?"

"Because everybody went back to their motels to sleep. We knew we were going to have a hard day."

"In what sense?" Hazard asked.

"Just, normal hard. That's the job."

"Really? Have you had much trouble while you've been with Zach?"

"What? No, I told you, everybody on the team's cool—"

"I meant with other people. People at the events where you're demonstrating, for example, or otherwise."

"Oh. Well, yeah. I mean, people don't like what we do, that's for sure. There's always some micropenis who wants to show off for his friends, prove what a tough guy he is. Sometimes they try to get rough, but Zach and I, we can handle them. For the most part, people want to talk shit or

87

give us dirty looks. It never goes beyond that." He played with the tape on his bandage and shook his head. "I mean, it never went beyond that before."

"Jalisa told us that Zach always insisted that members of the team stay in different motels."

Benji stared at him blankly. After a moment, he said with a note of confusion, "Yeah."

"Why?"

"Oh God! No, it's not like anyone was in danger. I mean, maybe that was what Zach told Courtney and Jalisa. That would be something he'd do. Zach kind of liked…drama, I guess. Attention. But the real reason he did that is he was, you know, slipping it to them. Both of them. And he didn't want the other one to know."

"Straight people are so charming," Hazard murmured.

"I mean, they're all adults," Benji said. "It's not like he was doing anything wrong. But he didn't want bad feelings to ruin the work. And, you know, sometimes he'd meet a girl in whatever town we were in, and…Well, it's like I said: he had this charisma. You should have seen some of the girls he got."

"Attractive?" Somers asked.

"Well, yeah, but I mean—they'd be super conservative, you know? Wearing their Trump shirts, that kind of thing. But they'd spend five minutes talking to Zach, and, I don't know. He had this weird mix of bad boy and hippie that was like crack to those girls."

"Do you think one of those girls could have done this?" Somers asked.

"Uh, I guess. I mean, as far as I know, he hadn't hooked up with anyone here yet."

"What about an angry father or husband?"

Benji shrugged again and spread his free hand in a *who knows?* gesture.

"What about anyone else who might have a reason to hurt Zach? Can you think of anyone? I'm sure you come across a lot of people who don't like what you do."

For a moment, Benji's expression was blank. "Well, yeah," he said slowly. "I mean, that's why I wanted to talk to you."

"What do you mean?"

"I know who killed Zach."

"You do?"

"Yeah. It was the Ozark Volunteers."

"I see," Hazard said. "And you have some way to corroborate this?"

"Yeah, of course."

"But instead of going to the police, you decided to hold on to that information on the off chance that you'd stumble across our path."

"What the hell? Of course I wasn't trying to 'hold on' to it. You're the police, right? You're supposed to find me."

"Yes, I forgot, there's absolutely no way that you could have figured out how to contact the police in an emergency. There's no phone number that everyone learns when they're a child, a number that's the same no matter where you are, that you could have used to contact the police."

"What the hell? What the actual hell? What are you trying to say?"

"I think it's interesting that the day after your brother is murdered, we catch you in the middle of an argument with one of the organizers of the gun show."

"She's trying to shut us down! And what the fuck do you mean, 'catch me'? You make it sound like I'm doing something wrong!"

"Are you?"

Red mottled Benji's cheeks, and he opened his mouth for more shouting.

"Ree, cut it out. Benji, let it go." Somers considered the young man again. Benji's eyes were hard and locked on Hazard. "You expected the police to contact you. All right, here we are. What's this information that you have?"

"That guy, the one who attacked Zach at the gun show? He was a big deal with the Ozark Volunteers."

"We've heard about Landon's ties to that group," Somers said carefully. "But Landon was one of the victims, and although I can't go into the specifics, it's clear that this was not a murder-suicide or a case of murder and self-defense."

"That's not what I'm saying," Benji said, squirming to the edge of the seat. "I'm trying to tell you, the Ozark Volunteers killed both of them."

"Why would the Ozark Volunteers—" Hazard began.

"What do you know about Landon's dad?"

Somers threw a sidelong look at his husband.

Benji spoke into that gap: "Yeah, you didn't think about him, did you?"

"Benji," Somers said, "you're acting like you know something, but I'm not connecting the dots. I know a little about Landon's father, but nothing that would suggest why he would kill his own son."

"No, that part was an accident. They didn't know Landon was going to be there."

"Kid," Hazard said, "what the fuck are you talking about?"

"I found this today. We've got a shared folder in our cloud storage, and I was looking for some of the nonprofit's paperwork; my dad said the family lawyer wanted a copy." He pulled out his phone, tapped the screen a few times, and turned it toward them. On the screen a video began to play.

It took Somers a moment to understand what he was seeing: only a narrow section in the center of the frame was visible, off-white bracketing a patch of gray. Then one side of the image stirred, and Somers realized he was looking out a window, through curtains that had been parted. The camera looked down on a patch of asphalt — presumably the parking lot of the Presidential, outside of Zach Renner's room.

The sound of a door slamming came across the video. A man stepped into view, and Somers leaned closer, trying to make out details. Then the man turned, and Somers knew his first guess had been right: he was looking at a man with a Tasmanian Devil tattoo on his upper arm. The camera wobbled again, and a second man stepped into view. Somers recognized him: the white hair, the lantern jaw, the coveralls. It was Gerrit Maas, Landon's father. And he was carrying an assault rifle.

CHAPTER SEVEN
APRIL 11
SATURDAY
8:31 PM

IN THE KITCHEN, Hazard ran water around the inside of the sink, rinsing the last of the soap and food particles down the drain. Music that was, he guessed, supposed to be ominous filtered in from the next room. *Ghost Hunters*. Colt's latest obsession. Hazard watched the spray run down the stainless steel. It wasn't ghosts that came back, he thought. It was everything else.

His phone buzzed, and when he saw Ramona Andrews's name on the screen, he answered.

"Mr. Hazard, I'm sorry to bother you," Colt's social worker said.

"It's not a problem. This is late for a work call; is everything all right?"

"I don't know about all right. I'm driving back from Cape Girardeau; it's been a weekend. I thought I might as well make the most of the hours."

"What can I help you with?"

"Well, I know we talked about this when we were formalizing the arrangements for Colt to stay with you and your husband, but we're required to regularly review Colt's permanency plan until it's finalized. I'd like—"

"Colt's permanency plan is finalized," Hazard said. "He's staying here. That's the end of the discussion."

The silence of empty miles came back at him. When Ramona spoke, her voice was calm. Almost gentle. "Mr. Hazard, a permanency plan is finalized when it's approved by a judge."

"All right. Let's have this meeting. We'll see a judge. We'll have him sign it or whatever he needs to do."

"It's not that simple—"

"It seems simple. I don't understand what the problem is."

"Mr. Hazard, as I was trying to say, I'd like for you and Colt and your husband to come in for a meeting. We'll talk about what Colt wants, what's best for Colt, as well as requirements by the state that need to be addressed—"

"What do you mean, requirements by the state? We did the trainings. We've done all the follow-up bits." A swell of eerie music came from the next room, and Hazard tried to clamp down on his voice, aware that his volume was slipping. He crossed the kitchen and passed into the dining room. He ended up at the windows that looked out on the street. He smelled lemon furniture polish. On the other side of the glass, pockets of light marked the lines of sidewalks and curbs and street, and then everything dropped away. "If there's some minimum mandatory hours—"

"The state of Missouri requires that we attempt placement of a foster child with a relative as the first option."

It was like the edge of a great river, Hazard thought, looking out at the night, the sidewalk and curb and hint of the street sliding under the darkness. All of a sudden, everything solid gave way.

He heard himself talking from a long way off. The other side of the river, maybe.

"I understood that his relatives were all either incarcerated or out of state."

"That..." Ramona took a breath. "That no longer seems to be the case."

"That letter," Hazard said.

"What?"

"Nothing." But he thought it: that letter, that fucking letter, Danny fucking Lee and his motherfucking letter.

"This is why I'd like to meet with you and your husband and Colt," Ramona said. "So we can review the permanency plan and talk about next steps."

"There is no next step," Hazard said. "Colt is staying here."

"Mr. Hazard, that's not entirely your decision to make."

He opened his mouth to tell her all the things he could do, all the problems he could cause, if she didn't drop this right now. And then a small part of him, a part that sounded like Somers, pointed out that he'd sound like a lunatic. He managed to shut his mouth.

"I've got an opening on my calendar next Thursday."

"No." Hazard's jaw ached. "It's—could we do it the week after? His birthday is the twenty-first, and—" The blankness of the world outside stared back at him. He was aware of himself, aware of sounding like he was picking the words up off the floor. "If we could wait until after." He closed his eyes. "Please."

Ramona was silent. All the miles. Missouri was a big, dark place. And then she sighed. "Nothing will happen immediately, Mr. Hazard."

His throat was dry. His voice was on the verge of cracking, and that hadn't happened since he was in his teens. "Please."

"I'll call back next week, and we'll make an appointment for after his birthday."

"Thank you."

She said goodnight—or she said something, anyway—and the call disconnected. Then it was like the tide pulling out, and he thought, for a moment, he might fall face-first into the window. He blinked. A truck or an SUV rolled past; it was a blur. He blinked some more, and then it was gone. A second car came a few minutes later—something sporty and low, a muscle car, the flow of the body suggesting a classic model. Then it, too, was gone. Horace Tomlinson's porch light came on. Then it went off. You could do Morse code with a light. You could stand there, flicking the switch short-short-short long-long-long short-short-short. And it wouldn't mean a fucking thing if nobody was looking for it, if there was nobody else out there in the big dark.

He pocketed his phone and went back to the kitchen. A joist creaked underfoot, and Somers called from the living room, "Ree? Are you going to come in here?"

Colt's voice was pitched low enough that they could all pretend it was a whisper, even though it was meant to carry: "Why'd you have to do that?"

Somers's answer was equally low when he said, "Stop."

"If he comes in here, I'm going upstairs."

"Bubs, cut it out." Then, in a louder voice, Somers called, "Ree?"

"Yeah," Hazard said. The word felt thick. His face was puffy, he realized now. His eyes hot. He fumbled with the trash can. "In a minute."

Trash in one hand, he let himself out the back door and crossed the patio. The April night was cold. It had a biting clarity that was a memory of winter, the stars like augur holes in the sky. Redshift, Hazard thought as he swung the bag into the can. It was trash night; he rocked the can onto its wheels and rolled it around the side of the house. Redshift and blueshift. The color of light changed depending on a star's movement relative to earth. Which goes to show, Hazard thought, the wet earth and young grass spongy underfoot, which just goes to show, his smile like a razor opening and closing, which just goes to fucking show, he pushed his hair back when the wind's cold hand raked it into his face, that any message, anything you want to say, gets fucked up the farther apart you are.

He lowered the trash can into place at the curb.

To his right, headlights flared to life. An engine growled. Hazard shaded his eyes, but he could only make out the silhouette of a larger vehicle. A truck or an SUV. He thought, vaguely, that he'd seen one drive past the house a few minutes before. Then the SUV—he was pretty sure it was an SUV was coming up the street.

It rolled to a stop in front of him. Yes, an SUV. Black. Tinted glass. The rumble of bass like a swarm of hornets. The window buzzed down, and a cloud of vapor rushed out: mango and marijuana. Hazard's brain assembled a composite of the man in the driver's seat: a beanie pulled low, thick eyebrows, a strong jaw, a diamond stud in each ear. His brown skin and his features suggested at least some of his ancestry was African. Hazard's eyes came to rest on the gun pointed at him. It was a pistol. Probably a nine-millimeter.

"Hands," he said.

Hazard displayed his hands. His mind laid out his options, branching and forking, possibilities and probabilities. He could run; having a gun wasn't necessarily the same thing as having the resolve to shoot. But, of course, he might get shot. He could call for help, but Somers's gun was locked in the safe under their bed, and worse, Colt might come to the door first—he might not, part of his brain put in nastily—and either way, he'd be putting people he loved in danger. He could try to get closer and hope this man made a mistake. That seemed like the best option. A part of his brain was reminding him that the standard advice about kidnapping was that it was better not to be kidnapped at all, no matter the cost, because your chances for survival dropped drastically as soon as you were taken.

All of that passed through his head in an instant.

"Be cool," the man said, and he laid a finger to his lips. It made Hazard think of Saint Nick—a brain flash, one of those uncontrolled associations. "Don't want to bother the kids."

And that was it, the deciding factor. They knew about Colt and Evie. Hazard nodded.

The passenger door opened, and a second man came around the front of the SUV. He was tall, and under the streetlights, he had a warmer tone to his skin, almost tawny. He wore a hoodie, the hood up in a loose, stylish way that Colt would have envied. The same strong lines to his jaw suggested a relationship to the driver. Gold and silver chains glinted around his neck.

"Put these on," he said in a softer voice, tossing a pair of handcuffs.

Hazard caught them.

"Now," the first man said. When Hazard snapped one of the bracelets shut around his wrist, he added, "Behind your back."

Hazard nodded. He wasn't sure these men were professionals — the way they dressed, their use of drugs while on a job, the fact that there had been time, if Hazard had taken advantage of it, for him to run back into the house while they were driving up the street, all suggested that they were opportunists instead. But opportunists or not, they weren't rookies either. He locked the second bracelet around his wrist, hands behind his back.

"Show me," the second one said in his softer voice.

Hazard turned around.

"Move your hands. No, man, really move 'em." Hazard complied, and then the man said, "All right. Don't do anything stupid, you hear?"

"Nothing stupid," Hazard said.

The second man opened the rear door and then moved a few steps away. No, Hazard thought with something like despair dropping in his gut. Definitely not rookies.

"Where are we going?" Hazard asked. It was a bid for time, for the chance that Somers would wonder what was taking so long and come to the window, that he might see what was happening. Hazard had to fight the urge to look back at the house.

"Don't worry about it," the driver said.

"Just get in, man," the second man said.

"Why should I? If you're going to kill me —"

The driver straightened in his seat. "Motherfucker, if I have to tell you to get in one more time, I'm going to fuck you up."

"Fuck, Larenz, shut up." The second man studied Hazard. "We want you to help us, that's all. We're going for a ride. Then you tell that kid we're legit. We get what we want, we leave, and everybody's happy."

"Fucking dumbass," the driver — Larenz — snapped. "What the fuck are you thinking, saying my name?"

"Korrin," the second man said, tapping his chest. "Now you know our names, and I told you we aren't going to hurt you unless you make us. Come on, Mr. Hazard. Nobody wants this to go bad. Let's get out of here before somebody sees us."

"Logically, the fact that you told me your names increases the likelihood that you're going to kill me."

"Logically, huh?" Korrin grinned. He was nice looking, younger than Hazard had first thought. "Because you're going to ID us, is that it?"

"That's it."

"Well, Mr. Hazard, Larenz and I have got bigger problems than you or the police. We want to get what's ours and get the hell out of here. We don't want trouble. We sure as hell don't want to add a murder charge to the sheet. So it's like I told you: we're going for a ride. You'll be back before your boy is asleep."

"Ten," Larenz said. "Motherfucker, don't make me get to one. Nine."

Hazard let his brain run through one last sprint of calculations. Then he climbed into the SUV's back seat. Korrin shut the door behind him and came around to climb in the front passenger seat.

"About fucking time," Larenz muttered and let the SUV roll forward.

They drove five over the speed limit down the block: a reasonable speed, nothing that would get them pulled over. They weren't going to rush. They weren't going to get sloppy—at least, not yet.

"When you say, 'that kid,' you're talking about Carson Maas?"

"Shut up," Larenz said.

"That's right," Korrin said, glancing back at him. "You're as good as everybody says you are."

"It didn't exactly take a genius," Hazard said. "You've been watching the house. Were you waiting for it to be empty?"

"God damn," Korrin said to Larenz. "He's like Sherlock Holmes."

"That's a meaningless comparison since Sherlock Holmes was a fictional character," Hazard said. "If you wanted to compliment me, you could compare me to William Burns—God damn it, now I'm realizing I've already had this conversation with John once."

"I said shut up," Larenz snapped, looking back. "What don't you understand—"

The car came out of nowhere at the next intersection: the driver was going twenty over, easy, maybe thirty.

"Stop!" Korrin shouted. "Stop!"

Larenz snapped his head forward and hit the brakes. The SUV screeched into a skid, but it was too late. They connected with the car, hitting it behind the rear wheel. The force of the impact rammed the car sideways—it wasn't enough to spin it around, but it did shove it a few feet before both vehicles came to a stop.

"Motherfucker!" Larenz screamed.

Through the windshield, Hazard watched as the driver of the other car turned in his seat, checking on the passenger. Then the driver's door opened, and a man got out of the car. He was tall, broad-shouldered, with a thatch of blond hair and a Cardinals tee. He was handsome in a rough trade kind of way, and right then, he looked royally pissed. Hazard tried not to groan.

It was North McKinney.

CHAPTER EIGHT
APRIL 11
SATURDAY
8:49 PM

"WHAT THE FUCK?" North shouted. He stood in the blaze of the SUV's headlights, and Hazard stared at him, his brain trying to catch up, trying to figure out how this was possible, what it meant, how he could use it to his advantage. "You hit my fucking car!"

Larenz laid on the horn.

"Get your ass out here!" North shouted when Larenz let the sound die.

Larenz honked some more.

When the sound cut off, North was in the middle of more shouting: " — don't know what you're honking about, you goddamn hump muffin! You hit me! Get out of that fucking Escalade before I drag you out!"

At that, Larenz picked up his gun.

"Cool it," Korrin said.

"Do you hear that cracker cunt?"

Korrin pushed open the door.

"Where are you going?"

"To pay him so he'll get off our ass."

And then Korrin was gone, walking out into the cones of the headlights, saying something in that soft, easy voice. North stood with his hands on his hips. The two men began to speak. Then the passenger door opened, and Shaw got out. He was North's partner or boyfriend or whatever they were calling it: average height, slim build, his long brown hair tucked up under his hat. He wasn't exactly handsome, but the sharp symmetry of his features was compelling—in spite of his batshit getup. Today, for example, he was wearing an ushanka, in spite of the relatively mild spring, and a saffron-colored sari, and although Hazard only got a glimpse of the footwear, he had a sinking feeling that they were what he thought of as Aladdin slippers, the ones with the curled toes. Bells optional.

Shaw came toward the SUV, and this time, Hazard did groan. Just a little. He had the brief thought that maybe his calculations had been wrong. Maybe it would have been better to let them shoot him. Then the slender man made a rolling motion with one finger. When Larenz didn't lower the window, Shaw shouted, "Do you have any ibuprofen?"

"Get back in your fucking car, man!"

"I can't hear you!" Shaw cupped one hand around his ear and then, his face lighting up with what was, for him, presumably a flash of genius, lifted the ushanka's ear flap. He offered a goofily triumphant grin. "I hit my head!" Exaggerating each syllable, he asked again, "Do you have any ibuprofen?"

"Motherfucker—" Larenz began, lowering the window.

Shaw's arm came up, and pepper gel streamed through the window. Larenz shrieked, thrashing in his seat, his free hand coming up to claw at his face. The hand holding the gun waved wildly. Hazard rocked onto his hip and kicked between the seats. It connected poorly; Larenz was moving around too much. Larenz howled, and Hazard kicked again. This time, the sole of his boot connected with Larenz's knuckles, and he dropped the gun.

Outside the car, Hazard glimpsed Korrin going for a gun in his waistband. North must have known what was about to happen, though, because he was ready, and he was faster. He caught the taller man—one hand catching Korrin's wrist to keep him from reaching the gun, the other latching on to Korrin's nape. He spun and slammed the man into the Escalade's hood.

Shaw, meanwhile, reached through the window, unlocked the door, and opened it. Larenz flailed at him, still trying to wipe his face clean, but Shaw dodged the blow. He reached down and plucked the gun from the foot well.

Hazard squirmed toward his door and turned around. His hands were still cuffed behind his back, and he groped blindly for the handle.

"Do you need some help?" Shaw asked between Larenz's screams.

"No," Hazard growled, his fingers closing around the handle. "I've got this whole fuckfest under control."

"I knew you did," Shaw said. "I knew it! I was telling North you had it under control, but he said you didn't. He said you were going to get your piss nozzle capped if we didn't help you, which I thought was a strange expression because I've heard piss nozzle before—it's one of North's Best of March 2020 swears—and I've heard the expression 'get capped' before, but

I'd never heard them together before, and it kind of made me think of a gas nozzle and a fuel cap, so I told North that, and he said I was a piss nozzle—"

Hazard yanked on the handle once, twice. It didn't budge. Between Larenz's screams and Shaw's yammers, Hazard had a sudden, vivid fantasy of smashing his head through the glass and, if he were lucky, cutting his jugular in the process. Instead, he gritted out, "Child lock."

"Well, yeah, I mean, North is definitely in some sort of state of arrested development, and I guess calling it child lock is actually pretty accurate. That's why I have to be the responsible one, you know, like doing surprise cheese-checks and making sure his salad gets tossed, which did you know actually has another meaning, and one time we were visiting this guy in prison and—"

"The door has the fucking child lock set!" Hazard roared. "Open the fucking door!"

"Oh!" Shaw hit the unlock button on Larenz's door and then opened Hazard's. "There you go. Wait, what was I saying?"

Hazard slid out of the SUV. It was harder than it looked on account of the handcuffs; four out of ten on the landing. Shaw steadied him, and Hazard shook him off. He straightened up in time to see North release Korrin. Hazard had a glimpse of Korrin's face—bloodied, nose almost definitely broken—as Korrin staggered to the SUV and hauled himself up into the passenger seat.

"I can't see!" Larenz was screaming. "I can't see!"

"Drive, motherfucker! Hit the fucking gas!"

That must have penetrated Larenz's confusion because the Escalade leapt forward. North sprang out of its path, and the Escalade jerked hard to the right, detouring around the parked car. It clipped a mailbox and knocked it, post and all, out of the ground. Then it cut right at the corner and disappeared from view.

The roar of the engine faded. Silence pressed in, cottony and thick, as lights began to come on in the houses around them.

"Motherfucker," Hazard said. He was surprised to feel himself shaking.

"Are you all right?"

"Of course I'm all right!" Then he heard himself, heard a little voice in his head that sounded like his husband, and managed to add, "Thank you."

"You're welcome," Shaw said, beaming. He was still holding Larenz's gun, and for a man in a sari, he looked surprisingly at ease with it. "What are best friends for?"

"We are not—" Hazard began.

"Will you look at this?" North was crouching at the rear of the car, his fingers tracing something. "Those donkey-wanking fucks scratched her!"

The whole thing felt like a bad dream. Hazard wanted to rub his eyes, but the cuffs made that hard. Instead, he took a few deep breaths. When he felt slightly steadier, he asked, "What are you doing here?"

"We're here for your surprise fucking birthday party," North snapped over his shoulder. "And thanks a fucking lot. Do you know what it's going to cost to get this fixed?"

"North! You told him!"

"Fuck my fucking life," North muttered, still looking at the car.

Yeah, Hazard thought. You and me both. But all he could manage to say was "My birthday isn't until April twenty-fourth."

Shaw looked happier than any human Hazard had ever seen as he screamed, "Surprise!"

CHAPTER NINE
APRIL 11
SATURDAY
9:07 PM

WHEN HAZARD STEPPED INSIDE—hands free of the cuffs, now, thanks to a key that North had grudgingly produced—he came face to face with Somers. The blond man had obviously been pacing; in one hand, he held the keys to the Mustang, and in the other, he had his phone pressed to his ear. Relief creased his face.

"Thank God," he said. "No, he's here. Never mind. Yes, thank you, I'll check in later." Sliding the phone in his pocket, he pulled Hazard into a hug and said, "Jesus, Ree, where did you—"

"Is that Pops?" Colt asked from the opening to the living room. He stood with arms wrapped around himself. Worry crinkled the corners of his eyes, and for a moment, all the sullen resentment was gone, replaced by fear stark and bleached in his face. "What happened?"

"I'll tell you later," Hazard said.

"Are you ok?"

"I'm fine."

"Hi, John-Henry," Shaw said as he stepped into the house, crowding Hazard and Somers, followed a moment later by North. "Oh, are we hugging? Hold on, I have this box where I've been collecting the ten most magical hugs of my life—North, where's my hugbox?"

"Kind of," Hazard added in an underbreath.

Surprise in Somers's face transformed quickly into a bewildered smile. "Hi, Shaw. North. What's—"

"Don't ask," North grumbled.

"Surprise!" Shaw shouted.

"My daughter is asleep," Hazard said.

"Surprise!" Shaw said in a whisper-shout, a chagrined flush filling his face. "It's Emery's surprise birthday party!"

"His birthday isn't until—" Somers began.

"They know," Hazard said. "That's why it's a surprise."

"Exactly!" Shaw was glowing. "That's why it's a surprise!"

"Please tell me you have a beer," North said. "I cannot do this shit without a beer."

Somers laughed. "No beers, sorry. We've got some Pepsis."

"Oh, I only drink Coke," Shaw said, but he had already looped his arm through Somers's and was half-leading, half-pretending to follow him toward the kitchen. "Pepsi is, you know, like the watered down—oh, wait, it's like the piss nozzle version of Coke!" He turned a beatific smile over his shoulder at North.

"No Pepsis," North said.

"I'm a guest," Shaw said, raising his chin. "It would be rude not to accept."

"He didn't offer you one. He stated a fact. They've got some Pepsis. That's a statement."

"It's an implied offer." Then, in a worried whisper, "John-Henry, it was an offer, wasn't it?"

"Sure—" Somers began.

"No Pepsi!" North said over him.

"For the love of Christ," Hazard said. "Get him a fucking Pepsi before I put a screwdriver through my eye."

Somers looked like he was trying not to laugh as Shaw towed him toward the kitchen.

"Great," North said to no one in particular. "This is fucking fantastic. You know what? You can deal with him when he decides to give all the drapes a 'kitten haircut' at three in the morning."

"What the fuck is a kitten haircut?" Hazard asked.

North folded his arms across his chest. "Really? That's the part you fixated on?"

A laugh burst out of Colt; when Hazard glared at him, he cut off and covered his mouth, but his eyes were bright. The boy had watched all of this from the opening to the living room. He was still hugging himself, wearing a filched pair of Somers's old Wahredua Wildcats mesh shorts and a Moosejaw tee that he had somehow talked Hazard into buying him.

"You might as well come in," Hazard finally said to North. "Unless you plan on standing in the doorway all night."

"Righteous thanks for somebody who hauled your ass out of the fire."

"I already said thank you. You were too busy bitching about your car."

Colt was peering between them. He blurted, "That's yours? The GTO, I mean."

North raised a blond eyebrow. "Yeah."

"This is my son," Hazard said. "Colt, this is North McKinney. He is...here."

After a moment of silent consideration, North said flatly, "My condolences."

And for some fucking reason, that was apparently the perfect thing to say because Colt grinned.

"Colt is currently in the process of trying to bankrupt me and John with a new car," Hazard said. "He's got cars on the brain."

"Do you want to take a look?" North asked, cocking his head at the door.

"Uh, yeah." Colt looked a silent question at Hazard, and Hazard nodded. "That'd be dope."

"Don't judge me," North said as he rocked the screen door open with his hip. "It just got scratched by some twatholes."

"He's a goddamn child, for fuck's sake," Hazard said. "Watch your motherfucking language."

North and Colt shared an eyeroll.

"What kind of car are you looking for? You recognized the GTO; do you want something classic?"

"He wants a compact sedan, three years old, under fifty thousand miles, with a low average cost of ownership."

"Oh my God," Colt muttered.

"Shut the door," North said as they stepped outside. "He might try to follow us."

And fuck of all fucks, Colt laughed and—traitorous little bastard— pulled the door closed behind him.

Hazard found Somers standing by the refrigerator, holding an unopened Pepsi in one hand. Shaw was halfway inside one of the cabinets, the sari riding up. The clatter told Hazard that he was going to spend his next free day organizing the kitchen again.

"Jesus Christ."

"Well," Somers said, "he told me he wanted to see if it was, uh, quote, 'drinkable,' if he put lime in it. I told him we didn't have any limes, and he said that was ok, he only needed the ethereal essence of a lime."

"There's no such thing."

"Yes, there is." Shaw extracted himself from the cabinet. The ushanka started to fall, so he clapped a hand to it. "Yes, you see, the ethereal essence of a lime is the part of the lime that exists on the ethereal plane."

"There's no such thing as the ethereal plane."

Shaw burst out laughing. "Oh my God. I forgot how funny you are. Your sense of humor is one of the one hundred and seventeen reasons we're a perfect match as best friends."

"We are not—"

"Let it go," Somers said in an undertone. "What happened?"

Hazard told him.

"Jesus Christ, Ree, you were kidnapped."

"In effect, yes."

"Right off the street in front of our house."

"I was on the sidewalk, actually." Something in Somers's face told him that wasn't the point, so he hurried to add, "It was a miscalculation on my part. I'll take appropriate precautions next time."

Somers shook his head. "That's not what I—Ree, God, I am so glad you're ok." He pulled him into another embrace. "All right. Give me descriptions—these guys, the vehicle, whatever you can remember. You think they were going to see Carson?"

"They wanted me to help them get inside the house; I think they assumed, because I was with you, that I could vouch for them. My sense was that they wanted to be able to search the house without causing a disturbance. I don't think they'll try anything tonight, not with one of them half-blind and the other with a broken nose."

"Still," Somers said, detaching himself. "I've got to call this in."

He was already on his phone as he excused himself.

"What are you doing?" Hazard asked.

"I'm looking for your juicer," Shaw said, voice muffled inside the cabinet. "That will be the easiest point of contact to extract the ethereal essence."

"We don't have a juicer."

"I'm pretty sure you do. I saw it in a dream."

Hazard had to blink a few times to de-stroke from that. He was about to follow up on the argument about the juicer when something clicked in his head.

Somers was on the phone.

Colt was currently being baited with car porn.

Evie was asleep.

"Stay inside that cabinet," Hazard said.

"What? Why?"

"I don't know. Maybe you know. Maybe you saw the reason in a dream."

"I did have a dream about us playing hide-and-seek. Is it hide-and-seek?"

"Yes," Hazard said. "That."

He crossed the living room double-time and hurried up the stairs. He let himself into Colt's room. He was met by the smell of the air freshener he had insisted on installing and the much more pungent odor of the hamper. He left the door open and turned on the lights.

In the months since Colt had moved in, the guest room had slowly transitioned into truly his room. The bookcase held his books now, instead of Somers's castoffs—Colt wasn't much of a reader, but he and Somers had passed a few thrillers back and forth. They'd gotten him a better desk for his schoolwork. Somers had even painted the room—a soft blue with a hint of gray that Colt had picked out. Those changes, combined with the arterial spray of cast-off clothing and plates and loose change and a frozen burrito wrapper, made the room unmistakably Colt's.

They also made it pretty damn hard to find something that Colt might want to hide.

Hazard started with the desk. He rifled the drawers. Then he pulled them out and checked underneath. He moved the desk away from the wall. Nothing. He tried the bed next, lifting the mattress and the box spring. Nothing. He tried Colt's backpack—another new purchase—and got nothing there either, except for an egregiously abbreviated handout on commas. He made a mental note to bring that up with Theo Stratford at their next unofficial parent-teacher conference.

Nothing.

He couldn't find the letter anywhere.

His phone buzzed. His mother's name flashed on the screen, and he considered letting it go to voicemail. Then he moved to stand in the doorway, where he could keep an eye on the hall, and answered.

"Bunny? Are you there?" Loose laughter came across the line, and with a slight slur to the words, Aileen Hazard said, "Oh my God, I slipped! Bunny, I walked right out of my shoes!"

"Mom, are you all right?"

More laughter came back to him. Then, breathlessly, she said, "I can't— I can't—oh Bunny, I have to sit down."

His attention sharpened. Most of the tests for stroke relied on visual assessment, but there was one that Hazard could try: "Mom, can you repeat, 'Don't cry over spilled milk'?"

"Don't cry over spulled—I mean spilt, spilled, spilled." With exaggerated enunciation, she tried again. "Don't cry over spilled milk. Oh, bunny, these shoes are so damn tight."

The last time Hazard had heard his mother swear was in 2002 when the Patriots beat the Rams in the Super Bowl, and that night she'd had—

"Good God," Hazard said. "Are you drunk?"

"Muffin!" The outrage was hollow. Then she giggled. "That's a terrible thing to say to your mother. I had some schnobs—some schnops—some—a few drinks at book club."

"What was the book?"

"Oh muffin, it was wonderful. There was this woman, a mature woman, and then there was this coxswain, and they were on a yacht of course, and then her horrible best friend who wasn't really her friend at all—Dolores says they're 'frenemies,' isn't that such a clever word?—she showed up in nothing but a nightgown right when the coxswain was about to—" With the sound of someone operating without power steering, she tried to turn her tone casual. "It's very silly, anyway."

Hazard thought maybe he had developed tinnitus. Into the ringing silence, he managed, "That sounds like some of the books John likes. There was one about a cruise, I remember. And something about the shrimp tower."

Another of those girlish giggles slipped free from his mother. "Bunny, I miss you."

"You're welcome to come visit." He thought about that and amended, "In a week, maybe? We're a little busy right now."

When she spoke again, her voice was heavy. "I miss your father."

And what, Hazard wondered, was he supposed to say to that?

His mother cleared her throat. "I'm sorry. I don't even remember why I—oh, yes, bunny, I do! I really need you to come take a look at your father's things."

"There's nothing I want. You can toss it or give it away."

"No, no, no. I want you to look through it. You never know what you'll find."

"Fishing lures. Bud Lite memorabilia. Cigar bands."

He could have broken the silence by breathing on it.

"Fine," he said. "When things calm down."

"That would be wonderful, bunny. The sooner the better."

Hazard ended the call; what he wanted to know was why it mattered, why now, why the phone calls and the urging and the wounded sense of expectation? It had been a year; it wouldn't hurt anything to let the shit sit in the garage for another year.

He went back into the bedroom and was starting on the closet when he heard Colt and North downstairs.

"—too much power for a new driver," North was saying.

Hazard stopped and headed down the stairs. His son and North were standing in the living room. North had his arms folded. Colt was staring at him with something ungodly close to worship.

"You want to start with the right amount of power for your skill level," North said. "Then you level up."

"That's what I told him," Hazard said.

Neither Colt nor North looked at him.

"Found it!" Shaw called from the kitchen.

"That's impossible," Hazard said. "We don't have a juicer, so you can't have—"

He stopped when Shaw emerged from the kitchen, juicer in hand. He offered a glowing smile. "Where's John-Henry? I think I'll have that Pepsi now."

"You surely fucking won't," North shot after him before turning his attention back to Colt. "Have you checked out a Toyota 86?"

Colt shook his head.

"That's what I'd get my kid if I had one."

Doubtfully, Colt said, "I guess a couple of my friends have Corollas—"

North burst out laughing. "No, it's not like that. Trust me; you'd like it. Do some research and let me know if you have any questions."

Colt nodded and opened his mouth, but before he could speak, Shaw reentered the room.

"John-Henry is still on the phone," he said. "I think he might have an ear infection. He kept putting his finger in his ear and turning up the volume on the call."

"Jesus God," North muttered and covered his face.

Colt was studying Shaw with something like wonder.

"Colt, that's Shaw," Hazard said. "Don't listen to anything he says, particularly in the areas of medicine, engineering, chemistry, biology, biochemistry, religion—in fact, don't listen to him at all. It's time for you to go to bed—"

"Hi, Colt," Shaw said with an enormous smile. "I can't tell if your soul used to be an eagle or a lion or a horse."

Colt's eyes got huge.

North breathed out something that might have been "For the love of fuck."

"This is why I said don't listen to him," Hazard called from the stairs.

Colt glanced at Hazard and then, for some reason, at North. A tiny smile curled Colt's mouth. With the voice of someone testing new ground, he said, "Maybe it used to be all three."

"Like a hippogriff," Shaw said excitedly. "Oh my God! A Hazard-griff! That explains why you have such an amazing aura. You're brave and you're strong and you've got a caring heart. Oh my God, and you're in love! That's wonderful!"

A hectic blush covered Colt's cheeks.

"Quit talking to my son," Hazard said.

"Have you ever considered how you'd look with a face tattoo?"

"Jesus Christ, thank you," Hazard said, coming the rest of the way down the stairs. "That's exactly what I need: something else to keep me up at night. Why the fuck are you two clowns even here?"

"The clown college burned down," North said.

"Our clown car ran out of gas," Shaw said.

"We got caught in the middle of a clown three-way."

"Gross, North."

"What? You've literally invited Hazard to be in a three-way like, I don't know, eight times, and don't tell me it's the clown part because clowns can have three-ways. It's their God-given right as Americans. Well, if they are Americans, I guess."

"No, I mean gross because—" Shaw nodded at Colt.

"I know what a three-way is," Colt said a little too loudly, his gaze sliding to North again, watching for whatever he was hoping to see there. Approval, Hazard hoped. Even that was a fucking nightmare.

North, on the other hand, seemed to be trying his hardest to look anywhere but at Colt, and his face looked like it was on fire.

"I would have said we're political refugees," Shaw said. "From an oppressive clown dictatorship. And now we're seeking asylum."

"That doesn't make any sense," North said. "An oppressive clown dictatorship? Asylum? You're asking me to do the work of imagining an entire clown sociopolitical system. That's just lazy joke writing."

"No! It's an allegory for resistance and ethical behavior! Colt needs strong role models! Oh, Emery, you know what? You and John-Henry should have an open relationship so Colt can be raised by a variety of men who come in and out of his life. North and I would be happy to be your first, you know, um, partners."

"No," North said. "We wouldn't. I'd rather have somebody run baling wire through my balls."

"Great idea," Hazard said, crooking a finger at Colt. "Let's start there. Colt, upstairs. Now. You two what's-your-nuts can get the fuck out of here now."

"Colt," Somers called from the other room.

Colt rolled his eyes, but he moved toward the stairs. "Don't listen to Pops. J-H wants to talk to you. He said you have to give him those guns."

"There's no birthday party," Hazard said as he trailed after his son. "There's no celebration of any kind. So you can go home now."

"I'm having a birthday party," Colt said over his shoulder. "Next week."

"No," Hazard said. "He's not."

"It would be fire if you guys came." When Colt looked back, his cheeks were pink. "Uh, North, do you want to come?"

"Mother of God," Hazard growled, and he gave Colt a nudge. "North and Shaw need to get back to St. Louis."

"No, we don't," North said. "We're working, for your fucking information. The only way I could get Shaw to come was if I told him we were going to your birthday party."

"You're my kryptonite," Shaw said with a shrug.

"No," Hazard said. "I'm not. Finish whatever work brought you here and go home. To be clear, you are not invited to any family celebrations of any kind."

Shaw waved his arms and pitched his voice like they were getting too far away. "Colt, when's your party? We're going to bring you so many presents! Do you have a lot of crystals already? Oh! How many clogs do you own?"

"We're not getting him a present," North said in a low voice.

Shaw answered, but it was too quiet for Hazard to make out. Thank God.

Hazard followed Colt to his room, and Colt dropped onto his bed. Hazard waited for the argument, the demand that he be allowed to stay up, for whatever the next battle would be, but instead, Colt sat there, looking up at him.

"Colt, for the next few days, I need you to be careful—"

"What really happened? I'm old enough for you to tell me the truth."

Hazard weighed the pros and cons of telling him. And then he nodded and told him.

"Holy shit, Pops!"

"Keep your voice down."

"But holy shit!"

"Language."

"They could have killed you. They were going to kill you."

"Most likely."

Colt looked gray, and he kept wiping his mouth. "And they're still out there, and you don't know what they want or—or—"

Hazard lowered himself onto the mattress. He sat next to Colt; their knees connected, and he put his hand on Colt's back. "Take a breath. I'm fine. We're all safe right now."

"Thank God North and Shaw showed up."

"Yes," Hazard said with a dryness he couldn't help. "Thank God."

"Why don't you like them? Shaw is trippy, but he seems all right." Hazard didn't miss the rush of color as Colt added, "And North is dope."

"I don't dislike them. They're unexpectedly capable considering who they are and how they behave, and they're an actuarial nightmare because it's unreal that they've managed to stay alive this long."

"So, you do like them?"

"Colt, the next few days are going to be unpredictable. I don't know what's going to happen. For these men to attempt something like an abduction on a public street, even at night, they must have little fear of reprisal. Until this is wrapped up, I don't want you home alone."

The second miracle of the night—although who was counting?—was that Colt nodded.

"I could go to Ash's after baseball. If you or J-H ask his parents, I mean."

"We'll let John handle that," Hazard murmured, trying to avoid his son's gaze. "If they're busy, you could come to the office. Or you could pick up some hours at the station. Or you could go over to Noah and Rebeca's."

"I don't want to do that," Colt said, shaking his head.

"I understand you don't like being treated like a child—"

"No, I think Rebeca treats me more like an adult than she does Noah. I meant, I don't want to go there because that's putting them in danger, right?"

Hazard weighed this question as well. "Possibly."

"I know it would be the same thing for Ash's family. But they're, you know, tough. They can shoot. They've got guns." He shrugged and looked at the ground. "Ash wouldn't let anything bad happen to me."

Hazard opened his mouth. The words invited a response: they were a childlike fantasy of security, the product of adolescent love, the untested assumption that this feeling, because it was so deep, was strong and true. And, of course, the whole premise offered about as much protection as a soap bubble. But then Hazard closed his mouth and rubbed Colt's back and nodded.

"Do you know Carson Maas?" Hazard asked.

"Not really. He's older. I mean, he plays baseball—varsity—so I see him at practice, and he's a nice guy. Quiet. He's good, but he's not a show-off or anything."

"Does he do drugs?"

"I don't think so."

"What about performance-enhancing drugs?"

"Like steroids?"

"Like that."

"I don't think so. I mean, nobody's ever said that. And he's nice, you know? He shows up and works hard and he doesn't talk shit or act like a jackass."

"Is he gay?"

That surprised a laugh out of Colt. "What?"

"Have you heard anything like that?"

"Uh, no. Why?"

"Shot in the dark." Hazard was quiet for a moment. "Do you have any idea what those men wanted to find in Carson's house?"

Colt shook his head.

"Ok," Hazard said. "Then you need to get to bed—"

"Pops," Colt said. The word was tense. Hazard waited, and when Colt spoke again, his voice was wrought with an emotion Hazard couldn't untangle. "What do you think about me visiting Danny Lee?"

Downstairs, Shaw was laughing, and Somers was saying something. The clock radio on Colt's nightstand showed 9:22 PM in blue digits. The springs in the mattress gave tiny protests so that Hazard was suddenly aware of every micromovement—aware of his own inability to be still.

"Is that what was in the letter?"

Colt shrugged.

Hazard's whole body felt weightless. His head in particular. As though his brain had been scooped out, and, in its place, something white and fuzzy had been stuffed into the cavity. Major blood loss could cause symptoms like this. Or any serious trauma. Shock. He touched his chest to make sure he was still breathing.

Inside that thick white cloud, he almost felt like laughing when he heard how normal his voice sounded. "If you want to."

Colt was silent. He was staring at the carpet again.

Say something, Hazard thought. Say something. Say anything.

And then it was too late, and Hazard heard himself saying, "Of course, now probably isn't a good time."

Colt's head came up. His face was splotchy. He was stiffening up, his body becoming armor, hard lines of steel to keep the world out, the hurt out, Hazard out. "Why not?"

Why not? Hazard thought, and he felt himself teetering on the brink of that manic laughter again. Why not? Why the fuck not? He knocked the shit out of you anytime he could get you in arm's reach. He about beat John to death. He's a liar and an abusive asshole, and whatever he wants from you, he'll only hurt you worse, and I can't stand it, seeing him hurt you again and again, because I'd rather die first than let anyone hurt you.

What he said was "Well, your grades are down."

"That was one quiz."

"One quiz on atomic structure. You should have aced it. And it wasn't just one quiz. You got a C on that World History project, and you turned in your paper to Theo late."

"Dr. Stratford said it was ok!" Colt had half-risen from the bed. "I've got all A's and two B's. That's really good!"

"If you've got two B's, it's not all A's."

"You're being an asshole."

"Good; we're back in familiar territory. I'm tired of your grades slipping, Colt. We talked about this. Your responsibility—your one responsibility right now—is to get good grades. You're exceptionally smart. That means straight A's. And when you wanted to go out for baseball—"

"Are you serious right now?"

"—and we agreed that baseball would be a good item to have on your college resume, to show that you're well-rounded—"

"I didn't do baseball to be well-rounded! I did it because I like baseball and because it's fun and because Ash said I should!"

"Oh, I'm sorry. I didn't realize Ashley was your college and career counselor."

Colt stared at him, mouth slightly open with what must have been shock. Then he shook his head and stood. "Can you go? You're pissing me off."

"We're not finished with this conversation."

"Yeah, we are."

"If you want to continue playing baseball, you will bring your grades up—"

"Grades don't matter! Quit fucking talking to me about my grades!"

It was getting easier now, everything condensing inside Hazard, everything below freezing: superchilled and clear. "You'd better believe grades matter. You won't get into a good college—"

"I told you, I don't even know if I'm going to college."

"Really? How do you think that's going to work out for you?"

Colt set his jaw. "There are lots of things you can do without college. Dr. Stratford talks about it sometimes."

"Theo isn't your father."

"Will you stop? I'm trying to—I'm trying to talk about this! Can you not go ape shit for, like, five seconds?"

It was like swimming, Hazard thought. Swimming in the Arctic, looking up from under an ice floe, the sun milky as it refracted in frozen crystals. All that light and air and you couldn't reach it.

"You want me to be calm?" Hazard asked, rising. "You want me to be rational? Here's rational: I am sick to fucking death of your mixed-up priorities. You had five games this week, Colt. Five. That's ridiculous. That's a waste of your time and energy, when you should be studying for the ACT and finishing your assignments on time—"

"I don't want to study for the ACT! Why don't you listen to me when I tell you things?"

"I don't care what you want! It doesn't matter what you want! You're a child; you have no idea what life is like, no fucking clue how hard your life is going to be. That's why you have parents. That's my whole job: to make sure you don't fuck up your life. You're done with baseball, Colt. I'm calling Theo tomorrow and telling him you no longer have permission to be on the team."

"You can't!" Colt looked on the brink of tears. "No, please, I'll get my grades up, I'll study—"

"It's too late for that." Hazard headed for the door.

Colt's voice chased him, choked with fury. "I hate you!"

"I can live with that."

"You're ruining my life!"

Hazard laughed drily. It was easy to laugh because it wasn't him laughing, not really. He was under the ice, hammering on it. He could barely see because something was floating in the center of his vision, a spot like he'd stared at the sun. "Colt," he said with the cool disregard he knew would hurt most. "Don't be so dramatic."

He shut the door.

Something struck it, hard. And then something else. And on the other side of the wood, Colt's breathing hitched toward sobs.

What am I doing? Hazard made his way downstairs. His hand trembled on the railing. What the fuck am I doing?

"—rough night," Somers was saying in a familiar tone—the easy social grace, a hint of apology and shared embarrassment. "I'm sorry you had to hear that."

"Don't worry," Shaw said, "we'll be back tomorrow."

"No," North said, "we won't."

"Let me know if you want to grab lunch," Somers said.

Then he made a grunting noise, which was explained a moment later by Shaw saying, "You give really good hugs. Almost as good as Emery's."

"Hazard's never hugged you, dumbass," North said.

"Of course he has," Shaw said haughtily. "In my dreams."

When North spoke, his voice was unusually serious. "He seems like a good kid, John-Henry. Maybe you should tell Hazard not to ride him so hard."

"He is a good kid," Somers said. "And Emery loves him more than just about anything in the universe. You guys—" He cut off, and then, in a different voice, he said, "This is Chief Somerset." Silence. And then, "Are you kidding me? At the motel? All right. Yes, I'll be there in a minute."

Hazard came around the opening to the entry hall. Shaw was leaning into the screen door, and North had a hand on his shoulder. Somers was pocketing his phone.

Shaking his head, Somers met Hazard's gaze. "Carlson's on duty at the motel, keeping Renner's room secure. Guess who she caught trying to get inside?"

"Who?"

"Benji."

CHAPTER TEN

APRIL 11
SATURDAY
10:03 PM

AT NIGHT, THE Presidential slept with its mouth open—a transgressive kind of accessibility that was grossly intimate. Doors stood propped open. Curtains billowed out of windows. Even in the car, Somers could hear shrill laughter; when Hazard lowered his window, the spring air smelled like mildew and the burnt-electric stink of meth. Unmistakable grunts and the slap of flesh reached them over the Mustang's rumble. Hazard put the window back up. The lack of privacy, in aggregate, turned into a kind of anonymity. As they rolled into the parking lot, Somers crossed gazes with the woman waiting for her next john at the edge of the asphalt. She was petite, hard used, in a halter top and with runs in her stockings. She had a mentholated cigarette drooping from her mouth and the flat, dark eyes of a resale-shop doll.

"Jesus Christ," Hazard said. "Someone needs to fumigate the shit out of this place and then burn it to the ground."

"Not exactly material for the tourist pamphlets," Somers said as he parked next to two cruisers already in the lot.

"For fuck's sake, there are police officers here," Hazard said, glancing back at the woman they'd passed. "Don't these people have any fear?"

"She's just waiting for a friend, officer." Somers started to open the door. Then he stopped and checked his phone. He dismissed the call.

"North and Shaw?"

Somers shook his head; they had asked the St. Louis detectives to stay with Colt and Evie, to which North had grudgingly agreed, at which point Shaw, talking faster and faster in a Pepsi rush, had attempted to convince Colt that maybe he was a baby witch and also maybe, just maybe, his familiar was a barn cat named Jambo. "Cora."

"What if it's about Evie?"

"If it's about Evie, she'll call back. But it's not. This is about Naomi, and I'm not ready to deal with that." As he got out of the car, he added, "Come on; we've got bigger fish to fry."

As they headed toward the motel, Yarmark appeared on the stairs. He made his way down from the second floor, nodding when he passed them, and headed toward the woman working the corner. By the time Somers and Hazard had reached the second-floor exterior corridor, Yarmark had gotten her moving. She'd be back, or another woman would take her place, but at least for the moment, they wouldn't have to arrest her.

Janie Carlson was standing outside the door to Zach Renner's motel room. She was slim, one of those women who melted off the pregnancy weight, and her long dark hair was escaping her hat. It was lots of little things like that: the stain on her cuff, her shirt misbuttoned, the shadows under her eyes. Having a new baby wasn't easy, and working patrol for the Wahredua PD didn't make it any easier. She gritted her teeth when she saw them and straightened up as best she could.

"Chief Somerset, I know I made a mistake."

Somers nodded. "Where's Mr. Renner? Benji, I mean."

"In my cruiser, sir. He's restrained."

"And have you notified Detectives Dulac and Palomo?"

"No, sir." Color rushed into her face. "I'm sorry, sir. I called dispatch, and then Officer Yarmark got here, and —"

"I called them," Yarmark said. "Chief, Mr. Hazard. I called Detective Palomo and told her what had happened."

Carlson shook her head; the gesture seemed directed at herself.

"Is Benji all right?"

"What? Oh, yes, sir. He didn't give me any trouble." But more color rushed into her face, and she opened her mouth to correct that statement.

"Slow down," Somers said, patting the air. He glanced over. "Sam, are you on your own tonight?"

"Yes, Chief." The dark-haired officer with the suspiciously familiar haircut had a steno notebook in hand, and he was jotting details. He glanced up now, eyes wide, ready to capture the next jewel of wisdom. Somers thought of the manual, that damn supervisor training course, and all the bullshit that came with a job he wasn't even sure he wanted. He tried to focus. Confidentiality. All performance-related communication should be kept private and confidential.

"Go down to the lot and keep an eye on Mr. Renner. See if he needs anything. Make sure he's comfortable. Don't take the cuffs off him until one of us is down there to back you up, but otherwise, make sure he's all right."

Yarmark snapped a salute, shoved the steno notebook in his back pocket, and jogged toward the stairs.

"Good Christ," Hazard muttered. "He almost clicked his heels."

"Be nice," Somers murmured. In a normal voice, he said to Carlson, "Let's start at the beginning. And don't go beating yourself up, Janie. Just the facts for now, please."

She nodded. More hair slipped out from under her hat, and she jabbed at it savagely, trying to get it under control. "I was on duty first tonight, Chief. We split the shift like you ordered, so that we don't get sloppy." That must have stung because she reddened again. "Nickels is taking over for me."

"All right. And what happened?"

"Well, sir, everything was quiet. As quiet as this place gets, you know. And I wasn't too worried about the, uh, traffic. The detectives told me that I wasn't supposed to get involved. My job was to watch the room."

"That's right."

Carlson swallowed, and her eyes drifted away to fix on something out in the night. "Well, sir, everything was quiet, like I said. But about nine-thirty, I hear screaming. And it's not like—it's not like them carrying on down below. This was somebody who was scared. I mean, terrified. And she was saying, 'No, no, please, help' —"

"She?" Hazard asked.

Nodding, Carlson said, "It got worse. 'He's killing me,' and then, 'help, help, help' over and over again." She shivered. "I—I reacted, Chief. I made sure the door was locked, and then I ran."

"Did you call it in?"

Eyes shimmering with unshed tears, Carlson shook her head. "No, Chief."

"All right." Somers eased some of the bite from his voice. "What'd you find?"

"Nothing, Chief. And me, I'm such a big dummy, I thought maybe she'd gotten hurt, dragged herself into some bushes, that kind of thing, so I started poking around, calling out, that kind of thing. And then it hit me, what an idiot I was being, and I sprinted back here. Well, I caught him, sir." She sounded bitterly disappointed even in that part of the story. "He was looking through the suitcase, over on the far side of the room. I messed up."

"And Benji didn't give you any trouble?"

"No, sir. He wasn't happy I busted him, but he was real calm, showed me his hands, got down on the floor, put his hands behind his back. I didn't even have to tell him."

Hazard's eyebrows went up at that.

"Anything else?" Somers asked.

"Like I said, Chief, I know I messed up."

"Everybody messes up, Janie. This was—"

"A fuck-up?" Hazard suggested. "A ruse so simplistic that even a child wouldn't have fallen for it?"

Fire flared in Carlson's face, and she shot Hazard a hard look.

"Ree, go teach Sam something about search patterns or fingerprint ridges or tool marks in cases of auto-erotic asphyxiation."

"You're saying that because I read one article, one, about distinctive leather textures from belts used in—"

"Ree." Somers took a breath. "Now."

Hazard grumbled something that didn't sound flattering, but he made his way to the stairs. When the sound of his steps faded, Somers forced himself to take another breath. This was one of the things he hated about the job, giving feedback, dealing with discipline, when his natural instinct was to let things slide, to be a buddy. But being a supervisor meant leaving behind those casual work friendships. Here, too, the manual was clear: like it or not, his role created a power dynamic, and all he could do was participate in that new dynamic as respectfully as possible. It was his responsibility to help his employees grow and improve, to provide correction when necessary, and most of all to want them to perform at their absolute best. And because, most of the time, he knew himself, he also knew that he could do that.

He made his voice even as he said, "You messed up big, Janie."

"I know, sir." A tear leaked from one eye, and she dashed it away. "I'm not crying, sir."

"You made a judgment call. That's a big part of this job, and I'm glad to know that you are willing to make a tough call and then take responsibility for it. But, Janie, your responsibility was to preserve the integrity of this crime scene. You'd been instructed not to respond to infractions or violations in the area. What were you supposed to do if you saw something that needed police involvement?"

"Call it in, sir."

"There you go."

"But she was screaming, sir. You didn't hear her. It sounded so real."

"I'm sure it did." Somers waited out the next few beats. "The point, though, is that you didn't know what was happening. You didn't know if she was being dramatic. You didn't know if she was being stabbed. You didn't know if it was a trick to get you to abandon your post. But you had your orders, and you could have called it in. I understand that it was a dilemma; you thought a woman's life was on the line, and you made your choice. But here's something to think about: we can't do everything. That's why we have assigned responsibilities; otherwise, this job would never end. So, you do what you're supposed to do, and you remember that there's an entire department ready to back you up when you need help."

Carlson nodded. Her jaw had a slight tremor.

"Anything you'd like to say, Officer?"

"No, Chief."

"All right. Go kick Sam loose and keep an eye on Benji. Send Emery back up, and don't take what he said too hard. He told me a few weeks ago I didn't deserve to have a badge because I kept losing at *Where's Waldo?*"

That got a drawstring smile from her, and she trotted toward the stairs. A minute later, Hazard had rejoined Somers.

"Do you have any commentary?" Somers asked.

"Why would I? You handled that adequately."

"God Almighty," Somers said under his breath and pushed open the door to Zach Renner's room.

Hazard knelt and inspected the strike plate and the latch and the keyhole. He shrugged. "The thing is scratched to shit; too many drunks with shaky hands. It wasn't forced, but it's impossible to say if he picked it."

Somers nodded.

"I grabbed these from the Mustang," Hazard said, handing over a pair of disposable shoe covers and then gloves.

"God, I miss working with you."

Hazard wore one of those tiny, Emery Hazard smiles as he tugged on the gear.

They stepped inside. The reek of old gore and urine met them like a wall, and Somers grimaced. The most obvious disturbance was across the room, in the overturned suitcase that Somers had noticed on his first visit. Now the suitcase was right-side up, and the pile of clothing and belongings had been scattered around it. They crossed the room as carefully as they could and crouched next to the suitcase.

Hazard frowned. "This is the one you told me about? The blood spatter indicated it had been overturned after the shooting?"

"Yep."

"So, we've got somebody looking for something."

"That's one possibility."

"The killer neutralizes Landon first, by the door. Then Zach, who's standing here." Hazard indicated the respective bloodstains. "Then the killer dumps out the suitcase looking for something."

"Maybe," Somers said. "It's too far from where Zach was lying for him to have knocked it over when he fell."

"Then someone else did it when they were tossing the room."

"Maybe," Somers said again. "Or maybe the clerk got brave after she found them and decided to see if she could pick up something valuable before she called the police. Maybe someone else was in the room."

"Who?"

"I don't know, Ree. I'm throwing around possibilities."

"The blood spatter only has one void. That suggests only one additional person in the room."

"Maybe they were twins. Maybe one was standing directly behind the other."

Hazard's eyes narrowed. "They'd have to be wearing the same clothes, and be holding themselves in exactly the same way, to avoid incidental irregularities in the silhouette."

"God, you make it no fun at all."

"What?"

Somers stood and began moving around the room again.

"What are you talking about, John?"

"Don't worry about it. Now help me check the rest of this place."

As they inspected the room further, it became clear that the suitcase wasn't the only thing Benji had searched. He'd moved through the room quickly—Hazard's phrase from earlier, *tossing the place*, came to mind—and the signs were there for Somers to read them: drawers not pushed shut completely; the bedding caught between the mattress and the box spring, the lamp shade askew. Fingerprint powder, which covered most of the surfaces, had been disturbed in places, and fresh prints trampled the carpet. Unofficially, Somers didn't think they matched the prints that he associated with the killer, but there were too many variables.

"He could have changed shoes," Hazard said; he was looking under the bed, and he spoke without looking up.

"Jesus God," Somers muttered. "How the hell do you do that?"

When they'd finished, they retreated to the exterior corridor and stripped off the disposable gloves and booties. A familiar set of headlights swung into the parking lot below them; Somers thought he could make out Palomo's shape behind the wheel of the Impala.

"The law of parsimony," Hazard said. "The most likely explanation is that the same person who killed Zach and Landon is also the person who searched the room the first time—in the process, overturning the suitcase— and the same person who broke into the room to search it tonight. That would be Benji."

Somers pressed the heels of his hands into his eyes and fought a yawn. "The law of parsimony, right. Ree, the thing is, that's a nice idea in theory, but it doesn't necessarily hold up in the real world. There are a lot of weird things about this case, and I don't think the law of parsimony should be our go-to."

"Have you done a background check on Benji?"

Sighing, Somers shook his head. "You're thinking the same thing I am?"

"I'm thinking that most people would not have memorized a 'best practice' list for when the police stop them. Most people—especially most people breaking the law for the first time in their lives—react with absolute terror. Benji should have been freaking out when Carlson caught him. Instead, he pretty much arrested himself and saved her the trouble."

"Yeah," Somers said, watching Palomo and Dulac make their way up the stairs. "That's weird."

When the detectives reached them, Somers ran them through the night's events. Palomo, as usual, didn't swear or bluster—Dulac did enough for both of them.

"You'll need to photograph the room again," Somers said, "and compare the before and after images. You'll also need to process the room again and see what new prints you can lift."

"Fucking hell," Dulac said. "Norman and Gross are going to kill me."

"Yeah, well, tell them there's some fat overtime in it," Somers said. "And then the city council can kill me when I have to give my next budget report. We're going to talk to Benji; why don't you take a look around, haul Norman and Gross out of bed, and then see what you can get out of Benji in round two at the station?"

"Fuck me," Dulac said as he spun and dug his phone out of his pocket.

"Are you going to charge Mr. Renner?" Palomo asked in that neutral, I'm-memorizing-everything-you-do-and-say tone.

"We'll see," Somers said. "Photos, Detective Palomo. Lots of them. Even if we don't charge Benji, we'll need to be able to explain this mess when the murders get to court."

Somers and Hazard took the stairs down, and Hazard said, "'When' seems like an optimistic choice of word."

"Christ, Ree, if this doesn't get to court, I'll be out of a job. I'm not exactly leaving other options open at this point."

In the parking lot, a low tide of red light lay over everything; neon letters reminded everyone they had options: WEEKLY AND SHORT NAPS. The smell of meth and cold asphalt mixed with a fried chicken smell— apparently somebody was including the Colonel in their catting around. The volume of the night's activities had faded; either most of the guests had been taking advantage of the SHORT NAPS policy and were now on their way again, or the presence of cops had finally percolated through God only knew how many layers of drugs and alcohol. Yarmark's cruiser was gone, and Carlson stood next to her own vehicle. Her face was clear now, her jaw set, her mouth a razor line. Benji sat next to the door, staring out the glass, his bruised and battered features pale. When Carlson saw them coming, she saluted, and Somers didn't know if it was compensatory or for Benji's benefit. Probably a little of both.

"How's Mr. Renner?" Somers asked.

"Officer Yarmark said that Mr. Renner assured him he was comfortable," Carlson answered. "When I checked on him, Mr. Renner repeated the same assurance. He asked to speak to the detectives and told me this is a misunderstanding."

"Well, let's see if we can clear it up."

Carlson responded to Somers's gesture by opening the rear door. Then, when Somers nodded, she backed off a few yards. She had her hand on her service weapon, and Somers hoped Benji got a look; it was a nice touch.

"Chief Somerset," Benji said with a wry smile. "Hi."

"Hello, Benji. What seems to be going on?"

"I fucked up," Benji said with a shrug. "It's kind of my MO." He twisted enough to wiggle his fingers at them. "Would you mind taking these off? I'm not a flight risk, officers."

Hazard made a sound that was a mix of skepticism and contempt.

"All right, Benji, I think we can do that." Somers motioned for him to slide out of the car and turn around. He undid the cuffs. Then, hand on Benji's shoulder, he guided him back onto the bench seat. He coiled the cuffs around one finger and gave Benji a long, assessing look. "Do you want to skip the part where you lie to my face? Or are we going to do this the hard way?"

Another wry smile. A shrug. It was the curse, Somers knew firsthand, of being too good-looking and, on top of it, smart. Ninety-nine percent of the time, you could smile your way out of anything.

"It was stupid, I know. I should have...I should have waited, I guess. But you know how these things go—evidence can get tied up for years sometimes. I thought—I mean, it's not like it's important, and I figured it couldn't hurt—"

"How do you know that?" Hazard asked.

"Huh? Oh, I mean, I guess I don't know for certain, but it's not like it's connected to what happened, so I thought if you didn't need it as evidence—"

"No, how did you know that evidence can be tied up for years? Most people don't know that, especially if their exposure to law enforcement is limited to television and movies."

This time, the smile was chiseled. "What do you want me to say? Busted?"

"I want an explanation."

"Yeah, I've done some dumb stuff, ok?"

"What kind of stuff?"

If anything, the smile got harder. "I said I've done some dumb stuff. I didn't say I'm stupid."

"Mr. Renner—" Somers began.

"Benji, please."

"Benji, you're in a bad spot right now. You broke into a sealed crime scene. At a minimum, that's trespassing, and we could add interfering with a police investigation. Is that how you want tonight to go?"

He sounded like Colt, sullen, his head hanging down. "No."

"Then why don't you start helping us understand what you were doing."

Benji blew out a breath and absently touched his hair, as though checking that it were still in place. "I was looking for some papers. They're for the nonprofit. Banking stuff. We can't keep operating if we don't have any money, and I thought—I mean, they're not even part of the investigation, so it's not like taking them could hurt, right?"

"Right," Hazard said. "Because money has never been a motive in a murder."

Somers tried not to roll his eyes. "That's the story you want to go with?"

"It's the truth."

"How did you get in the motel room, Benji?"

He shifted on the seat and checked his hair again. He was studying the asphalt; the yellow lines of the parking stalls had worn away almost completely, but maybe he could read something there.

"Yeah," Hazard said with satisfaction. "Because that whole story is a crock of horseshit."

"Ok," Benji burst out. "I waited until it was night because I thought maybe you'd be done with the place."

"Or nobody would still be watching it."

He looked up, and his face tightened. "And she—" He indicated Carlson. "—was there, and as soon as I saw her, I knew she wasn't going to let me go inside. But I need those papers, you guys. I hung around. I thought maybe—I don't know what I thought."

The noise Hazard made could only generously be described as skeptical.

"I swear to God! And then, all of a sudden, someone starts screaming, and the cop takes off running. So, I, you know…"

"Committed trespass, burglary, interference with a police investigation—"

"I didn't do any of that!"

"Enough," Somers said.

Flushing, Benji sank back onto the cruiser's rear seat. "Ok," he mumbled. "Maybe the trespassing."

"Benji," Somers said. "Come on."

The young man's flush darkened, and he glared down at the asphalt again.

"Nice fucking story," Hazard said.

"Fuck you!"

"Here's what we're going to do," Somers said. "Benji, you're going to take a ride with Officer Carlson. You're going to get printed. And then you're going to have a longer conversation with Detective Dulac and Detective Palomo. I'm going to let them decide if they want to charge you with trespassing, so I suggest you tell them the truth."

"I am telling you the truth!" His voice was scraped raw with emotion. "My dad is going to kill me if he has to bail me out again."

Hazard snorted. "Asshole dads aren't a soft spot with us, I'm afraid. You'll have to try that one on a couple of guys who weren't royally fucked up by their own fathers."

"Yeah, tough guys." He rubbed his arm over his eyes. "You couldn't give two fucks, right?"

He wouldn't say anymore, and so Somers set about coordinating what needed to happen. He gave Carlson her assignment and then, with help from Benji, called Yarmark back and sent him to retrieve Benji's car, which he'd hidden a few blocks over. He filled Dulac and Palomo in about the conversation, and then he rejoined Hazard on the strip of uneven sidewalk. It was almost midnight, and any other night, the Presidential would have been hopping. The increasing presence of the police, though, gave the place a yawning emptiness. The wind rolled a tin of Skol, and for a moment, that was the only sound.

"He's lying," Hazard said.

"That's what I think too. So, what was he lying about?"

"All of it seems like a safe starting place."

Somers made a considering noise.

"What does that mean?" Hazard asked. "You didn't buy that story about paperwork, did you?"

"I don't know. I don't believe the bit about wanting to keep the nonprofit running, but I could be convinced that he was looking for some sort of financial paperwork."

Hazard grunted.

"I didn't particularly buy that part about showing up without a plan, though," Somers said.

"For fuck's sake, he could have at least made an effort to sound believable."

"What do you think the deal was with the distraction?"

For a moment, Hazard was silent. "The fact that he parked somewhere else and approached the motel on foot makes it clear that he was planning on getting into the motel room somehow without being noticed. It's possible that he had some sort of plan and that the scream was a lucky coincidence."

"But coincidence is like a paper bag full of shit."

"Doesn't hold long," Hazard finished sourly. "The other option is that Benji arranged for the distraction."

"Which means he has an accomplice."

"Not necessarily. He might have lucked into someone—there are plenty of women working tonight, and he could have paid her fifty bucks to scream."

"Or he had an accomplice."

"Or," Hazard said with a shrug, "he had an accomplice."

"That seems like it's worth finding out, doesn't it?" Somers asked.

"There aren't any cameras here."

"No, there aren't. That would make things too easy. Carlson said she heard the scream coming from that direction, right?"

Hazard nodded, and they set off walking. The night had an urban restlessness: a cat streaking down an alley, the clatter of disturbed cans, the sound of distant traffic and, closer, the occasional solitary engine. Ahead of them, a strip mall opened up, with the usual offerings: a tattoo parlor, a payday-loan store, a Chinese restaurant. Number 1 China Wok made the next block smell like an industrial fryer that needed its oil changed and hot chilies, the heat biting at the back of his throat.

"Too many people," Hazard said, gesturing at the strip mall, where the tattoo parlor and Number 1 China Wok still had lights in the windows.

Somers nodded, and they kept going.

They passed a little storefront church—the letters on the glass had flaked away, but the cross was still visible. They passed a Gulp and Go, four of the pumps bagged and obviously out of use. They passed La Jolla Gardens, an apartment complex where cigarette butts seeded the cracks in the parking lot. On the next corner, an abandoned shop with roll-up doors had faded words in the glass: E-Z-Lube. A standalone building with stained stucco had a blue and white illuminated sign: GARNACK FAMILY DENTISTRY. They had a second sign, also illuminated, of a cartoon molar. It was grinning as it brandished an enormous drill, which seemed like a poor choice of advertising.

"Are they trying to drive customers away?" Hazard muttered.

Somers squeezed his arm.

"What?"

"I love you."

"What's this about?"

"Nothing. I'm just telling you I love you."

"I should fucking hope so. You married me. John, did they even think about the fact that people don't like getting their teeth drilled? I mean, did they do any kind of focus group?"

Somers laughed a little too long, and Hazard yanked his arm away.

A block later, the commercial section ended, and tract housing began: block after block of frame houses, eyes of light winking in the distance.

Somers came to a stop. "This is too far."

Hazard turned back the way they had come. "We could ask at the tattoo parlor. I don't think he'd have risked staging the distraction at the strip mall, but maybe that's where he found someone who was willing to help him."

The Gulp and Go, La Jolla Gardens, the E-Z-Lube with its roll-up doors—

"The oil change place," Somers said.

Hazard cocked his head. After a moment, he said, "Because it has a parking lot behind the structure?"

"I think so. Everywhere else, you're at risk of being seen. It's the only spot that's not in use and has an area that's not visible from the street."

"He could have gone a street over."

"Houses."

Hazard frowned. Then he shrugged, and they started walking.

When they came around the side of the E-Z-Lube, the smell of motor oil and stagnant water and something else—a food smell, something pungent and slightly processed that he associated with Colt—reached them. He recognized it a moment later as a whiff of sour cream and onion potato chips. The back of the E-Z-Lube had a matching set of roll-up doors so that patrons could drive their vehicles forward after an oil change. Two dumpsters were pushed up against the cinderblock wall, with flattened cardboard boxes wedged between them. Apparently the locals had, at some point, decided to drop off their own garbage after the E-Z-Lube closed— Somers could make out the shapes of a Morris chair, a CRT television, and a mini-fridge wedged inside the dumpsters. A swatch of orange behind the dumpster caught his attention—an old sleeping bag, and then a rustle, a mercury flash—an empty bag of chips caught under one wheel of the dumpster. Sour cream and onion, Somers guessed.

His brain was still processing all of that as he scanned the rest of the parking lot behind the oil change shop. Then he stopped. The only light came from a street lamp, but it was enough for him to make out three things: the buckled asphalt; the water and oily sludge that had gathered in a shallow trough near the entrance to the parking lot; and the tire tracks that ran from the oily water.

Two sets of tracks.

"Motherfucker," Hazard swore.

"You see it too?"

"I see two sets of tire tracks. At least two. There might be more; they overlap in places, and it's hard to tell."

Somers picked a path toward the tracks, making sure not to step in the dirty water or to mar what might be evidence. He crouched and used the flashlight on his phone. The tracks were clear and fresh; under his light, they had an iridescent shimmer. He touched one, and his finger came away wet. Hazard followed the tracks, playing his own light over them as he bent to examine them.

"One of them drove in first—" Hazard began.

One of the dumpsters boomed hollowly, and Hazard spun toward it. Somers shot up from his crouch, hand going to his service weapon. Nothing. Nothing. A white hiss filled his ears.

Then, after what felt like an eternity, a rat crept out from the garbage.

"Fuck my fucking bones," Hazard growled and wiped his forehead. "Can we please raze this part of the town and start over?"

"I'll bring it up at the next city council meeting," Somers said, "but you should probably come up with talking points and action items."

Hazard flashed him a glare. In clipped tones, he repeated, "One of them drove in here first, and they circled and were facing out. See? Then the other entered—you can tell they're different vehicles—"

"Because of the tires, right. I got that. This one has a defect."

"Typically, tire tracks are analyzed for class markings, meaning the markings that are associated with that make and model of tire, and then for individual markings—defects, damage—and then wear patterns."

"Uh huh. And I'm telling you," Somers pointed to the slight irregularity in the pattern, "this one has some sort of damage. Hold on, I want to check something."

He turned off the flashlight and placed a call to Yarmark.

"It's right where he said it would be," Yarmark said in answer to the question. "I'm waiting for Nickels to show up with his keys; we're going to drive it over to the station."

"Don't do that," Somers said. "Not yet. I need you to look at his—what do you think, Ree?"

"Rear passenger."

"Rear passenger tire," Somers said. "You're looking for some sort of damage to the tread."

"It should be on the exterior of the tire," Hazard said.

Somers conveyed that detail.

"I don't know," Yarmark said. "I don't see anything."

Somers shook his head.

"Let me talk to him," Hazard said, taking the phone before Somers could respond. "Yarmark, we're switching to FaceTime."

Somers could faintly hear Yarmark's distressed "Oh, uh, is that ok with Chief Somerset?"

"Don't worry about Chief Somerset," Hazard said. "Worry about me."

While Hazard bossed Yarmark around and watched the video feed, Somers followed the tracks across the parking lot. Now that Hazard had pointed it out, he could see how the tracks from the first car swung around. Then the second car had entered, veering to the right. He pictured the cars lining up in his head, facing opposite directions so that the drivers would be next to each other. So they could talk, Somers realized.

Another of those hollow booms came from one of the dumpsters.

"Fucking rats," Hazard said, throwing a glance over his shoulder.

"Uh, Mr. Hazard, I should probably be talking to the chief about this, since it's a police matter and—"

"And what?"

Silence.

"Be nice to him," Somers whispered.

Hazard made an annoyed shooing gesture. Into the phone, he said, "Did you want to finish that statement, Samuel?"

"Uh, no, sir." But then apparently the strain was too great because he asked, "Are you sure Chief Somerset isn't available?"

Somers tuned out the rest of Hazard's bullying. The intuitive part of his brain, the part that could take a hundred different invisible cues and put them together without anything ever reaching the surface of consciousness, was stirring now. He could feel it, like a word he couldn't remember. It was the hollow sound of flexing metal. It was the cardboard wedged between the dumpsters. It was the flash of orange. It was the smell of sour cream and onion chips that made him want to wash chip-dust off his fingers.

And then he let out a slow breath and walked toward the garbage.

Hazard was shouting, "Samuel, I said left. Do you know your left from your right?" Yarmark's answer was swallowed up as Hazard shouted, "Then left, brainfuck. Left!"

When Somers reached the dumpsters, he crouched down. He could smell it then: not just the chips, but the oniony heat of an unwashed body.

"You can come out," he said quietly. "Nobody's going to hurt you."

The person—whoever was hidden back there with their sleeping bag and their convenience store food—must have moved because the dumpster's metal gave another of those shivering chimes.

"I'm a police officer, and I'd like to help you, but you have to come out right now. Slowly. That's an order."

Scuffling. Wheezing. Labored grunts. It took almost two minutes for the woman—Somers was fairly sure she was a woman—to emerge from behind the dumpsters. She was white, her skin grimy, and the smell was much, much worse. She wore a puffer vest and flannel and mismatched duck boots. Her hair was gray, curly, matted with sticks and leaves and scraps of paper and plastic. When she turned toward Somers, her face had a scrunched-up quality, her eyes almost completely closed, that made him think of a mole.

"Hello," he said. "Could you show me your hands, please?"

She held them out. They were surprisingly white, her fingers small and stubby.

"Thank you. I'm John-Henry. Who are you?"

"Didn't do nothing. Didn't bother nobody."

"I'm sure that's true," Somers said. "Could you tell me your name?"

"Didn't do nothing to nobody." She had a way of speaking into the collar of the vest. "My place. Don't bother nobody."

"Ree," Somers said in a slightly louder voice. "I need you, please."

He knew the moment that Hazard turned because there was a hitch in the steady flow of invective. Then Hazard disconnected and was silent. He approached with even steps.

"The tire is damaged in the correct place," he said. "Yarmark is photographing it. That puts Benji here."

Somers nodded without looking back. He kept his gaze on the woman in front of him.

"Too loud," the woman said. "Squeak, squeak, squeak."

"He drives a Scion," Hazard told her. "A worn belt is probably the least of his problems."

"Did you see the man who was here?" Somers asked. "Did you see who he was talking to?"

She shook her head, and her hand lifted in a partial gesture toward her eyes. She was blind, Somers realized. Or mostly blind.

"Did you hear anything?" Somers asked. "There was a man here, and—"

"Man. Woman."

"That's right. That's great. Did they say anything? Did you hear what the man said to his friend—"

The woman shook her head so violently that Somers cut off. "Not a friend. Not a friend. You have to! You have to! He told her, and she said no, and—" Her voice broke. "This is my place. I don't bother nobody."

"They weren't friends," Somers said. "Is that right? He was angry at her? He was yelling?"

"She said no. You have to! You have to! Bad. Makes her cry. It's my place. It's mine. I don't bother nobody."

Somers blew out a breath and looked up.

Hazard asked the question. "Who the fuck did Benji scare into helping him?"

CHAPTER ELEVEN
APRIL 12
SUNDAY
9:11 AM

WHEN THEY GOT TO Gerrit Maas's property the next morning, the gate was shut.

Somers eased the Mustang to a halt on the gravel drive. On the other side of the wire fence, a hill rose, capped by trees, limiting his sightline to less than a hundred yards. Mounted above the gate on a telephone pole, a camera looked down at them.

"The hillbilly version of a gated community," Hazard said as he yanked on the door handle. "Like anyone would want to bother these goat-fuckers."

The big man jogged over to the gate, rattled the chain, and came back shaking his head. When he got back in the car, he said, "Locked."

"Did you see an intercom?"

"Yes, John. I buzzed up to the big house and spoke with Jeeves. The master is busy at the spring jubilee."

"Were you always this sarcastic?"

"No. You've been a bad influence. What are we going to do?"

"Buzz up to the big house," Somers said and laid on the horn.

He kept it up, on and off, for five minutes before a golf cart trundled into view and rolled down the hill toward them.

"Thank fuck," Hazard muttered, working a finger in his ear.

"Baby."

"Hearing damage is real, John. I'm not looking forward to spending my twilight years with hearing aids."

"Maybe Shaw could lend you one of those Victorian ear trumpets. We can ask him."

"Absolutely not. If there's a merciful God, those two nut-drips have gone back to St. Louis."

Somers considered reminding Hazard that North and Shaw had come to Wahredua for work, but he figured that his husband had already had a rough morning. They'd been up late the night before, trying to get more information out of the woman they'd found by the E-Z-Lube and deciding what to do with Benji. By the time they'd finally sent the younger man back to the motor court, it had been past two. Then Dulac and Palomo had caught Hazard and Somers up on their work verifying alibis—they'd managed to place Courtney and Jalisa at a bar near Wroxall College, where they were easily visible on a security camera until almost midnight—which put them out of the running as suspects.

That morning, Somers and Hazard had slept in—although still not enough—and as they'd gotten ready for the day, Somers had had to watch while Hazard tried a variety of nonverbal apologies and Colt iced him out: a full breakfast, bacon, egg, waffles, and fresh fruit, that Colt refused to eat; the offer of cash money so Colt could spend the afternoon with Ashley at the movies, which Colt refused to accept; the baited hook of a discussion about cars—Colt refused to bite. Then, later, Somers had caught Hazard sitting on their bed, phone in hand, Theo's contact information pulled up on the screen. When Hazard had seen Somers, he had locked the phone and put it away and dropped his head into his hands.

As the golf cart motored up to them, Somers dragged himself back into the present. The driver was a big man, wearing a camo jacket to ward off the spring morning's chill. He had long, wiry hair and a long, wiry beard. His complexion was wind burned. He got as far as the gate, stopped the cart, and shouted something.

Somers and Hazard got out of the Mustang, and the golf cart driver ducked and came up with an assault rifle—what Somers thought was an AR-15. Somers stopped, the Mustang's door like an apron between him and the rifle. He put a hand on the Glock holstered at his hip and shouted, "Drop that gun!"

"This is private property, Officer," the man called back. "I got a Constitutional right to carry this bad boy."

"Are you out of your fucking mind?" Hazard shouted. "Put down that fucking gun!"

The man shook his head. "You two turn around. This is private property, and you're creating a disturbance."

Somers took a breath. He eased his hand off the Glock, displayed both hands, and approached the gate. The man stayed on the cart, staring at him, the assault rifle leaning against his shoulder.

"Sorry about that," Somers said, resting his arms on the dusty steel bar. "You startled me is all."

That got him a sneer.

"Would you mind coming over here so I don't have to yell?"

Gravel crunched behind Somers as Hazard approached. "Don't bother, John. He feels nice and safe in his go-kart."

The man's face tightened behind the wiry beard, and the golf cart rocked as he climbed down. He approached the gate with the rifle at port arms. "Now listen, I know who you are, and you're not welcome here, so get back in your fancy car—"

"I need to talk to Gerrit Maas," Somers said. "Mr. Maas. Is he here?"

The breeze stirred the weeds already springing up on the side of the drive, and they gave off a rasping whisper.

"Answer him," Hazard said. "We don't have time to wait for your balls to drop."

"This is private property, so unless you got a warrant, you need to get back in your car—"

"This is police business," Somers said. "It's about the murder of his son. I think Mr. Maas would want to talk to us."

"You think," the man echoed with a sneer. Then he trudged back to the cart. He backed up, did a three-point turn, and zipped back up the hill.

"God damn it," Somers muttered.

"King," Hazard said.

"What?"

"That's what he had engraved on the stock of the AR. Didn't you notice?"

Somers turned a look on his husband.

"Oh," Hazard said. "Well, I suppose from where you were standing, the angle was different—"

"Don't."

Somers turned back to the Mustang and called the station on speakerphone. He got Peterson, who—as part of Somers's attempts to modernize the department and, in the process, keep himself from going crazy—had recently been promoted to lieutenant over the day watch patrol. It hadn't been much of a change, in truth; Peterson had been coordinating schedules and helping hammer out the watches unofficially for as long as Somers could remember. Once Somers had realized he needed to reorganize his department, promoting Peterson had been the obvious decision. There was still a long way to go, in terms of bringing the Wahredua PD into the twenty-first century, but Peterson had already made Somers's job significantly easier.

"Dougie King," Peterson said when Somers sketched out the encounter. "He's a limp-dick. The closest he ever comes to getting his rocks off is shooting his gun."

"That sounds familiar," Hazard said.

"You know him?" Somers asked.

Peterson answered, "He's been around a year or so. Moved here for— God, I don't know, actually. Maybe work at Tegula? I got that humming around the back of my head for some reason."

"What a fantastically reliable source of information," Hazard muttered.

Somers asked, "Does he have a record?"

"Shit, hold on." The sound of typing came, and then Peterson said, "No, sir. Nothing that comes up for me, anyway."

"What about an outstanding warrant?"

"No, sir."

"You gotta give me something, Peterson. Even a parking ticket I can hang over his head would be one step closer to getting me onto the property."

"Sorry, Chief."

Somers disconnected and said, "Shit."

Hazard frowned. "I swear to God, I know that name."

"Is it humming around the back of your head?"

Hazard's glare was even darker this time, and Somers smirked.

"I'm going to let that slide—" Hazard began.

"Oh, not on my account."

"—for the sake of marital harmony." He was silent for a moment, considering the wire fencing, the rippling prairie grass, a crow that had settled on a tilted post. "I suppose that, in light of yesterday's events, you are not open to the idea of jumping the fence?"

"No, Ree. I'm currently not accepting any suggestions that involve trespass or, in this case, wandering onto the land of territorial gun nuts."

"That seems shortsighted—"

Something in Somers's face must have convinced Hazard to think, again, about the importance of marital harmony. He pulled out his phone and placed a call on speaker, saying, "Maybe Nico can find something on his social media profile."

"On whose social media profile?" Nico asked. Then he giggled and, speaking away from the phone, said, "Stop it! I'm serious!"

"What are you doing?" Hazard asked.

"Oh my God," Somers breathed. "Don't ask him!"

"Nothing," Nico said. But then he had to say again, his voice shifting, "I'm serious! Oh my God, you are insatiable!"

"Who is insatiable? Who's there? What's going on?"

"Just a minute." The ambient noise faded, and Somers guessed that Nico had gone into another room and shut the door. "Ok, what's up?"

"Where are you?"

"Uh, Em, that's kind of my business."

"It's going to be my business if I have to come find you because your trick steals your kidney. What's his name, age, address, occupation, and, if you remembered to conduct your first date conversations the way I instructed you, his Social Security number?"

"I'm going to jump in here," Somers said. "Hi, Nico. Sorry to bother you on the weekend. We're trying to dig up something on this guy Dougie King. He's out at Gerrit Maas's property acting like some sort of guard, and we need him out of the way."

"Holly's cousin?"

"What?" Hazard asked.

"Who?" Somers asked.

"Holly Brainard. She was the one who had that guy following her, remember? And he broke into the building laundry and stole some of her underwear?"

Hazard scowled. "How do you remember that?"

"You worked that case a month ago."

"I know when I worked the case. I'm talking about the relationship."

"She talked about her cousin, I don't know, a hundred times when she was filling out the contract. She was so glad he moved here. He always used to come visit. He was going to help her, but he got too busy with this new important job. She went on and on about him, even after you told her, quote, 'At this point, the client is no longer obligated to talk' and then 'I don't need your family history.' Which, it turns out, you kind of do."

Hazard's jaw was tight.

"Good thing you've got me, right?"

"Yes," Hazard bit out. "Wonderful. While I've got you on the phone, Nico, why don't we talk about your new work schedule, which will involve nights, weekends, holidays—"

"Ok," Somers said. "Thank you, Nico. Any chance you've got her number?"

"Not with me, but it should be on the contract, and all those documents are in the secure cloud storage. Em has the app on his phone. So, if you guys don't need anything else…"

"No," Hazard said. "I'm sure you want to get back to Chase."

"Nice try," Nico said. "I'll see you at work tomorrow."

"Drop me a pin, Nico. Better yet, share your location with me."

"Goodbye."

"You will regret this when you wake up in a bathtub full of ice."

Nico was laughing as he disconnected.

Somers didn't bother trying to hide the grin when Hazard looked over.

"What?" Hazard snapped.

"It's cute."

"Nothing is cute."

That made the grin bigger. "It's very cute that you feel protective of him. I'm glad you guys are getting along, especially after, you know, how bad things were for a while."

"You could at least have the decency to be jealous."

Somers couldn't help it; it caught him by surprise, and it made him laugh so hard that he had to try three times to get the door open. By that point, Hazard was already out of the car, stalking away, the phone pressed to his ear. Somers got himself under control, and after a minute, Hazard turned around and gave a thumbs-up. Leaning into the car, Somers laid on the horn. He tried for a staccato pattern. For some reason, he thought Shaw would like that.

The golf cart whizzed down the hill. This time, the big guy didn't stay in his seat; he launched himself out of his seat toward the gate, his face twisted in a snarl, the assault rifle swinging at his side.

"Listen, you dumbshits—"

"Talk to your cousin," Hazard said and tossed the phone.

It looked like something of a miracle that the guy actually caught the phone. When he pressed it to his ear, Somers could hear the woman shouting on the other end, even at that distance. The shouting went on for a few minutes. The man's color slowly dropped. Then he started doing some vigorous nodding, and when he realized that wasn't effective, he started talking. "Yes, yes, yeah, I know," seemed to be the general refrain.

When it ended, he glared at them and pitched the phone back at Hazard.

"You got me in trouble," he whined as he stomped toward the gate. He unlocked it, rattled the chain loose, and swung it open.

"Get used to it," Hazard said, pocketing his phone. "I'm not sure Gerrit is going to be much happier with you."

The man hesitated, his hand still on the gate, and glanced back at the hill.

"You can tell him we lied to you," Somers suggested. "Tell him we said we had a warrant."

He brightened up a little at that as he opened the gate the rest of the way. Then he stood aside while they drove through and locked the gate again. He led them up the hill, through the trees—blackjack oaks, with a scrub of wild blackberry and overgrown tangles of what Somers thought might be lilac. The road hugged more hills, the trees pressing in close—a few dogwoods flowering early, some of the white blossoms tinged with pink—and even with the windows up, Somers smelled new leaves and forest litter and the resin of a mammoth pine.

When they rounded another hill and a stretch of open pasture met them, Hazard muttered, "What the actual fuck?"

Somers wanted to echo the sentiment. Acres of pasture had been converted into a kind of tent city, and at first glance, he thought maybe this was another gun show. Then his brain began to catch up, and he noticed that it wasn't like the gun show at all. The gun show had been made up of large, commercial tents. Here, though, the outer ring consisted of camping tents—everything from pup tents to big, twelve-person cabin tents. Then, moving in, the camping tents thinned out, and several larger structures covered the ground. They weren't tents at all, although his brain had supplied that term for want of something better.

"Why the fuck does he have temporary structures on his property?" Hazard asked.

That was a much better term, Somers decided, because although the structures clearly weren't meant to be permanent—they consisted of some sort of vinyl fabric stretched tight over a steel frame—they also were designed like buildings, with reinforced steel doors on some of them that suggested at least an attempt at security, and at least one that had an attached HVAC system. They were also much, much bigger than any tent Somers had seen—even bigger than the commercial tents at the gun show. Some of them, Somers guessed, were big enough to serve as warehouses.

The only permanent structure—now that Somers had that language in his head, it was hard not to see things that way—was a sprawling farmhouse at the center of the compound. It had white siding and raw wood shutters and a generous screened-in porch. It was clearly old, and the style—with an emphasis on the vertical that manifested in tall, narrow windows and sharply pitched rooflines—made the damn thing look almost gothic.

"Where's the red barn?" Hazard muttered.

"I'm sure it's around here somewhere."

"John, there has to be—Christ, I don't know, two hundred people here. And that's a conservative estimate."

"I see that."

"And they've put up these goddamn temporary buildings."

"I see that too."

"Well, how the fuck haven't we heard about this? What the fuck is going on? And who the fuck is letting it happen?"

"Those," Somers said as he followed the golf cart through the maze of tents, "are excellent questions."

Their guide stopped outside of the largest temporary structure—this one with a pair of steel fire doors on the front and an HVAC system plugged into the side. It didn't have windows, Somers noticed after a moment, and that pinged his weird meter. When the golf cart driver got down, the assault rifle back at port arms, Somers let out a breath and reached for the door.

"Let's try to keep this from escalating," he said.

"And what the fuck is that supposed to mean?"

Somers let that one lie and got out of the car.

Their guide stood next to the fire doors, shifting his weight. His color was still bad. He wiped sweat from his forehead, although the day was still on the pleasant side of cool, and glanced at the fire doors. "You can wait for Brother Gerrit—"

"Like fuck," Hazard said and hauled open the door.

Somers followed him inside.

For the second time that day, Somers had to take a minute to figure out what he was seeing. People seated in rows of folding chairs. A raised platform at the far end of the building. A man at a podium—pulpit, Somers's brain suggested—shouting into a microphone. Fluorescent lights hammering down on more men gathered behind the speaker. A meeting. His brain said, Church.

Then more details processed: the men and women in the congregation looked hard used, exhausted, and to judge by their clothes, poor; the men on the stage were dressed in satiny magenta robes and held assault rifles. Port arms again, of course. To a man, they looked fleshy and white and old. And the man at the pulpit, the one screaming into the microphone was Gerrit Maas, wearing a crown of bullets, a gold-plated assault rifle hanging from a strap across his chest.

"Jesus Christ," Hazard said.

"Yeah," Somers whispered. "I think that's the idea."

At the pulpit, Gerrit continued his sermon, his eyes scanning the room, restless. No, Somers corrected himself. Zealous. When he spotted Hazard and Somers, his gaze paused, although the flow of words continued uninterrupted.

"—will be a sanctuary from the Deep State, we will be a refuge for all who fight against tyranny, we will serve God and honor the covenant that the Founders of this great nation made with Him!" He had a deep voice, and it shook with the force of the emotion behind it. In another congregation, the words would have been met with an amen or hallelujah, but here, the worshippers huddled together, their faces solemn, and Somers remembered that the word at the root of reverence was fear. "I ask you, brothers and sisters, have you done everything in your power to reject political satanism and the machinations of the Beast? Have you warned your neighbors about the international Marxist globalists who seek to reduce this great country to a fiefdom of the United Nations? Have you withdrawn yourself from the influence of the Rothschilds and the Rockefellers, the satanic lineages who sit in high places, and are working this very moment to turn our great Christian nation into the Jewnited States?"

The questions, at least, provoked answers, and now men shouted from their seats, syncopated yes's and no's, furious assent and denial, as the question demanded. Only men. The women sat, faces blank, and clutched their children.

"Not everyone in our midst will join the Black-Robed Regiment." Gerrit pointed to a cluster of men, maybe thirty of them, ranging in age from late teens to early forties, who wore denim and black leather jackets—a kind of biker aesthetic meets '50s greaser culture look that made it hard for Somers to take them seriously. Hell, some of the older ones even had their hair slicked back. "Like the men of God who left their flocks to fight the mad King George, they are warriors for Christ, and they will lead us to victory against those who bear the mark of the Beast!"

More shouts, mixed with envious looks from the men who sat with the rest of the congregation. The women were looking too, devotion and desire mingling in their faces.

"Like they're the fucking Rolling Stones," Hazard growled.

Somers whispered, "I can't engage with that right now."

Gerrit changed course now, belting out a warning about the World Bank, but it faded into the background for Somers. A man from the Black-Robed Regiment stood and made his way toward them, followed by two more. The first man was older—if he was forty, it was a hard forty—and his iron-gray hair was pomaded into a sharp part. He had a face like the backside of a shovel, with about as much warmth. The ones who followed him were younger—one of them had a big pimple on his jaw, while the other had grown out his peach fuzz in a vain attempt to look, presumably, like he was out of grade school. All three of them carried assault rifles on straps.

Dougie King, stripped of his golf cart and the bravado he'd shown at the gate, was wringing his hands. "Brother Newell—"

"Outside," the hard-faced man said.

"We're here to speak to Gerrit Maas," Hazard said.

"Outside. You're disrupting worship."

The congregation didn't look particularly disturbed; with the exception of a child who couldn't have been more than four, who was currently hanging upside down from his mother's lap, nobody even seemed to have noticed them. But Somers nodded, and they followed Dougie out of the temporary chapel.

Outside, the air smelled like wood smoke and wet laundry and vinyl, a hundred times cleaner than the trapped body odor and warm polyester combination inside.

"I'm John-Henry Somerset, chief of police—" Somers began.

"Your instructions, Brother Douglas, were to admit no one," the hard-faced man—Newell—said. Dougie flinched. "And yet here I stand with two unbelievers who have defiled our holy place."

"I had to," Dougie protested. He must have realized that being browbeaten by his cousin wouldn't be an acceptable excuse because he threw a pleading glance at Hazard and said, "They told me they had a warrant."

"Technically," Hazard said, "I only suggested that."

Newell ignored him. "Did you see this warrant?"

"No, Brother Newell, but—"

"Return to your post, Brother Douglas. I will tell Brother Gerrit about this dereliction of duty. You will, of course, have a right to explain yourself before the council of the elect."

Dougie was sweating more heavily now, his face a curdled white. He opened his mouth and then seemed to think better of it. He hurried toward the golf cart with the tight, abbreviated stride of a man trying not to shit himself.

"I'm going to follow you off our land," Newell said to them, his voice flat. One of the boys behind him was cleaning his nails with a knife. Hazard snorted. "You'll be hearing from our lawyers about misrepresenting your authority to be on private property."

"I think there's been a misunderstanding," Somers tried. "But regardless, we need to speak to Mr. Maas about the investigation into his son's murder."

Newell considered this for a moment. He had dark, unreadable eyes. "What do you need to ask him?"

"This is a conversation for Mr. Maas."

"I handle Brother Gerrit's secular affairs—"

"Bullshit," Hazard said. "You're his guard dog, and you want to make a big show of how important you are. You want to know what we want to talk about? Let's start with Gerrit Maas being at the Presidential Friday night. Then we can talk about his dead son, somebody looking for paperwork, a missing gun—"

Newell's blink was like the shutter and rattle of an old slide projector; when his eyes opened again, there was something different in them, and Somers didn't like it. Newell studied them for another moment. Then he nodded. "This way."

When he started walking away from the tent, Somers hesitated. He caught Hazard's gaze. The representatives of the Jets watched them with hand-me-down tough guy routines; the one was still cleaning his nails. Hazard gave a tiny shrug, and Somers turned to follow.

Newell led them through the ring of tents and campers and into a line of trees at the edge of what had once been pasture. A narrow footpath led down a hill, winding between more blackjack oaks and white pines, the smell of mud and last year's leaves and balsam thick in Somers's chest. The sun speared through the new leaves overhead, so thin and fresh they were translucent. When Somers turned his head up, they looked like thousands of pieces of stained glass rippling in the breeze.

"Where the fuck are we going?" Hazard growled, stopping to scrape mud from his boot on an exposed root.

"Keep moving," the one with the dirty fingernails said from behind them.

"Listen to me, you overgrown sperm—" Hazard started.

"Brother Gerrit keeps a private house of prayer for these kinds of meetings," Newell said without looking back. "Hurry; the worship is almost over."

"Like fuck he does," Hazard whispered as he came close behind Somers.

Somers gave a compressed nod.

But when three men with assault rifles suggested you start moving, that didn't leave many options. And, Somers reminded himself, nothing had happened. Yet.

When they reached the bottom of the hill, the trees were shorter, stunted, and the ground softer. Prairie grass grew as high as Somers's chest, and he could make out a line of last year's reeds, so straight it was like someone had drawn them with a pencil. The air was different—the mud smell was stronger, and now it was mixed with stagnant water and moldering vegetation.

"Where the fuck are we?" Somers muttered. He'd had the vague idea they were walking in the direction of the highway, but now he was completely turned around.

"Missouri has wetlands," Hazard said. "I think this technically constitutes a fen."

"Perfect," Somers said as one shiny black boot sank an inch into the mud. "A swamp."

"No, swamps are different because they can support woody plants, but as you can see—"

"Watch your step," Newell said a moment before his shoes rang out on wood. Then Somers made out a narrow plank laid over a stretch of water; it was almost hidden by the thatch of dead grass and sedge. When Somers crossed it, it bowed under him.

"Careful," he whispered back.

"Very funny," Hazard snapped, but Somers didn't miss the single, ominous crack when Hazard came behind him.

They made it to the other side without the plank giving way, though, and after crossing two more planks, the ground grew more solid, and the stunted blackjacks appeared again. Twenty yards later, where the trees grew taller, they reached a clearing. It looked like it had been cleared with drip torches at some point; the trees ringing it still had black marks along their trunks. At the center stood a wooden shack with a tin roof. No windows here either, Somers noticed. Maybe that was a design principle for cults.

Newell undid a padlock and opened the door.

"No fucking way," Hazard said.

"You're trespassing on private land. Lot of bad things can happen to a trespasser."

"I'm sure you've gotten used to terrorizing chickenshit twelve-year-olds and little old ladies, but I've got news for you, dick-drip: you're dealing with something else now. There is no fucking way we're going in there."

"Go on, then." Newell weighed the padlock in one hand as he looked back at the fen. "The same way we came down here."

The Jets moved back, and the one with the pimple swung the assault rifle into a two-handed grip.

"You wouldn't dare," Hazard said.

"Ree, let's just go inside."

"Dare?" Newell asked. Iron-gray eyebrows quirked. "What?"

"People know us," Hazard said. "People know we were coming out here."

"I don't know what you're talking about."

"Enough," Somers said. "Ree, come on. We'll wait for Mr. Maas."

Hazard turned on him, eyes wide, but Somers nodded. Then, without waiting for a reply, he stepped through the door. He had a brief impression of a shadowy space, cooler than the April day outside, and the musty smell of weathering wood and dust. Hazard followed him a moment later. The big man turned around as soon as he crossed the threshold, but Newell was faster, shutting the door and, a moment later, sliding the padlock home.

"Motherfucker," Hazard shouted, hammering on the wood. "You're going to regret this!"

"Cool it," Somers said.

"When I get out of here, I'm going to find you, and then I'm going to break every fucking bone in your body!"

"Emery Hazard!"

Hazard shot him a look that was clear, cold, and controlled, but when he pounded on the door again, he sounded unhinged. "Let us out of here!"

The world seemed to take a breath after that, and in the quiet, murmured conversation filtered into the shack from outside. The words were too low for Somers to make out. Then, a moment later, steps moved away from the shack.

"Let us out, let us out, let us out!" The door reverberated under Hazard's blows.

"Ree, I know this is freaking you out, but we didn't have a choice. If we'd tried to go back—"

"For the love of God, John, I know. I'm not an idiot." He worked something out of his pocket and passed it over; it was a single-piece multi-tool, surprisingly light—although maybe not so surprisingly, because Somers thought he remembered Hazard saying it was made out of titanium. "I can't get a signal down here, so we can't call for help. Would you please hurry and find us a way out? I'm trying to create a distraction, but I'm running out of things to say."

It took Somers a moment to process that. Then he grinned. "Why don't you channel some of your feelings about that cut-rate shipping company that got Evie's Christmas present here late?"

Hazard brightened and pounded on the door again. "You shit-burrowing fuck weasels!"

While his husband made new friends, Somers took the multi-tool and did a more thorough assessment of their surroundings. His eyes were adjusting to the gloom, and he saw his first impression hadn't been far off: the shack consisted of a single, open room. The boards of the walls were fitted together loosely, and the only light came through the cracks. It was cool bordering on cold in the darkness. Aside from mouse droppings and what looked like a nest in the low-pitched rafters above, they were alone. Then Somers saw something and crouched.

"What?" Hazard asked quietly between cries of "You diseased horse pizzles" and "Slut nuggets."

Round, dark drops stained the wood. Somers straightened and shook his head. "Nothing."

He moved around the shack, testing the boards and getting nowhere. They were all nailed in solidly, and when Somers tried to work the multi-tool into place and use it as a lever, the angle was wrong, and the opening was too tight.

"I will fuck you with a rotary hammer—" Hazard snapped his fingers, and when Somers glanced over, he pointed up. "—you McLovin ass clowns!"

Somers moved to the far wall, away from the door, and mimed a stirrup. Hazard joined him. The bigger man laced his fingers together and boosted Somers up, and then Somers planted a foot on a length of blocking. He used the horizontal length of wood to stand and steadied himself by grabbing a rafter. When Hazard looked up with a silent question, Somers gave him a thumbs-up, and Hazard resumed pounding on the door.

"You crotch-biscuit, Cheeto-dick, shit-sprayers!"

"If you find yourself running low," Somers suggested *sotto voce*, "summon up the memory of when you borrowed a welding torch to cut up the barbeque grill and I caught you saying, 'Take that, motherfucker.'"

Hazard flipped him the bird.

Grinning, Somers pushed on the sheet of tin above him. It was nailed down, but unlike the boards, some of the nails had come loose, and he was able to shift it a few inches. He raised it up and got the multi-tool under it and then applied pressure, using the multi-tool like a pry bar. The sheet of tin shot up, the nails tearing free, and it was so easy that Somers barely caught the metal before it fell back into place with a clatter.

After that, he worked steadily, still grinning. It was stupid—he ought to have been scared for his life, and at one level, he was. They'd miscalculated what they were walking into. Badly. But that was lack of information as much as anything else, and he didn't know how he could have been expected to predict a congregation of assault rifle-wielding lunatics. But even with all that, he was also riding an adrenaline rush, and he was with his husband, and they were so fucking good at this—well, most of it—especially together.

When Hazard drew a breath again, Somers whispered, "Got it."

Hazard nodded. He launched into "You sandpaper-assed human excuses for dickholes—" as he made his way across the shack. At the same time, Somers eased the sheet of tin sideways. He had to angle it in order to pass it down to Hazard, and for a moment, Somers was sure he'd chosen the moment wrong and that the guard—or guards, since he wasn't sure if both the Jets had stayed behind—would see. But then he passed the sheet of tin down, and Hazard carried it across the shack to prop against the door. It wouldn't hold anyone for long, but it might buy them a few seconds.

Somers lifted himself up through the opening in the roof, pivoted on his stomach, and then leaned back down to stretch out a hand. Hazard eyed him and shook his head. Somers nodded. After a moment, face twisting with what might have been embarrassment, Hazard grabbed him. Somers grunted at the sudden weight, but he hauled up, and Hazard jumped. Hazard scrabbled for a moment at the top of the wall before he steadied himself on the blocking. Somers whoofed a breath.

"My stomach is going to have bruises for a month," he whispered

Hazard turned adorably red. He whispered back, "Can we go, please?"

With a smirk, Somers pushed back and let himself fall. He landed easily, and then he straightened and pulled his gun from the holster. The rules had changed now, and more importantly, he had the advantage. For the moment, at least.

Hazard dropped down next to him. He glanced around. Then he jerked a thumb in the opposite direction of the shack, where the trees thinned into the fen. Somers nodded, but before they could move, a voice came from nearby.

"Open it, open it, open it!"

It was Newell, and the man's cold authority had sharpened with panic. Running footsteps came toward the shack. Somers and Hazard crouched.

The lock rattled, and then Somers heard the sound of the tin sheet flexing as Newell tried to open the door.

"God damn it!" Newell shouted.

Hazard's eyes widened, and he bore Somers to the ground without a word. A moment later, shots rang out; bullets tore through the wall of the shack, and splinters struck Somers's coat. The clap of the shouts rang in Somers's ears, and a moment later, he tasted gunpowder.

Newell must have realized they were gone because he let out a wordless howl. Then he shouted, "You stupid fuck!"

"But they were in there the whole—"

Another shot came. The Jet—whichever one he was—cut off with a scream.

"Get off," Somers whispered, and he rolled away from Hazard and came up on his knees. The Glock floated in his hand like a thundercloud.

"He's down here!" That was a new voice.

"This way!" That was another.

Newell let out another of those furious shrieks. Then pounding footsteps moved away from the shack and away from the incoming voices. Somers slid to the end of the structure and peered around. He caught a glimpse of Newell as the man tore up the next hill, obviously trying to escape whoever was coming after him.

"What in the—" That was another fresh voice, although this one, Somers recognized. He'd heard it growing up, when Landon Maas played football. And he'd heard it not too long ago in the temporary chapel. Gerrit Maas called out, "Chief Somerset? Hello? Chief Somerset, if you're still alive, I need you to respond."

"Nice fucking try," Hazard muttered. His face was white; dirt clung to the sweat snaking down his cheeks.

"Chief Somerset, if you're alive, I want you to understand that I am delivering myself into your custody. My people—the true ones—had nothing to do with what happened. When I couldn't find you after worship—" He cut off with a distressed noise. "Please accept my unconditional surrender."

"That was easy," Somers breathed.

"John, no."

"Ree, listen. There have to be twenty of them. We can't run, not now."

Before Hazard could argue, Somers stood. He kept the Glock at his side even though it kept wanting to drift up. He checked around the corner of the shack. Then he stepped out.

Gerrit Mass, in his magenta robe and crown of bullets, stared at him. There weren't twenty men behind him; there had to be at least thirty, all of them robed, all of them carrying assault rifles. Gerrit smiled. He had fine, white hair that looked, in texture, like a baby's. Then he knelt, laid the gold-plated assault rifle on the ground in front of him, and raised his hands in the air.

CHAPTER TWELVE
**APRIL 12
SUNDAY
11:28 AM**

IN THE KITCHEN OF Gerrit Maas's old farmhouse, Somers tried to think. He knew he only had a little time; the sheriff and his deputies and detectives had turned out in force after Somers had called. For the moment, Sheriff Engels was busy organizing a search for the fugitive Brother Newell, but Somers knew that wouldn't last forever. Eventually, he and Hazard would have to give statements, and the sheriff would take over the interview with Gerrit. In other words, they needed to hurry.

But hurrying didn't seem to be on the menu. With the sheriff's permission, Gerrit had gone upstairs to change out of his church regalia, and Somers and Hazard had been left in the kitchen to wait. Through an open doorway, Somers had a line of sight on Neecie Weiss, the deputy who was currently making sure nobody in the house decided to make a run for it. Weiss was favoring her bad leg, but her face was impassive.

The house was like many of the old family homes in the area: the main floor broken up into smaller rooms with low ceilings and few windows, the plank walls painted white and the floorboards honey-colored under the varnish. The furnishings weren't exactly *Little House on the Prairie*-era—the leather sectional crammed in the living room, for example, had clean modern lines—but many of the pieces were obviously antiques, some of them repurposed.

In the kitchen, Somers and Hazard sat at a table with a red-check cloth, smelling something that definitely contained a lot of butter and sugar, with undernotes of what he thought might have been brass polish. Quiet chatter came from the radio in the next room—he thought it was an AM band, either conservative talk or conservative religion, maybe both. Then steps came, and through the open doorway, Somers saw Neecie Weiss smile and nod, and a moment later Gerrit stepped into the room. He'd ditched the satin robe and the crown of bullets and even the gold-plated AR, and now, as he sat at the table in denim overalls and a flannel shirt, he looked a lot more like the man Somers had seen at football and basketball and baseball games.

A woman followed him into the room. She looked older than Gerrit, although that might have been partly her choice: she wore her graying hair long, in a braid that came almost to her waist, and no makeup. A simple gray dress. A clean white apron. She might have been pretty or even beautiful—she had the right bone structure—but frown lines marked her forehead and eyes and mouth. She was the kind of woman Somers couldn't imagine ever having been a child, much less out of an apron. As though responding to Somers's thought, she moved to the oven and opened it.

"Crack pie," she said. "I'm afraid it's no good warm. I planned it for Father's supper, plenty of time to cool."

"It's only a name, Chief Somerset," Gerrit said. "You ever had a gooey butter cake?"

"Sure," Somers said with a smile. "Is it something like that?"

"Tastes the same."

"Oh," Hazard said. "Artificial vanilla extract, bleached flour, and enough sugar to make your teeth hurt? Delicious."

"He ate three-quarters of the one we got when we were in St. Louis," Somers said. "And he brought home two in his suitcase."

Hazard flushed. "That was for an experiment. I think they added almond."

Gerrit laughed quietly. "I am sorry about earlier, Chief. I saw you in the congregation, and I knew that we needed to speak, but I had a responsibility to tend to my flock first."

Hazard was making a noise, and Somers kicked his foot under the table.

"When I finished delivering the word," Gerrit said, "I went to find you, but you were gone. I asked around, and fortunately, some of the brethren had seen you being escorted out of the chapel by Brother Newell. Well, I went to find him, and eventually I found someone who'd seen you heading down into the fens. I knew something was wrong, so I took some brethren I trust with me." He shook his head. "I was too late for Ricky, I'm afraid."

"Ricky should have known the risk when he became an accomplice to kidnapping and attempted murder."

At the stove, where she was setting the pie to cool, the woman made a noise of contempt—actually, now that Somers thought about it, a lot like the one Hazard had made.

Gerrit shook his head. "I'm sorry; this is my wife, Pamela."

They exchanged greetings, and she said, "You didn't know Richard Smith. That young man was a sweetheart."

"Let me guess," Hazard said. "He was the sweetheart who was cleaning his nails with a knife to make sure we knew how scary he was."

"He wouldn't have hurt anyone. He was a child. You wouldn't know this, but children do all sorts of foolish things."

"Believe it or not, I managed to pick that up."

"He wouldn't have hurt anyone. And for Newell to cut him down like that—"

"Mr. Maas," Somers said, "do you have any idea why Newell acted the way he did today?"

Gerrit hesitated.

"Let me help," Hazard said. "He got real jumpy and started planning to murder us after we told him we needed to talk to you about your son's murder."

"I don't understand what you mean."

"I mean he acted like a shitty accomplice."

"We don't use that language in this house," Pamela said.

"I mean," Hazard said as though he hadn't heard her, "he acted like he was trying to cover his own ass." Then scarlet slashed his cheeks. "Butt. Whatever."

"You think Brother Newell had something to do with Landon's death." Gerrit shook his head as though dazed. "You think I had something to do—I can't—what—"

Somers played the video that Benji had given them, the one that showed Gerrit and Taz crossing the Presidential's parking lot, carrying their assault rifles with them.

Pamela shook her head and made that noise of disgust again.

Gerrit leaned back and covered his face. After a moment, he lowered his hands. "I'm an old fool."

"What does that mean?" Hazard asked.

"I have a temper. I'm a man of God, but I'm still only a man, and even though anger is a sin, I fall sometimes."

"Less Biblical self-flagellation. More facts."

"Yes. I went to that motel. I went armed, with Brother Josiah—"

"That's this fellow with the Tasmanian devil tattoo?"

Gerrit nodded. "We went to confront that...that man."

"Who?" Somers asked.

"The one who assaulted my son."

"You know his name," Hazard said.

"Renner." The color in his face was muddled and wine dark now. "I went to warn him. He had touched a member of my family, and regardless of my feelings about Landon, that couldn't be allowed to stand. I told him, I warned him, that he needed to leave town. If he didn't, there would be consequences for his behavior."

"Nice," Hazard said. "Threatening him. It's always easier when a culprit confesses to assault and premeditation. Keep going; when did you shoot him?"

"I didn't hurt that man! I didn't hurt anyone! Family is sacred—"

"He doesn't understand that," Pamela put in from near the stove. She was still standing, and although her face was smooth and her voice neatly clipped, she twisted a towel in her hand, her knuckles popping out from the strain. "His type can't."

"Family is sacred," Gerrit said. "Family honor. Family name. What he'd done to my son—"

"Helping him suck some cock?"

"Get out!" Pamela snapped the towel down to her side and pointed with her free hand. "You can't talk like that—"

Gerrit raised a hand, and she cut off instantly. He watched Hazard with a new wariness. "You come at me tooth and claw, but I haven't said a word against you or yours."

"You don't have to," Hazard said. "I can hear the members of your flock stacking wood for the bonfires already."

"Let's calm down," Somers said. "Ree, maybe you should wait outside—"

"I preach the word of God."

"You preach a poorly understood amalgamation of received writings that span thousands of years, and you do it with no sense of historical or cultural specificity or instantiation." Drily, Hazard added, "And you do it while looking like a *Heart of Darkness* fuck-around action figure."

"That's enough," Somers said. When Gerrit opened his mouth, Somers spoke first: "Mr. Maas, how did Mr. Renner respond to your suggestion that he leave town?"

Gerrit's voice was thick with anger, and his eyes stayed on Hazard. "He said he wasn't going anywhere."

"And what did your son say?"

That brought his attention back. "My son?"

"What was Landon's part in this interaction?"

"Landon wasn't there."

"That doesn't make any sense—" Hazard began.

Somers spoke over him. "Landon didn't go with you to visit Mr. Renner?"

"No." Gerrit seemed to struggle with what to say next. "My son and I—"

"That's enough, Father," Pamela said.

He raised his hand again. Her face colored, and Somers thought Bible or not, church or not, crown of bullets or not, Gerrit Mass might be sleeping on the couch for the next month.

"My son and I have not spoken in months."

"Why?" Hazard asked.

"Personal reasons."

"You'll need to be more specific."

Pamela wrung the towel between her hands. "That woman."

Gerrit nodded.

"Naomi?" Somers asked.

"That doesn't make any sense," Hazard said. "She's a political force, and she's aligned with the particular brand of bat-shittery you're peddling here. Her relationship with Landon was a smart strategic move."

"You wouldn't understand," Pamela said. "Your kind never does."

"You've used that line before," Hazard said. "Find something new, or figure out something useful to say, or go make another fucking pie."

"You cannot talk to my wife like that," Gerrit said.

Hazard's eyes met the older man's.

"Did you hear me?" Gerrit asked quietly.

After jerking out a nod, Hazard growled, "My apologies," and he sounded about as apologetic as the time he'd poured all of Somers's energy drinks down the drain.

It was enough, though. Gerrit nodded. Pamela wasn't smiling except on the inside, and it shone out of her.

"What was the problem with Naomi?" Somers asked.

"She is a smart woman." Gerrit sounded like a man picking his words carefully. "She is driven. She would, as you say, be a strong match in many ways. But she is not a good woman. Not saintly, I mean."

Pamela nodded. "Impure."

"In what way?" Somers asked.

Gerrit flushed and looked over at his wife. "Pamela, do you mind?"

She nodded and left the room. A moment later, the front door clicked shut.

"It's not a thing to speak of in front of women," Gerrit said. "That's not how I was raised, to talk about this kind of thing in front of a woman."

"Sex," Hazard said in that drily brittle tone again.

Gerrit nodded. "She has been promiscuous in the past. There is good reason to believe that she was not faithful to my son during their relationship. When Landon was growing up, I was not a man of faith. God was calling me, but I was too stubborn to listen. All this—" He gestured around them. "—came when God shook me by the scruff of the neck and told me it was time. The Herdsmen came out of that."

"The Herdsmen?" Hazard muttered. "Christ."

"One of my regrets is that I came to the truth after Landon was an adult, when I could no longer guide him. When I told him about this woman, about her carnal pursuits, he laughed."

Hazard snorted. "God, it's like we never even had a sexual revolution."

Somers barely heard him. What Gerrit said was off-putting for a number of reasons, but it made sense, in a way. Naomi had told them the marriage was a political one, and if there had been a physical component, Somers didn't find it hard to believe that it had been out of convenience instead of love or loyalty. He certainly wouldn't have put it past Naomi to have been involved in other relationships, even if they were purely sexual, while she was engaged to Landon—although the irony was something fierce. But it raised an interesting possibility. Had the murders been motivated by jealousy?

"When I left that motel," Gerrit said, "Renner was still alive. And he was alone. I don't know why my son was there. I wish to God he hadn't been."

"You mentioned your feelings toward Landon," Somers said. "Was Naomi the only reason you were estranged?"

He hesitated and shook his head. He was a pastor, and pastors, by trade, probably weren't supposed to be good at lying, but it was still a little disappointing how transparent he was.

"What else?" Somers asked.

Gerrit shook his head again.

Somers glanced at Hazard, and the big man's face was blank, almost empty, the way he looked sometimes when he got deep in thought. When he spoke, he had the tone of someone laying out the pieces of a puzzle. "Newell didn't seem particularly worried about us until we told him why we were here. But if you're telling us the truth, then that doesn't make any sense. He wouldn't have been worried because he knew you hadn't killed

Zach Renner. He certainly wouldn't have freaked out and tried to sequester us and then, when his panic escalated, to kill us."

"I don't think I have anything else to say."

"I told him we needed to talk to you about someone looking for paperwork, about a missing gun—"

Gerrit flinched.

"What?" Somers asked. "What is it?"

The old farmer-turned-pastor shook his head.

But the pieces were falling into place for Somers now too. "Landon was a sales rep for a gun manufacturer. And your congregation, the Herdsmen, you believe in carrying guns—"

"We believe in the Second Amendment. We believe in the Constitution that the Christian Founding Fathers of this great nation—"

"Save it," Hazard said.

Gerrit was taking little shallow breaths now. "All those purchases were legal. Even though the background checks are unconstitutional, we complied. Landon has all the paperwork to prove it."

"But Landon wasn't worried about us coming here," Somers said, still trying to think his way through the dark. "And neither were you. Newell was."

Jaw tight, Gerrit stared at them.

"They were working together," Hazard said. "Newell and Landon. They were doing something illegal, and you didn't like it. No, that's not quite right. It made you furious."

"You need to leave now."

"What were they doing?"

"If you don't leave now, I'll get the sheriff."

The connection was one of those bright, trailing flares that came up from the base of Somers's subconscious, and he said it as the thought was still processing: "You put that guard on Landon's house. The family friend, the one who was with Carson's aunt and uncle."

"My daughter and her husband are good people."

"You're avoiding the issue." Somers decided to gamble. "Did you know that two men in an unmarked SUV tried to abduct my husband last night?" The surprise in Gerrit's face looked genuine, so Somers continued, "They wanted him to help them get into Landon's house—they wanted him to make them seem legitimate, so they could search the property."

"That won't happen," Gerrit said stiffly. "They'll be taken care of."

"Mr. Maas, you're missing the point. Whatever you're not telling us, it's putting Carson in danger. Now, either you can help us, or we can put the pieces together ourselves. It'll take longer, but we'll get there eventually, and the only thing that will happen is Carson will be in danger longer. That's not what you want for your grandson."

Something caved in Gerrit's expression. He rested his chin in his hand for a moment, and when he spoke, his voice was soft. "He's a good boy. In spite of his father, I think. Maybe in spite of his grandfather too." Then he shook his head, and his voice strengthened. "I did not want to believe it, and so I chose not to. Until today. I don't know why Newell locked you up; I think he wanted to know if I had seen you. I think he was hoping I hadn't, so he'd have time to come up with a better plan. When he learned that I was looking for you, though, he must have known he didn't have time. That's why he rushed back to the fens and tried to kill you. To cover his tracks."

"What didn't you want to believe?"

"When I went to confront Landon about...that woman, I saw the papers. The forms. For the background check."

"The ATF Firearms Transaction Record," Hazard said. "Forty-four-seventy-three."

"He had them all spread out on the kitchen table. He was filling them out. Names from my flock. My congregation. Listing the guns they'd bought. And I knew those people, knew those families, and I knew what he was writing was all lies."

"But why bother with the paperwork—" Then Hazard's face hardened. "He wanted the commission, is that it? God, what a dumb fuck. He's supposed to keep those records for twenty years; did he think nobody would come looking for them eventually?"

"Landon was lying about gun sales?" Somers asked. "Using names from your congregation?"

"Names, dates of birth, Social Security numbers. The information had to come from someone inside the Herdsmen. I thought—" He shook his head, his smile bitter and disbelieving. "Well, I suppose I'm reaping the whirlwind. I didn't want Newell to be responsible; now, he's killed one of our young men."

"In all likelihood," Hazard said, "he's killed before—it's possible he also killed your son and Zach Renner."

Gerrit nodded slowly. Then he paused and said, "I'm not sure—I know you'll think that I'm being a fool, but I'm not sure that Brother Newell—" He cut off, seemingly unable to speak the words.

"Why?" Somers asked.

"I went over there once more after I learned what Landon was doing. We fought, again. About the names. The guns. He was upset. Afraid. And then he told me he'd done something stupid. It wasn't stupid enough, I asked him, to help those men traffic guns to Mexico?"

"What did he do?" Somers asked.

Gerrit's throat worked, but he only shook his head.

"He stole from them, the gunrunners." Pamela stood in the doorway, her cheeks apple bright, her eyes like a fever. "Somewhere around three million dollars."

CHAPTER THIRTEEN

APRIL 12
SUNDAY
2:45 PM

ON THEIR WAY TO Landon Maas's home, Hazard ran searches on his phone while Somers placed phone calls. In spite of their best efforts, neither Gerrit nor his wife had been able to tell them anything concrete about the gun runners, and so Hazard had to rely on the limited information he'd gathered from his brief encounter with them: the men were black or, possibly, mixed; they were young, in their early twenties; they were competent and dangerous; and they were looking for something. After the conversation with Gerrit and Pamela, Hazard had a pretty good idea that they were looking for the stolen money.

When Somers disconnected, he tossed the phone in a cup holder and said, "Dulac and Palomo say they verified Naomi's alibi with the donors and the hotel. They're going to meet us at the Maas's home and do a more thorough search, and they're also going to grab all the paperwork. Maybe we can match up some of the ATF forms to guns that have been seized in crimes."

Hazard grunted. "Going after the guns is pointless."

"It's not pointless. That's part of building this case—hell, if Gerrit is telling the truth, and if Landon has been buying guns and then running them down to the cartels, putting together those links is going to be a big part of a lot of cases."

"I mean it's pointless for our investigation."

"No, it gives us motive. Three million dollars is enough of a reason to kill someone."

"It gives us two motives. The gun runners—Larenz and Korrin—definitely have a reason to kill Landon. I'll even be willing to stretch that theory and include Zach as an ancillary killing."

"So generous of you," Somers murmured.

"But it also gives Gerrit motive. He admitted that he was furious when he found out Landon was using information from his little cult to move guns. It might be more than that; Gerrit plays the nice old farmer turned pastor, but keep in mind that he raised Landon, and Landon was an unmitigated fuck. I could see that argument escalating. I could see Gerrit wanting to kill Landon for compromising his cult."

"Ok, fair. Two motives."

"Two motives. But motive doesn't help us put a gun in anyone's hand, and motive doesn't help us put anybody in that motel room. That's what we need."

"I know. And we're going to do it. You know how it goes: you follow this thread, and then you follow the next, and eventually you get what you need."

"Or you don't, John. Not every murder gets solved."

Somers nodded. He rested his elbow on the car door and propped his head in one hand. The afternoon sun dappled his face in gold and shadow.

They drove a mile like that before Hazard, gaze fixed on the windshield, added, "We do have a higher-than-average close rate, though."

The smirk was so fast that it had to have been waiting, and Somers said, "God you're a softie."

It wasn't punishment for that little joke, spending the rest of the drive on his phone while the miles flicked by in bursts of new leaves on the maples and elm and haw, in the patches of still-damp pavement where the canopy had thickened enough to block out the sun, in the smell of Somers's cologne and the faint hint of the fens that still clung to them—waterlogged rushes and trampled sedge and mud. It wasn't a punishment at all. Hazard was just busy trying to solve this fucking case.

When they turned onto the gravel drive at Landon Maas's property, Somers made a noise, and Hazard looked up. He followed his husband's gaze along the state highway.

"Motherfucker."

The muscle car with a damaged rear panel, the one that North and Shaw had been driving, was parked on the side of the road.

They followed the driveway up into the trees, and Hazard lost sight of the car. He turned forward, peering at the Maas house as it came into view. It looked normal—or, better said, it looked the way Hazard remembered it. There was no sign of North and Shaw.

"What the fuck are they doing?" Hazard asked.

"I don't know."

"If they're fucking around in my case, they are going to seriously fucking regret it."

Somers's voice was mild. "Your case?"

"You know what I mean." Hazard leaned forward as the car rocked along the gravel. "God fucking damn it." He twisted again in the seat, scanning the open stretch of farmland, and pointed. In a fallow stretch that bordered the state highway, a clear line had been trampled through the prairie grass and weeds toward the house. "Jesus Christ, they might as well have used spray paint. Anybody can tell they walked through there."

"Go easy on them. They're city boys. And I think North might be sensitive, and you ride him hard sometimes."

"That fucker doesn't know the meaning of rode hard, but he is sure as fuck going to find out. I'm going to ride the shit out of him."

Out of the corner of his eye, Hazard was aware of Somers's eyebrows going up.

"You know what I mean," Hazard snapped.

Somers shook his head and breathed, "Good God."

They parked in front of the house and went up to the porch, but when they knocked, no one answered. After a minute, Somers knocked again. Nothing.

"Perfect," Hazard said. "Those two twits waited for the house to be empty, and now they're tossing the place. Get your handcuffs ready."

"Oh Lord."

"If you haven't already bought me a birthday present, I'd like to make a request: I'd like to be the one to put the cuffs on North. And put him in the holding cell."

"Cut it out."

"It can be birthday and Christmas."

"I know you like them," Somers said as he went down the steps. "Hell, I know North is your friend. You've got him on speed dial. So, I don't get this whole thing between the two of you."

As they walked to the back of the house, Hazard took advantage of the time to list in bullet-point format his objections to that statement.

He was barely getting started on subpoint 2B, speed dial signifies nothing on a personal level, a follow-up to 2A, speed dial is a professional concession, when they reached the back of the house and Somers said, "Ree, I love you, but you've got to shut up now."

"Fine," Hazard said. "That will give me an opportunity to organize the rest of my rebuttal."

It might have been the breeze, but he thought Somers sighed as he took steps up onto the back deck.

Hazard's brain was half-busy formulating 3F, the irresponsibility of using vague language like 'this whole thing' to describe a relationship between two non-sexually involved men, when he bumped into Somers, and he realized his husband had stopped. Hazard glanced up, and then he swore.

On the other side of the wall of windows, in the Maas' enormous living room, North and Shaw were sitting on the couch. North was in a tee and jeans and the Redwings again; Shaw was in, of all things, a pineapple-patterned romper, complete with neon yellow Nikes. It was enough to make Hazard want to turn around and go home. All the signs of distressed teenage living could be read in the room: empty Pringles cans, a twenty-four pack of Mountain Dew Code Red, a flattened box that had once held s'mores Pop Tarts, a drift of silvery wrappers. A man who must have been Murphy—the guard who, according to Angela, Gerrit had stationed at the house—was holding a shotgun on the two private investigators. Kurt stood in the opening that connected to the kitchen; he looked like he might be sick.

"Shit," Somers swore.

Then Kurt seemed to see them, and he said something, and Murphy glanced over. North and Shaw did too. Shaw waved and beamed at them.

"God damn it," Hazard muttered. "If we'd been five minutes later, he would have shot them."

"Put the gun down," Somers shouted through the glass. He had his hand on his Glock, his coat pushed back. "Murphy, drop it right now."

Murphy made a face, but he lowered the shotgun and stepped back. He kept his hands out and open.

A moment later, Kurt was struggling with the lock on the door, and then he must have figured it out because it swung open. "Chief Somerset, uh, we didn't—"

Somers advanced into the house, and Kurt fell back. Hazard followed.

"Kurt, are you armed?" Somers asked. "Mr. Murphy, stay just like that."

Kurt flushed. "I have a Swiss Army knife in my pocket."

"Put it on the table over there. Where are Angela and Carson?"

"In the kitchen. Nobody—" He broke off. He looked close to hyperventilating. "Chief, it was a misunderstanding, and—"

"Knife on the table, Kurt. Then I want you to do like Mr. Murphy over there and keep your hands where I can see them. Call Angela and Carson, and tell them to move slowly and keep their hands visible as they join us."

Kurt called their names and repeated Somers's instructions; from the kitchen came the murmur of voices and then Angela's voice: "We're coming in." Steps came toward the living room.

"I knew Emery would rescue me!" Shaw crowed. "I told you Emery would rescue me. Well, us, actually. But I knew North wouldn't want to be rescued, on account of his toxic masculinity—"

"First of all," North said, "what the fuck?"

"—and so when I encoded my telepathic message, I made sure I omitted North, you know, to protect his dignity, especially that part about how he might have peed a little when this guy tried to bunghole him with his gun—"

"What the actual fuck?" Horror pulled at North's features. "Nobody tried to bunghole me with anything."

"Well, you did a lot of bending over—"

"He told me to drop the paper! And I didn't pee at all, not even a little." He set his jaw and looked like he tried not to say any more, but then words slipped out: "And I sure as fuck did not need to be rescued."

"See?" Shaw said with syrupy patience. He even tried to pat North's head until North swatted his hand away.

"I can't do this," Hazard said. "Let's go. We'll let Murphy shoot them and call it justified homicide."

"You want to bitch?" North asked. "You didn't have to sit here for the last ninety minutes of Shaw coaching this fuckwad on how to awaken his spirit guide and avoid gluten-interactive micronutrients and use his anal rings to dial into the cosmos's fucking subconscious or whatever the fuck he's been talking about."

"What?" Hazard asked.

Murphy, of all people, opened his mouth.

"That's totally wrong," Shaw said. "I wasn't talking about spirit guides. I was talking about spirit selves. And it wasn't gluten-interactive foods. It was gluten-reactive foods. And it wasn't—"

"Let me guess," Hazard said. "It wasn't the cosmos's subconscious, it was the cosmos's unconscious or some such bullshit."

"Oh my God, that's amazing! I was just thinking about the cosmos's unconscious! We are so in tune!"

"No, we aren't," Hazard snapped; he had the feeling that somehow he was already losing control of the conversation. "If anything, we're—"

"Anal sphincters," Shaw said triumphantly.

North choked on his spit.

Hazard gaped.

"I wasn't talking about anal rings," Shaw continued. "I was talking about sphincters. The innie and the outie, although those aren't the anatomical names."

Hazard stared at Murphy.

Murphy looked like a man who wanted the earth to swallow him up.

Carson began to laugh. It was a galloping, frenzied laugh. Angela shushed him, and the boy began to laugh harder. His shoulders shook, and then it was hard to tell if it was laughter or tears.

Shaking his head, Somers said, "Angela, what happened here?"

"They were sneaking around outside." She nodded at North and Shaw and then patted her mink-like hair to make sure it was still in place. "They came yesterday and wanted to talk to Carson, but Kurt said no. Because they're not police or anything." She sounded outraged by that fact. "We told them they had to leave. We told them they were trespassing. But they came back, and Murphy caught them poking around in the fire pit."

Kurt chose that moment to pipe up: "You can defend yourself in your own home. It's legal. It's called the castle doctrine."

"The castle doctrine doesn't cover taking people at gunpoint and forcing them inside your house," Somers said. "That's false imprisonment. That's a felony."

"That's what I told these needle-dicks," North said. "Didn't I?"

"Well, kind of," Shaw said with an embarrassed shrug. "I mean, you peppered in a lot of 'dongfuckers' and 'assmunches,' and it was kind of hard to know exactly what you meant."

North was making a noise Hazard wasn't sure he'd ever heard before. It made him feel like he had tinnitus.

"Is that correct?" Somers asked North.

"It's fucking bullshit. For one thing, I never said assmunch. I said assgobbler, and—"

"Assgoblin! I knew I was forgetting assgoblin!"

"Assgobbler, shit for brains!" North heaved several breaths. "And anybody could have understood—"

Somers sounded like a man trying to hold his shit together. "I meant, were you trespassing?"

"Ask my lawyer," North said, adjusting his Carhartt tee and smirking.

Somers turned to Shaw.

"I was in a fugue state," Shaw said. "I'm sorry, John-Henry. I looked into the astral impression of Friedrich Nietzsche, and I got lost in the void."

163

North's smirk changed to a scowl. "What's-his-nuts took a nap on the drive over and has been bitching ever since about how he needs to complete his REM cycle."

"I did not! And you stole that from Emery. He called us 'what's-your-nuts' yesterday, and now you're using it like it's your own."

"I surely fucking did," Hazard said.

"Who the fuck cares who said it first? It's an expression. And I never pretended it was my own. If anything—"

"Everybody needs to stop talking!" Somers said. Loudly. Probably, to judge by Hazard's expression, a little more loudly than he intended. And he was rubbing that spot at the center of his forehead again. At a slightly more moderate volume, he said, "North, Shaw, you were warned to stay off private property, and you didn't. That's trespassing. Murphy, on top of false imprisonment, I could slap you with assault and brandishing a weapon. I'm taking the shotgun; you can pick it up when things cool down."

Murphy glowered, but it was Angela who cried out in protest. "You can't! What if those men come back?"

"North and Shaw won't bother you again. I'm going to make that a personal promise."

North muttered something, but when Somers looked over, he had the decency to flush.

"Not them," Kurt said. "Those other guys, the ones in the SUV. They—they could kill us!"

"My detectives are aware of the situation. We can talk about providing a security detail. What I'm not going to do is let you have Murphy running around with a shotgun like it's the Wild West." Somers blew out a breath. To Hazard, he said, "Anything?"

"I don't suppose any of you want to comment on gun runners, falsified federal documents, or three million dollars being stolen?"

It was hard to read Murphy's face, but Angela, Kurt, and Carson all stared at Hazard with identical expressions of disbelief.

"I thought not."

"Detectives Dulac and Palomo will be here in a few minutes," Somers said. "Like last time, they're authorized to search the victim's belongings. This time, the search will be more extensive. You should plan on uniformed officers arriving as well. During the search, you will be asked to remain outside." A knock came from the front door, and Somers said, "Good. That should be them."

He was right, and while Somers made arrangements with Dulac and Palomo to search the house—again—this time, for the stolen money and to take into evidence any documentation relating to firearms sales, Hazard broke open the shotgun, emptied the shells, and led North and Shaw toward the front door.

North stopped in front of Carson on the way out and cocked his head at a stack of books that Hazard hadn't examined yet; he could read, at a distance, some of the spines: *Howl's Moving Castle* and *Smile* and *The Sad Ghost Club*. "If you like shōjo," North said, "you should try *Sailor Moon*. It's a classic for a reason."

Carson hunched his shoulders and looked away.

"All right," Hazard said. "Outside."

"I knew you'd save us," Shaw said when they stepped out of the house. He undid his bun of auburn hair and redid it. "I could feel your psychic weight approaching."

"My psychic what?"

"Like gravity. The dark well of your presence."

"That sounds like his asshole," North said.

"No, no, no, it's more like, well, I mean, look at him, he's obviously got a lot of physical mass—I'd describe him as a man of carriage—"

It took that long for Hazard's brain to catch up. "What the fuck?"

"Well, I mean, your derriere—"

This feeling, Hazard realized, was horror. "Stop. Talking."

By that point—thank God—Somers had finished his instructions, and Carson and his aunt and uncle were climbing into their car while Dulac and Palomo headed into the house. Somers made his way down from the porch. When he reached them, his face was coldly perfect porcelain.

"Well?" Hazard asked.

"Kurt says Carson's pretty shut down. He reads. He eats junk. They found him messing around with his bedroom window last night, upstairs. Kurt won't say it, but I think they're afraid he's thinking about hurting himself." Somers turned toward North and Shaw. "All right. What's going on?"

North flushed again and messed with the thatch of blond hair. "Nothing's going on. That ball-swinging hoosier got the drop on us is all. We thought the house was empty and—"

When he cut off, Hazard said, "No, go on. You told me you were here for my birthday, which isn't for another two weeks and, in case you were wondering, you're not invited to. So, what the fuck are you doing in Wahredua?"

"Delivering newspapers," Shaw said.

"Political campaign," North said. "I'm up for state rep."

"Federally licensed Lunchable inspector."

"Pizza delivery, the kind where the guy has a really big piece of Italian sausage."

"Gross, North. Um, oh! Singing telegram!"

"Selling wrapping paper door-to-door."

"Oh my gosh, that's so cute!"

North shrugged and blushed some more. "I was trying to make up for the Italian sausage."

"You did! That one was so sweet. Like, maybe you're a Boy Scout. Oh! And there's another boy in your troop, and he's been pitching his tent, and you've been pitching your tent, and now you want to pitch your tent together, and if you sell enough wrapping paper, you'll get an even bigger tent—"

"That's not how door-to-door sales work!" Hazard shouted. "Or Boy Scouts! Or tents! Or anything! How the fuck does anyone put up with you two?"

"You know what?" Somers said. "This isn't productive. North, Shaw, we're going to escort you back to your motel. Are you going to give me any trouble about that?"

"I don't know," North said. "How much trouble is it going to be following the GTO in that teenybopper's first squirt that you call a car?"

"For your information, the 2017 Mustang was highly rated—" Hazard began.

"Ree, stop giving him what he wants. North, Shaw, where are you staying?"

"Something something motor court."

"The Bridal Veil? All right, let's go."

"I think Emery should ride with me," Shaw said, "on account of I might do something irresponsible."

"No," Hazard said.

"He's not wrong," North said sourly, folding his arms.

"Why me? Why is that my responsibility? And what don't you understand about no?"

"Actually, Ree," Somers said in an apologetic tone, "it's not that bad of an idea. Just to the motor court—"

"Are you out of your mind?" Too late, he caught the shimmer of Somers's underwater grin. "Fuck you. Fuck all of you. Now start walking before I shoot you fuckers like you deserve."

North and Shaw traded grins as they headed toward the gravel drive; they reminded Hazard of Duane Harris and Trevor Brown, kindergarten dumbshits who had gotten themselves hauled to the principal's office week after week for sniffing rubber cement. He watched them go until they'd crested the hill, and then he stalked toward the Mustang.

When Somers got in the car, he said, "I'm sorry. They're such doofuses, but the look on your face." He started to laugh. Then there must have been another look on Hazard's face because he cut off abruptly.

Hazard indulged his husband with a lecture on his failing sense of humor, the responsibilities of being chief of police, how to handle a couple of shit-for-brains, and general policies on teasing. It wasn't one of his best performances; North—and particularly Shaw—had a way of knocking him off balance. At one point, Hazard heard himself reciting part of the national anthem.

The Bridal Veil Motor Court was a dilapidated, Art Deco confection— if you could still call something a confection when it had crumbling tuck-pointing and a screaming mildew infection. Hazard had stayed there when he'd first arrived in Wahredua, and the rooms actually hadn't been half bad, but it was by no means a luxury accommodation. North and Shaw parked at the end of the small lot. The two men got out of the GTO, and Shaw gave an overly enthusiastic wave.

When Somers started to turn the Mustang around, Hazard shook his head.

"Ree, we've got stuff to do, not the least of which is getting back to Landon's house and trying to figure out what the hell is going on."

"They might be lying. Park there."

"They might be—oh. God damn it, if they're trying to pull a fast one, I'm going to lose my mind."

When Hazard got out of the car, Shaw's voice carried clearly in the still spring afternoon.

"—the clinical use of vibrators—"

"Stop talking," North said.

"It's scientifically proven, North! It's a time-tested method for curing hysteria."

"You're not hysterical. You're not nervous or anxious or whatever the fuck you're talking about. You don't need cold baths or hot baths or plunges or, Christ, Shaw, I don't know. You saw a mouse. You tried to kiss it. You screamed when it bit your hand. That's the end of that particular episode of horse-fuckery."

This was approximately the moment when Hazard reached them.

"I thought it was a prince," Shaw explained.

"I don't care," Hazard said.

Turning a dark look on North, Shaw said, "I thought it would turn into someone who would be nice to me and make me soft-boiled eggs and wash my dentures and watch *Antiques Roadshow* with me and not say things like 'The Blues are playing' or 'my dick is engorged.'"

"Mother. Fucker." North wheeled on his boyfriend. "Never in my life have I said 'engorged,' and sue me if I think watching a bunch of saggy tweed-dicks cream themselves over an end table—"

"You bought the PBS subscription!"

"Both of you shut up!" Hazard took a breath. "Where is your room?"

Shaw pointed toward a door at the opposite end of the parking lot.

"Why'd you park—" Somers began. "Oh, right, the car."

"It's his baby, and possibly the only baby we'll ever have because my hysterical uterus—" Shaw cut off with a cry when North pulled his hair. "North! What if that had been a wig?"

"Let's separate the two of you," Somers said, nudging Shaw toward Hazard. "Before my husband has a stroke. Ree, would you—"

"Yes, fuck, anything to get this over with faster." He grabbed Shaw's arm and marched him toward the door Shaw had indicated.

"You're not a treat yourself," North called after him.

Somers said something, and a moment later, footsteps came after Hazard and Shaw. North laughed quietly. He said something, and Somers said something, and Hazard would be fucked on a fence post if he hadn't heard his oh-so-devoted husband say something about "The Star-Spangled Banner."

Hazard was ten feet from the motel room door when he stopped. The door hung ajar, the frame splintered where it had been forced.

"God fucking damn it," Hazard said.

Shaw let out an annoyed cry when he spotted the damage. He wiggled free from Hazard's grasp and hurried forward. "Oh my God, I brought my whole stash of that really good—" The sentence took a tumble, and then Shaw was saying, "—crystals that Master Hermes sold me. If those asswipes stole it—"

Hazard wasn't exactly sure what he was planning—a half-formed fantasy was swimming in the back of his head, a dream of locking up both these idiots for possession. For the night at least. He hurried after Shaw. The phrase *catch him red-handed* had a nice ring to it.

He was three feet behind Shaw when he saw the red dot of a laser sight gliding across the motel bricks.

CHAPTER FOURTEEN
APRIL 12
SUNDAY
3:59 PM

AS THE RED DOT of the laser sight rushed toward Shaw, Hazard threw himself forward. He crashed into Shaw, bearing him down, and Shaw let out a startled squawk. When they hit the sidewalk, Hazard rolled, carrying both of them toward the row of parked cars in front of the motel. At the same time, a chunk of the wall exploded, spraying chips of brick. They stung Hazard's head and arms. A moment later, glass shattered overhead, and the car next to them rocked on its suspension as though it had been shoved. The car's alarm activated. Then the clap of gunshots reached Hazard, a fusillade that left his ears ringing.

To Shaw's credit, the wiry man had rolled free of Hazard's grip and was now lying on the ground next to Hazard, his eyes alert, his face focused. Hazard reached for the Blackhawk, but of course, he'd left the gun at home. He was a consultant on a police investigation. For the second time that day, he swore never to take what that meant for granted.

Then the gunfire broke off. Hazard's ears felt packed with cotton. Even the blare of the car's alarm sounded distant.

"Ree?"

"Shaw?"

"Fine," Hazard called back.

"I'm ok," Shaw shouted. "Emery saved me." His voice brightened. "Oh my God, again! Just like in my sex coma dream!"

North's answer was a litany of swears; Somers's voice was taut and low as he spoke, presumably into his phone.

"Backup's coming," Somers shouted. "Everybody stay put in case that son of a bitch is waiting for us to move."

"Or daughter of a bitch," Shaw shouted in what he must have considered a helpful tone.

"Yeah, John-Henry," North said, sounding like a man trying for solid ground. "It's the twenty-first fucking century."

It was the adrenaline. It was the fact that, for the second time that day, Hazard found himself grinning into Death's ugly fuck of a face. It was everything from the day before catching up with him now, the awful fight with Colt, his fear of Danny Lee rising like a specter in their lives again, the phone calls from his mom about cleaning out his dad's shit, all the baggage—literally and figuratively—that he didn't want to deal with. It was the sheer unreality of this moment, of these two dumbfucks who couldn't keep their mouths shut for five seconds.

He started to laugh. He smothered it after a moment, burying his face in the crook of his arm, but his body continued to shake.

"It's ok," Shaw whispered, patting his shoulder. "You were very brave."

The sirens saved him.

It took time to lock down the scene. And then it took time to be examined by paramedics—Hazard had gotten away with nothing worse than a bad case of road rash on one arm, where he'd hit the cement, and some nicks and cuts from the flying pieces of brick. Shaw, of course, was untouched. It took time to give statements. And then they had to hang around while North and Shaw's room was processed, which North didn't like, although after Somers pulled a few officers aside, no one said anything about Shaw's collection of baggies. The whole process took hours.

But eventually, all the Wahredua PD officers left except for Norman and Gross, who would continue to look for the spot where the shooter had taken those shots, along with any potential evidence they might have left behind. Hazard found himself alone, finally, with Somers, North, and Shaw. The April evening was the color of crushed lilacs that darkened to the bruised throat of the horizon, and the air still smelled like gunpowder and antibiotic ointment and what Hazard could smell of himself, the lingering sourness of his flop sweat.

"We're past the point where you can blow this off," Somers said. His hair was mussed worse than usual, and he had a smear of dirt on his cheek. "What are you two doing here, and why did someone try to kill you?"

The men shared a look. Shaw shrugged.

North rolled his eyes, but his voice was cautious when he said, "We might, possibly, have been hired to look into those murders."

"Are you fucking kidding me?" Hazard asked. "Is this some kind of fucking joke?"

"No, it's not a joke, nut sac. We're good at our job, believe it or not. And we've handled some pretty hot cases before. You two aren't the only decent detectives in the state."

"Who's your client?" Somers asked.

Another shared look. "I don't think we can tell you that," North said slowly. "The client requested confidentiality, and I don't have any reason—"

"You're shitting me," Hazard said.

"I don't have any reason," North said a little more loudly, "to believe that compromising our client's confidentiality would help. Look, I'm not trying to be a hard-ass about this, but we've got a job and a reputation to think about."

"You don't think it would help? Glad to hear your oh-so-fucking valuable opinion. Now, why don't you tell us who the client is, and let us be the judge of whether the information is useful or not."

Color made circles in North's cheeks. Shaw touched his arm, and he shook him off. "Emery, I'm trying to be cool about this. You—what you did for Shaw, Jesus Christ, man. You saved his life. And I owe you for that. But you're asking me to break my word, and I can't do that, not without a good reason. I swear to God, if I thought it had any bearing on the case, I'd tell you."

"Bull-fucking-shit."

"Let's calm down," Somers said.

"Emery—" Shaw tried.

"You come here, into our town, and you don't even have the decency to tell us to our faces that you're working on one of John's cases. That's a professional fucking courtesy, motherfuckers—leaving aside the fact that we're supposed to be friends. And now you won't share information. Do you want to tell us why you were trying to talk to Carson? Do you want to tell us anything that you fuckwads have managed to put together?"

"We wanted to talk to Carson because he's the son of one of the victims." North's voice had a buckled-down quality. "And yeah, I'll admit, it was dumb not to tell you why we were here. We thought—you know, it would be fun. Kind of like a race. That was before those assholes held us at gunpoint. And it was sure as fuck before we knew somebody was trying to put a bullet in us. We were going to tell you as soon as we got back to the motel—"

"Of course you were," Hazard said.

"—only somebody set us up. That's what this was, right? The door forced open like that, but nothing got taken, nothing was missing? The door was bait. Somebody wanted us to see the door like that and get careless—"

"Why? What do you know? Or what does the killer think you know?"

"I've got no clue."

"For fuck's sake."

"We don't know, Emery," Shaw said. "We don't!"

"Fuck this," Hazard said. "And fuck both of you. John, let's go."

"Give me a minute."

"Sure," Hazard said, spinning toward the other end of the lot. "Why not?"

But when he got there, he had to stand at the car door because, of course, the Mustang was locked. The murmur of voices floated toward him. Then a sound that was distinct—Shaw was crying, rubbing his eyes while North put an arm around him. And Somers, of course, pouring oil on troubled waters, knitting up the social tissue, finding words and ways to make it all work. When it ended, North still had an arm around Shaw, and he guided him into the motel room. Somers's shoulders slumped as he came across the parking lot, his face cast like wax, the hint of gold stubble on his cheeks and dark hollows under his eyes.

"I read them the riot act about operating in my city without letting me and my officers know," Somers said as he unlocked the car. They got in, and Somers started the engine. "And I told them that if they're going to operate in my city, I expect their cooperation with the official investigation."

"Perfect. I'm sure the problem is completely solved, then."

"Do you want to do this right now?"

Hazard had to count himself down from ten. His breath leaked out of him, and he rubbed his eyes. "I'm sorry."

"For what it's worth, North is—well, upset, is one word. Freaked the fuck out might come closer. He wouldn't let go of Shaw, and he knows you saved him, knows he owes you. He would have kissed your boots if you'd asked him to."

"That sounds like a good place to start."

A weary smile lifted one corner of Somers's mouth. "And Shaw is officially heartbroken."

"They knew what they were doing, John. And they did it anyway."

"Ree, they're, what? Ten years younger than us? Maybe not quite that, but they're—well, they're still dumbasses sometimes. And they like you, and they're upset they made a mistake, and they want to fix it."

Hazard made a disgusted noise.

"Give them another chance, all right?"

"I'd like to go home."

Somers let out a slow breath and nodded. As he shifted into gear, he said, "Dulac and Palomo found a match, by the way."

"What?"

They rolled out of the motor court's parking lot as Somers spoke. "The guns they took from those guys who tried to kidnap you? At least one of them is a match to a gun that Landon sold; according to the paperwork, it went to a guy named James Staten. Want to guess where he is?"

"Living at Gerrit's compound?"

"Yep. He's one of the Herdsmen."

"Well, that means Gerrit was telling the truth about part of it, anyway." Hazard thought as they drove, the city sliding by him in the glass. "Landon was helping traffic guns. He was using the Herdsmen as cover. We haven't verified the stolen money, but I think it's clear that there was some sort of falling out—Korrin and Larenz want something, and they were willing to kidnap me to get it." He shook his head. "Why would they kill Landon before they got the money, though?"

"Well, maybe they didn't mean to kill him. Maybe they followed him to the motel and tried to kidnap him, the way they did with you, only things went wrong. Landon might have been carrying, and he tried to defend himself, and it turned into a shootout. Zach got caught in the crossfire."

"You didn't mention finding a gun at the scene."

"No, we didn't find one. But if Landon was carrying, they might have taken the gun with them when they left."

"Why?"

"I don't know, Ree. I'm brainstorming." They drove several blocks in silence. The dogwood blooms looked yellow, like old teeth, at the edge of the headlights. "Korrin and Larenz strike me as the kind of guys who wouldn't mind setting a trap like the one at the motel and then picking us off with potshots."

Hazard grunted. "Gerrit Maas has plenty of gun nuts who wouldn't mind the chance to play sniper, either."

"Fair enough."

"Someone's out there, John. And they're willing to kill again to cover their tracks."

"Yeah," Somers said. The light from the dash glinted in his eyes. "I know."

When they got home, Ashley was sitting on the front steps, his face visible under the porch light.

"What's that about?" Somers asked.

"That's very fucking much what I'd like to know."

After they parked in the garage, Hazard made his way to the front of the house. The spring evening was mild, and the air tasted like rain and new grass and something frying in one of the homes nearby. Ashley wore a jacket, and he looked comfortable enough perched on the steps.

"Hi, Mr. Hazard." Ashley craned his head. "Did Colt go inside, or…"

"What are you doing?"

"Um, oh my God, Chief Somerset, hey—"

"Ashley," Hazard said.

"Just waiting for Colt." He craned his head again. "Is he…"

"Colt's not with us. Colt is supposed to be home right now."

"Oh, he probably is. I probably didn't knock hard enough. I'll just—"

Hazard grabbed his arm and shot a look at Somers.

"Ash, hang tight," Somers said. He let himself in through the front door. The slightly warmer air, stuffy from a day of being shut up, drifted out with the scent of Old English.

Hazard's brain ran ahead of Somers through the darkness: Colt on the floor, Colt at the bottom of the stairs, Colt fallen in the shower. A brain aneurysm. A seizure. Undiagnosed diabetes. Korrin and Larenz. One by one, he staved off the images. His hand tightened, and Ashley shifted in his grip; it was enough to bring Hazard back. He tried Colt's phone and got nothing. Then he tried Rebeca next door, but as soon as she started to say that she hadn't seen Colt all day, he disconnected.

"All of it," Hazard said, dragging Ashley a step closer. "Right now."

"Mr. Hazard, I swear to God, I don't know—"

"Tell me everything you can about Colt today."

"I don't know!" The words were a terrified squeak, but then a dam broke, and more came rushing out. "We were messaging this morning, and he was really, um, mad."

"At me."

Color rushed into Ashley's face. "About a lot of stuff, and he wanted to come over, only my mom said she had to talk to you first, and then he was mad about that, and then, you know, we talked about stuff, and then we played Fortnite, and then he said maybe I could come over for dinner, and he said it was all right with you, and so I asked my mom, and she said it was all right with her if it was all right with you, only when I got here, nobody was home, and I thought maybe you guys were running late, but—" His voice cracked. "He's not answering me."

The front door opened, and Somers emerged. He shook his head once and put his phone to his ear, already speaking into it in a low voice, and ducked back inside.

"You have no idea where Colt is?"

Ashley shook his head.

"Because Ashley, if I find out you're lying to me, you will learn the hard way how seriously I can screw up your life."

"Mr. Hazard, I swear!"

Hazard ran back over Ashley's account in his head and asked, "What did you talk about?"

"Um."

"What?"

Ashley ducked his chin; his eyes skated away. "It's not, uh, you know—"

"Have you or Colt committed a crime?"

Wide-eyed, Ashley shook his head.

"Is either of you doing drugs?"

"No, sir."

"Were you watching porn?"

Hazard could practically feel the heat off Ashley's face. "No!"

"Is it sex? Is Colt involved with someone I don't know about?"

Ashley was trying to wriggle free again. "No, Mr. Hazard, but, um, if you could let go—"

"If it wasn't any of those things, then I don't understand your reluctance to talk to me."

"Colt's, you know, private. He knows he can talk to me about whatever, and I won't say anything."

Somers reappeared in the doorway to say, "He's not at the station; I thought maybe he'd gone in to pick up a few hours. I had them put out a BOLO. I'm trying the baseball boys now." Then he was gone again, the screen door swinging shut behind him, his voice batting like a moth against the mesh.

"What did you talk about?" Hazard asked again.

Ashley had stopped trying to get away, but now he was staring at his boots.

"If he wanted to talk shit about me, trust me, Ashley, I can handle it."

Ashley hesitated. Then he gave a tiny shake of his head.

"Then what?" Hazard's voice slipped, volume rising. His brain showed him Larenz and Korrin rolling up in a black SUV. His brain showed him the red dot of a laser sight tracking across the wall. His brain showed him the sun-on-gold glare of Gerrit Maas's assault rifle. "You'd better start talking, Ashley, because my son is missing, and I'm about to lose my fucking mind."

A moment passed between them like an in-drawn breath. Then Ashley looked up. The porch light turned the tears in his eyes bronze and strangely hard. His voice was a teen-boy record scratch, but it had iron at the core when he said, "I promised I wouldn't tell."

Something like a scream built in Hazard's throat, and for a heartbeat, he had a vividly satisfying image of shoving Ashley, of following after him, towering over the boy when he fell back against the stairs.

He wrenched his hand away from Ashley's arm and turned toward the garage. As he fumbled the keys to the Odyssey out of his pocket, his phone rang. He grabbed it, answering blindly.

"Bunny, I know you're busy, but I wanted to see if one day this week you could take a quick look at your father's boxes—"

"Mom, I can't do this right now."

"Muffin?" His mother's voice dropped into concern. "What's wrong?"

Hazard had to steady himself for a moment, his hand tightening around the keys, the metal biting into his palm and grounding him. "Colt is—I don't know." He wrapped his hand more tightly around the keys. It was like a red light at the back of his head. "It's been a bad couple of days."

And then, coming up the block, a familiar silhouette appeared against the dead-lilac evening.

It was like something breaking inside Hazard: a sundering that relieved the tremendous weight that had been crushing him but, at the same time, left him fractured and sagging, all splintered bones and stretched-out sinews. The black SUV rolling up, rumbling with bass. The red dot sliding along brick and mortar. The assault rifle like gold leaf shaking in a wind. He closed his eyes so he wouldn't cry.

"Mom." His voice was so thick he wasn't sure she could understand him. "I've got to go. Colt's here. He's fine, I think. I'll call you back."

She was saying something as he disconnected.

By then, Colt had coalesced out of the dusk: taller than in Hazard's memory, broader shoulders, filled out, almost a man. He hadn't shaved, and the stubble was patchy and thin. His hair was freshly shorn. He was wearing the old Budweiser frogs tee, the one he'd had when he'd come into Hazard's life, and a pair of jeans worn at the crotch and sagging in the ass, and old boots. The clothes were threadbare and, now, too small. It was a funhouse mirror of the past, and it made Hazard's stomach flip.

Hazard took two steps forward, already moving into a hug, when Colt angled his body away. The boy kept his head locked forward, but he was staring at something in the middle distance, his eyes never coming to rest on Hazard. Hazard stopped, and Colt kept walking, veering around him like he'd been a traffic cone.

"Colt," Hazard said. But the name was small in his mouth, and the night swallowed it up, and the boy kept walking.

"Sorry about that," Colt said to Ashley, and the tone was frighteningly adult in its pretense that everything was normal, everything ok.

Ashley's eyes went from Colt to Hazard and back to Colt. "Bruh, I mean, it's fine, but like…"

"Come on," Colt said and took the steps two at a time up the porch and into the house.

Ashley followed. He didn't look back, but the desire was written on his body, as though he were fighting the urge.

And then it was Hazard, alone, and a hammering noise picked up from somewhere down the street, and then the protest of distant hinges, and the darkness crawling up the dead-lilac sky like the coldest fire imaginable.

And then he was cold too, inside and out. Numb. Which was nice, honestly. Nice not to feel anything, not that broken, splintered, stretched-out relief after the fear that had been crushing him.

He went inside.

The main floor was bright, all the lights on. Of course, he thought. Somers had searched the house. So, of course the lights were on.

Up the stairs, one by one, the old treads groaning under him. He felt strangely light. He'd backpacked a few times, days and miles with the same weight on his back, until it became part of him, and the strangeness at the end was this, feeling light, feeling like nothing was dragging you down.

"—but J-H might let us order a pizza," Colt was saying.

"Uh, yeah, bruh. But, like, are you ok?"

Hazard pushed open the door to Colt's room on the heels of Ashley's question. Colt was still pulling off a boot. Ashley had his arms wrapped around himself.

"The door was closed," Colt said without looking at Hazard.

"You know the rule," Hazard said. Even his voice sounded easy. Relaxed. He wondered, briefly, why this had ever seemed hard. "The door stays open when you have friends over."

"I'm sick of that rule," Colt said and tossed the boot toward the closet. "Here's the new rule: if I close the door, you don't come in unless I say it's ok."

That brought out a smile on Hazard's face. "Ashley, go downstairs."

"No," Colt said. "You don't have to leave."

Hazard waited.

Hugging himself tighter, Ashley looked back and forth between Colt and Hazard. "Bruh, maybe just for a minute—"

"No. You're not going downstairs."

Hazard didn't shift. He didn't speak. He wasn't even sure he was breathing anymore.

"I'm just gonna..." Ashley trailed off as he slunk toward the door.

"Oh my God, you are such a pussy. Fine. I'll be down in a minute. Don't order the pizza without me." After Ashley had pulled the door shut, Colt looked up and said, "What?"

It was a shock again, always a shock to see the frozen amber of those eyes, the strange symmetry of face and features across the genetic divide. To see himself and not himself, and to remember that in some way, this was a deeper truth, maybe what everyone was at some level: a stranger to himself. This grappling in shadows with the thing that you thought you were, the thing that you thought you understood. It wasn't just about having a child. It was always there; you just didn't see it until you had the right mirror.

Colt stood. "Ok, if you're going to creep there, I'd like to—"

Hazard put a hand on the door. Now it was hard to breathe. "Do you want to say something?"

"Uh, move, please."

Hazard didn't know what to call the expression he felt on his face. It was shaped like a smile. It felt sharp enough to cut the inside of his mouth.

Seconds thumped past, a silent tattoo like a pulse.

"Get out of my way, I'm—"

Hazard pushed him back. The shock on Colt's face lasted only a moment, and then a rage flush lit him up.

"Do you want to say something?" Hazard asked again.

"Yeah, get the fuck out of my way."

"Fine. If you don't have the decency to tell me where you've been and what you've been doing and why it was worth scaring the shit out of me and John, I'll ask: where were you?"

"What do you care?"

I stay awake thinking about all the wrong turns life can take, Hazard thought. That's why. I stay awake with numbers and charts and averages running through my mind. I stay awake thinking about what I can do, what I can possibly do, to prevent the worst of them. I stay awake, and it's you driving, and it's you at college, and it's you on a date, and it's you at your first job, and it's you getting cracked in the head with a fly ball, and it's you sliding into a turn on a rainy stretch of road, and it's you getting bit by the tsetse fly, and that motherfucker only lives in Africa. That feeling was back, that feeling of being riven by the weight he had tried to carry so long, and Hazard felt like his hand on the door was the only thing keeping him up.

"Where were you?"

Colt flashed a hard smile, the crooked eyetooth exposed and then gone. "Relax, Pops. I went to see my dad, that's all."

From downstairs came the drone of the television. Hazard shifted his hand, and his skin squeaked along the wood.

"You did what?"

"I went to see my dad. I figured today was a good time."

"How did you get—JCC is almost two hours away."

"I hitched."

"You hitched."

"It's fine; I've been taking care of myself for a long time." Colt rolled his shoulders. Then he dropped into the chair at the desk, his body loose, a puppeteer's play at casual. "It was a good visit, actually. My dad was proud of me for getting out there on my own. And it meant a lot to him, that I made an effort to see him."

"What else did he say?"

"Oh, you know, father-son stuff. We talked about old times. Not all of it was bad; a lot of that was the drugs, and he's clean now."

Hazard was distantly aware that he was breathing through his nose and couldn't get enough oxygen. The edges of his vision fogged.

"He kept calling people over, telling them about me. About baseball. About how I'm doing this season."

"You told me you didn't like it when he bragged about you to other people."

"And he wants to meet Ashley. He thinks it's smart, you know, what we've got planned."

"I didn't know you had a plan."

"Yeah, well…" A shrug. A smile that was meant to hurt. "I think after I graduate, I'll stay and work on the farm with Ashley. The Boones need the help, and Ash said they could pay me fifteen dollars an hour."

The laugh tore itself from Hazard's throat. "Did he?"

"That's just to start."

"Sure."

Color rushed into Colt's face as he straightened in the seat. "This is why I don't tell you anything—because you're such an asshole. Ash and I work great together, and pretty soon he's going to be running the farm, and he said we could be partners."

"Ash won't be running that farm for twenty years," Hazard said. "And if you think for one second that I'm going to let you throw your life away—"

"But it's not your choice," Colt said with a bright pleasantry. "So, we don't even have to talk about it. Hey, my dad really wants to see me play, so maybe you could record some of the next game—"

It came again, that feeling of something ripping apart under tremendous strain, and Hazard heard himself speaking as though his voice were echoing back to him from down a long corridor. "What next baseball game?"

"Uh, I don't know, I think we have one on Wednesday."

"Did you forget? Was there some sort of misunderstanding? You're not playing baseball anymore, Colt. That's what we decided."

"That's not what we decided. That's what you said because you were being a douche canoe, and I am playing baseball."

"No, you're not. And you're not going to see Danny Lee again. I don't like how you're acting, and I don't like his influence on you."

"You can't tell me what to do. He's my dad; I can see him whenever I want."

"No, you can't. I forbid it."

The words seemed to startle Colt into a laugh. "Who the fuck do you think you are?"

"I'm your legal guardian. And whether you like it or not—whether you hate my guts or not—I have a responsibility to do the best I can to make sure you're safe and healthy and that you don't throw away your life before you're even sixteen years old—"

"You can't tell me what to do! You can't tell me anything! My dad said so, and—"

Hazard shouted over him, "—and that's why I'm also forbidding you from seeing Ashley. You will not see him again. Is that clear? I'll speak to your teachers about changing your seating assignments, and at semester, you'll switch classes."

Fear cleaved Colt's expression. For an instant, it laid bare how much Hazard had hurt him. Then anger clouded everything, and he launched himself up from the seat. "You can't keep me from seeing Ash!"

"Of course I can. I'm going downstairs to tell him, and then I'm going to call his parents, and that's the end of that."

"You can't!" Colt sounded on the verge of sobs. His face was almost purple with a flush. "You can't!"

This made it easier, somehow, Hazard coiling his own rage, the sense of control growing as Colt fell apart. "I'll have John bring you up something to eat."

"I hate you! Why do you have to ruin everything?"

"Hate me if you want."

"I wish you were dead!"

"I'm doing what's best for you," Hazard said as he pulled the door shut. "You'll thank me when you're older."

CHAPTER FIFTEEN
APRIL 12
SUNDAY
6:58 PM

HAZARD RAN INTO SOMERS halfway down the stairs. Literally. His vision was cloudy, and he was navigating by touch, his hand tight on the rail.

"Jesus, Ree, what is going on up there?"

Colt's muffled screams chased after Hazard.

"He's upset because I won't let him ruin his life," Hazard said. He continued down again, and Somers stepped out of his way. "He'll calm down."

Somers said something, but it slipped away from Hazard, and then the blond man was hurrying up the steps.

Hazard passed Ashley in the living room. He registered impressions: a black Nike slide poking out from under the sofa; red Beats wedged behind a cushion; a batting glove pinned under the leg of the coffee table; the smell of lanolin and leather that had become perennial since Colt had tried out for baseball. Ashley sat with his shoulders curled, his hands clasped between his knees. Some of his auburn hair had slipped free and now hung against his cheek. His eyes tracked Hazard. Hazard turned his gaze toward the kitchen and pretended he hadn't noticed.

In the kitchen, he opened cabinets and shut them, ran the water and hammered it off, took out the cast-iron skillet and set the stove to medium-high and then slapped the blackened iron of the handle so that the pan skittered in an uneven circle. *I wish you were dead.* Really, Hazard thought. Really? He took a few breaths, trying to glue together shards of thought. They could have pasta tonight. Something with the half a cabbage he still had in the crisper. *I wish you were dead.* He made a noise kind of like a laugh, righted the pan on the heating element, and turned it down to medium.

He got out the half cabbage. He got a cutting board and a knife. He quartered the cabbage and cut out the stalk. His brain was already halfway back up the stairs. You wish I were dead? What the fuck do you know about anything? He turned the cabbage and began to slice at an angle, sending gray-green ribbons fluttering down to the board. What the fuck do you know about life, about how hard it is, about how big the world is and how dangerous? What the fuck do you know about me, about what I'm doing and why I'm doing it? What the fuck do you know about this fucking garbage disposal of a planet, how quick it is to chew people up and shit them out? What the fuck do you know about anything, and how fucking dare you? The knife came down too hard, too fast. It slashed open Hazard's index finger and then hit the board and came loose from his hand, spinning across the countertop.

No, he realized. No, it hadn't cut his finger. That had been his synapses playing hopscotch, jumping to the conclusion before anything had even happened. But his guts cramped, and he felt like his lungs were full of something inert, something filling them almost all the way up, so each inhalation could only top off the tanks, and it wasn't enough. He reached for the knife. His hand was shaking too badly, so he propped himself on the counter instead and put his head in his hands.

The memory swam up at him; it was on him before he realized it was coming, before he could get away from it. He was in his childhood bedroom in that tiny house where he could hear everything. He lay under a too-thin quilt. The darkness was like burlap against his face; the only relief was where light scored an opening under the door. *He's confused.* That was his father, speaking in the tiny house where you could hear everything. *He doesn't know what the fuck he's talking about.* And later, the breaking of glass, the smell of cheap whiskey, *I'll beat it out of him if I have to. I will not have a fag for a son.*

I wish you were dead. I wish you were dead. I wish you were —

"Mr. Hazard?"

Hazard had to screw down the noise in his throat, fix it in place before it could get away from him. He had his back to Ashley. Thank God, a small part of him thought. Thank God. And then he wiped his eyes, wished he could wipe away the heat in his cheeks.

"What?" Hazard asked when he trusted his voice. He took up the knife and went to work on the cabbage again.

"Are you —" Ashley must have sensed the jaws of the question because he stopped and asked instead, "Is everything ok?"

"No, Ashley, everything is not ok."

The slight crunch and whisper of the knife through the cabbage.

"Is Colt—could I talk to him?"

Hazard focused on the cabbage, on the smooth, even rocking of the knife. But another part of him was trying to shake off the memory, packing everything up, storing it away. It wasn't the same thing at all. It wasn't. With his own father, it had been completely different.

I wish you were dead.

And then that section of his brain that never turned off heard the words and played them back to him differently, against the backdrop of gym equipment and sports videos and the silent, empty house where a boy spent most of his life alone. It was the old escape pod, the one he ran to when the airlocks blew: work. He could seal the hatch behind him, and it was like being someone else, someone who could breathe, someone who had his shit together.

He turned around. Ashley's cheeks were hectic, and his lip looked raw from worrying it. Hazard met his eyes and asked, "What do you know about Carson Maas?"

Ashley glanced toward the opening to the living room. He looked back. "Carson?"

"Do you know him?"

The boy nodded. "He's a senior."

"And what do you know about him?"

"His dad, he got murdered, right?"

"Yes, Ashley. I'm asking you about Carson, not about his dad."

Ashley made a face, and then he must have realized he was making one because he gave Hazard a worried look and his features smoothed out.

"What?"

"Nothing—"

"No, you thought of something. What?"

"Well, I know you said you weren't asking about his dad, but with Carson, it's like—well, that's the first thing anybody would think of."

"What do you mean?"

"Did you ever meet Mr. Maas?"

"I knew him. Not well."

"He wasn't—" Ashley seemed to struggle. "He wasn't a good person, I don't think."

"He was a first-class asshole," Hazard said. "He was a bully. And he was a condescending prick. In high school and after, he always thought he was God's gift to the world."

"Yeah, like that. I mean, I've never talked to him, but you can tell, you know? When he's at games, he's the loudest one, and he's always picking fights with the ref or the ump, and he gets in fights with other parents. My dad had to break one up last year; it was a varsity football game, so I wasn't even playing, but we went because it was Homecoming. Carson fumbled a pass, and somebody shouted something, and Mr. Maas—he went ape—uh, he went ballistic. He ran at the guy and started swinging. It was unreal; I'd never seen somebody lose it like that."

"I've only interacted with Carson briefly, but he doesn't seem like that."

"No." But Ashley's word held doubt. When Hazard raised an eyebrow, he said, "No, Carson is nice. I think. But it's hard to tell, actually. He's so quiet. I mean, he's a senior, so I don't have any classes with him, but I see him in the locker room, and I see him in the commons, and other places—he's in the library sometimes when I have study hall. I don't think he has any friends. Or, he has friends, but, you know, only because they're on the same team. All he cares about is sports. And winning. He signed to play baseball for IU in the fall, you know, so I guess it paid off."

"Why?"

"Well, he must have got a scholarship—"

"No, why doesn't he have any friends?"

"Oh. Uh, well, some people say he's stuck up. You know, he really is good. At everything, basically. And he doesn't, you know, hang out with girls either, although one time I heard him say he had a girlfriend in St. Louis. But some people say his dad won't let him. And somebody else said he just sits around at home on the weekends and gets drunk when his dad's not home. Like, blackout drunk. But that's just a story."

"His dad won't let him what? Have friends?"

Ashley nodded. "I think—" He cut off and blushed and shook his head.

"I'd like to hear what you think."

"I don't think he's happy."

Hazard's brain played back a detail from earlier that day. "What does he read in the library?"

"Um, manga, I think. Well, he always grabs one from the graphic novels section, and it looks like he's reading, but he never checks them out, so maybe he just doesn't want the librarians bothering him."

In his mind, Hazard could see the stack of graphic novels in the Maas house. He tried to remember what North had said. "What kind of graphic novels does he read?"

Ashley's face was blank, and he shrugged. Then, pushing back his hair, he said, "Mr. Hazard, um, it might be, you know, made up, but—but there's a story about Carson. About freshman year."

"What do you mean it might be made up?"

"I don't know if it's true. I mean, some kids say they have pictures, but I've never seen them. Nobody I know has, but people still say they have them, or they say they saw it themselves."

"Saw what?"

"Well, I guess Carson skipped football practice freshman year to hang out with this girl, and the next day, his dad made him come to school in a dress. And Mr. Maas came to school with him. He went to every class with him to make sure Carson didn't change clothes or anything. Like I said, I don't know if it's true, but—but why would somebody make that up? I mean, all the seniors would know about it, right? They'd say if it wasn't true."

"Maybe," Hazard said. He tried to wrap his head around that detail; it fit nicely with what he'd already been laying out. *I wish you were dead.* Plenty of kids had said it before. And some kids had done more than say it. "Give me his phone number."

Ashley tapped something on his phone, and a moment later, Hazard's phone vibrated. Then the boy said, "Mr. Hazard, is Colt ok? I'm kind of worried—"

"Then I've got good news for you: you don't ever have to worry about Colt again."

For a moment, Ashley's face held only confusion. Then something changed, worry annealing into anger. "What does that mean?"

"It means grab your coat. I'm taking you home."

Face blotchy, shoulders hunched, Ashley shook his head. "I want to talk to Colt—"

Steps came from the living room, and then Somers stood in the opening. His mouth was hard, his eyes flat. "Ash, I'm going to give you a ride. Colt's upset, but he's fine; he needs some time to calm down. Go wait in the garage for a minute."

Ashley hesitated. Then he grabbed his coat and headed to the garage.

When the door had closed behind him, Somers turned on Hazard. "Are you out of your mind?"

"I don't understand the question."

Somers shook his head. His eyes widened. His mouth relaxed into a hard laugh that sounded surprisingly hurt. Then everything contracted again. "I expected better of you, Ree. I really did. And you are better than that; I know you are."

"If you're referring to my interaction with Colt—"

"Of course I'm referring to that. What the fuck else could I be referring to?"

The words veered into a shout at the end, and in their wake, the silence felt tinny.

"What has gotten into you?" Hazard asked. "He hitchhiked to a state prison, John. To see that abusive, meth-addict piece of shit. The same one who has already tried to ruin our lives once. The same one who almost beat you into a coma. On top of that, when I tried to have a rational conversation—"

"Don't do that." Somers shook his head again. "You're better than this."

"—he refused to handle things like an adult—"

"Stop it." The words were crisp and clear; they were belied by the way Somers drilled a finger through the air, by the faint tremor in his hand and arm. "Stop it right now. You like giving ultimatums? Here's one for you: don't you fucking dare call Ashley's parents or the school or anyone and try to enforce that horseshit decision you just made upstairs—without consulting me, without even talking to me, Ree, after we agreed that we would handle things together."

"What was there to talk about? It was the logical—"

"Finish that sentence," Somers said over him with that same cut-crystal evenness. "See what happens."

Hazard tried to count the seconds. All he could hear was his own labored breathing, the cymbaling of his pulse in his ears.

"Get out of the house," Somers said.

"What?"

"I don't want you in the house with him while I'm gone. Take a drive. Go for a walk."

"He might run away—"

"He won't. I talked to him. Get your coat, get your keys, whatever you need. Then get out of the house."

The silence limped past for a second, then another. Then Hazard headed for the garage. Somers gave him a head start and followed. The blond man stood near the door that led into the house, watching, as Hazard started the Odyssey and backed out of the garage. He stopped halfway. He was aware of Ashley huddled near the Mustang, of the keen edge of the boy's presence, but something dark and deep was washing in over Hazard, and the lights were going out one by one. He lowered the passenger window.

"John—" He scavenged for words. "I'm sorry."

Somers shook his head again and looked down, bouncing the Mustang's keys in his palm. Without looking up, he muttered, "Jesus Christ, Ree."

CHAPTER SIXTEEN
APRIL 12
SUNDAY
8:02 PM

THE FIRST MINUTES WERE blind, and he came back to himself in increments: the blat of a horn, the blazon of a stop sign, the brake pedal compressing underfoot. Wiping his mouth with a shaking hand, Hazard signaled and turned when he had an opening. He stayed in the right-hand lane. Then it was only one lane. And then it was a gravel lot under an old elm, the branches creaking as squirrels raced overhead. The last light of day had a fallen-down quality, as though it had been tipped over. It gave more shadow than light. He was parked in an old cemetery, he saw now, and the light on the uneven ground made the tombs look like hummocks.

He didn't believe in ghosts, but he thought there might be some sort of ethical conflict in smashing gravestones. He considered his other options — smashing a branch to flinders seemed like a promising alternative. But instead, he sat behind the Odyssey's wheel, night coming in like the tide. It was some time before he could sit up straight and pass a hand across his face. When he started the van, when the headlights came on, the illumination shocked him; he had felt, until the light carved out the night, that he had been seeing clearly.

Work.

He drove out of Wahredua and decided to borrow a page from North and Shaw's book. The two might be insufferable dumbasses, but they weren't entirely incompetent. He parked on a familiar stretch up the state highway, got out of the car, and made his way up the wooded slope until he had a line of sight on the Maas home. The lights were on. Against the cupola of stars, it had a charmed look. He thought of Ashley's story. He thought of the workout equipment, the training equipment, the recordings of old games and practices, the empty bedroom with the closet full of women's clothing. It was like raking through ashes and finding the heart of the fire still alive, embers already stirring. He had been a boy like that with a father like that. Different, of course. But in so many ways the same.

The crunch and crack of branches behind him made him tense. He reached for the Blackhawk, but it was still locked up at home, and the pepper gel was in the van with his gear. When he turned, he saw the glimmer of blond hair, and for a moment, his belly tightened at the thought that he might have to deal with North and Shaw's bullshit. Then Somers's features took shape in the gloom: the mussed hair, the glimmer of tropically blue eyes, the familiar cut of his jaw, the new weight dragging at his shoulders. He smiled, but it looked like it needed a tune-up.

"I suppose I shouldn't be surprised," Hazard said, settling back into a crouch and turning to face the house again. "You have a habit of tracking me down."

"If it's any consolation, it was more difficult than usual. I went to Zach Renner's motel. Then I tried Gerrit's property; the Herdsmen haven't gotten any friendlier. I even drove by the gun show."

"I had a conversation with Ashley that made me consider a new course for the investigation." Hazard filled in Somers and then looked a question at him.

"I mean, we talked around the possibility of a conflict between Carson and Landon," Somers said. "When we visited the house, right?"

"We talked around it, yes. Now, based on new information, I'm focusing on it."

Somers was silent for several moments. When he spoke, his voice was gentle. "Ree, I was scared too when we couldn't find him. And I was scared after I talked to him, when I saw—" He broke off; it was the end of a safety line, something for Hazard to grab on to, haul himself in. "We need to talk about what happened."

Hazard shook his head. Something swam in his vision, black specks he told himself were gnats. When he could, he said, "Not now. Please."

"You aren't going to do anything about Colt and Ash until we talk?"

Hazard shook his head again.

"Soon, Ree."

"I know." Hazard cleared his throat. "I think there's a way to test our hypothesis. About Carson and Landon, I mean." He took out his phone and placed a call to Carson. "Hello, Carson. I wanted to let you know that we've been authorized to conduct a full search of the premises, including your bedroom. I couldn't reach your aunt or uncle, so I need you to pass along this information. We're coming in—" He paused long enough, he hoped, for verisimilitude. "—about forty-five minutes, so you'll need to have removed yourself from the house and the surrounding property by then. Sorry for the short notice."

"I need to—" Carson began.

Hazard disconnected.

"We don't have a warrant to search the property," Somers said.

"No, we don't."

"And since I assume you remember our conversation about legally obtained evidence and trials and judges being particular about things like that—"

"Conversations, John. Multiple. And yes, I remember. We're not going to do anything illegal, although I don't recall you having any objections to infiltrating the gun show."

"That was a gray area," Somers said. And then, hastily, he added, "Don't ask why."

It was enough of an opening for a smile to slip through the crack, for Hazard to feel, for a moment, like they were back on the same side.

At the house, the lights came on in the garage, and then the carriage house doors began to roll open. Taillights flared. The Jeep backed out of the garage while the door was still rising, barely clearing it.

"I guess we should follow him," Somers said.

"We'll trade off. Shit, John, run."

They ran back to their cars, and Hazard pulled out first—there were few things more anonymous than a dark-colored minivan. He managed to flip around on the state highway in time to see the Jeep's taillights wink out ahead of him at the next turn, and he accelerated hard. For the first few minutes, the night was a blur of shadowy limbs and the lighter patches of sky between the branches. Then he caught the red flare of the Jeep's brake lights, and Hazard slowed until he was no longer closing the distance. His speedometer read sixty-five, and the speed limit was sixty. Carson might have been panicking, but he still had enough sense not to get himself pulled over.

When they reached the city limits, Hazard spotted the Mustang's headlights in his rearview mirror, and he called Somers.

"Ready?"

"Ready."

At the next light Hazard moved into the left-turn lane, signaling, and Somers glided past him like a dream of smoke. Hazard turned, turned again, and began following a parallel route. He accelerated to make up the distance.

"Where are you?" he asked.

"Still following Market. Ok, he's turning onto Jefferson. Damn, this boy signals like he's got the driver's ed manual on the seat next to him. Maybe he could give Colt lessons."

"That's a great idea, John. Let's have a murderer give our foster-son pointers on road etiquette. Maybe they'll count it toward his community service."

"I'm just saying, it couldn't hurt. I've been in a lot of dangerous situations, but the first time I genuinely feared for my life was that time Colt turned the wrong way up a one-way street, and then he immediately turned onto another one-way street against traffic. I think I broke the oh-shit handle."

"I'm glad to see your version of a sense of humor is back."

A grin carried in Somers's voice. "You shook something loose; I'm excited. Where are you?"

"About to hit Jefferson—there he goes. Ok, fall back."

Hazard signaled and turned, picking up the tail as Somers cut down another side street. The Jeep was going thirty in a twenty-five, and Hazard had no trouble keeping it in sight. As far as he could tell Carson had no idea he was being followed. Most people—people without any training— wouldn't have any idea they were being followed, not unless the tail was obnoxiously bad, and even fewer ordinary people would suspect that a pair of drivers was tag-teaming to follow them. He hoped that, aside from being a potential murderer, Carson was a regular, oblivious teenage driver.

They drove another few blocks, and then Hazard knew where Carson was going.

"It's the high school, John." As though on cue, Carson signaled and turned into the parking lot. "Shit, I can't follow him in there."

Somers was silent.

"John, did you—"

"I know where he's going. I think I know, anyway. Park down by the baseball fields."

Hazard drove to the end of the block, and as he signaled to turn, the growl of a much more powerful engine reached him. Headlights rushed up alongside the minivan, and a moment later, the Mustang was turning at the same time—in the wrong lane, Hazard noticed—and then gliding forward to pass him. Somers, the little asswipe, even tapped his brakes twice in salute before shooting forward again.

When they parked by the baseball fields, the smell of crushed clover and chain fencing and gravel met Hazard. He got out of the minivan and told his husband, "You're a child."

Somers grinned.

"That was completely unnecessary, not to mention unsafe, and this part feels like it should be obvious, but, since apparently it isn't, I'll say it anyway: as chief of police, you probably shouldn't be breaking traffic laws."

The grin had transformed into a smirk, and Somers gave him a jaunty, two-fingered salute.

"Lane divisions exist for a reason, John."

"Come on, love. Before we're too late."

Hazard trailed after his husband toward the doors that led into the school's lower level, where the pool and gym and locker rooms were located. It had helped, the ridiculous immaturity of it all, that damn smirk. It had untangled some of the mess in Hazard's chest. As Somers must have known it would.

"It still doesn't make it ok, John," Hazard said. "That was a moving violation at a minimum."

His husband laughed quietly as they approached the steel fire doors.

"I can pick that," Hazard said, eyeing the lock on the fire doors, "if my bump keys don't work—"

Before he could finish, Somers did an easy, lazy jump and struck the right-hand fire door on its inside corner. The door popped open.

"God, I hate jocks," Hazard said.

"What?" Somers asked, barely stifling another laugh.

"You know what."

Hazard pushed his husband out of the way and headed inside.

The smell of old vinyl tiles. The smell of chlorine. The smell of commercial cleaners with cheap, synthetic perfume. Only the emergency lights were on, and they created spaced-out ruptures of light in the darkness. Like any other building that was meant to be well lit and full of people, at night, empty, the school offered a creep factor that Hazard couldn't entirely shake off. Somers passed him, taking the lead as he trotted toward the locker rooms.

"If he—" Hazard began in a whisper.

Somers shook his head. "This is the other place he knows, Ree. His house and the school athletic facilities. And people run to the places they know."

Hazard couldn't argue that point, although he did try to think of exceptions.

When Somers eased open the boys' locker room door, a wall of light met them, and then the locker room funk rolled out—a mixture of teen sweat and mildew, aged for decades in a cinderblock shell. It had been here, Hazard thought. That day when he had seen John-Henry Somerset with steam wicking off golden skin. Then the sound of heavy breathing echoed off the bare concrete, and he came back to this moment. Somers pushed his coat back and rested a hand on the Glock.

They followed the curtain wall until the hallway turned, and then they were looking into the locker room itself. The echoes distorted the sounds of breathing, making it hard to tell where it was coming from. At Somers's gesture, they split up, with Somers walking the rows of lockers to the left, and Hazard turning right. He had gone three rows before he stopped.

Carson knelt in front of one of the small, square lockers—the kind where you kept your gym clothes during the week, not the tall, rectangular ones you only used when dressing out. He was trying to cram something into the space. A garment of some kind. Larger and bulkier than Hazard expected, and the disconnect of place and expectation made it take a moment longer than it should have. Then he recognized it as a woman's dress. A woman's dress spattered with rust-colored stains that Hazard was sure were blood.

"Hands where I can see them," Hazard said evenly.

The words jolted Carson, and he rocked back so fast that he connected with the bench.

"Hands!" Hazard barked.

Carson put his hands in the air.

"Ree?"

"Here," Hazard called back. To Carson, he said, "Don't move."

The boy stared up at him. His face was pale and empty. Then a nervous giggle slipped free, and he squeezed his eyes shut.

"What the—" Somers began as he reached Hazard.

"I want to confess," Carson said. His voice was light. It might have held relief. "I killed him. I killed my dad."

CHAPTER SEVENTEEN
APRIL 12
SUNDAY
10:22 PM

HAZARD WAS HALF-asleep in Somers's office when the door opened, and he sat upright too quickly and banged his knee against the desk.

"Sorry," Somers murmured. "I didn't realize you were sleeping."

"I wasn't sleeping," Hazard said automatically. Then he rubbed his face. "God, John, maybe I was. It's been a rough few days."

And a rough few hours; Carson had gone with them willingly, but when Somers had notified the boy's aunt and uncle, everything had gone sideways. Instead of Kurt and Angela showing up, Gerrit and Pamela had arrived with a squad of the Herdsmen, and they'd demanded that Carson be released immediately. They hadn't actually gone so far as to bring their assault rifles into the police station, but they'd stormed the bullpen and turned what should have been a solid interview into a fucking three-ring circus. It had only ended when Somers had officially taken Carson into custody, based on Carson's confession, and ejected the Herdsmen from the station.

"He's talking to his lawyer now," Somers said; instead of taking his seat behind the desk, he dropped into the chair next to Hazard and laced their fingers together. "Ree, it's going to be a shit show."

"It already is. Does he want Gerrit in there with him?"

Somers shook his head. "Believe it or not, he wasn't interested in having his estranged grandfather, who also happens to be a gun-loving cult leader, be part of his legal team. He seemed genuinely hurt that Kurt and Angela didn't show up; that poor kid gets let down every time he turns around." Somers opened his mouth to say something else, but a yawn overtook him. When he could speak again, all he said was "God, I'm tired."

"Did he say anything else?"

"He says he and Landon had a big fight on Friday. Landon found some of those manga or graphic novels or whatever you want to call them, and he burned them. Carson didn't exactly come out and say this, but I guess Landon didn't think that kind of stuff was appropriate reading material for a three-sport athlete. Then, Carson says, after baseball he got wasted, blackout drunk. He says when he woke up, he was at home, naked, with blood on his face and hands. The dress was there with him. Apparently he kept us from finding it when we searched the house by hiding it behind the downspout; that's what he was doing when Kurt found him messing around with the window. He claims the mud on the Jeep is from parking behind the Presidential, where some of the asphalt is torn up; we'll have to check if we can verify that. So, that's his story. Now."

"Fuck," Hazard said.

"The obvious question is if he was blackout drunk, how could he know what he did or where he went? How could he have known where his dad was that night?"

"Because we told him in the death notification." Hazard grimaced and shook his head. "Whether he's lying or genuinely believes he's telling the truth, his brain is filling in the blanks with what we told him."

"DNA testing will take weeks, but the blood type matches Landon's—O-positive."

"Which happens to be the most common type."

Somers shrugged and yawned again.

"And what about Zach?" Hazard asked.

Another shrug. "I asked him. He obviously hadn't thought that far ahead. The best he could come up with was that maybe Zach got in the way."

"Yeah, sure, from all the way across the room. What the fuck, John?"

"I don't know, but if I had to put money down, I'd say Carson is telling the truth."

"You're joking; you think he killed his dad over some burned manga?"

"It was more than that, Ree, and you know it. Landon was emotionally abusive and, most likely, physically abusive too. The kind of humiliation he put that kid through, the isolation, the demands—"

"You told me Carson might like that. He might appreciate it because it was the only form of positive attention from his dad."

"Yeah, well, I said that before I knew he'd made his kid go to school in a dress and wouldn't let him have any friends." Somers blew out a breath. "I'm not saying I believe Carson did this. But I think he thinks he's telling the truth. And, if I'm being honest, Ree, I think it's possible he did do this.

He blacked out. He wore the dress. He went after his dad; I mean, he reached some sort of breaking point."

"This version requires him to be operating with some degree of logical reasoning, deduction, and fine motor skills for an extended period of time while in a blackout. How feasible is that?"

Eyes closed, propping himself up with one hand, Somers shook his head.

"On the other hand," Hazard said, "a blacked-out teenager with tremendous rage and guilt issues would be an ideal person to take the fall for the murder of his father."

Somers cracked an eye. "That is also a possibility."

"Gerrit would have had access to the house; he would have known about the incident with the dress and about their complicated relationship. Those same points are true for Naomi."

"What about the gun runners?"

Hazard paused. "I don't know. It's clear they're after the stolen money, but I'm not sure why they would have framed Carson. That might explain Naomi's behavior, though; if she had been involved with the theft, she might have gotten greedy and wanted to keep the three million for herself. I really don't know."

"Hell," Somers said, "the money is reason enough for Naomi. I have a hard time believing Landon thought up a scheme like that on his own; she's got to be involved. What I want to know is why the gun runners went after North and Shaw."

"Maybe they were trying to do a public service."

Somers flashed a surprisingly wicked grin. "Shaw brought you a present."

"Jesus fucking Christ."

"And I know what it is."

"You had better be joking."

Somers stood. He kissed Hazard and squeezed his arm. "Go home, love. I'm going to be here all night dealing with this mess."

"John, I need you to tell me you're joking. Usually I can tell, but —"

His husband passed out of the office with a backward smirk.

"God fucking damn it," Hazard muttered as he dragged himself up from the chair.

He drove home. It was almost eleven by the time he let himself in through the garage. The lights were on in the kitchen. A bag of Doritos was empty on the counter; a box of pizza, meat lover's, with only two slices missing, sat next to it. All the lights were on in the living room too. And all the lights upstairs. The lights in Colt's room. The lights in Hazard and Somers's.

But no Colt.

Hazard took out his phone and placed a call. He got Colt's voicemail.

"I understand that you're upset with me, but I'm worried about you. I need you to call me back and tell me where you are." He forced himself to add, "Please."

A minute went by. Then another. He tried Colt again; nothing. He tried the parent app, but Colt's phone was off, and the last location showed that Colt had been home shortly before nine that night. Hazard placed another call.

Ashley sounded half asleep. "Mr. Hazard?" Then, more clearly, "Is Colt ok?"

"He's not with you?"

Silence.

"Ashley, I need you to tell me the truth."

"No, sir. I mean, no, he's not here." More sounds — the whisper of fabric and the protest of springs suggested Ashley scrambling out of bed. "I can call him—"

"Do that," Hazard said and disconnected.

His body was too heavy for him; its own, particular gravity felt like it would drag him to the ground. How many times? How many times could he do this, feel this way, like something had been carved out of him and left a gaping hole of raw nerves? How did everyone else do this, day after day, grappling with the fear that today might be the day that what you loved most in the world could be ripped away from you, that you couldn't stop it or save it, that—in fact—what you loved most might be responsible for its own destruction? Christ, how did anyone ever take a full breath again after they had a child?

He found himself in Colt's room. The bed was unmade. Colt's backpack lay on the floor near the desk, and it looked like Colt had dumped out the bag; papers lay everywhere. Some of them were schoolwork: a geometry assignment, two chemistry labs, his World History textbook with the missing page where Hazard had objected—violently—to an incomplete and highly prejudicial description of the role of cuneiform in the rise of ancient Mesopotamian agrarian society. An essay for his English class, with Theo's familiar red marks along the page. The first line taught Hazard what it must feel like to be disemboweled: *The most important person in my life is my dad, even though we don't always get along.*

He closed his eyes.

Some people claimed they could feel the earth's rotation. A thousand miles an hour, spinning in the void. His own personal gravity dragging him along with that spin.

He had to open his eyes because he thought he might throw up.

And then he saw it, on top of everything else, where he would have seen it first if he hadn't been blind with panic.

Emancipation and You: A Guide to Legal Independence for Youth Under 18.

It was a kind of form, Hazard saw, with blanks to fill and spaces to write. Colt's spiked letters covered the page.

Ok, Hazard thought. He settled one hand against his stomach. He told himself to get to his feet, but he stayed there.

When had Colt gotten that material? How long had he been planning this? Why hadn't he said anything?

The answer to the last question, at least, was obvious.

Hazard pushed himself up, and this time, his body responded. His phone buzzed in his hand, and he saw Ashley's name. When he answered, his voice sounded anesthetized.

"Mr. Hazard, he's not answering. I think his phone's off because—"

But Hazard's phone buzzed again, and out of reflex, he pulled it away to look at the screen.

A single message floated over the call with Ashley. From Colt.

One word.

Help.

CHAPTER EIGHTEEN

APRIL 12
SUNDAY
11:14 PM

HAZARD DISCONNECTED THE CALL from Ashley and stared at the text from Colt.

Help.

He wrote back: *Where are you? What's going on?*

Nothing. The screen timed out.

For a moment, his mind blanked out. He unlocked the phone and stared at the messaging app. No reply. No composition bubbles.

He tried Somers. He got voicemail and left what was probably, a part of his brain suggested, an incoherent message.

When the screen darkened, his hand jerked, tapping to keep the phone awake. He took one deep breath. Then another. Panic wouldn't help Colt. Standing here, frozen like a rabbit, wouldn't help Colt. Whatever was happening, it was happening now, and seconds were trickling away.

He reverted to what he trusted most: facts.

Fact, Colt needed help.

Panic surged up again, threatening to fog him. He saw Korrin and Larenz rolling up. He saw Gerrit Maas, assault rifle gleaming. He saw—

He fought it down. Facts. Facts. Facts—

Fact, Colt had messaged him for help. Therefore, fact, Colt had his phone. Therefore, fact, Colt had some degree of freedom and, fact, Colt was conscious, and—

And, holy fuck, Colt had messaged him for help. Colt had messaged him.

Which, fact, fucking fact, meant the phone was back on.

Hazard opened the parenting app, and his whole body tensed. Colt's location had been updated; a red pin marked a spot in the section of

Wahredua known as Smithfield—one of the most dangerous areas in the city.

Without thinking about it, he grabbed the emancipation packet and, as he ran into his bedroom, wadded it up in his back pocket. He pulled out the gun safe, unlocked it, and took out the Ruger Blackhawk he kept there; Somers liked to call it his cowboy revolver, but the fact was that it was big, it was powerful, and it was very fucking accurate. The checked rubber grip felt warm under his touch like something alive. He unlocked the ammo next, chambered six cartridges, and grabbed a speed loader. It took him two tries to belt on the holster; he couldn't get the belt through one of the loops, and he had to stop and breathe and try again.

On his way out of the house, he stopped at the door to pull on a windbreaker—the weather was still mild, but he wanted to cover the gun. That was a last resort.

Help. The letters burned a mile high at the back of his brain.

He called Somers, got voicemail again, and left the house. He was backing the van out of the garage, checking left and right as he did, because the neighbor kids apparently had a complete disregard for their own safety and more than once had run directly behind the Odyssey. It was late, too late for the kids to be out, but the movement was automatic now. Then he tapped the brakes, and red flooded the cement behind the van.

Someone was pressed up against the front window of his house—not the window near the porch, where the light would have picked out the figure, but the window farther along, the one that looked in on the formal living room. The one where the light from the porch didn't reach. The figure—a man, Hazard guessed—was barely more than a silhouette against the relatively lighter darkness of the inside of the house, and it looked like he was trying to make himself as small as possible.

Hazard's hand hovered on the gear shift.

Help.

Five seconds, he told himself.

As he dropped out of the van, he shouted, "Hey!"

The figure near the window startled. For a moment, it looked like he might run, but then he slunk forward, the light etching his features by degrees until Hazard recognized Benji Renner.

"What the hell are you doing?"

"I'm sorry!" Benji had his hands up, and once again Hazard was struck by Benji's automatic reaction to challenges from authority. "I knocked. Swear to God! Nobody answered, but the lights were on, so I thought if I checked—"

"Benji, what the fuck are you doing here?"

"I wanted to talk to Chief Somerset about those nonprofit papers. If they turned up, or if his detectives have them—"

It was unusual. It was weird. It was shady—what Colt would have called sus. But it was an order of magnitude less important, in that moment, than Hazard's other problems, so he filed it away.

"Go back to the motor court, Benji. John isn't coming home tonight, and even if he were, this would be totally inappropriate. If you need to talk to him about work, you go to him at work. Understand?"

"Right, yeah, but this is an emergency—"

Hazard was already climbing back into the van. He slapped the remote, and the garage door started down, and then he was pulling out of the driveway.

The drive across town was a blur of impressions: elms with dead-men arms clutching at each other; a small, black bullet against the stars—bat, his brain said; the strap-like petals of a fringe tree in bloom; a redbrick church on an overgrown lot; the harsh brilliance of TONI'S FOOD MARKET – KITCHEN NOW OPEN – PIZZA PUFFS – CHICKEN GIZZARDS – FRIED OKRA – NACHOS, and the smell of a hot fryer and fish.

Smithfield was an ulcer, where poverty and neglect had abraded the city's tissue and left a sore. It was where kids went to bed hungry and woke up hungrier, where people made money dealing or hooking, where other people stood on their necks to get a cut, where people clawed to keep from falling any further. Many of the streetlights were out, and the ones that were on had a tremulous, gray-orange glow that barely gave any light at all.

KRIS-KROS AUTOMOTIVE's sign was dark, and it looked old enough that Hazard suspected they could make a fair argument that they weren't infringing on any hip-hop intellectual property. It hung on the front of a tar-and-gravel roof building, white brick with decorative red and green tile. It had a steel security door on the front and, on the side, another security door plus two roll-ups. The windows looked like they hadn't been cleaned since the first Bush, and from a distance, driving past, Hazard could make out nothing on the other side of the glass except the weak amber glow of an incandescent bulb. A blue-gray Ford Ranger, probably purchased around the same time that the windows had last been cleaned, was parked in front of one roll-up door. On one side, someone had hand-lettered in white paint: FLAT EARTH, and below, NASA IS A HOAX.

Hazard parked in front of the building and killed the van. He checked the gun. He took a steadying breath, and then he retrieved the pepper gel from his gear bag. The gun took everything to its ultimate—and final—level.

He would use it if he had to. He'd rather not. Then he checked his phone. On the parenting app, Colt's phone still showed as on, and the pin was here, in this building. He thought about calling 911. And then he thought about what kind of trouble Colt might be in. The kind that might stick to him, even though he was a minor. Hazard let himself out of the van.

He walked a circuit of the building, peering in windows, but the front window and the glass on the roll-up doors was too dirty for him to see anything but blurred shapes on the other side, and on the back, the windows were glass block. The incandescent light was brighter here, but the thick glass warped everything beyond recognition.

He tried the front door first. Locked.

He went to the side and tried the second door. It caught, and for a moment, he thought it was locked. Then he realized that the slow shift of the building had put the frame out of true, and when he pulled harder, it opened.

A rush of only slightly warmer air washed over him, with the smell of motor oil and rubber and what he thought might be kerosene. Boxes and barrels cluttered the space; one of the grease pits was filled with more garbage. Amidst the clutter, he saw signs that this had once actually served as a mechanic's garage—a rolling tool chest, a portable work light, a mechanic's creeper tilted on its side, a work bench covered with spray cans and the remains of a ratchet set. Even a floor jack, although God only knew why they needed it with the grease pits available.

On the other side of the garage, a woman and two men sat around a portable heater—the source of the kerosene smell, Hazard judged. All three of them were staring at their phones; they hadn't noticed Hazard yet, and he took a moment to study them. The woman was in her bad thirties or her decent forties: hair bleached, an inch of dark roots already showing, a round face hard as a frying pan. She was fleshy, in a thin leather jacket and camo cargo pants capped with engineer boots. The two men might have been brothers, although one had clearly come from the shallow end of the gene pool. One might have been handsome, if you were into greasy-haired white boys with sunken eyes and patchy scruff. The other had similar features, but rawboned and pinched, his hair falling in a bowl cut that Hazard was willing to guess he'd given himself. At the very least, he'd been an accessory to it.

Hazard yanked the door shut behind him, hard enough that the clap of the door striking the frame echoed back from the bare brick walls. The woman jerked upright; Scruffy spun around in his seat, and Bowl Cut dropped his phone. When it bounced off the portable heater, it made a tinny noise that the silence swallowed up. Bowl Cut grabbed it and started to swear.

The woman spoke over him: "Who the fuck are you?"

"Emery Hazard. Where's my son?"

Her lip curled in a sneer. She settled back in the folding chair, spreading her legs, shifting until her jacket fell back to expose the chain that led to a wallet. "He's not your son. He's Danny Lee's."

"Not according to the state of Missouri," Hazard said. "Right now, you're going to go down for kidnapping in the first degree, which is a class A felony. If you give me my son and if you ask nicely, I imagine the county attorney may consider reducing the charges to false arrest or assault."

"Oh yeah?"

"Tera." That was Bowl Cut, and he was shifting a worried look from Scruffy to the woman. "You didn't say nothing about—"

"Shut up."

"I'm not going to ask you again," Hazard said.

"You didn't call the police, though." The woman—Tera—spoke with a trace of amusement. "You came over here your own self. And you're standing here talking about kidnapping, but you still haven't called the police."

"I call the police when I get into a situation I can't handle myself. Plus, if I'm being completely honest, I'm in a terrible fucking mood, and I would really like to fuck someone up."

Tera's sneer returned. "You can have the boy as soon as you pay what he owes me."

"What?"

"You heard me. He called me, on my personal number, and he told me what he wanted. Fine. I gave him the price. I drove up from Joplin. I told him where to meet. Then he walked in here tonight, spouting some shit about Danny Lee told him this, and Danny Lee said that, like I was going to hand over a pound on credit. Well, fuck, son, Danny Lee might be my cousin, but he was about as much use as a shit-stain on your drawers when he was living in Joplin, and he's not any more useful now. When I told him it didn't matter what Danny Lee told him, I wasn't giving him shit without cash, he grabbed Madd's baggie—" She indicated Scruffy. "—and tried to run for it."

"It was a fucking eight-ball," Scruffy—Madd, apparently—said. "Dumb-fuck kid."

It was central Missouri; it was Ozark Volunteers' territory. Hazard didn't even have to ask a pound of what or an eight-ball of what. Meth.

"My son—"

"You can have him," Tera shouted over him, "when that little cunt pays me what he tried to rip me off. And that's a lesson to him and to you and to Danny Lee."

The echo died slowly against the brick. When it had faded, Hazard said, "An eight-ball is, what? Fifty dollars? Sixty? Fine; I've got cash—"

"Not a fucking eight-ball, man. I put my ass on the line for that pound; that shit ain't free. I'm getting my money tonight."

"A pound—"

"Five thousand. Make it six, because I don't like your face and because you and that cunt Danny Lee are pissing me the fuck off."

"No. I'll pay you for what he tried to steal; then we're leaving."

"Go on, then," Tera said, settling herself in the seat again. "Call the cops. Madd will give the boy a quick hit, and then maybe he and his daddy can be bunkmates up at JCC."

Something melted inside Hazard—the days and weeks of tension and worry, all of it draining out of him, leaving him feeling loose, almost relaxed. "I'm taking my son," he said, heading toward the door he spotted in the corner behind Tera. "And we're leaving."

"Madd," Tera said. "Brady."

The two men rose from their seat. They weren't exactly huge, but they both carried some mass, and they both moved like they knew how to throw a punch. Brady—presumably Bowl Cut—was closer, and he came first. He must have been eager or stupid or both because he came way too fast.

Hazard flipped the creeper onto its casters and kicked it toward Brady. Surprise flickered in his face, and he dodged, but by then, Hazard had grabbed the portable work light. He swung it by its cord, and the wire-enclosure for the bulb connected dead-on with Brady's nose. Brady howled, stumbled, and crashed into the creeper. He went down, and rolling as the creeper carried him sideways.

Madd's face twisted, and he slowed down, fishing in his pocket for something. Hazard took advantage of the delay. He set his shoulder to the rolling tool chest and shoved. It must have been emptied—the tools sold off or stolen—because it practically flew away from him. Madd didn't try to dodge like Brady; instead, he caught the tool chest with the sole of one boot. Then he planted himself and pushed it back toward Hazard.

But Hazard was still moving, and by then, he'd reached the floor jack. He twisted, and the handle came free. It was thirty inches long, and it was steel. When the tool chest came hurtling toward Hazard, he sidestepped it. Madd must have realized his mistake; he should have been pressing the attack instead of trying to out-macho Hazard. He started fishing in his pocket again. The jack handle made a whistling sound as it cut through the air, and then the sound ended with a hollow thunk as the steel connected with Madd's head. He dropped, boneless.

"What the fuck are you doing?" Tera was screaming as she reached behind her. Some sort of small semiautomatic, Hazard guessed, shoved into the back of her cargo pants. He grabbed a spray can from the bench, aimed, and depressed the nozzle. A jet of something hit her in the face, and she screamed, hands coming to claw at her eyes, the gun forgotten. WD-40, Hazard saw when he looked at the can. He gave it a shake and kept spraying as he walked toward her.

He kicked her in the knee. Then he kicked her in the head. She rocked backward, and her head connected with the brick wall, and then she stopped screaming. Hazard rolled her over and found the gun. It was a Canik—Turkish, Hazard thought. He checked the load, shoved it into the waistband of his jeans, and then he found Colt's cellphone and took that too. He checked on the other men. Brady—Bowl Cut—had apparently been carried into the grease pit by the creeper; at least, that was Hazard's best guess, based on the moaning he could hear from down there. Madd wasn't moving except for the rise and fall of his chest.

Hazard bent, hands on knees, and shivered as he tried not to be sick.

After a minute, maybe three, when he trusted himself, he stood and opened the door in the corner. The room was dark and small, and it smelled like wet concrete. Hazard guessed it had probably been intended as an office. The only light came from the garage, but it was enough for Hazard to make out Colt sitting on a folding chair, hands and feet duct taped together, a rag tied around his eyes.

Taking the EDC tool from his pocket, Hazard crouched next to Colt. His throat felt like steel wool as he said, "You're ok."

Colt must have recognized his voice, because his whole body hitched, and he made a noise like a gasp mixed with a sob.

Hazard cut the tape; he let Colt reach up to remove the blindfold. Amber eyes stared back at him, filling with tears.

"Come on," Hazard said.

Colt blinked, tears spilling down his cheeks, but after a moment he nodded. Hazard made the boy walk behind him, but nobody moved in the garage, and the only noise was Brady's moaning.

They drove home in silence. A streetlight fluttering like wings beating against a cage. A skyline of low roofs and red maples and light pollution. A cat caught in the white cone of the headlights, one paw raised, motionless, like something embalmed. The smell of flop sweat and the lingering, machine smells of the garage filled the car, and Hazard lowered the window and chuffed air that was crispy cold and tasted, the closer they got to home, like new mulch.

When Hazard pulled into the driveway, Colt covered his eyes. His body hitched again. He finally spoke, his voice breaking on every word, the rush of tears lying in wait. "I'm sorry."

Hazard clutched the steering wheel. He locked his arms, like he was pushing himself away from—what? Away from everything, he thought. Why the fuck not?

"Pops, I wasn't—I swear to God, I—"

Hazard tossed Colt's phone onto the boy's lap. "Get out of the van."

"I'm so sorry."

"Colt, get out of the van."

"I knew you'd come. I knew. I'm sorry I was so stupid, but thank you— thank you—thank you for—"

"Get out of the fucking van!" The words exploded out of him. "What the fuck don't you understand?"

Colt stared at him in hiccupping, staggered silence. He opened the door. His movements were slow, drained, as though enfeebled, and when he stood on the cement, he looked bent, folded at the corners.

"Pops, please, I want to explain—"

Hazard shifted his weight to one hip and pulled out the emancipation packet. He threw it, and it struck Colt in the chest. The boy caught it, more luck than anything else, and stared at it. Recognition shattered his face.

Hazard couldn't look at him anymore. He shifted into reverse and backed out of the driveway, the passenger door winging as the air caught it.

CHAPTER NINETEEN
APRIL 13
MONDAY
1:46 PM

HAZARD HEFTED THE CARDBOARD box labeled EMERY'S SUMMER UNDIES and carried it toward the dumpster.

"Bunny," his mother said from behind him, "dear, I really think you should—muffin, no, don't—"

The dumpster was one of those haul-away kinds; Hazard had gotten it delivered late that morning, after a flurry of phone calls. The box of summer undies—whatever the hell those were—made a satisfying boom against the metal base.

"Well," Aileen Hazard said, settling back onto the stacked twenty-four packs of canned peaches she was using as a stool, the old Ford behind her serving as a backrest, "I guess we'll never know if that one had any treasures in it."

"It had underwear, Mom. I looked. I have no idea what summer undies are, and frankly, if you were seasonally changing out my underwear, I'd like a thorough explanation."

"I meant garage sale treasures, bunny."

Hazard dropped onto the five-gallon bucket he was using for his seat. He had to hitch up the jeans to do it, and he was practically swimming in a LAKE WAPPAPELLO t-shirt that showed a bass leaping happily into a fisherman's boat. Fleeing your home in the middle of the night because you were terrified by the emotions that a child raised in you wasn't exactly easy on the ego; on the other hand, dressing in your dead father's too-large clothes wasn't much better. He dragged a box over, this one labeled DESK – JUNK. Pencils, pens, a scattershot of paperclips, manila folders—he thumbed through these briefly and found water bills dating back to 1979, the old house, the one in Wahredua. He heard himself saying, "If someone considers finding my old summer Jockeys a garage sale treasure, Mom, they should drive home and put a bullet in their head."

"Bunny, that's a terrible thing to say."

Hazard grunted and flipped over a pad of stationery: the top contained an illustration of what he took to be a paddlefish. It was spearing a piece of paper that said "Honey-Do," and below it were words in block letters some graphic designer had obviously considered kooky: GONE FISHIN'.

"They could at least buy some of your father's old bullets before they left," Aileen Hazard finished in a murmur.

It caught Hazard so quickly that he barely had time to stifle the smile; when he glanced up, his mother was wearing a tiny, hidden smile of her own. She was always older than he expected, when he caught her like this, when he saw her in the moment again, really saw her. She'd been beautiful; that wasn't just Hazard's opinion. People had told him they'd never understood why she'd married Frank Hazard; Hazard had puzzled over that particular question himself a time or two.

Last night had been one of those times. It had been easier, lying in a bedroom that wasn't his bedroom, in a house that wasn't his house, without even the insulation of childhood memories to buffer him, to think about his father, to breathe that particular fire back to life, than to think about Colt, about the packet of emancipation pages, about the brief, abortive phone call to Somers, in which Hazard had explained where he was and, when Somers had tried to sort out the confusion of words, Hazard had said goodnight and disconnected.

Now, after a morning spent "catching up"—whatever that meant, when his mother made weekly phone calls to Hazard and, he was fairly sure, an undisclosed number of texts and phone calls to Somers—Hazard was determined to get as much cleaned out of the garage as possible. It wasn't only his dad's old belongings in here; apparently, his parents had decided to use this for storage when they'd moved from Wahredua. Some of the boxes were clearly filled with Hazard's possessions. In one of them, he'd found the comforter he'd slept with during his teenage years, navy blue and stitched with walleye. He'd put that box in the room where he was sleeping. It needed laundering, but otherwise, it was in remarkably good condition, and he remembered it having a high fill power.

After a few more minutes of sorting through binder clips and a wire desk organizer and a Missouri Conservation Department's 1988 *Fishing Regulations and Guide to Game Fish,* Hazard hoisted the box and made toward the dumpster.

"Oh, bunny, let me just—"

Yes, Hazard decided. That boom at the end was distinctly satisfying.

"Well," his mother said, "that's ok. We'll find some other treasures."

"No one is going to find any treasures, Mom. That's not how garage sales work."

"Oh no, bunny, on *Antiques Roadshow*—"

"People who buy things at garage sales are either hoarders, the viciously cheap, or the desperately lonely. Nobody in their entire life has needed to pick through someone else's garbage in order to buy a ceramic ashtray for five cents."

"That's the dime box, dear." His mother was examining a tablecloth that had probably once been white and was now tinged yellow. Through the open garage door came a breeze that tugged at the fabric. The April day was beautiful, the weather mild, cotton ball clouds drifting through a bright blue sky. The sweet spring air carried away some of the sting from the open dispenser of disinfecting wipes that Aileen Hazard had open at her side, to be used whenever a treasure looked particularly grimy. "And people find treasures at garage sales all the time—"

"Mom, it's a rare occasion when I'll speak ill of public television, but I can say categorically that *Antiques Roadshow* is a manipulative, engineered showpiece on par with *Jersey Shore* or—"

"No, muffin, I don't mean treasures like that. People find all sorts of things. They find things they need or they might need, and they get a good deal on them. Or they find things they want. Or things they didn't know they wanted, but now that they've seen it, they want it. Or they find things that remind them of something from their childhood. That's nice, when you find something that reminds you of your childhood."

"Is it?" Hazard muttered as he opened yet another box full of fishing tackle.

"Oh, yes, muffin. Last summer, June Louise and I went to this flea market outside Lebanon, and I found—well, can you guess what I found?"

"A modicum of regret for choosing to spend your day that way?"

His mother laughed. "No, bunny. I found Little Miss Echo!"

She said it with so much excitement, and the pause after it teetered like the face of a collapsing bluff, and she was his mother, and Hazard was, after all, only human, so he finally gritted out, "Who or what is Little Miss Echo?"

"Oh, she was the best toy. You could move her head and her arms and her legs, and she had the cutest little dress, and you could comb her hair, but the best part was that she had this magnetic tape in her, and she'd record whatever you said and play it back." Some of the enthusiasm ebbed as she added, "Only this one was broken because she couldn't record anything new, and when she talked, you heard this woman saying, 'Sharon, did you hear your father?'"

"Good God." Hazard slid the box of fishing gear into the to-be-tossed-when-mom-isn't-looking pile. It might sell at a garage sale; Hazard would have preferred to give his mother the thirty-five cents out of his own pocket.

"I know," Aileen said. "I would have bought it for Evie, but—"

"Her name isn't Sharon," Hazard guessed.

"Exactly, bunny. It was so sad. But June Louise did find this pair of jumping shoes—"

"What does that mean?" Hazard tried to stop himself, but the words came pouring out. "All shoes are jumping shoes."

"Oh no, these were like little platforms, and they had springs underneath, and you could bounce on them like a trampoline. June Louise took them to her McDonald's group, and she let Sally Trautman try them on, and she was showing off for the men because she never could be alone, and she fell and broke her hip." Hazard's mother suddenly became focused on the placemats she was sorting as she added in a guilty voice, "I laughed so hard when June Louise told me, and I know it's terrible, but that woman has the wickedest sense of humor."

Hazard couldn't help it; he groaned.

"Bunny!"

"I'm sorry, but my patience—"

"You must be starving. Here we are, just chatting away, and we've worked right through lunch."

"In the first place, I have never in my life been 'just chatting away,' and in the second place—"

"I'll make you a ham and Swiss sandwich, how does that sound? I can put the potato chips on it the way you like. June Louise taught me that."

"I'm not hungry. I want to finish this, Mom. There's still half the garage to sort through." He had to force himself to add, "Thank you, anyway."

"Is it your back?"

"My back is perfectly fine."

"I could hear you tossing and turning last night. That bed is murder on your back."

"It's not my back."

"I have a back brace inside. Let me take a look."

"No, Mom, I don't—"

"And I'll whip up a couple of sandwiches while I'm at it. In case we get the nibbles."

"I have never once 'gotten the nibbles'—"

"And think about how we're going to sell your father's truck. I was sending messages to this nice man on Craigslist, but he wanted to meet me so late! Three in the morning all the way out at that state park. I said I had to talk to you first."

"No, Mom, you are not going to meet the Craigslist killer—"

But she was already gone.

Hazard sagged on the bucket, resting his head in one hand. Then he grabbed a box marked DO NOT TOSS in his father's familiar chicken scratch—not too different from Hazard's own—and opened it to find two quarts of Valvoline MaxLife.

"Motherfucker," he muttered as he pushed it aside with his foot. "When I die, just burn the fucking house down."

"That seems like it goes against the manifesto on property ownership and intergenerational wealth you made me read before bed last week."

Hazard glanced over his shoulder.

Somers stood under the garage door. His hair was mussed. His tee—a Wildcats Baseball parent fundraiser purchase—was pulled askew. The day wasn't quite warm enough for knit shorts and sockless sneakers, but it was hard to argue with legs like that. At the street, Colt stood next to the Mustang, arms folded across his chest as he kicked the curb, his gaze down.

"I didn't hear you drive up." That was the closest thing to neutral that Hazard could manage.

"I killed the engine half a mile away and coasted. Black ops style."

"That seems unlikely. The terrain is too flat for you to coast that distance, not in a vehicle that wasn't engineered specifically for—"

"You were talking to your mom, dummy." Somers smiled to soften the words. "Am I allowed to come inside?"

Hazard stood, and Somers must have taken that as an invitation because he crossed the distance between them. When he reached Hazard, he studied his face for a moment and then took him in a hug. Hazard's body felt stiff; he couldn't seem to unlock his joints.

"Hey," Somers whispered in his ear.

Hazard's face was suddenly hot and tight. He didn't trust his voice, so he squeezed Somers tighter.

Then he felt the buzz of a phone.

They separated, and Somers extracted his phone and glanced at the screen. He seemed to weigh the decision for a moment, and then he said, "Sorry."

"No, go ahead."

"I'll get Colt settled inside. Or do you want him to wait in the car?" Somers rushed to add, "He fell apart, Ree. Last night, I mean. Completely. It was kind of scary, if I'm being honest. Otherwise I would have left him with Noah and Rebeca until the two of you were ready to talk."

Hazard had to try twice to get the words out. "I'm an adult. It's not a problem, John."

Somers nodded, still watching Hazard with those eyes that never missed anything. His phone had stopped buzzing. Without looking over his shoulder, he called back, "Bubs, you want to go inside?"

There was no verbal answer, so Hazard said, "He's shaking his head."

Somers's phone began to buzz again.

"Answer it," Hazard said. "We'll be fine."

Somers took the call, his voice fading as he moved away around the side of the house toward the backyard—it must have been a work call since it apparently required a degree of privacy. Colt remained at the curb, the soft thud-thud of his sneaker against the concrete the only sign of life. Hazard watched him for a moment and then dropped onto the bucket, his back to the street, and pulled over another box. This one was marked POWER TOOLS.

He tested four electric drills. None of them worked. When he glanced over his shoulder, Colt was lurking near the garage door, hands in his pockets, face down.

"Grab a box," Hazard said. The words didn't come out the way he wanted; too brusque, too hard, too hurt. "If it's junk, toss it in the dumpster."

He went back to the box, taking out a circular saw this time. A few seconds later, Colt's sneakers scuffed the cement behind him. They worked in silence for a while. The saw didn't work. Neither did the cordless ratchet. Neither did the reciprocating saw. All of which begged the question, in Hazard's mind, of why the fuck his father had kept any of them. Probably for parts, he guessed. Frank Hazard had believed you could fix anything. Then Hazard heard the thought, felt the lash crack after all the years, and decided maybe, for his father, that had only applied to power tools.

The squeak of rubber soles. Colt pushed something in front of Hazard and mumbled, "Do you want this?"

It was a newspaper clipping, although it took Hazard a moment to recognize what he was seeing: an article from the St. Louis *Post-Dispatch*. It was about a shooting that had happened twelve years ago; Hazard knew because he'd been involved in the shootout. A color photo showed the aftermath of the shooting, and in the corner, a much younger Emery Hazard—he was still in uniform back then, still on patrol—was leaning forward to ask something of a witness. In a blunt pencil, in that familiar chicken scratch, his father had drawn an arrow and written, *Emery Hazard*.

Hazard didn't even realize he was taking the clipping until it rasped against his fingers, the old paper's texture rough and hinting at crumbling. His voice, when he spoke, was unrecognizable to him: "Where did you get this?"

Colt must have sensed the shift because he rocked on his heels and pointed. "There's more of them."

He knelt next to the box. A shoebox. New Balance. The box itself had to be almost as old as Hazard was. He dragged his fingers through it, disturbing the stacks of newspaper clippings, press releases, four-by-sixes, school photos. One of them he recognized, a tiny wallet-sized one with a grim-faced boy, his hair slicked into a perfect part, as kindergarten. His hand kept moving; he felt like he was blind, like he had to see it all by touch. News stories on cases he'd worked. Announcements about promotions. A photo of his college dorm. A photo of his first apartment in St. Louis. A photo of himself, and God, he had to be seventeen, maybe younger, asleep on a blanket in the sun. Hazard had no idea where the photo had been taken. He didn't remember it at all.

It was like something breaking in him, tearing loose, old iron that couldn't stand up to the force of whatever was rushing through him. He couldn't breathe. He closed his eyes, but that wasn't enough, and he pressed one hand there against the hot sting. Another day, another time, it might not have hit him like this. But it was everything in the last few days. It was everything from his whole life—or what he thought of as his life.

"Pops?" Colt said with that tone of teenage anxiety when they witness adults caught up in strong emotions.

"I'm fine." Hazard choked the words out. It took him longer, wrestling the thing inside his chest, to muster the rest of it: "I need a minute. Alone. Please."

Colt dropped into a squat. He put his hand on Hazard's arm, the touch light, uncertain.

"Go on," Hazard said. He cleared his throat. He tried to blink his eyes clear. "Find John, or my mom—"

Darting in, like if he moved too slowly Hazard might stop him, Colt wrapped him in a hug. The boy was shaking—sobbing, Hazard realized. His own eyes stung, and he closed them as he pulled Colt against him, stroking the boy's hair, rubbing his back, saying something—he didn't even know what—and trying to hold all their broken pieces together.

CHAPTER TWENTY
APRIL 13
MONDAY
2:19 PM

THEY SAT ON THE patio out back, in wrought-iron chairs that, even padded out with yellow-and-pink floral all-weather cushions, were still uncomfortable as all fuck. Between them lay a plate of sandwiches—ham and Swiss, of course. And lemonade. And two slices of chocolate cake. One was noticeably bigger than the other.

"In case we get the nibbles," Hazard murmured.

Colt cocked his head.

Since the flood of emotion, they had both been quiet, aside from answering queries from Somers and Aileen. It had been Hazard's mother who had gotten them settled out here. The April sun was warm on Hazard's face; it felt even better when he closed his eyes and tilted his head back. Tulips were coming up, vivid shocks of red and yellow, and pansies in purple and blue and pink. He could smell the forsythia coming in, a green, vegetative odor that wasn't exactly pleasant, but that made him feel like the world was waking up again.

"Something my mom said," Hazard explained to Colt's questioning look. "I'm sorry. I'm not really myself today."

"That's ok," Colt mumbled and looked back at the plate.

"Do you want to eat?"

Colt shrugged.

"The one without onions is for me," he said. "And I'll be willing to bet she crushed up extra potato chips for yours."

Colt checked; he had a ghost of a smile when he pushed one plate toward Hazard. "You like onions."

"Now. They're fine when they're cooked, and I can eat them raw, on a sandwich for example. But I was…selective about my food when I was a child. My mom remembers things like that."

Chewing his first bite, Colt nodded. He looked like he was processing this information, like it might be the most important thing he'd ever heard.

A wren fluttered down to land on a forsythia branch, the yellow blossoms trembling as the branch dipped under the weight, the slight arch to the limb almost catenary and then gone as the wren took flight again. When it landed the next time, on a scraggly pin oak on the property line, it burst into song.

"I didn't know he had any of that," Hazard said. He kept his eyes on the bird. "I didn't know he knew about half of that. Or that he cared."

"He cared," Colt said through a mouthful of ham-and-swiss and potato chips. Wiping the back of his mouth with his hand, he swallowed. "He was your dad."

Hazard let that one fall broke-back between them, and after a moment, Colt colored and took a huge bite. In the pin oak, the wren was checking its feathers. Its head came up. It looked around. Maybe it could hear Hazard's heartbeat. Maybe it could hear whatever was galloping toward them in this moment, the thing that had slipped its reins in the garage, riding roughshod over Hazard. The thing he couldn't call back, didn't even know if he wanted to.

"It would be easy to say that all our problems were because I'm gay and he was a homophobic asshole, but I'm not sure that's actually true."

"J-H said—" Colt stopped and flushed again and looked down at his sandwich.

"What did he say?"

"He said he didn't like that you were gay."

"That's putting it mildly. But I meant, I don't know if that was the root of the problem. Even before I came out, I was a disappointment to him. Nothing I did was good enough. Coming out to him, well, that made it worse. But I think that dynamic was there for a long time before that."

"Sometimes people get mad when they're scared. You screamed your head off when I burned my hand on that cookie sheet."

"I did, didn't I?"

"And then you used those tin snips to cut it up and said you were going to make a shit bucket out of it."

A laugh tore free from Hazard; the wren startled, a flicker of brown, and then was gone. "I did, didn't I?" He saw again the shoebox, the old photos, the yellowed sheets of newsprint. "That might have been part of it.

Maybe I've been too hard on him; maybe a lot of it was worry or fear. But that might be too simple. He was a complicated man, a fact that today has only reinforced. I don't think there's an easy answer to any of it."

For a moment, it was just them and the sound of the breeze stirring new leaves.

"Pops—" Colt began.

"Let me finish, please." Hazard turned to face his son—if that's what he still was. "My whole life, I told myself what a shit father he was to me. I never thought I'd have children, but I was perfectly confident that if I did, I wouldn't treat them the way he treated me. And here you are, Colt, and you are one of the three best things that has ever happened to me, and I didn't know that I could be so happy and, at the same time, scared shitless. Every day. Every minute. I'm scared you'll get in a car accident. I'm scared you'll slip and hit your head wrong. I'm scared you'll fail your classes, that you won't get into college, that you won't get a good job, that you won't have a good life." *I'm scared,* he thought, not brave enough to say the words out loud, *that Ashley will break your heart over and over again, and I don't know how to keep you safe from that.*

"I don't—" Colt began.

Hazard held up a hand. "I'm scared about all of that and so much more. And I'm not saying it's an excuse for…for when I lose my temper. But I'm trying to explain—I don't know. I don't even know how to explain it to myself. I get scared, and then we start fighting, and then lately, sometimes, it's like somebody else is talking, and I'm in the background watching it get worse and worse, and—and I sound like my dad, and I hate that." The last words punched out of him, and he had to struggle for another breath. He only sounded slightly steadier when he said, "I hate it, Colt. I told myself my whole life that I wouldn't be like him, and here I am, and I'm doing it. It's like I can't shake him. He's dead, and there's still this part of me carrying him around, letting him fuck things up." The laugh sounded weird, on the brink of teary. "Anyway, that's more than I meant to tell you. What I wanted to tell you was that I'm sorry for how I've treated you. I am afraid, all the time, that if I don't do everything I can, you won't have a good life. But it's your life. And I'm proud of you, and I want you to be happy, whatever that means for you."

Colt nodded, still chewing slowly. He lowered the ham-and-Swiss. His eyes came to Hazard's face and darted away again. Back, and then away. A wren. The arc of a forsythia branch.

"Sometimes," Colt said, "I say things, and I sound like my dad. In my own head, I mean. I can hear it."

Hazard nodded.

"One time, the first time they took me, you know, someone like Ramona, and they had me in this group home, I was little. Really little. And I kept doing, you know, stuff to get attention, like I'd take other people's toys, or I'd get glue everywhere. That kind of thing. And we had to talk to this woman; I guess she was a therapist. So when it was my turn to talk to her, she wanted to talk about why I was acting that way, and she asked me about my dad, if my dad ever paid attention to me, or did my dad take things from other people." He wiped his mouth with the back of his hand again. "I was little, but I wasn't stupid. And I think about that sometimes, when I can hear myself sounding like him, if I want his attention or his approval or something, even if that's never something I'd think in a million years, that maybe it's deep down in there somewhere, and maybe it'll never go away." He flushed and picked at the crust—white bread, of course, the nutritional equivalent of a sponge made out of carbohydrates. "Maybe sometimes that's why I come back at you. Because he never let people tell him what to do, and I—I don't know what I'm saying."

"You're not wrong," Hazard said slowly. "About either of us. People inherit behavioral patterns from their parents. And part of perpetuating those patterns is an unconscious search for approval, a way of holding on to a parent, repeating those behaviors, hoping somehow, irrationally, this time the relationship will be different."

Colt raised his eyebrows.

Face hot, Hazard shrugged. "It's easier for me when we're talking about someone else."

For some reason, that made Colt laugh softly. He picked at the crust some more.

"I want to be a better father to you," Hazard said. "I don't want to keep repeating my dad's mistakes. But I know I might have—you might not want that, anymore. John warned me that if I tried to come between you and Ashley, I'd lose you, and Colt—" He had to stop. Something stitched his chest tight. He fought it; he lost. He offered the boy a tight, fractured smile and a helpless shrug.

Colt was still looking down; if he'd seen any of it, Hazard couldn't tell, but after a moment he started to speak. "I shouldn't have gone to see Tera. I know that. I shouldn't have done any of it, going to see my dad like that, not telling you, even though I knew it'd make you crazy. I just wanted—I don't know. Maybe it's like you said. In my head, I know he's not going to be any different." His voice took on a dry bitterness much too mature for his age. "Same old Danny Lee, center of the universe, epic fuck-up. But I guess I'm fucked up too. He beat on me my whole life. Said awful shit to me. Made me feel like I was worthless. And he sent one letter, one, and I hitched a ride two hours to see him, and—and I know he's never going to be any different. I walked around with that letter, telling myself no fucking way would I go see him, no fucking way, and then I was in that fucking truck riding north, and I didn't even know why. So, you want to talk about fucked up?"

"Not fucked up," Hazard said. He reached without thinking, before he remembered that it might not be safe, and ran his hand over Colt's buzzed hair. "Complicated. Everybody is, in their own way."

Colt nodded. He laid down the ham sandwich and wiped his eyes. "He was so nice. Like I told you. Like he cared. Talking to me about how sorry he was. Telling everyone else in the visiting room about me. Fucking baseball." Colt broke off with a watery, indignant laugh. "And I ate it up. By the time he told me what he wanted, I'd swallowed all his shit. Then I came home, and we had that fight, and I talked to Ash about what—about what was going on, and Ash told me I was crazy." Colt dashed his hand across his eyes again and dried it on his jeans. "So I called him; Danny Lee's got a phone in there, even though you're not supposed to. And I told him I didn't want to do it. I mean, it was night and day. No more chatting. No more good guy. He told me I was going to get it, or he was going to take me away from you. I said he couldn't because he was a fucking felon, and he started to laugh. He's got this way he sounds when he knows he's got you. And he told me. Tera was back—she'd been in Arkansas for a while—and if I didn't do what he wanted, he'd tell the state, and they'd make me go live with her. He says they can do that. He says in Missouri, they make you go with family if you've got any."

"Maybe," Hazard said, thinking of Ramona's call. "I'm not sure it's quite that straightforward. We need to meet with Ramona and figure out what's going to happen next."

"I won't go live with her. I won't. I'll run away first."

"We'll figure it out, Colt. If you—" He had to take a breath. His face felt hot and cold at the same time. "If you want to be on your own—"

"No! No, that's not what—I thought maybe if I was emancipated, I wouldn't have to go live with Tera, and maybe I could stay, you know, a couple more years with you and J-H. J-H said you probably saw that essay I was writing, the one about you. He said you don't miss much. I know it's probably too late, but I meant what I wrote; you're the most important person in my life. But that was before..."

"Before?"

"Before I fucked up so bad," he said in a small voice. "I shouldn't have done that. I know you're tired of me fucking up your life. I told myself I was going to handle it on my own. Only Tera and my dad are always fighting about something, and my dad either lied about getting the stuff on credit or didn't know Tera would be pissed, and I didn't know she was going to go crazy like that, try to keep me there and get the money, and I panicked, and I sent you that message before they took my phone because—because I knew you'd come, no matter how mad you were. I'm sorry, Pops. I really, really fucked up."

He started to cry, turning in his seat to put his face in his hands, the ham-and-Swiss toppling from his lap to spill lettuce and crushed-up Lays across the concrete slab. Hazard knelt next to Colt's chair. He pulled the boy against him, and Colt cried harder. Hazard closed his own eyes. He remembered being young, nightmares, his father's weight bearing down the mattress of the twin bed, the familiar smell of cigarettes and beer and machine grease, the arm around his shoulders. That had happened too, he thought. Along with all the rest of it. That was his father too.

CHAPTER TWENTY-ONE
APRIL 13
MONDAY
5:01 PM

UNDER THE PRETENSE OF checking the grill, Somers let himself out onto the back patio, where Hazard was reading. The big man was holding a book that Somers hadn't seen before, a little paperback, the corners bent, the cover design—a few watercolor flowers—suggesting it was thirty years old, minimum, and no one had ever expected it to be a bestseller. Hazard looked better than Somers had expected; the big man's color was back, and his hands were steady as he turned the pages.

After their talk on the patio, Hazard and Colt had made a brief appearance to inform Somers and Aileen that everything was all right, at which point, Aileen had drafted Colt into looking at some of Frank's old clothes in case he wanted any of them. To Somers's surprise, the to-keep pile of flannels and beer-sponsored tees was growing steadily, and he thought he and Hazard might have to do a careful weed-through of the selection. Hazard, meanwhile, had escaped to the patio. Somers had given him time and, instead, worked on prepping burgers and a salad and potatoes and onions for the grill. He knew his husband. So he waited.

As Somers inspected the coals, which were beginning to catch, Hazard said behind him, "All right. You've been admirably patient. Go ahead and ask."

Grinning, Somers turned around.

Hazard was trying to glower. After another moment, he said, "Well?"

"Oh, no, I'd hate to get involved in a private conversation."

"Excuse me?"

"I'm sure you handled it perfectly. I don't need any details."

Hazard's eyes narrowed. "You're an ass."

"If you wanted to talk about it, however..."

"Sit down. You have five minutes to tell me what happened after I dropped Colt off at the house yesterday. And then I will apologize. And then I will tell you what happened here. And then you will tell me what I did wrong. And then I will make another attempt to fix things."

"I don't think you did anything wrong. Colt's smiling and trying on a shirt that says, 'I like my fish like my women: after a beer, and not too much work.' So I think our parenting job is done."

"You have four and a half minutes now, thanks to that little display of humor."

"He really is trying on that shirt, Ree."

"Four minutes and twenty seconds."

Another grin exploded on Somers's face, and he lowered himself into the chair next to Hazard's. His face settled into seriousness. "He called me. Last night, after you dropped him off. He was...well, hysterical isn't a great word, but I guess it comes close. He was crying so hard I couldn't understand him. I thought he'd gotten hurt or — well, I didn't know what. I called you, and you didn't answer. I saw on the app that he was home, so I drove back and checked on him. He was on the couch, Ree. Sobbing. I thought he might be having a fit. I finally gave him a Xanax because I thought he was going to hurt himself. By then, you had called and told me you were going to your mom's, so I had an idea the two things might be related. The next morning, Colt told me what had happened, and then I got a couple hours of sleep, and we came here."

Hazard studied him. He reached out, and his hand cupped the side of Somers's face. "You stayed up all night. With him."

"Leaving him alone didn't seem like a good idea."

"God, I did a piss-poor job of handling that."

"Well, I wasn't exactly happy with you last night. After Colt told me all of it, including the bit about the emancipation papers, I understood a little better." Somers's jaw cracked when he yawned. "I won't object to a better night's sleep, though."

Hazard was silent for a moment. He dropped his hand. "I fucked up your work last night."

"Not really. I mean, I was mostly there because the stakes are high, but Dulac and Palomo were handling it. Palomo's almost as tough in an interview as you are, and Dulac plays off her well. They're turning into a good pair. Carson has the bloody clothing, but there are still a lot of holes in his story. He might be telling the truth. God, in some ways, it would be easier if he were telling the truth." Somers rubbed his forehead. "You wouldn't believe the phone calls I'm getting about this. The last one was the lieutenant governor. If one more Jeff City asshat uses the phrase 'political powder keg' to try to motivate me to do my job, I'm going to turn in my badge and take up fishing."

"They're worried about the fallout," Hazard said. "If this comes back on an Ozark Volunteer killing a wealthy progressive activist, or if it comes back on a crazy liberal nut killing a conservative leader, either option could ignite a firestorm."

Somers offered him a flat look.

"I know you know," Hazard said quickly. "I'm just talking it out."

"My point," Somers said, "is that a personal motive for the killing, like Carson's, would actually make that simpler. And someone is leaking our business; the lieutenant governor knew Carson had confessed and told me in not so many words that I needed to accept his confession and close the case."

"Someone told him?"

"Someone told someone," Somers said drily.

"Who?"

"Carmichael, I think. She's gone off the deep end, Ree. The tech guy sent me a list of flags from her computer; she's been going to a lot of extremist sites. On her work computer. During work hours. Domestic terrorism shit. I talked to her about it, and she said it was research. What the hell do I say to that?"

Hazard grimaced and shook his head. "I don't know. About the only thing we can do is figure out what happened. And fast."

"Oh, gee, I hadn't thought of that yet. It'd be nice if we could get some straight answers out of somebody in this case; Dulac and Palomo have been hounding Naomi, trying to get her to talk about the guns, but she's stonewalling them."

"Boys," Aileen called from the back door. "How are those coals coming?"

"Almost ready, Aileen," Somers said.

"He's sucking up to you, Mom. Five seconds ago he was being snarky as hell."

"Oh muffin," Aileen said, laughed, and shut the door.

"Did she giggle?" Hazard asked.

"I have that effect on women."

The look on Hazard's face was worth whatever that was going to cost Somers down the road. After a silent struggle, he managed to say, "John, I'm sorry. About last night. About everything. If I'd listened to you about Colt—"

"It's ok. He's here. He's ok. You're here. You're ok. We're going to figure things out, one day at a time."

"But if Danny Lee is determined to take him away from us—"

"They're not going to put Colt with Tera, Ree. Not after what happened last night."

"But he'll have other relatives. Cousins, aunts, who the fuck knows?"

"Ramona is a reasonable woman," Somers said with more confidence than he felt. "And Colt knows what he wants. We'll figure it out."

"But—"

"Ree, I love you, but not today, ok?"

Hazard rubbed his eyes, nodded, and accepted a kiss. The quick kiss was starting to turn into something more serious, with Hazard's hand sliding up the back of Somers's shirt, when a shout of "Oh my God, why?" came from the back door. Colt stood there in an old tee, obviously stolen from Frank Hazard's closet, printed with COORS and then a cattle skull.

"Go away," Hazard told him.

"You were alone for, like, five minutes!"

"Sorry," Somers said, wiping his mouth. "Got caught up in the moment."

"It's your mom's house. It's the middle of the day. Don't you have any decency?"

"My mother is perfectly aware—" Hazard began.

Colt shouted wordless frustration and turned back into the house. Then he was complaining, the volume not quite loud enough for Somers to make out the words. A moment later, Aileen's surprisingly wicked laughter floated out.

"God," Somers said. His cheeks were hot. "Do you think she…"

"We're grown men. We're married. It was one kiss." But Hazard's face was red too, and he stood up a little too quickly for casual and gave Somers a shove. "And you're letting the coals burn down. Go get the burgers."

Together, they cooked the burgers and hot dogs, Hazard with a Bud Lite in one hand, Somers drinking Diet Coke because Aileen didn't have any Pepsi. The day warmed up. The smell of the charcoal, of meat seared over open flames, of the slight yeastiness of Hazard's breath, when he snuck another kiss and his hand rested on bare skin at the small of Somers's back, made Somers feel like he'd stepped out of one world and into another.

When they carried the food inside, Colt and Aileen were sitting at the kitchen table, going through the shoebox that Hazard had found among his dad's belongings. Colt had changed into a D.A.R.E t-shirt, gray with red letters, that fit him just about perfectly.

"That's mine," Hazard said.

"Bunny, I didn't think you'd mind."

"Not the shoebox. The shirt."

Colt glanced up and flashed a grin so bright it exposed his crooked eyetooth. He indicated a center part in his hair and then held up a picture. It was too small for Somers to make out anything more than a serious little boy, probably no older than four or five. "You had a butt cut."

Somers burst out laughing.

"Thank you, Mom," Hazard growled as he set the burgers on the counter and picked up the box of foil. "I'm so glad you thought it would be a good idea to give away my belongings and, at the same time, take a walk down memory lane. Is there anything else you'd like to do? Would you like to give Colt my vaccination records? Are you going to write me out of the will and put him in?"

"Bunny, you're being terrible."

"He's always like this," Colt said.

For some reason, that made Aileen burst into fresh peals of laughter, and Hazard's face reddened again.

"He liked Frank's old things so much that I thought maybe he'd like some of your clothes."

"Key word, Mom: mine."

"And look, it fits him perfectly. Doesn't it look nice on him? He's the most handsome boy, and that t-shirt hangs just right on him."

Colt blushed almost as hard as Hazard. He grabbed another photo and held it up. "J-H."

Somers took a step forward.

"No," Hazard said a beat too late. He grabbed Somers's arm.

"Frosted tips," Colt said with a huge smirk.

"Oh my God," Somers said. He tried to get loose, but Hazard wouldn't let him free. It turned into wrestling, with Somers and Colt and even, surprisingly, Aileen, laughing harder and harder as Hazard's growls got fiercer and fiercer. It ended when Colt brought the photo close enough for Somers to make out what he guessed was a fourteen-year-old Emery Hazard with frosted tips, glaring at the camera like he might bite off the lens. Somers laughed so hard that he had to lean against the sofa, and Hazard released him with a snarl and retreated to the kitchen.

"It was one summer," he shouted as he ripped off a sheet of foil to tent the burgers. "And it was a mistake."

"You looked—" Aileen said, gulping air between laughs. "You looked very nice, muffin."

The sentiment was somewhat spoiled when she burst into laughter again.

"Please tell me there's more," Somers said when he finally managed to stand upright and totter toward the kitchen table. "Bubs, are there any pictures from middle school? He used to wear this Walkman—"

"On his belt!" Colt finished in a shout. "Oh my God, it's right here. He was such a nerd!"

"Fuck you," Hazard said, stabbing a finger at Somers. "And fuck you." The finger stabbed at Colt. "And—" He seemed to be at a loss when he got to his mother, so he settled for wordless outrage.

That was when the doorbell rang, and Hazard stomped away to answer it.

Somers stared at the photo of eleven-year-old Emery Hazard, tall for his age, rail thin, the Walkman at his belt and the foam-padded headphones hanging from one hand. Dark, wary eyes looked back at him. The boy next to him, Somers knew too; Jeff Langham, the boy who would eventually become Hazard's first boyfriend. The photo had been taken before Hazard had come out to his parents. He must have been on the cusp of puberty. Had he suspected, even then, that there was something different about himself, something to keep secret in order to protect himself? Somers stared into those dark eyes, his thumb teasing the corner of the photo. The game didn't seem quite as fun then.

Colt continued to root around in the box. "Jaydog, why aren't there any pictures of you in here?"

The hurt of it surprised Somers more than the question itself; he had known, someday, Colt would learn some of it—hopefully not all of it, hopefully not the worst parts. But it still hurt. He had to clear his throat before he said, "Emery and I weren't friends back then." He could have left it there, but he owed Hazard more than that. He owed himself more than that. "I wasn't very kind to him. Especially once we got to high school."

There was a question in Colt's face, but also a kind of preemptive understanding. Before Somers had to answer either of them, Hazard reappeared.

"You will not believe—" he began.

"Surprise!" Shaw shouted as he darted around Hazard and into the living room.

"Surprise," North echoed sourly from behind Hazard.

"Oh my God," Shaw said, stopping to turn around in a circle before his eyes came to rest on Aileen. "You must be Emery's sister."

"I don't have a sister," Hazard said. "She's obviously my mother."

"Bunny, don't be unkind. He was being polite." Aileen smiled at Shaw. "And you are?"

"I'm Shaw. I'm Emery's best friend. Well, soulmate."

"What the fu—" North seemed to catch himself, and he darted a guilty look at Aileen. "Excuse me?"

"Quantum entangled soulmate," Shaw said. "Not romantic soulmate."

"Uh huh," North said.

"That's you."

"Fu—freaking fantastic."

"Probably."

"What the fu—" By now North was starting to sound strangled. "What do you mean, probably?"

"My best friend," Hazard said, "would have known that I don't have a sister."

Shaw waved that away airily. Then, without any warning, he wrapped Aileen in a hug. "Did you know Emery saved me once? I was about to be run over by a truck or a van or maybe it was a stampede, and North had eaten bad shrimp, so he had the heaves, and I think maybe there was a talking fish and I got three wishes—"

"It was none of those things," Hazard began. "I was driving—"

"He was driving the van," North said at the time, "and he didn't come close to running you over—"

Both of them cut off and offered the other a suspicious look.

"You did such a great job raising him," Shaw was saying as he continued to hug Aileen. "And now you've got this amazing family, and everyone loves everyone, and oh my God, did you know your hugs are like catnip, only if the cat were made out of clouds, or maybe that toilet paper with the commercials about the family of bears who are always talking about their dumps."

"Ok," Hazard said. "That's enough."

"I'd put this hug in my hugbox, only North ran it over and said that was a lesson for—North, what was it a lesson for?"

"Who the fu—who knows? And it wasn't a hugbox, whatever that is. It was an old Huggies box you filched out of a dumpster." The whole time he was talking, he was disentangling Shaw, the movements surprisingly gentle considering the stream of words. "He had four Cokes before I caught him," North added, steering the slender man toward the kitchen. "Let me get him some water."

Aileen stared after them. Her face was unreadable to Somers, which was rare, and she was touching her arms where Shaw had hugged her. "Would you like to stay for dinner?"

"No," Hazard said.

"Yes," Shaw called back.

"No," North said over his shoulder. "Thank you."

"Do not touch those burgers," Hazard shouted after them.

North gave him the finger without looking back, then he flinched and dropped his hand.

When Somers glanced over, Colt's eyes were wide. "Those guys are nuts."

Somers laughed. "That's one word for it."

Colt watched them across the room, where the open floorplan connected with the kitchen. Shaw was drinking water. North stood with his arms crossed, glaring at Shaw. When he seemed satisfied that Shaw wasn't going to somehow choke to death or drop the glass or spray water like an archerfish—all of which, based on Somers's limited experience with the man, seemed like equally probable possibilities—North turned back to the rest of them.

"Sorry to crash you like this. We heard about the Maas kid getting arrested, and then our client called and told us our contract was canceled, so we were going to head back to St. Louis—"

Shaw made an indignant noise between gulps.

With a weary sigh, North nodded. "Only Shaw refused to leave until we apologized for, you know, not handling this the best."

"You can apologize over the phone," Hazard said. "Preferably from two hundred miles away."

Glass to his lips, Shaw made another of those noises.

"And," North growled, "Shaw insisted that we give Emery his birthday present in person. I'm going out on a limb here, but I'm guessing that's because the birthday gift is a psychic soulgaze or the breath of a baby sparrow or the echo from a wind chime that Robert Frost liked to shove up his own—" North's eyes cut toward Aileen, and he mumbled, "—exhaust pipe."

"It's not any of those things," Shaw said with what, Somers guessed, was supposed to sound like tremendous dignity. He set the glass on the counter. "It's a three-part gift, and it's a very good gift, and Emery is going to love it because, yes, I admit that I stumbled a little the first few times, but now that I really know him, you might even say now that I've been inside him—"

Somers choked on his spit.

"Excuse me?" North asked.

"You have never been inside me," Hazard snapped.

"Psychically," Shaw said with a beatific smile. "Because of our entanglement. Now I know the perfect gift."

"Great," Hazard said. "Send it in the mail."

"J-H," Colt whispered. "Can they please stay for dinner?"

"Yes," Aileen said. "You're staying; that's settled. Any friend of muffin's is a friend of mine. Now, Shaw, Colt, help me set the table."

North waited until she turned away. Then he looked Hazard in the eye, smirked, and whispered, "Muffin."

"Say it again," Hazard whispered back. "And you're going to be pulling Robert Frost's whatever-the-fuck out of your own exhaust pipe."

For some reason, that only made North's grin bigger.

Shaw and Colt set the table while Aileen and Hazard—with a great deal of grumbling—transferred the food to serving dishes. Shaw tried to get drinks for everyone, which North immediately put a stop to and extracted no fewer than six Diet Cokes from various pockets in Shaw's pants—which, Somers was now noticing were apparently made from hemp. North and Hazard had beers. They'd immediately started talking shop, each of them shooting down the other's ideas, both of them listening and cutting in and waving their beers dramatically.

"Oh my God, they're, like, best friends," Colt said in an undertone.

"I know," Somers said. "It's kind of annoying. Don't tell him, bubs. He thinks he doesn't like them, and weirdly, that actually makes it easier in some ways."

"Oh, yeah," Colt said, nodding. "I can definitely see that."

Then they ate, the conversation fragmenting and reassembling with an easiness that Somers hadn't expected. He held himself back, listening, making sure everyone had someone to talk to, so he heard when Hazard started talking about the case.

"If your client canceled your contract," Hazard said, "then I don't see the problem in telling us who hired you to investigate these murders."

"Nice try." North tore off another bite of burger. "Still confidential."

"That seems—"

"Not giving you the name, Hazard. Stop sniffing around."

"Oh," Shaw said excitedly, breaking off from whatever he'd been telling Aileen—Somers wasn't sure what, but he'd heard the word *dilation*, and Aileen's cheeks were red. "I caught North sniffing around the other day."

North set his burger down. He wiped his hands on the napkin. He stared at Shaw. "Really? You want to do this right now?"

Shaw beamed at him. "He was on his hands and knees, and his head was under the bed, and he was sniffing and sniffing. I used to think that in a previous life, North had been a baby cow." In a rush, he added, "A calf! But now I think in a previous, previous life, North was a drug-sniffing dog."

"I didn't have to be a drug-sniffing dog in a previous life. I've spent enough of my life around your candy ass, living with the stink of you smoking joint after joint of—" He cut off and looked, of all people, at Colt. "—uh, white sage."

Colt's snort sounded so much like Hazard's that Somers had to hide a grin.

"I smelled something burning," North said, his voice growing stronger. "Why don't you tell them about the time you decided to use your tote full of wrapping paper and tissue paper and blank greeting cards as an impromptu luminary?"

"Oh God," Shaw said. "It was amazing! It was one tiny candle, but it went up so fast! It would have been so interesting to watch, only North kept shrieking, 'My house, my house, you're burning down my house!'"

Colt laughed; when Somers looked at him, he had the decency to bury his face in his elbow.

"So forgive me," North said, throwing down the napkin, "if I thought I smelled something burning, and I decided to find out if you'd tried to invent your own heated mattress by building a bonfire under the bed or who the fu—who the hell—or who knows what else."

"He was looking for my birthday gift to Emery," Shaw said to Colt. "He's always going through my stuff. The secret is if you have something valuable, something you don't want anybody to find—"

Colt snagged something from the shoebox, which was on the floor next to his chair, and held it up. "Like a Vanilla Ice Superstars Musicard?"

"Oh my God," North said, and then he grunted—because, Somers guessed, Hazard had either kicked or elbowed him. Elbowed, most likely. Because North had those clodhopping boots.

"That is the single most amazing thing I've ever seen," Shaw said.

"Don't be impressed," North said. "He said that about a ketchup bottle at lunch."

"It was a Hello Kitty one! The ketchup came out of the kitty's mouth!" Shaw drew himself upright and, with a visible effort, restrained himself. "Ok, yes, for the sake of example, a Vanilla Ice Superstars Musicard. Which makes absolutely perfect sense that my best friend, Emery, would own."

"Ricky Dunphy put it in my locker and told everyone I had a crush," Hazard said. "I didn't buy the damn thing."

"But you do still have it," North muttered.

"Twenty years later," Somers murmured into his Diet Coke.

Hazard turned a betrayed look on him.

"So, if you want to keep it safe—for example, because even though your boyfriend says he doesn't like, um, smoking Vanilla Ice Superstars Musicards, sometimes you come home and your stash is significantly lighter, and the house smells like someone has been smoking Vanilla Ice Superstars Musicards, and when you ask him, he makes up an excuse and has to go out to the garage for six hours and listen to AC/DC—"

"Get on with it!" Hazard roared.

"Do you blame me?" North asked. "It's the only time I'm not listening to him talk."

"So," Shaw said more loudly, "if you want to keep it safe, you have to hide it really, really well, and then you have to let him think he found it so he'll stop coming in the bedroom with made-up excuses like vacuuming and changing the sheets and cleaning the windows."

"All real things," North said. "All things that normal adults do."

"So," Shaw said, "while he's pretending to 'wipe down the blinds,'" Shaw gave a laugh like he'd never heard anything crazier, "you let him stumble across, oh, I don't know, a little dime baggie."

"Of incense," North said.

"Yeah, yeah, yeah, of incense. And then he thinks he found your stash—"

"Of incense."

"Yes, exactly, of incense, and then you don't have to worry about him pulling the bed away from the wall, quote, 'because you have dust bunnies the size of the puppy down there.'"

Maybe it was because the empty chatter let his brain relax—kind of the conversational equivalent of the shower principle. Maybe it was because something hadn't felt right about it from the start. Whatever the reason, Somers felt a piece of the puzzle click, and he looked over at his husband.

Hazard was shaking his head as he tossed his napkin onto the table.

"You think so too?" Somers asked.

North swore under his breath, flinched, and glanced sidelong at Aileen. "You've got to be kidding me."

"What?" Shaw asked. "North, what?"

"Pops, what's going on?"

"Muffin, what's the matter?"

"The ambush," Somers said as he got to his feet. "At your motel. We missed something."

"We?" Hazard snapped, although he had the good grace to blush when Somers cocked an eyebrow. "Everyone assumed that because someone took a shot at us, the fact that your motel door had been forced was irrelevant. It looked like bait, a way to make us focus on the room so that we wouldn't notice the sniper."

"So, they—" North began.

"—searched our room!" Shaw shouted triumphantly, scrambling up from his seat. "We figured it out together! Teamwork!"

Somers stared at him.

Hazard stared at him.

North cuffed him on the back of the head. To Hazard, he said, "What the fu—what the hell—" He made an impatient noise. "What were they looking for?"

"Good question," Hazard said. "What did you take?"

"Nothing," North said. "I would have told you; we're not trying to blow up your case."

"Does having your third soul imprinted with the essence of despair and grief count as taking evidence?" Shaw asked. "Because I'm very sensitive to psychic impressions and—"

"No," Hazard said. "Stop talking." He fixed his gaze on North again. "The killer or killers think you took something. That's the only reason they would have tossed your room. And they stuck around for target practice, which means they didn't find it. So, why do they think you took something, and what do they think you have?"

"We didn't take anything! Jesus, man, we barely even got close to that kid's house before the bodyguard grabbed us. We never had a chance to take something."

And there it was.

"Did you sneak into Zach Renner's motel room?" Somers asked before Hazard could.

North grimaced. Shaw looked carefully at the hamburger on his plate.

"Look," North said, "it was right at the beginning, before I realized how stupid this was—Shaw and I popped inside for a quick look when the cop on duty went downstairs; someone in an SUV was idling. She told them to move along, and it turned into an argument. It felt like a lucky break, that's all. I didn't want to waste it."

"Jesus Christ," Hazard said under his breath. "John."

"Yeah. Aileen, can we—"

"Go, go. We'll be fine."

"You two," Hazard snapped, pointing at North and Shaw, "get your asses in gear. You're going to show us every single thing you touched."

Somers followed Hazard out of the house, and they headed toward the Mustang. Behind him, North and Shaw were talking as they came out onto the lawn.

"—just saying it was very, very manly the way you did exactly what he said," Shaw was saying. "Like, when he pointed at us and started barking orders, 'you two, blah, blah, blah,' and then you were practically quivering like when a dog is really excited and it can't wait to—oh my God, oh my God, oh my God, North, my balls!"

"Yeah? How do you like it, somebody twisting your nuts like that?"

"Jesus Christ," Hazard growled as he dropped into the passenger seat. "How are those two still alive?"

CHAPTER TWENTY-TWO
APRIL 13
MONDAY
5:40 PM

THEY DROVE THE MILES back to Wahredua, Somers pushing the Mustang as fast as he dared on the back roads. The spring fields were furrowed and black, some with tiny hints of green poking through the dark soil, the air smelling like manure when they drove along freshly fertilized acres. The roadside wildflowers were beginning to stir, chips and stripes of green among the tangle of dead brown winter leavings. The evening was gold and darker gold as the sun fell behind windbreaks and old-growth stands of trees. The light, almost horizontal, gave everything a static look, an illusion that shattered in the Mustang's wake.

"Benji Renner was desperate to get back in that motel room," Somers said.

Hazard grunted. He was tapping at his phone, reading something on the screen. Then he placed a call and put the phone on speaker. To Somers, he said, "I don't want any commentary about this, understand?"

"About what?"

"Hello?" The woman's voice suggested boarding schools and the Hamptons and gin.

"Uh, yeah." Hazard's voice was unnaturally deep. "This is North McKinney."

Somers looked at his husband, who flushed and used one hand to turn Somers's face back toward the road.

"Yes, Mr. McKinney. How may I help you?"

"I wanted to follow-up about that job—"

"The job, as you call it, is over. I thought I made that perfectly clear. I hired you to find whoever murdered my son. I understand now that was a mistake; I should have let the police do their work. It's a tragedy about that boy and his father. But it's more of a tragedy that their — that their business carried over into that motel room. I hope they try that boy as an adult, and I hope they —" Her voice broke. "I hope they stick a needle in his arm. There. How's that for vicious?"

"Mrs. Renner —"

"White-Renner, thank you. Just as it's written on the check."

Hazard's voice sounded a little too much like Emery Hazard again when he said, "I'm trying to ask you a question. What was Zach and Benji's relationship like?"

"What's that supposed to mean?"

"It's a question."

"The police already have this boy. He's confessed. I have it on good authority."

"Mrs. White-Renner, there are some irregularities —"

"I told you the job was done. Did you not understand that? The police have the killer; the case is closed, or however I'm supposed to say it. Now, I don't want you sticking your nose into family things, and I don't want you bothering Benji. That money would have turned up eventually; it was a misunderstanding or a miscommunication or what have you. Zach knew that too. They'd had their disagreements before, and Lord knows it wouldn't have been the first time that Zach sent Benji packing. He always did have a temper. But they would have worked it out — they always did, and Zach always took Benji back." Her voice sharpened. "Now, I want you to leave this alone. I want you to leave my family alone. There, have I made myself perfectly clear?"

And then the call disconnected.

"Shit," Hazard said staring at the phone.

"If Benji was stealing from his big brother," Somers said, "that would explain why he was so desperate to get into that room. There must be some kind of financial paperwork that will show a trail back to him. That's motive. Maybe this is the opposite of what we thought; maybe Benji showed up for an argument with Zach and somehow Landon got caught up in the crossfire. Only, damn it, that doesn't work with the forensics; Landon was definitely shot first."

Hazard was nodding slowly. "And it doesn't explain what's going on with Carson. I'd put money on the DNA from the blood on his clothes coming back as a match for Landon, and possibly Zach as well. Where does he fit?"

Somers shook his head. "We'd be a hell of a lot closer to an answer if those numbskulls hadn't kept their client a secret."

"They didn't know that it would have bearing on the investigation, and it wasn't that hard to guess. There are only so many people who would have paid to have the deaths investigated. Besides, they do have a code of ethics. Don't look at me like that; I'm only saying this because there's a degree of professional loyalty."

"I'm North McKinney," Somers said in an unnaturally deep voice.

"I said no commentary."

"I drive a fast car."

"All right," Hazard said, slouching in the seat and crossing his arms. "Go for it. Have a fucking blast."

"Babe," Somers said with a laugh, and he reached over to rub Hazard's leg. "I'm teasing—"

Hazard caught his wrist and flung his hand away.

Somers laughed again. "Come on, Ree."

"Did I hurt your hand?"

"What? No, of course not—"

"Good. Because you're going to need it. And you can think about this next month, and the month after that, standing in the shower with nothing but your hand, and remember this moment the next time you decide to be a fucking comedian."

"Oh my God," Somers said. "Love, it was a joke."

"Listen to me laughing."

After a moment, Somers grinned. "I'm North McKinney."

Hazard turned slowly to glare at him.

"Babe," Somers said, turning up the heat, the grin boiling into something a hell of a lot hotter. "You can talk big, but we both know that by the end of the week, you're going to be humping the mattress."

Hazard raised his middle finger.

"Yeah," Somers said, reaching down to adjust himself. "That's exactly the idea."

After that, Hazard refused to say anything for the rest of the drive.

When they reached the Presidential, night was settling down, purple darkness brooding over the canopy of sodium lights. A woman stood at the curb in stiletto heels, a short skirt, and a halter top. Her nose was red, and Somers was pretty sure the brown paper bag held a bottle of Nyquil. Someone was partying; '90s Will Smith was blasting from a room on the first floor, recommending that everyone get jiggy with it. A black-and-white was parked under one of the lights, and when Somers glided into the parking lot, McGraw shot out of the car, straightening his uniform and his hair and looking exactly like what he was, a twenty-two-year-old who had decided to take it easy on his shift.

"Chief Somerset," he said when Somers got out of the car. "I was just checking—"

"No, you weren't." Somers jogged past him, Hazard hard on his heels. "We'll talk about this tomorrow."

The GTO barreled into the lot a moment later, the throaty rumble of the engine died, and two car doors opened and shut. Heavy steps rang out on the stairs below as Somers and Hazard reached the second-floor landing. Somers was opening the motel door when Shaw elbowed past North and shouted, "I won!"

"It wasn't a race, fuckwit," North said. His breathing was heavier than Somers would have expected; the blond man looked fit, but the breathing suggested he was skipping cardio.

"Of course it was," Hazard said. "And we won."

"Oh my God," Somers said as he pulled out disposable gloves and booties and handed them around.

"Well, I was talking about just North and me—" Shaw began.

"I don't care," Hazard said. "If it was a race—and it was—then Somers and I won."

"Right, but in the sub-race—" Shaw tried.

"If anyone won," Somers said, pushing open the door, "it was me. Now will the three of you quit screwing around and help me?"

They shuffled after him into the room.

"John, technically, in our situation, it was not a race, which means you aren't technically the winner—"

But whatever else Hazard felt the need to quibble about, it dried up when Somers turned and looked at him.

Somers took in the room. It looked pretty much the same as it had the night they'd caught Benji in here, only with even more fingerprint powder covering everything; Norman and Gross must have printed every available surface again, and it looked like they'd done a solid job of it, as always.

"Am I going to have to explain why your latents are in this room?" Somers asked.

North snorted.

"All right," Hazard said. "Where did you look?"

"Everywhere," Shaw said brightly. "We're very good."

"Apparently not," Hazard said. "I have reason to believe Benji was stealing from Zach. On top of that, Benji was apprehended trying to recover something from this room. The next day, someone tossed your room and tried to make it look like they wanted you dead. Taken together, those facts suggest that Benji is looking for some sort of financial paperwork and that he still hasn't found it."

"How do you know Benji was stealing from his brother?" North asked.

Somers couldn't help it; the grin slipped out.

"What?" North asked.

"Really?" Hazard asked Somers. "After everything that happened in the car?"

Somers grinned harder, but he shook his head. Then, fighting to keep his voice steady, he said, "An informant."

"John," Hazard said in a warning tone.

"Deepthroat." That did it; his control slipped, and he had to move deeper into the room before he burst out laughing. He squatted next to a love seat and began to search the cushions.

"What's going on with him?" North asked.

"He thinks he's a comedian," Hazard said. "It's an ongoing issue."

"North thinks he's a comedian," Shaw said. "Actually, he is pretty funny. The other day he did this drawing, and it was—well, it was kind of lopsided. You know, cattywampus. And I said, oh, this is so nice, when did a preschooler give you this, and he said—"

"Shut the fuck up," North growled.

"You remember! And then he told me it was—" Shaw fought through a laugh to get the rest of the words out. "It was about how much dairy we should eat."

"It was the USDA's MyPlate," North snapped. "And it's a scientific fact that you're supposed to get three cups a day."

Shaw laughed even harder. "See? He's hilarious. And he comes up with stuff like that off the top of his head."

To judge by Shaw's startled squawk, Somers guessed that North had pushed him. "Go do some actual work, dickbag. No, go over there. No. Over there. Thank you. I'm going to check the bathroom."

Somers turned the love seat onto its back. He worked the staples loose and checked behind the dust cover fabric on the underside. He ran his fingers along every seam of the love seat itself, checking for any sign that it had been tampered with.

"Toilet tank is a bust," North called from the bathroom.

"I checked the pictures and the frames," Hazard said from the other side of the room. "Nothing."

"No luck with the curtains and valance," Shaw said.

"Ree, I'm sure they took a look when they processed the room, but will you give the mattress another check?"

Hazard's steps moved across the room. Then, a minute later, as Somers was working open the tissue box holder—a favorite for idiots wanting to hide their stash—Hazard spoke.

"Go away. I'm doing this."

"I know," Shaw said, "and you're doing such a great job. And I'm helping, and I'm doing such a great job too."

"No, you're not. If anything, you're making this more difficult by— God damn it, we're moving the mattress this way. Stop pulling it that way!"

"Maybe I'm helping in an alternate universe. Maybe we're pulling the mattress, and that's why I keep pulling it here too."

"Maybe in that alternate universe you never became a private detective and you're not here at all. Maybe you're somewhere else. Maybe we never met."

"Oh my God," Shaw said, voice thrilled. "Maybe I'm a lion tamer! Oh my God, oh my God, and maybe you're the lion!"

For a moment, Hazard's silence sounded helpless. Then he bellowed, "North!"

The clang of pipes was followed, a moment later, by vicious swearing. "What the actual fuck? I just about decapitated myself in here."

"I need you to deal with this," Hazard called toward the bathroom.

"You seem tense," Shaw said. "You know what would make you feel better? One time, North was so stressed because all of his bills went into this box, and I think the box used to belong to a magician because they all turned into confetti, and it was probably a really good trick only it wasn't so good for North because he has this, like, mania about bills, and he's always looking at them and writing them and putting them in envelopes with stamps. It's like an addiction."

"It's called keeping the fucking lights on." North stood in the bathroom doorway, massaging his scalp. "And that's why I can't keep a shredder at home anymore."

"And since North was so stressed," Shaw said, picking up the television remote, "I decided to help him with a guided meditation, and I found this channel on the TV, only it wasn't a guided meditation at all, it was—well, have you ever encountered a diabolical presence? It was like that, only blond and with an eating disorder, and she had her own news ticker—"

"Ann Coulter, for anyone who gives a fuck," North said sourly.

"—and that wasn't soothing at all, so then I changed the channel and I found this educational program—"

"Not educational at all. It was one of those things you leave on for dogs to supposedly watch while they're home alone all day."

"—and North was out like a light!"

"In case anyone gives any additional fucks," North said, "I'd worked a twenty-six hour stakeout with no sleep, and I came home to find the March gas bill jammed in the shredder. Fucking eat me because I needed to close my eyes for five minutes."

"He was dreaming like a dog, too," Shaw added in an aside. "You know, those little kicks and whimpers. Oh my God! Emery, it's like the sniffing. Remember what I said about the sniffing?"

"Give me that," Hazard said, reaching for the remote. "The last thing we need is you two creating even more of a disturbance—"

But Shaw twisted, pulling it out of reach, and jabbed the red power button at one end.

Nothing happened.

Hazard was stretching now, still trying to get the remote. But he stopped. Somers could see the thoughts flashing across his face.

"Oh my God," Shaw whispered. "This is our moment."

Hazard yanked the remote from his grip and opened the compartment for the batteries. Inside, a piece of paper had been wadded into the shallow cavity. Too small, Somers thought, for financial paperwork. And at first he felt a faint flicker of disappointment that they'd been wrong yet again.

"We found it together," Shaw was saying. "Teamwork!"

Hazard elbowed him out of the way to lay the paper down on an end table. Then, carefully, he unfolded it and smoothed it out against the veneer. Somers joined him, and North and Shaw crowded around.

It was a photograph, and it took Somers a moment to process what he was seeing. The picture looked old, from maybe as much as fifteen or twenty years ago. It showed a group of people, all of whom were dressed to varying degrees as what Hazard would undoubtedly call hippies. Somers's attention fixed, though, on a man and a woman against a backdrop of sand-colored brick. A tall, pointed archway opened the wall behind them. The man had a beard and long hair, and he wore a loose white tunic, jeans, and Birkenstocks. The aquiline features were even sharper in youth. Next to him, the woman wore a hijab and a long-sleeved dress, but her face and her bright smile were turned toward the camera. The frame of the picture cut off a sign, but Somers could still read the words: ISLAMIC CENTER OF—

Shaw made a considering noise and leaned closer. "North, I didn't know they were Muslim."

"That's Zach Renner," Hazard said. "He looks like he's barely out of high school—hell, he looks about Benji's age."

Somers didn't trust his voice, but he managed: "And that's Naomi."

CHAPTER TWENTY-THREE

APRIL 13
MONDAY
6:38 PM

COMING BACK ALWAYS FELT like coming home, Somers thought as he parked the Mustang in front of the little house where he had once lived with Cora. Not truly like coming home; his home was with Hazard now. But like someone playing back a recording for him. His grandmother had loved recording shows off TV onto VHS tapes, and sometimes when she played them back, there was a kind of ghosting effect—a fuzziness that tracked movement on the screen. Coming back was like that. And you played it over and over again until the tape broke.

"I can talk to her if it's easier," Hazard said quietly.

"What? No. I'm fine."

"Tell that to the steering wheel."

Somers relaxed his grip. "It's just—well, I knew there was something weird between Naomi and Zach. He'd threatened her, and now it's obvious he had blackmail on her. But I never would have guessed—"

"That the de facto leader of a white supremacist group converted to Islam when she was in college?" Hazard asked drily. "No, I should think not, John. And I'm not sure that's what's bothering you."

Silence again. The creak of the leather. The dusk was the blue of river stones.

"This feels like I'm using her for work," Somers said, directing the words at the windshield. "I don't like that. I know things have been good between us for a while now; they've been better than I ever thought they would be, actually. But—God she hated when I brought work home."

Hazard's breathing was slow and relaxed.

"And, if I'm being honest, I haven't really talked to her about Naomi, about what Naomi did, about—about Naomi at all, I guess, since you and

I—" He broke off. "What I'm trying to say is, Naomi was always the worst part of our relationship, even back when things were good, and this feels like I'm digging that all up again."

When Hazard's hand came to rest on his leg, the touch was gentle but firm.

"I don't want to hurt her," Somers said, letting his head drop back against the seat. "God, not again. Not like this."

"Then let me talk to her. She'll understand."

"No." A little more forcefully, he said again, "No. This is my job. I'll do it. I sure as hell won't like it, though."

"Are you sure?"

Somers nodded and turned off the ignition.

North and Shaw—in spite of Shaw's objections—had gone back to the motor court, which meant that Hazard and Somers were alone when they reached the porch. Somers knocked, and Cora answered a moment later. She was tall, her dark hair free of its curls today, and she was pale in a way that was beautiful, without her sister's reliance on a tanning bed. She smiled, and then her smile faltered, and she tugged on the sleeve of her grey Henley.

"Hello. Why the long faces?"

"Cora," Somers said. "We need to talk."

"Sure, come in. Evie's in her room. Let me get her—"

"No," Hazard said.

Surprise painted itself on Cora's face, and Somers looked away.

"Is this about Evie next week?" Cora asked. "Because she doesn't have to go to Kansas City with me if—"

Hazard nudged Somers, and that got him through the door at least. They stood in the small living room, where, at a different point in his life, Somers had stripped the floorboards and sanded them, where he had sworn a blue streak and sulked after getting his thumb with the hammer instead of the nail he was aiming for, where he'd passed out and, more than once, pissed himself. Cora had moved the TV and the couch, and she'd taken down a painting and hung shiplap in its place. She was staring at them.

"It's not about Evie," Hazard said. "It's Naomi."

"Oh." Cora was silent for a moment. She wiped her palms on her jeans. Then she gestured, as though they couldn't see the couch, and said, "Would you like to sit down?"

They sat, and she took the armchair in the corner, sitting on the edge of the cushion, her hands locked around each other. Her face was so painfully neutral that Somers had to look at the coffee table and direct his words toward a copy of *Vogue*.

"I've tried not to do this." Somers was wiping his own palms now, scrubbing them on his jeans. "When it comes to Naomi, I've tried to leave you out of it."

"I know, John-Henry."

"I never wanted you to feel like I'd—I don't know, put you in that position."

"What did she do?"

"If you're not comfortable with this, I could try talking to your mom—"

"You're being silly. What did she do? Emery, what did she do?"

Hazard produced the photo, now secure inside an evidence bag, and passed it to her.

For a minute, and then another, Cora studied it. Then she held it out to Hazard like someone pushing something away and said, "She looks so young."

Hazard nodded.

"She was at college. Well, she was at Mizzou, anyway. We both were, but we weren't—we weren't close. We still aren't, as I'm sure you can tell."

"You're very different people," Hazard said.

Cora laughed. "It's funny you say that because when we were girls, people couldn't tell us apart. And my mom always looked young. When we were teenagers, people would mistake the three of us for sisters—God, Mom ate that up. Naomi and I did everything together when we were girls. We're only two years apart. Close enough to be friends. We needed that. Our dad was gone from as early as I can remember, and our mom, well, she loved us, but she had her own demons."

Somers remembered a meal with his parents when he'd still been in high school, when he'd first been starting to date. They'd been eating some sort of chicken with the bone still in, which he'd found vaguely disturbing at the time. And he'd sat there, pushing on the bone, spinning the chicken thigh in a circle around his plate, while his mother told him, in not so many words, that Cora's mother was a whore and that he would stop seeing her immediately. That hadn't been the first rebellion, but it had been the first one that had come out of a decent place inside him, and now, sitting here, asking someone he loved to pry open her hurt and her past for him to paw through, he had to focus on the texture of the fabric under his clammy hands. He grabbed one leg of his pants, pulling it tight in his fist. Hold on, he thought. Hold the fuck on.

"But you and Naomi aren't close now," Hazard said.

"No." Cora brushed at the arm of the chair, cleaning away something invisible to Somers. "In high school, I was such a bitch."

"We've talked about this," Hazard said. "I don't agree, and furthermore, there's no need—"

"But I was. You're kind, kinder than I deserve, but I was terrible. Not only to you. To lots of people. It was a…a defense mechanism, I suppose. I was always uncomfortable. Always insecure. No, not always. But once I knew why people looked differently at my mother when we went out in public. Once I knew why women, in particular, didn't seem to like her. Why men came over late at night. I was six or seven when a woman attacked my mother in the Savers parking lot. Came up behind and started pulling her hair, trying to drag her to the pavement. Of course, my mom was a lot tougher, and she wasn't in any danger, but that's scary to a child." She smoothed the upholstery again. Her eyes were restless. "It stays with you."

"You were the first person who saw me, the real me," Somers heard himself saying. His head came up. "You don't know what that meant to me."

Cora nodded, but the silence drew out, attenuated, until Somers had to look down again.

"When I got to college," Cora said, "I realized I was sick of that person, who I'd been. I liked being with you, John-Henry. We were good for each other." She smiled and added, "In that way."

The smile hurt. "In that way."

"You know what I mean. We both wanted to be done with who we'd been back home. But we had each other, and that was a kind of lifeline to the past, so we weren't completely adrift. That was what we both needed. Naomi didn't have that. When Naomi left Wahredua, she was…lost. For a long time, I think. She was like me, defensive, hostile, looking for the first hint of a threat. But nobody wants to be like that, and I think she was looking for an alternative. She wanted a father so badly; I don't think I understood that until later, but I should have known. She talked about him a lot, even though neither of us remembered him. She'd talk about what he might be like, or how she might meet him one day. I thought about that too, I guess, but with Naomi—with Naomi it seemed like that was her lifeline. Even when she left for college, she was still…still hoping she'd meet him some day."

"And instead she met Zach Renner," Hazard said.

"I don't know about that. I don't even know that name. Is that the man in the picture?"

Somers nodded.

"I'd never seen him before. But—but I do know something. A little. Naomi disappeared during my freshman year of college. For almost a year, actually. She didn't tell me she was leaving. She didn't tell my mother. She just vanished. It was horrible. For the first few weeks, I thought she was dead. Then I started hearing rumors. She was living out at a farm, sleeping in a barn, with a bunch of people who smoked grass and had sex all day. It didn't sound like my sister, but I borrowed a friend's car and drove out there. And there she was. She was wearing a scarf like that; I suppose it's a hijab, isn't it?"

"It appears to be," Hazard said.

"I didn't know that back then. And she was wearing a long dress. And if she was smoking weed, I couldn't tell—honestly, she seemed more sober than I'd ever seen her since high school. I would have said she looked good, clean, healthy for the first time in a long while. She'd even put on some weight; she always struggled with that. But she was so strange. She talked to me like she didn't know me. She knew my name, sure, but otherwise we might as well have been strangers. She told me to leave. She just kept telling me to leave. So, finally, I left. I called my mom. God, the hours we spent on the phone. We figured she was in a cult—and yes, I know Islam isn't a cult. But what she was involved in, the way she was acting, it felt like a cult. We planned the whole thing, how to hire someone to get her out of there, how to deprogram her. It never went anywhere; I'd tell myself that she looked so much healthier, so much happier, that it couldn't all be bad." Cora shook her head. Her lips compressed into a white line, and then she closed her eyes and shook her head harder.

"Cora," Somers shifted on the couch, "you did what you thought was best—"

She held up a hand, and he stopped. After a moment, she cleared her throat, and she dabbed at her eyes with her fingertips. "She came back to school the next year. She showed up after one of my classes, stood there outside the building like it was something she did all the time, and we went and got coffee. She was back to normal, kind of. She was…harder, I guess. She laughed and smiled and acted like herself, and she didn't seem like a stranger, like the person I'd met out on that farm. But she was different. And I remember we were standing up, grabbing our stuff, when she said kind of off-hand, 'That was his farm.' So, I asked who she was talking about. 'Dad,' she said. 'That's why I went out there.' And I was honestly too stunned to say anything. She shrugged, and she said, 'Biggest mistake of my life. It was just another of his scams.' And she left. Walked away." Cora laughed. "I found out later, he didn't own the farm. He'd been squatting out there with his little commune, and they'd try one religion and then another. The farm was abandoned, but eventually somebody wanted it, and when the police showed up, he took off. He left them. He left Naomi. Abandoned her, again. I think that was—well, the next semester, she was in pre-law classes, and she was a Young Republican, and then the Young Republicans weren't conservative enough for her, and…you see?"

Somers nodded. He risked a look up. He had seen her cry before. He had seen her struggle with tears. During a commercial for wedding rings. When Evie had gotten croup, and Cora hadn't slept three nights so Somers wouldn't have to call in. All those compressed moments near the end, when he had made it so easy for her to hate him as he struck match after match and burned down everything they'd built together.

Hazard rubbed his jaw. "You think that Naomi was radicalized because of that experience with her father."

"I think that I've done a lot of reading about radicalization," Cora said. "And I think it's rarely simple. But I think Naomi wouldn't be who she is today if she hadn't had that experience."

"This man." Hazard tapped the photo. "Did you see him at the farm with her?"

"I don't know, Emery. I don't remember anything from that day except her; for heaven's sake, my father was there, and I didn't even know that."

"John?"

Somers cleared his throat. "Cora, we believe this man was blackmailing Naomi with this photo."

"For what?"

"For appearing to be a convert to Islam. That would have destroyed her standing with the Volunteers—"

"No," Cora said. "What did he want from her?"

"Money is usually the answer," Hazard said. "We have reason to believe that Naomi might have helped Landon steal several million dollars. Zach Renner might have wanted some of that money."

"And you think Naomi killed him."

Somers was still looking for a way to soften it when Hazard said, "Yes."

In the silence that followed, Evie's sing-song voice floated from the back of the house.

"I don't know." Cora's voice was toneless. "It's possible. But isn't there someone else? I thought a boy—"

"There are a lot of possibilities right now," Somers said. Hell, he even sounded like the chief of police sometimes and not the shit-face who used to sleep on the couch and puke into a Crayola bucket he kept close at hand. "We're still considering all of them."

"We know Naomi would have wanted this photo destroyed." Hazard shrugged. "We know two people were involved in an attempt to break into Zach's motel room after his death. One of them was caught, and he has his own reasons for wanting Zach dead. His accomplice was an unidentified woman. It's not hard to string it all together."

"Jesus Christ, Ree," Somers muttered.

"No," Cora waved the words away, "it's all right. I want to know. If you're asking me if she's capable of it—I don't know. Maybe. She's my sister; I—I don't feel like I can say yes, not the way you want me to."

"What we want," Hazard said, "is anything that can help us understand what's going on. You're sure you don't remember anything else about Naomi and Zach?"

"Aside from that visit to the farm, I didn't see her that whole year. All of this—" She gestured to the photo. "—is completely new to me."

"All right," Hazard said. "We should probably talk to your mother as well."

Cora hesitated. "You can try. If she thinks you're after Naomi, she won't give you anything. And to be honest, Emery, I'm not sure she'd remember much. We were scared, but she didn't go looking for Naomi. She knows even less about that time than I do."

Hazard nodded, but what he said was "We'll see."

They all stood at the same time. In the back room, Evie was still singing to herself.

"She won't—I won't tell her you were here." Cora said, and then she let out a bewildered laugh and gave a tiny shake of her head. "I'm sorry. I don't know what I'm supposed to say right now."

"Thank you for talking to us," Hazard said.

Somers met her eyes, the same dark eyes their daughter shared. Her eyes when she shaded them against the sun's glare. Her eyes when she laughed. Her eyes when she watched TV. Her eyes when she closed them to go to sleep.

"I'm sorry," he said.

She shook her head again, and her throat moved, but she didn't say anything.

At the door, though, she spoke. "She wanted a relationship with our father. Badly. She wasn't ever the same after he left her again. I think part of her—I think part of her refused ever to be hurt like that again. If she did something, well, I think that's why."

"You understand that you can't disclose this conversation?" Hazard asked.

"I won't call her and tell her to book a trip to Mexico, Emery."

Deep waters, Somers realized. It felt like being out in waders, the water hitting him at the thigh, threatening to carry him downstream and, at the same time, making it difficult to move in any direction.

"I'll be in the car," Hazard said, stepping out onto the porch.

The sound of his steps changed when he reached the sidewalk. They faded into the distance.

"I am sorry, Cora. I wouldn't have—"

"You were always sorry when it came to work, John-Henry." Her mouth trembled, and she firmed it before saying, "When it came to a lot of things, actually. But you never let it stop you."

CHAPTER TWENTY-FOUR
APRIL 13
MONDAY
7:17 PM

SUNSET WAS THAT BURNED brown and black that made Hazard think of harvest corn, black-eyed Susans, sunflowers. The colors were too old for this time of year. Maybe they were all too old now. If so, nobody had told the dogwoods. Nobody had told the bright pink blossoms of the redbuds that danced in the headlights.

They tried Cora's mother at home, but the little apartment was dark, and the neighbors didn't know when she'd be home. They tried Cora's mother on the phone, but she wasn't answering.

"Doesn't she like to gamble?" Hazard asked as they returned to the Mustang. The night smelled like cigarillos and the spilled can of Mountain Dew that had drained into the gutter. "Would she have her phone if she were playing the slots?"

Somers made a noncommittal noise. He started the Mustang, leaned back in the seat, and stared out the windshield. His eyes were unfocused. He might have been planning on driving them to Mars.

"John?"

"Hm?"

"You've been like this since we left Cora's house. What's going on?"

"Nothing." He ran a hand through his hair, squeezed his eyes shut, and when he opened them again, he was smiling. "Sorry. Kind of got to me, but I'm back."

Hazard studied him, the smile, the voice, the bright eyes. "You don't have to do that."

"Do what?"

"Act like it's ok."

The smile stayed, but it was glassy now around the edges. "You know what? I think maybe I do. I think we've all got ways of dealing with our own shit. Don't you think so, Ree? Don't you think maybe you've dealt with some of your own shit without letting me through the door? What do you think? Maybe once or twice?"

Hazard shifted back. He didn't recognize the movement for what it was—withdrawal, maybe retreat—until he bumped into the door handle. The man he'd been a few years ago was still there, still rattling the bars, shouting that this was a threat, and a threat meant a fight. But that guy didn't run the show anymore—most of the time, anyway—and after a few deep breaths, Hazard had the cell locked tight again.

He took his husband's hand.

"Sorry." Somers squeezed his eyes shut again, and the smile came off. "It—shit, I am really sorry."

"It's all right."

"No—"

"John, it's all right. You're not wrong; we all have ways. I'm sorry I didn't realize—"

Somers stopped him, eyes still shut, with another smile—a real one, this time, small and broken—and a shake of the head. When his eyes came open, their blue was so deep it was almost purple. "We can talk about this another time, I promise, but please not right now."

Hazard nodded.

"You were—what were we talking about?"

"Cora's mother."

"Christ, right. I don't know, Ree. She likes to gamble; she might have her phone off, or on silent."

Hazard was trying to be a good husband. He had read a lot of books on the subject. He decided to let this one go.

"For what it's worth," Somers continued, "I think Cora's right. Even if her mom knew something about Naomi, she wouldn't tell us. She's protective of her girls; she always has been. Talking to her might just send her running to Naomi."

"Naomi can't be unaware of the fact that she's a person of interest in this investigation."

"Not unaware, no. But I don't want her to know how much we've put together. She and Benji are in this together, I'm sure of it."

"They both have motives, but I think Naomi's are stronger. Eliminate Zach, and she gets to keep her position of authority with the Ozark

Volunteers. Eliminate Landon, and she gets to keep the three million dollars they stole from the gun runners. Benji might be involved—"

"Naomi helped Benji try to break into Zach's motel room."

"That's one theory. It could have been another woman. It could have been his friends from that ridiculous nonprofit."

Somers looked exhausted when he rubbed his face. "All right, that's fair. I'm jumping to conclusions. So, who took those shots at North and Shaw? Who tossed their room?"

"Either Benji or Naomi."

"Christ, we're back where we started."

"We know they both had motive. We know that they both had reason to want this photo. That's more than we knew a couple of hours ago."

"Great," Somers said with a lopsided smile. "But why doesn't it feel like it?"

"Naomi?"

"I think so," Somers said as he pulled away from the curb. "With Benji, all we have are theories. We've got something Naomi wants; let's see if it's enough to make her roll over."

They drove out of town, into the wilderness of bare fields and the past year's corn stubble, the white flash of cockspur flowers, like imperfect pearls caught in the headlights. They found Naomi's house, the modernist monstrosity tucked away behind a curtain of oak and white pine and fallow fields. The gibbous moon was waning, but what was left of it poured silver onto the blank faces of the windows. Darker, Hazard thought, looking at the moon. He tore his gaze away. Everything was getting darker.

Benji's Scion xD looked the color of an overripe avocado in the leached light of the moon. He had parked in front of the door again.

"Like he owns the place," Somers said as he came to a stop, the crunch of gravel falling silent under him.

"What's he doing here?"

"Probably not selling Girl Scout cookies." When Hazard looked over, he flushed. "Sorry—North and Shaw might be rubbing off on me."

"God Almighty, don't let them hear you use that phrasing."

They were at the door when they heard the crack of a blow and Naomi's sharp cry, both sounds distinct even muffled by the door.

"That sounds like probable cause," Somers said, pushing back his coat to ease the Glock out of its holster. He took out his phone and placed a call back to the station for backup.

"Motherfucker," Hazard swore. "I left the Blackhawk in the Odyssey. Why do I have a fucking gun if it's always locked up in a fucking safe?"

"Yeah, I've got thoughts about that, but let's save them for later. Do you have your picks—"

But as Somers asked the question, he was trying the handle, a reflexive action. He cut off as the door swung open. The smell of vanilla and sandalwood and a cold, dry something that his brain read as *crypt* floated out to them, along with voices too quiet to make out the words.

Somers went first—Hazard decided that the Blackhawk had just been promoted to every-day carry, even if it meant more hassle—and Hazard gave him room to maneuver before following.

Inside, the entry hall was dark. Light filtered out to them from somewhere deeper in the house, barely enough for Hazard to make out the shadows of his surroundings. He shut the door and set the deadbolt. When Somers took off down the hall, Hazard grabbed the most offensive trinket, an abstract metal sculpture, and followed. How abstract, he wondered with a dark glitter of satisfaction, would it feel to have your head smashed in with a third-year art student's B- effort?

Ahead, a rectangle of light marked an open doorway. Raised voices came from within.

"—I'll do it." That was Benji. "Not everybody. I'll show that human nut sack who follows you around. And he'll tell somebody else. And you might still have a chance, then. You might be able to convince them it's a trick or a lie. But if you still won't give me what I want, I'll show somebody else. And then you'll really have to hop to it, won't you?"

"Benji, please, I'm—"

"I don't care who you are!" The words were distorted with rage. The sound of flesh striking flesh followed, and Naomi cried out again. "I'm getting out of here, and I want that fucking money! They're talking to my family about me now. Do you understand that? And I am sick and tired of being pushed and shoved and pulled and dragged wherever the hell everybody else wants. I'm not going to do it anymore. That money is mine! It should be mine!"

"I don't have it!" That, at least, sounded more like the Naomi Hazard knew—full of rage, unyielding. "Why can't anyone get that through their thick heads? You're as bad as those two assholes he stole from. I'll tell you what I told them: I didn't know about that money, I didn't have anything to do with that money, and I sure as hell don't have that money. If you want it, you can get it from Landon. Good fucking luck!"

The silence that followed had a ragged, torn quality like a wound.

Then, in a too-calm voice, Benji said, "I think you're lying."

That was when Somers reached the door. Hazard felt the silent three-count before Somers spun, kicked open the door, and shouted, "Down, down, everybody down!"

"What the fuck?" Benji shouted.

"John-Henry?" Naomi sounded stunned.

"Get your asses down!" Somers shouted. He pressed into the room. "I said down!"

When Hazard stepped through the doorway, he took a heartbeat to assess the situation: Benji looked like he was still waffling between doing something stupid and following Somers's orders, but Naomi had dropped onto the floor. The bedroom was large, and it was decorated mostly in white: an enormous white bed, white carpet, white paint. Small decorative touches were silver or stainless steel. The only color was a painting of an enormous red flower that reminded Hazard, uncomfortably under these circumstances, of Georgia O'Keeffe.

"He's got my gun," Naomi said.

The flicker of surprise on Benji's face went out almost immediately, but it had been there.

"Keep those hands up," Somers told him.

"You cunt," Benji said. "You stupid fucking cunt, I am going to ruin you."

"Ree?"

"Don't do anything stupid," Hazard said as he approached Benji from the side. "You don't want to end your existence the victim of some fucking Bard grad student's art portfolio."

Benji made a face, but he kept still as Hazard patted him down. He found the pistol tucked into the back of his waistband, and he removed it carefully—a SAR 9, textured black polymer frame and grip, usually seventeen in the magazine and one in the chamber. Usually. If it was fully loaded. Hazard's quick search yielded nothing else, and when he stepped back, Somers motioned with the Glock, and Benji dropped onto the floor.

"Jesus Christ," Hazard said. He was breathing faster. The SAR's polymer felt greasy in his grip.

Somers's pulse was up, his color high, his pupils dilated. "Everybody's going to stay right where they are until my officers get here. Is that clear?"

"Fuck off," Benji said. "We were having a conversation, that's all."

"I've seen conversations like that before," Hazard said.

"Shut the fuck up."

"I don't know, I think we've got a lot to talk about. We could start by talking about the money you've been embezzling from the nonprofit. Or were you stealing from Zach directly? Or both?"

"I want my lawyer."

"Sure. It won't be that hard to figure out once we have access to the paperwork; you're not exactly a criminal mastermind."

"I'm not saying anything until I've got a lawyer."

"Did you hear that, John? He wants his lawyer."

"I haven't decided if I'm taking him into custody yet," Somers said. "I'm waiting on my officers to arrive so we can sort this out."

"I don't have to say anything!" Benji sounded like a child. "I have a right to remain silent!"

"For somebody who's not saying anything, you sure open your mouth a fucking lot." Hazard kept his grip loose around the SAR. He was aware he was ruining prints, but that horse was out of the barn as soon as he took it away from Benji. And right then, he wanted a gun. "What were you going to do if she didn't pay?"

"We're not talking," Naomi said. "We're not saying anything."

"Let's assume she's telling the truth, although with Naomi, that's a stupid assumption. But for the sake of argument, let's assume she didn't know anything about the money Landon stole from those gun runners. Fine. A bit stupid on her part not to be more involved, but fine. What were you going to do when you kept pressing her and she wouldn't give up the money because she couldn't, because she didn't have it? What then?"

"Don't talk to them," Naomi said.

"John, how effective is blackmail if you're not willing to deploy it?"

"Well, it's kind of a catch-22 situation," Somers said. "If you use it, you blew your shot. But if you don't use it, well, they might call your bluff."

"You don't know what you're talking about," Benji said. "We were having a conversation."

"I know that you were trying to blackmail her with a photograph belonging to your brother."

Naomi flinched. Benji's hands, open against the carpet, tightened and then relaxed again.

"And," Somers said, in that oh-so-casual-buddy-next-door voice he'd perfected, "I know that you don't have it."

Naomi's head came up. Surprise painted her face.

"How—" Benji began. Then he shook his head as best he could while lying on the floor. "This is all bullshit."

"Oh no," Hazard said. "We found the photo. That's what you were looking for the night you got busted in the motel, isn't it? You weren't worried about the financial paperwork; your family would have found a way to sweep those irregularities under the rug. You wanted the picture. And you told Naomi that if she helped you distract the police officer on duty, you'd give her the photo. Is that about it?"

Naomi had lowered her head again. A wall was going up, her face blank and unreadable. Benji was wriggling on the floor, obviously pissed and unused to being unable to vent his anger.

"I figure we've got, oh, ten minutes before the other officers arrive. Is that about right, John?"

"I'd say seven. We've got an excellent response time, even for out-of-the-way hidey-holes like this one."

"I think seven is optimistic, but you're the chief of police, so I assume that part of your job is projected optimism about the competency of your officers."

"Not at all. My job is to be realistic and to expect peak performance."

"All right. Just to be safe, let's go with John's number. Seven minutes. That means one of you has seven minutes to convince me that the other killed Zachary Renner and Landon Maas." Stretching the truth as much as he dared, Hazard added, "I've got motive and evidence on both of you, so you'll need to be extremely convincing. Ready, set, go."

The silence had a staticky, stunned quality to it. Then Benji said hoarsely, "You're out of your fucking mind if you think—"

"I did it." Naomi spoke clearly, even with her face pressed against the carpet again. "I killed Zach and Landon. I shot both of them. I did it."

It took a moment. "What—"

Naomi got up on her knees.

"Stay down," Somers ordered.

She got to her feet.

"Get on the floor!"

Next to her, Benji got to one knee, gauged everything for a moment, and then surged up.

"You're in violation of a direct order," Somers said. "Naomi, Benji, get back on the floor right now."

"There's no need for any of this." Naomi's voice was iron, but her color was hectic, and her eyes were wet. When she turned to speak into the middle distance, not meeting anyone's gaze, the lamps caught the unshed tears like lightning strikes. "I've confessed. Arrest me, and then take me to the station. Under the advice of my attorney, I will make a full written confession."

"We'll get into all that." Somers gestured with the Glock. "For now, I want you both to get down and wait until my officers arrive."

"Why? What don't you understand? I followed Landon to the motel. I knew he was going to confront Zach; he wanted to continue their argument from the gun show. I needed to remove Zach, of course. I never thought I'd see him again, let alone that he'd kept photographs from that time. I can only assume he planned to blackmail me; that's the only explanation for why he brought that picture with him to Wahredua. But he was always stupid. He was stupid enough to get dragged into Daddy's cult out at the farm, and he was too stupid to know what to do with himself when Daddy disappeared. Honestly, you should have heard the nonsense Daddy got them to swallow. Muslim this week, Hindu the next, then Buddhist, then a different kind of Buddhist." She shook her head and smiled. "Don't you want to record this?"

"Naomi—"

"Landon had ruined everything by stealing that money. He was stupid; I told him not to do it. But he was always greedy and overconfident. He always wanted more. More money than he could earn peddling guns for a third-rate manufacturer. More attention than he could rightfully get as an out-of-shape high school star. More from his son than his son was capable of. More, more, more. When I saw them together, I realized how much easier my life would be if they were both gone. After, I framed Carson. He had drunk himself unconscious; he made it so easy. The only thing that went wrong was that I couldn't find that picture. Zach must have known I'd try to get it back. He wasn't going to give it up easily."

An alarm was ringing in the basement of Hazard's brain. He knew something was wrong—the blotchy emotion filling her face, the urgency of her voice, the confession itself, which was completely out of character for a woman who had fenced herself in with lawyers. His brain tried to build an answer, but all he had were impressions, bits and pieces: the photo of Naomi in a hijab and dress, her face fuller than Hazard had ever seen it, standing next to Zach outside the mosque; the story of Naomi's search for her ex-con father, Cora saying, *She'd even put on some weight*; tonight, Benji saying, *I don't care who you are*; Benji himself, so young, stamped with Zach's features, his face a mixture of wariness and fury, no hint of compassion or grief for the brother he'd lost—

It was like turning a piece of a puzzle round and round, and all of a sudden it slid home.

He heard Somers's breath catch.

"You're not Zachary Renner's brother," Hazard said.

Benji swiveled to look at Naomi; that was all the confirmation Hazard needed.

He followed Benji's gaze to study Naomi. She was staring back at him, and he was surprised to read there a splinter of something. Pleading. Somers might have considered it, but Somers was a much more forgiving person than Hazard was.

"He's your son," Hazard said. "Yours and Zach's, and you—"

"Ree," Somers shouted, "watch out!"

Hazard looked over in time to see the red dot of a laser sight gliding across the carpet.

CHAPTER TWENTY-FIVE
APRIL 13
MONDAY
7:36 PM

THE RED DOT OF the laser sight rushed toward them.

Hazard had an instant to process everything as Somers dragged him toward the door to the bathroom and shouted, "Everybody down!"

Naomi screamed wordlessly and flung herself sideways. In front of Benji. Her body jerked once, and she stumbled. Benji caught her under the arms. It all had a bizarre gracefulness to it, like something out of a ballet, Benji sagging as he tried to keep her upright. Blood was spreading across Naomi's shirt. The crack of shattering glass and, a deeper note, the gunshot, came an instant later.

"Get in the bathroom, get in the bathroom," Somers was shouting.

Benji's face twisted, and he caught his balance. He shoved Naomi away from him. She stumbled and went down, letting out a cry when she hit the floor.

The next shot caught the wall above Benji's shoulder. Gypsum dust exploded in a tiny cloud, spackling the side of Benji's face. He shrieked, the noise competing with the clap of the gunshot.

Somers had taken up position in the doorway, kneeling now, and he fired through the window. The thunder of the gunshots made Hazard's ears ring. These guys were good, he reminded himself, but they weren't pros, and the fact that Somers was firing blind through the window didn't matter—the natural reaction, until you got it trained out of you, was to go for cover when somebody started shooting in your direction.

He took advantage of the brief seconds that the shooter—or shooters—was pinned down. Tucking the SAR into his waistband, he launched himself toward Naomi. He reached her in two huge strides. She was facedown, shaking, and blood was already staining the carpet under her. When Hazard flipped her over, her eyes were rolled up in her head. He didn't have time for more than a cursory glance at the wound, but it was bad: a mess of ruined flesh high on her abdomen, thick blood pumping out steadily. He lifted her; she felt like she weighed nothing, but that was mostly the adrenaline talking. Two huge strides later, he was past Somers, in the safety of the windowless bathroom, lowering Naomi onto the white tile floor.

White towels. A frameless shower. A little white soap shaped like a swan. He yanked one of the towels from the bar and began packing the wound. It was as ugly as it had always sounded in training, forcing the fabric into the damaged flesh, violating her body in yet another way. Naomi screamed and tried to lurch upright, clawing at Hazard's arm, her bloody hands slick against his skin. Then she went still. She was the color of cold ash, but she was breathing.

"John!"

Somers's breathing was ragged; he was still crouched by the doorway, the Glock in one white-knuckled hand. "You ok?"

The clap of the gunshots still rang out in Hazard's ear, and all he could smell was gunpowder. "Fine. You?"

"Fine. Motherfuckers. It's got to be those goddamn gun runners. How is she?"

"Not good."

"We just need to hang on. Officers will be here any minute. They're going to light this place up. We can—shit! Where the hell is Benji?"

Hazard weighed his options. Then he said, "I don't know, but I need you to come over here."

Somers scooted back from the door.

"Press here," Hazard said. His own hands were dark with blood now as he indicated the towel. "If you can pack more into the wound, great, but that's as much as I could manage."

Somers laid the Glock on the tile and leaned on the towel, using both hands to direct as much of his weight onto the packing as he dared. "Ree, what are you—"

"Going to get Benji."

"Are you out of your mind? No. No fucking way!"

"John, they'll kill him. And we need him to figure this shit out."

"I said no—"

"This isn't a discussion. Someone needs to stay with Naomi. You need to call your officers and alert them that there is an active shooter, more likely multiple shooters, so they don't walk into this blind. You can't do that and find Benji, so that means I'm doing it."

"Let them kill him! You know what he is, what he did."

"Yeah?" Hazard asked, settling the SAR in his grip. "Is that what you'd be saying if we switched right now?"

Somers set his jaw. "I'm the chief of police. I should —"

"Call your officers," Hazard said as he edged toward the doorway. The smell of blood and gunpowder still filled his nose, but now, faintly, another odor reached him: the cool, chill air of a spring night filtering through the broken window. "Take control of the scene. That's your job."

"God fucking damn it."

"I know."

"Please be careful."

"Obviously."

"I will murder you if you get yourself killed."

Hazard decided to leave that one; this level of shit wasn't covered in the good husband books, but he figured it might not be the right time to quibble about logic.

"Love you," he said instead.

He was out the door, sprinting across the room, as Somers echoed the words back to him. He ran at full speed until he cleared the door to the hallway, and even then he was waiting for the impact, for the second-after crack of gunfire. But nothing came, and after another moment, he realized he'd cleared the first hurdle.

The smell of stomach acid came to him, and up the hall he spotted a puddle of vomit, presumably where Benji had stopped to be sick after getting free of the bedroom. Good. That would have slowed him down, bought Hazard a few extra seconds to make up for time lost saving Naomi. He scanned the hallway, spotted the closest light switch, and ran for it. He slapped it off and kept running, his eyes locked on the huge windows at the end of the hall. Darkness came down around him like a noose, but he figured unless these guys had some sort of night gear, dark was better than being taken down by a potshot. He kept running, weaving from side to side in case they did have night gear, until he rounded the corner. This hallway was already dark, so he kept going. Ahead, maybe ten feet away, an archway connected with the entry hall.

He slowed as he reached the opening. From nearby came panicked breathing and sobs of frustration. The front door rattled and thumped in its frame. The deadbolt, Hazard guessed. He had thrown the deadbolt when they'd come inside, and now Benji, blind with terror, couldn't get it open. He exhaled, trying to steady the hand holding the SAR, and darted into the entry hall.

In the gloom, Benji stood at the front door, yanking with both hands, making those choked noises as he tried to escape.

"Benji," Hazard said softly.

Benji turned the handle again and pulled, a sob building in his throat.

"Benji!"

The boy flinched and spun around.

"What the fuck are you doing? You think they're going to let you walk out of here?"

Benji stared at him. His eyes were hard and feral.

"Come on," Hazard said. "We're going to hole up until—"

Glass shattered behind him, in the hallway where he had just come from. Not the shatter of a bullet cracking glass—this was longer, cascading, the sound of someone knocking all the glass out of a window.

"Fuck," Hazard said. He crossed the room, grabbed Benji's arm, and hauled him toward the opening on the opposite side of the entry hall. "We can't go that way. Come on, we've got to find somewhere those asshats can't pick us off."

They passed the dining room with its massive table set with what looked like service for fifty. They passed more of the little side tables and end tables set with sculptures and figurines and little bowls full of polished pieces of metal, like chips of frozen mercury. Ahead, an opening connected with Naomi's enormous living room, where a wall of windows looked out on the rolling hills—

The sweeping shatter of glass came from ahead of them.

Hazard stopped

"What are we—" Benji tried to say; it was almost blubbering.

"Be quiet."

Voices behind him. Low, confident.

Then, ahead, so clear that it sounded like they were in the same room: "I told you, I saw those spooks go inside." Someone must have said something in the pause because then the man continued, "I don't give a good God damn what Brother Gerrit says; I'm not letting them walk off with three million dollars."

"For fuck's sake," Hazard said under his breath, turning Benji back toward the dining room they had passed. "Could I catch a fucking break? For once in my fucking life?"

"What—"

"I said be quiet," Hazard snapped.

More windows looked out on the rawboned hills and cornfields, and the light that made it into the dining room was so attenuated that it was more like smoke. This wasn't where Hazard wanted to make his stand; there was a doorway at the back of the room that connected with the kitchen, and he had no way of fortifying himself in this space. He kept Benji moving. All the fight had been scared out of him, and he stumbled along under Hazard's prodding. They passed through the swinging door into the kitchen; the smell of some sort of floral cleaner met them, along with the cool blue glow from digital clocks, the light twisting along stainless steel and granite.

Two openings, one to his right and one to his left, and another door directly across the room.

"Fuck," Hazard said as he pushed Benji forward.

The door opposite them led into a pantry, which was a small win. He shut Benji inside, ignoring the boy's wordless whine of protest. He returned to the door that connected with the dining room and yanked at his laces until his boots came loose. He wedged first one, then the other under the door. It wasn't perfect; someone who tried hard enough would be able to force the door open. But it would buy him seconds.

Voices were drifting toward him through the opening that connected with the living room, and Hazard controlled his breathing to keep his heart rate from rocketing. He slid open drawers and eased open cabinet doors, trying to be as quiet as he could as he assessed his situation. He found the knife block. He found a fire extinguisher. He found kitchen twine. He found shears and a sharpening steel and an end-grain butcher's block that made him think of a checkerboard. He found the flatware and had an idea. Carrying a handful of knives and forks, he crossed to the microwave and opened the door. He laid the flatware inside and set a delayed timer. Two minutes.

Through the other opening, the one that led toward the bedrooms, voices were getting louder. That was Korrin and Larenz, Hazard guessed; the gun runners had obviously planned this better than the Herdsmen, and after sniping through the window, they were most likely making their way toward Naomi's bedroom. Sure enough, a moment later Hazard could hear Somers's voice, loud enough for him to identify the tone as a challenge, even though the words were indistinct.

Please, Hazard thought. It was a wingless prayer, but he let it loose anyway.

He opened the pantry door again, and Benji whispered, "Oh thank God—" before Hazard shoved him back again. Hazard took a broom and, after a moment of scanning the shelves, a bottle of cooking oil. He shut the door again. There was something surprisingly satisfying about the look of disbelief on Benji's face.

Across the opening that led to the living room, he laid the broom at an angle, wedging it under the cabinets to keep it from falling. Then he poured the cooking oil across the tile. He grabbed the fire extinguisher and retreated to the corner that was exposed to the opening that led to the bedrooms; he figured that was the lesser of two evils.

The timer on the microwave had seven seconds left.

He realized, in that instant, he'd forgotten to check his load. The SAR 9 usually had seventeen in the magazine, plus one in the chamber. If it had been fully loaded. If some of the cartridges hadn't been fired.

The microwave dinged, and then it activated with a hiss of static and fizzing light.

"What was that?" a man said from the living room.

Everything happened quickly: the hammer of footsteps from the living room, the shadow in the opening, the crack of his leg connecting with the broom, and then a startled cry changing into something that sounded almost cartoonish—a "whoa-oa" as the man came down on the other side of the broom, trying to catch his balance, and slipped in the oil. The crack of his head against the tile didn't sound good. The assault rifle he'd been carrying fell from his hand and skittered along the ceramic flooring. Dumbass should have used a strap.

The microwave was still crackling and hissing.

"Denny?" another man shouted; the name was a cocktail of confusion and outrage. "What the hell—"

Another shadow appeared in the doorway and then stopped, pulling back before the broom. Then the assault rifle dropped down, the barrel pointed off into the darkness, and the muzzle flash gave a stuttering illumination.

Hazard aimed. Breathed. Squeezed off two shots.

Silence swallowed up the roar of gunfire. Darkness pulled tight, and the shadow in the doorway dropped away.

From the other end of the house, gunshots erupted. Korrin and Larenz trying to get to Somers.

Fire extinguisher hanging from one hand, SAR in the other, Hazard started off at a jog.

He had gone two paces when a shadow appeared in the opening ahead of him.

Stupid, Hazard told himself. Stupid, stupid. Just because one of them was shooting at Somers didn't mean they both were.

The silhouette of a pistol came up, and the glimmer of night sights swung toward Hazard.

He squeezed off a shot and threw himself to the side. Something buzzed past his cheek. Bee, he thought. No, bullet. The thunderclaps from the guns made Hazard's ears ring. He fired again, only nothing happened. He depressed the trigger. Still nothing. It took precious moments for realization to penetrate the adrenaline haze.

Seventeen plus one. If it's fully loaded.

The shape in the opening was turning, trying to track him; whoever it was, his own night vision had been ruined by the muzzle flash, and he was having trouble finding Hazard again. It wouldn't last long. The kitchen was too damn small.

"I thought it was the other guys who were going to be trouble." The voice belonged to Larenz. "The big blond one and his twink. When we checked out Renner's motel, thinking maybe that bitch Landon had stashed our money there, they were snooping around. I thought for sure they'd beat us to the cash. And then you fucked up my shot outside their motel, and I realized all y'all might be trouble. Tell me—"

Hazard didn't wait for the rest; whatever question Larenz wanted to bait him with, Hazard refused to bite. He chucked the SAR. His shot might have gone wide, but the pistol itself made a satisfying thump as it connected, and the figure in the opening grunted. Then Hazard pulled the pin on the fire extinguisher, aimed the nozzle, and depressed the lever. A spray of chemical powder shot out. The man in the opening shouted in surprise, his hands coming up to protect his face. The stink of ammonia mixed with the fresh burn of gunpowder. Hazard's eyes watered; he kept the nozzle aimed at the man in the opening and scooted backward. He'd get out through the dining room—

But the man brought his gun down and began to fire blindly. The first shot went wide; Hazard saw it punch through the oven door. The next one shattered the tile next to Hazard's right hand.

And then the gunman jerked. He took a step, and even in the dark, Hazard could tell something was off: it was undirected, almost exploratory, like he'd stumbled into the kitchen and wasn't sure he was allowed. Then he went down, and the gun cracked against the ceramic flooring.

Hazard sucked in a breath. Then another. The fire extinguisher was empty now, but he couldn't let go of the lever, and his lungs were hot with gunpowder and ammonia. Static hissed in his ears; too many gunshots in a too-small space.

The voice sounded far off, small: "Ree?"

He got onto his knees, slipped in the dry but surprisingly slick powder that the extinguisher had discharged, planted both hands, and got up again.

"Ree?"

"Here." He managed to drop the extinguisher. It made a hollow, metallic ding when it hit the floor. "Clear. In here."

Somers appeared in the opening, the shape of him familiar even in the darkness. He kicked away the fallen man's gun. A moment later, lights flared overhead, and Hazard blinked and squinted, trying to inspect his husband. His coat was askew, and his hair was mussed worse than ever, and he was pale, but he didn't appear to be hurt.

"Are you—"

"Fine."

Somers collided with him, pulling him into a hug, and Hazard grunted. Then he hugged his husband back.

From the front of the house came the sound of wood splintering, and then a voice called, "Police!"

"Seven minutes," Hazard muttered in his husband's ear.

Somers squeezed him tighter. Hazard could sense him looking around the kitchen.

"What?" Hazard asked.

"I thought you had a gun."

CHAPTER TWENTY-SIX
APRIL 14
TUESDAY
2:11 PM

SOMERS'S HEADACHE WAS A low-intensity klaxon that seemed determined to ramp up into something a whole hell of a lot worse. The brightness of the April day didn't help. He hurried across the parking lot toward Wahredua Regional, shading his eyes and wishing he hadn't left his sunglasses—and his Tylenol—in the Mustang.

The rest of the night had been the kind of procedural morass that followed any shooting, but magnified by the involvement of a major figure from the Ozark Volunteers, as well as one dead man and one injured man who could be traced back to Gerrit Maas's Herdsmen, and the presence of two dead men whom Hazard identified as the gun runners Korrin and Larenz. It had taken all night and into the morning to make a dent in processing Naomi's house; the sheriff's department had turned up in force to help, and Somers's father had been on the phone with Missouri Highway Patrol to wring whatever resources he could out of them. The search was on for Gerrit and his wife, who had vanished, and for Brother Newell, who was still in the wind. Somers thought Newell, at least, might never be found—at least, not if the Herdsmen found him first.

Eventually, Somers had sent Hazard home. Hours later, when he had gotten five minutes to run home and shower, he had found the big man asleep in their bed. Somers had been extra quiet. He had tried not even to splash. For a while, he had stood there under the spray, turning the water colder and colder until his face and neck and shoulders felt numb. The pounding water took on a rhythm that sounded like falling bodies, footsteps. The first gunman hitting the ground after Somers dropped him. Shots from deeper in the house. His own steps slapping the boards as he raced to find Hazard, hoping he wasn't too late. He blinked into the water, the water needling him. He closed his eyes again. He stood there until he didn't hear anything anymore, and the numbness had changed to dull, pinprick hurt.

Now, after a few hours at the station dealing with the logistics of the mess waiting for him, he was heading into the hospital. He grimaced at the rush of cleaner and what he thought might be the beef-and-noodle casserole from the cafeteria. He checked in at the desk, rode the elevator up, and let a weary smile slip out when the doors opened.

"I thought you were napping."

Hazard looked up from his phone, already scowling. "I'm not a child, John. I don't 'nap.'" He invested the word with particular scorn. "And I heard you in the shower. You were supposed to get in bed with me. I had plans."

Somers kissed his cheek. "Did those plans involve snoring? Because you were sawing logs when I came out of the bathroom."

A hint of red dusted Hazard's cheekbones as he pocketed his phone. "That was a decoy. Did you talk to Jalisa?"

"Yep. Dulac already checked it out." He let Hazard wait a beat, because sometimes the big man was too smart for his own good, and then he said, "You were right."

Hazard looked so damn pleased with himself, and trying not to show it, that Somers had to bite the inside of his cheek

He checked the room numbers, but he didn't need to—at the end of the hall, he could see Patrick Foley, former beat cop and current all-star desk jockey, sitting in a tubular chair outside a door. He was examining his phone raptly, and he didn't look up until they were within twenty feet. Then he made a face and turned back to the screen.

"Maybe instead of watching porn," Hazard said, "you could do your job and guard a dangerous prisoner."

"Yeah, but I'd rather watch porn."

Then a woman's voice came over the phone's speakers, saying, "Today I'm going to be unboxing the Fashionista Fillies hair salon, complete with Jezebel and Rhonda, who are exclusive to this set—"

Face bright red, Foley tapped the screen frantically until the voice stopped. He stared at it for a moment. Then he muttered, "Chloe's birthday is in a couple of weeks."

Hazard snorted.

"Fuck you, you know?"

Grinning, Somers held out his hand for the sign-in clipboard. He added himself and Hazard to the list, and then he passed it back to Foley.

"The better value," Hazard was saying, "is the salon with the hoof-and-nail parlor expansion because you get six of the Fillies, including Kandi, that's with a K and an I, and you can't get her anywhere else, and your dollar-to-Filly ratio comes out at—"

"Ok," Somers said. "We'll set up a playdate later."

"Yeah," Foley said, "Chloe and Evie—"

"I meant the two of you."

"Fuck you, Chief, and I mean that with the utmost respect. Fuck both of you motherfuckers."

"John, it's simple math, and if he's going to be buying toys while he's supposed to be on the clock, he might as well do so economically. The formula I wrote for the spreadsheet calculates toy-to-child happiness in one column and a toy utility index that is based on the cost of the toy, the child's satisfaction, the relative difficulty of acquiring the toy—"

"Come on." Somers steered him toward the door.

Foley shifted in his seat. "Uh, Emery, so that spreadsheet—"

When Hazard tried to turn around, Somers breathed, "Good Lord," and redirected him.

Inside the hospital room, the air smelled faintly like urine and loose bowels and a stronger chemical disinfectant. The April day's brightness fell in thin lines through the closed blinds, the only light, which left the room dim except for the illuminated displays of the equipment. Naomi looked smaller inside the hospital gown. The tan, the hair, the elegant lines of her body—they were the same, and yet they were different, like the edges had been taken off with a grindstone. Some of that was the light, Somers thought. But not all of it.

Her eyes stayed closed, and voice was crackly when she said, "I was wondering when you'd come."

"It's been a busy night," Somers said. He took one of the chairs; Hazard sat next to him. "And a busy day. How are you?"

Her eyes opened. Dark. Lusterless. Ink that had already dried. "I'll survive."

"Yet another trait you share with cockroaches," Hazard said.

To Somers's surprise, Naomi smiled—a tiny, razored thing that she pocketed again almost immediately. "Are you ready for me to repeat my confession? I assume it will need a little more official standing than this. I'd like a lawyer. And the county attorney, of course. And you should probably have a few witnesses; our history isn't exactly a secret, and I wouldn't want anyone to think that anything untoward was happening."

Somers raised his eyebrows. "What are you planning on confessing, Naomi?"

"I killed Landon and Zach."

"No, you didn't."

"Of course I did. I'm telling you right now. I needed to obtain that photograph before Zach attempted to blackmail me. And I wanted the money that Landon had stolen from those gun runners."

"Right," Hazard said. "The same money you told Benji you didn't have."

"Can you corroborate any of that?" Somers asked. "How do I know you're not making this up?"

"I've told you how I followed Landon. I've told you my motives. I've told you how I framed Carson—how many other people would have remembered Landon's favorite way of humiliating that boy, making him wear his mother's clothes? The blood-soaked dress, that was a nice touch. And he really thought he'd done it. Isn't that the most spectacular part?"

"That's all circumstantial evidence, Naomi. Don't you have anything that puts you at the scene?"

"Like what? I didn't write my name in their blood; I assumed, John-Henry, that I would get away with this."

"How about the murder weapon?" Hazard asked. "That'd be a nice start."

"Don't be ridiculous. I disposed of it. I threw it down a storm drain; I don't even know where, so I won't be able to help you retrieve it, unfortunately."

"You told us you were in St. Louis," Somers said quietly. "To meet with donors."

"I lied."

Somers shook his head. "We verified with the donors and with your hotel—"

"They lied."

"They've got a picture of your car on their doorbell camera."

"I checked in early at the hotel and then immediately turned around and came back to Wahredua."

"Not unless somebody else was in your room. I finally got the hotel statement this morning, Naomi. You charged an on-demand movie to the room a little after ten. You couldn't have come back to Wahredua, killed them, and gotten back in time. It's not possible."

"I had a friend—"

"For fuck's sake," Hazard growled. "We know it wasn't you. Cut the bullshit. We know it was Benji. We know he's your kid, yours and Zach's. Do you want to know what I think happened? I think Benji didn't know about you, did he? Not until he and Daddy Dearest came to Wahredua. And then, after you and Zach had your face-off at the gun show, he found out. Zach told him. That was it, wasn't it? He had no idea who you were, no idea you even existed, and then all of a sudden, there you were. Do you think maybe that was Zach's plan all along? Do you think he wanted Benji to meet you?"

Naomi looked bloodless. Her mouth was clamped shut, her lips white.

"Play it," Hazard said, dropping back in his chair.

Outside, somewhere in the parking lot down below, a horn honked, and a woman shouted, "Fred, knock it off!"

Somers took out his phone and pressed play.

Benji's voice came over the speaker: "He was such a dick. He'd put on this big show about how important I was, how much he loved me, and we'd do family photos and we'd go on vacation and he'd take me to dinners with his friends. And then the next week, he'd be off on some other stupid bullshit, like he was going to be a monk or live in a commune or just wanted to get a college girl to suck his dick, so he was going back to school for the fourteenth time—and whatever it was, it didn't include me. So he'd send me to boarding school. And when that didn't work, he'd send me to these—to these camps. For troubled teens. And some places, they wouldn't give you food, and some places, they'd hit you, and some places they'd tie you up so at night—" Benji's breathing was harsh, labored. "And then, six months later, a year later, he'd want a son again, and he'd pick me up, and—and it was supposed to be normal. Like nothing had ever happened. I think he honestly believed that. I think if it had been up to him, he'd have just put me in the fucking attic until he was ready for me again."

"Turn it off," Naomi said, her voice thick and pitchy. A tear had slipped free; it ran down the side of her nose.

"He was going to hurt my dad. He was saying these things, these awful things, and my dad was yelling back, and—and I don't know, I grabbed his gun and shot him. He was going to hurt my dad. He was going to kill him!" His voice rose, urgent and insistent. Then the imperfect silence of the recording hissed in the background. He spoke again, quieter now, but still insistent. "I had to do it. And my dad, the look on his face. 'You did that. You did it. You have to tell them you did it.' That's when I figured it out. He was going to do it again. I'd just saved his life, and he was going to throw me to the cops, let them have me, so he could save his own ass. I—I wasn't going to do it again. I wasn't going to go to one of those places again. Especially not for him."

Somers's voice came on the recording: "You shot Landon Maas and Zachary Renner."

"I shot them." Benji snuffled. "I didn't know what to do. And then I did. I knew who would help me. She'd help me. She had to help me; she was my mom." His voice brightened, as though he'd been struck by a sudden idea. "Hey, she did a lot of bad stuff to cover it up. If I tell you about it, can I get, like, immunity or something?"

"You'd do that to your own mother?"

Benji's answering noise blended contempt and amusement. "I just met her. I was going to tell you she did it—her prints are all over that gun; I made sure she touched it a bunch of times. She wanted to use it to set up Carson, but I figured I should hold on to it. You know, kind of like a backup? Plus she's got a good motive. She told me about the gunrunners that night when she came to help me. She said maybe we could make it look like they did it, all that money Landon stole. I didn't think she'd have such a good alibi."

Somers turned off the recording.

More tears had leaked free. Naomi stared straight ahead, her face rigid, but after a moment she reached up to wipe them away.

"He confessed," Somers said gently, "because we found the murder weapon, and it has his prints on it as well as yours. It was a pretty good hiding spot, actually. Emery figured it out."

"What better place to hide a gun than a gun show?" Hazard said with a grim smile. "Or an ass-backward non-profit dedicated to gun control? He slipped it in with the other guns that Zach had put there as 'seed money' to convince other people to trade in their firearms. Unfortunately, his backup plan to frame you didn't pan out."

"He would have been better off dumping it down a storm drain like you said," Somers said. "But he's barely more than a kid, and he's a smart one. Sometimes the smart ones are too smart for their own good."

One of the machines beeped steadily. Naomi's tears had stopped. She wiped her face again, and her fingers tracked a crescent smear across her cheek, a salt-glitter in the weak light. "Yes," she said thickly. "That was Zachary too. Terribly smart, but not much of a planner. As you said: too smart for his own good. He wanted so desperately to be good. But he wanted attention more; even when I knew him, he was like that, jumping from one project to the next, trying so hard to be an activist, to change the world, but wanting that first flash of satisfaction and approval more. It drove his parents crazy." Her lips trembled in what might have been a smile. "It drove me crazy."

"Where did you meet?"

"At my dad's—" She swallowed. "At the farm. We were together six months, give or take. It would have been longer—" She smiled, a twisty little thing. "But I was worried my father would disapprove. That didn't last. Obviously. I found out my father was...not who I thought he was. But by then I was pregnant with Benji. Zach was thrilled. But I was angry. I was so angry. Angry at my father for all the years I wasted—it doesn't matter. When I had Benji, I left him with Zach. The family had money. I knew he'd be taken care of." She tried twice before she got the rest out. "I might have changed my mind, but by then it was too late. My life was different. My priorities were different. I didn't know what his life had been like, bouncing around like that, until he came back and told me, and then it was too late. Why is it always too late?"

"Naomi, when did Benji call you to ask for your help covering up the shooting?"

She shook her head. "I saw him in the tent at the gun show, and I knew. I knew it was him before I saw Zach. I always thought it was silly, a mother knows, all of that. But I knew. He was mine; I knew it the minute I saw him."

"When did Benji—"

"I killed Landon and Zach."

"No," Hazard said. "You didn't."

"Naomi—"

"I killed them. I can provide a detailed account of my movements that night. I can give you details that only the killer would know."

"You're being an idiot," Hazard said. "His lawyer is scraping together a plea for him right now. He's already confessed. He's not waiting for you to swoop in and save him; he knows he's busted, and he's covering his own ass by throwing you under the bus."

Somers shook his head. "Naomi, work with us here. Benji's going to face two murder charges, and you're going to be an accessory. If you can fill in some information—"

"I killed Landon Maas and Zachary Renner."

"Why try to frame Carson? Normally, you're a pretty cool customer. Why not just walk away? There wasn't anything tying you to the scene." Silence distilled, drop by drop, until Somers said quietly, "I think you panicked. I think your kid was in trouble, and you couldn't think straight. You needed somebody else to take the fall; that's the only thing that mattered."

"It was a logical precaution." Her voice was stiff. "I thought I had been careful, but I couldn't be sure; I might have missed something. Better to point you toward Carson."

Hands on his knees, Somers sat still for a moment. "What about your mom? What about Cora and Evie?"

Naomi looked past him. The salt tracks had dried. A shadow of a bruise darkened her temple, something to remember Benji by.

"What about the money?" Hazard said. "Do you have it?"

Another tiny smile hooked the corner of her mouth, and she glanced at him. "Does it matter what I say?"

"It might, if you told the truth."

Something moved in her face, something so deep that Somers caught only a hint of it riffling the surface. And then her face was smooth, and she looked at him, and he had the sense that for the first time, they were seeing each other, and he felt naked and raw under that gaze.

"When he came back to me, it was a miracle. Someone had turned back the clock. I had a chance to make things right."

"You can't make things right," Hazard said. "You can only try to do better next time."

No matter what they tried, after that, she would say nothing. By the time they left, the light had fattened between the slats of the blinds, and the room had turned coppery and hot. Somers's head pounded. In the elevator, he rested against the wall of the car, the stainless steel cool beneath his hair.

"She can't explain away his fingerprints on that gun," Hazard said as they emerged into the warmth of the late afternoon. Warmer, really, than April should be. Somers massaged his forehead as Hazard continued, "As long as Benji and his lawyer keep going under the impression that they're fucked, you'll be able to wrap this up, and it won't matter what Naomi says."

"You know it's not going to be that simple."

Hazard sighed. One hand came to rest on Somers's nape. "No. Most likely not."

"Come on; we'll be late."

"John, you've got a million things to do. You're exhausted. If anything, you should be home in bed—"

Somers shook his head. He took Hazard's hand as they started across the parking lot. "What are we going to do if Ramona wants to place Colt with Tera?"

Hazard snorted.

"What's that supposed to mean?"

"I did some digging after I woke up this morning. A contact gave me Tera Larsen-Raven's Arkansas arrest record. If Ramona wants to push for placement with a relative, I hope she's ready to do some bedtime reading. And if Tera wants to cause me any problems, I've got her gun with her prints all over it; let her try."

"That was fast."

"It was one phone call." He came around the Mustang and opened Somers's door, and the gesture was old fashioned and courtly, and it made Somers smile. His smile got even bigger when Hazard's eyes got distant and he said, "Danny Lee is a fucking idiot if he thought that was going to work."

CHAPTER TWENTY-SEVEN

APRIL 18
SATURDAY
8:48 AM

HAZARD GOT HOME LATER than he expected; he'd woken before dawn so that Somers could drive him out to his mother's, but on the return trip, he'd gotten stuck behind a farmer moving his tractor, and then he'd gotten delayed again at a traffic light that had been out, and then again for some sort of emergency work on a water line. Today, he thought. Today of all fucking days.

He would have planned it better, of course, except the idea had come to him Friday night while he and Somers were talking through Colt's presents and plans for his birthday. The idea had been like a high-tension wire. He hadn't been able to sit down for an hour after it came to him. Somers had finally put him out in the hall and shut the bedroom door, and twenty minutes later, Colt had opened his door and said he couldn't sleep with Hazard, quote, *clomping the fuck around out here.*

As he stepped into the house, the sound of the usual last-minute panic greeted him, along with the smell of oatmeal and fried eggs.

"But I left it right here," Colt was saying, his voice tight. "I have to have my glove!"

"Bubs, I don't know what to tell you." That was Somers, and some of the good nature had been scraped off his voice. "I didn't move it. Evie didn't move it. Maybe you put it in your room?"

"No, I left it—" Dressed in his baseball uniform, Colt cut off when he stepped into the entry hall and saw Hazard. "Where have you been? We're going to be late. I thought you were getting donuts."

"Your glove is with the rest of your equipment," Hazard said. "In the garage. Where it belongs. Where we've discussed, at length, that it belongs. Even if, to borrow your words, you're 'just having a catch with Ash.'"

Colt spun on his heel. Then he spun back. "I told Ash we'd have donuts."

"Come here for a minute."

"Pops, Coach is going to skin my ass—"

"Language!"

"—if I'm late. We've got to go, and J-H is still getting Evie ready, and Ash already texted me twice asking why I'm not there yet, and he said if I don't get there, like, now, he's going to get put in charge of the pitching pocket, and—"

"Colt Kimble Ballantyne, come here for a minute. Please."

Something in the tone of Hazard's voice must have caught Colt's ear because the boy hesitated. He pulled up one sagging sock. Then he padded toward Hazard.

"Shoes," Hazard said.

"Where are we going?"

"To the driveway, but—"

"Then I don't need shoes."

Hazard would have argued the point, but Colt was already out the door, so he called toward the back of the house, "John?"

"You two go ahead. I'll finish getting Evie ready."

Hazard followed his son out of the house and almost collided with him when Colt came to a dead stop on the porch.

The truck was a Ford, an F-150, a brown that had probably been an aftermarket choice by Frank Hazard because it was cheap and did the job. The front fender was dinged up; the rear one was even worse. One of the headlight lenses was cracked, held together by what looked like superglue but otherwise, as far as Hazard could tell, functional. The passenger window only rolled down two inches, and the suspension sounded like an old man getting out of bed. But it was safe. Perfectly safe. This had been part of the conversation last night. As safe, anyway, as it could be to strap a teenager into two tons of metal and send him rocketing down a public road.

"That's Aileen's truck," Colt said.

"It was my dad's truck," Hazard said. The next part was the hardest because it was, in its own way, part of letting go. "And now it's yours. If you want it."

Colt turned to stare at him.

"I know it's not much to look at. It's twenty years old, it's got close to two hundred thousand miles on it, it's beat to hell on the outside, and the inside is even worse. If I'd known how much coffee that man spilled, I never would have felt bad about one fucking Dilly Bar when I was nine." Colt still hadn't said anything, so Hazard stumbled into the rest of it: "You're going to be sixteen in a few days, and you're becoming an adult. I don't want you hitchhiking anymore. You've got a job and school and baseball, and you shouldn't have to depend on me and John for rides. You need some independence—some, Colt. Some. Because it's your life, and this is the next step. And I know you and North were talking about cars, but I don't think we can afford to buy something right now, so if you can make this work for a while—"

"Are you serious? About giving it to me, I mean?"

"Yes. And yes, you will have to replace the headlight lens yourself, and yes, you will have to pass my personally designed driving test before you get the keys, and yes, you will be paying for your own insurance, and—"

Colt crashed into him, hugging him so tightly that Hazard heard himself make a noise similar to one he'd heard when Evie had been two and squeezed a cat too hard.

"Thank you," Colt said, his voice thick.

"You're welcome. I know it's not what you want, but—"

"Pops—" He pulled back, a huge smile unrolling, and wiped his face. "—it's the shit."

"Language."

"It's fire. It's dope. Oh my God, Ash is going to be so freaking jealous. Can we drive it to the fundraiser?"

"Yes, but—" He cut off at the sudden look of worry on Colt's face.

"I know Ramona said I can stay a few more months, but maybe I shouldn't take it if—" The boy looked at the truck, and his longing was almost physical.

"We'll figure it out. A little bit at a time, Colt. Don't worry about it right now."

He nodded.

"I said don't worry about it."

The grin was back, a little floppier this time.

"Go on," Hazard said and pushed him toward the door.

"J-H," Colt shouted, tearing into the house. "Did you see the truck?"

"It's a gift from John too," Hazard called after him. "Grab your gear and let's go!"

A moment later, Somers appeared in the doorway, massaging his side.

"He seems like he likes it," Hazard said, trying to keep his voice neutral.

Somers offered a mock scowl. "I think he broke a rib." Then he gave a lopsided smile. "He loves it, Ree. I'm pretty sure you just gave him the single best present of his entire life."

"He wants to drive it over to the fundraiser."

"Of course he does. Go on; Evie and I'll follow you over in case you break down."

"Ha ha."

That lopsided grin got bigger as Somers ducked back inside the house.

"I didn't realize I married a comedian."

"I love you," Somers sang back.

Before they could go, Colt had to take pictures. And then he had to text Ashley. And then he had to text Ashley some more. And then more pictures. Hazard heard the familiar chimes of FaceTime when he said, "I thought we were late."

Colt fixed him with a look of distilled disgust. Apparently, best gift of his life or not, teenage patience still had its limits.

"Bruh," Ashley was saying, "it's freaking sick."

"We're going to be late."

"Is that your dad? Hi, Mr. Hazard. Good morning."

"Be quiet, Ashley. You're making me late."

"Yes, sir, Mr. Hazard. It's nice talking to you."

"No, it isn't. And I don't want my son spending time with liars."

"Oh, no, I wasn't lying, Mr. Hazard, I meant, you know, in a general sense, like, it's a pleasure, because, um, you're Colt's dad, and you're so smart, and—"

"Why are you doing this to me?" Hazard whispered to Colt. "I got you a truck. Why are you torturing me?"

Colt wore a tiny smirk that looked a hell of a lot like Somers as he said, "Bruh, you're so weird," and disconnected the call. Then he looked at Hazard, and the smirk might have been invisible, but it was sure as fuck still there. "And technically, I'm torturing both of you."

In the truck, Hazard issued instructions. "Hands at nine and three."

"Oh my God," Colt mumbled as he strapped himself in.

"Nine," Hazard said with a hint of murder. "And three."

Colt grabbed the wheel and glared at him.

"Foot on the brake."

"I know, jeez. We do this every time."

"Foot on the brake."

Colt stomped on the brake. "You don't have to tell me!"

"Start her up." When Colt reached for the gear shift, Hazard barked, "Are you out of your mind? Mirrors!"

"I was going to look!"

"Really? Was that before or after you ran over a child?"

A rap at the window pulled Hazard's attention; out of the corner of his eye, though, he caught Colt shifting into reverse with something that bordered on rebellion.

Somers stood on the other side of the glass, Evie on his hip. Hazard rolled down the window. Then he was forcibly reminded that it wouldn't go lower than two inches.

Somers, God damn him, looked like he was trying not to smile. "How's it going?"

"Fine," Hazard said. "We don't need any help."

"Terrible," Colt said over him. "I want J-H to drive with me."

Somers was definitely trying not to smile.

"I go with Co," Evie announced.

Hitching Evie up, Somers shook his head. "Not today, baby. We're going to head over to the fundraiser. I assume that you'll be there in time for lunch."

"Hardy-har, John."

"Unless you're stuck on the side of the road, flagging down Triple A."

"Why does he always think he's funny?" Colt asked.

"It's a defect," Hazard said. "He doesn't have many, but Jesus Christ, the ones he does."

"All right," Somers said, grinning openly now. "Drive safe, boys."

Colt had the grace to wait until Somers had belted Evie into her car seat before easing his foot off the pedal.

"Are you out of your goddamn mind?" Hazard roared. "Mirrors!"

"Oh my God!" Colt screamed. "I already looked!"

That, of course, was exactly when Somers passed them. He was pretending not to notice as he backed out of the driveway. Hazard thought by the end of the day, one of them might be sleeping on the couch.

After that, though, it didn't take much longer to get to the school, where the baseball fundraiser—a carnival theme—was getting started. And by the time he started showing the truck off to his friends—and to Ash in particular—Colt had even forgotten that he wasn't talking to Hazard.

Hazard lingered for a while, watching, making sure every now and then to catch Ashley's eye. It was psych ops. A mindfuck. And it never hurt to rattle the boy a little extra, like a bonus.

"All right," Somers said, catching the sleeve of Hazard's tee and towing him away. "You're done."

"I'm making sure nothing happens to the truck."

"You're glaring at Ashley like you're about to pistol-whip him."

"That's actually not a bad idea. Let's see what he thinks."

Instead, though, Somers kept tugging, and Hazard followed him over to their friends, who had turned out to support Colt: Nico, in shorts that barely hit mid-thigh and a tank printed with rainbow-colored sunglasses and a rainbow mustache, all of which probably meant something to someone under thirty; Dulac, with a kind of white-knuckled smile, and Darnell smiling too but looking tired; Cora, in a summery dress, who kissed everyone's cheek but immediately separated herself off into a bubble with Nico; and Noah and Rebeca, their brood swarming toward the carnival midway, already screaming about the various forms of sugar they were going to ingest.

"They'll wear themselves out," Noah said with a bright grin.

"Or they'll get amped up on sugar and chew holes in your car door," Hazard suggested.

Noah turned a sour look on him, then a considering look at Rebeca, and then he swore under his breath and jogged off after the kids. "Roman, Rafe, no cotton candy!"

By any standard, it was a well put together carnival and — to judge by the amount of cash exchanging hands — fundraiser. They had the balloon pop, where Somers dropped twenty dollars trying to win Evie a stuffed panda. There was Gone Fishin', which Hazard objected to on grammatical grounds until Nico said loudly, "I need to take a walk," and he and Cora were both giggling as they left. At the bean bag toss, Darnell won a stuffed ocelot for Dulac, and it softened some of the sharp-edged control in the younger detective's face, and he kissed his boyfriend. After Somers dropped another twenty dollars, Darnell took pity on him and won a panda for Evie. Hazard started to say thank you, but when Somers turned around, there was a vividly familiar expression in his eyes, and Hazard remembered sometimes saying nothing was the best option. From a distance, Hazard spotted Theo with his arm around Auggie, the two of them talking to another gay couple that Hazard didn't recognize.

Along with the sickeningly sweet smell of cotton candy, the midway was alive with the aroma of hot dogs on a roller grill, nacho cheese dispensed out of an industrial-sized plastic bag, pretzels rotating inside their glass cases, the sizzle of funnel cake batter frying up, purportedly homemade lemonade sloshing in giant plastic pitchers.

When Colt and Ash found them, the boys were sweaty faced, and Colt started speaking before they even came to a stop.

"Pops, it's an emergency."

"You can say no, Mr. Hazard." Ashley shrank back when Hazard looked at him and mumbled, "If you want to, I mean."

"Coward," Colt muttered. More loudly, he said, "They won't let us do the dunk tank if we're under eighteen. It's not fair! Coach said that's not what they told him when he rented it. And Ash and I were supposed to do it, but now we can't, and Coach won't do it—"

"That's interesting," Hazard said. "It's his fundraiser. Why the hell not?"

"—and it's our game and now we're not going to raise any money for the team!"

"What about Theo? Hell, what about Auggie? What about any of your other teachers? People love to see an authority figure humiliated."

Colt looked at him.

Ashley, with what must have taken a lot of daring, looked at him.

Somers burst out laughing.

"No," Hazard said. "No goddamn way."

"I'll do it," Somers said. He plucked at the white tee he was wearing and grinned. "Although I might have dressed differently if I'd known I was going to do this."

"J-H, you are seriously the coolest, you are—"

But then Somers's phone rang, and he pulled it out, made a face, and answered it. After a moment, he said, "All right, but why can't Carmichael handle it?" He listened, covered the phone, and whispered, "I'm sorry, I'll be as fast as I can," before turning to stride away.

The weight of those gazes settled on Hazard again.

"What about Noah?" Hazard said. "Or Gray? Or Darnell?"

The disappointment was only a flicker before Colt turned and said, "Detective Dulac—"

"Oh for the love of God," Hazard said. "Fine."

"For real?"

"Can we just do this? Before I change my goddamn mind?"

Colt whooped, and he and Ashley took off at a run.

Hazard trailed them. Slowly. He did not miss the fact that his alleged friends were following him, laughing and talking behind his back. He was starting to get a firsthand understanding of why public executions had drawn such a crowd.

The dunk tank had a plastic base with a window set into it—the better, Hazard assumed, to enjoy the spectacle. Above, there was a cage of cyclone fencing and the seat. To the right of the tank itself, a sheet of vinyl marked with a bullseye waited for the first pitch.

A line was already starting to form. Word spread fast; Hazard heard his name more than once. Patrick Foley was arguing with Dulac about which one of them got to go first. Hazard glared at them as he heeled off his sneakers, and both men burst out laughing. Foley, the Irish fuck, had to lean over, hands on knees.

"I'm in jeans," Hazard growled as he took off his socks. "And I'm probably going to get some sort of fungal infection."

"Thank you, Pops. Thank you so, so much. I'll be right back. I've just got to get the balls."

"Um, me too—" Ashley tried before Hazard caught his arm.

When Colt was a safe distance away, Hazard said, "Ashley, I hope we're perfectly clear about what's going to happen when you take a turn."

Ashley didn't say anything. To be fair, it looked like he couldn't say anything. On a hike once, Hazard had stumbled onto a fawn, and the poor thing had stood there, trembling, staring at him.

"You've got a decent arm," Hazard continued in a whisper, "and decent speed. So it's going to be a real surprise when you miss that target by a mile, isn't it?"

Ashley offered a jerky nod. "Yes, Mr. Hazard."

Hazard watched him. Then he released him and said, "Go away now."

Colt came back with the balls. Dulac had apparently won the argument—Hazard heard the phrase "broke my nose" more than once—and was pretending to be a pitcher, winding up and then relaxing, a grin pasted across his freckled face. Hazard climbed onto the seat. At least, he thought with a kind of secondhand relief, he hadn't been stupid enough to wear a white t-shirt.

Studying the line—it had to be thirty people deep now, Hazard guessed—Colt said to himself, "We're going to make so much money."

"Fantastic," Hazard said. When Colt looked up, though, he managed a smile and said, "Let's get this over with."

Colt headed over to Dulac, already asking for money.

"Emery!"

The voice made Hazard wish, if only for a moment, to be dunked. He glanced over; Shaw and North were hurrying toward the tank.

"You're supposed to be back in St. Louis."

"What's-his-nuts," North jerked a thumb at Shaw, "wanted to spend a few days at Lake of the Ozarks."

"And anyway we couldn't go back to St. Louis—not without giving you my present." Shaw beamed up at Hazard. "I wrote a haiku. For your birthday. On account of our soulmatedness."

"Not a thing," North said, slouching against the tank.

"Is that a unicorn sodomizing an elephant?" Hazard asked.

Shaw glanced at his tee, which featured exactly what Hazard had described, and looked back up. "Yes, but don't worry; it's consensual."

"That wasn't what worried me," North muttered.

"Oh, you should always worry about consent. Even last night, when you'd had too many beers and it was more of a pushing rope kind of situation, only I, um, might have made it more of a pulling rope situation—"

"For fuck's sake," North said, covering his eyes. "Give him his fucking present so we can leave this shithole!"

"Shaw and Emery. That's five syllables."

North was making a strangled noise, and his face was surprisingly red.

"Shaw and Emery," Shaw began again, a little more hurriedly this time. "Two souls, one heart, one body—"

"One body?" Hazard asked. "What the fuck does that mean?"

"Yeah, Shaw, what the fuck?"

"Besties forever," Shaw finished. "It's ok if you don't have a present for me, Emery. I wasn't expecting one."

"I don't know why you would be. It's my fucking birthday. Next week."

"Oh, in lots of countries the person celebrating their birthdays gives gifts—"

"Pops!" Colt shouted.

Hazard looked forward in time to see the wicked grin on Dulac's face, and then the baseball cutting through the air to slam dead center into the bullseye.

He hit the water with a splash and went under.

Even under the water, the cheers and laughter reached him. He found the bottom, pushed up, and broke the surface.

"Ouch," North said as Hazard wiped his face. "That's super embarrassing."

"No, it's not embarrassing," Shaw said. "It's just, you know, emasculating. But he's going to cover it up with lots of swearing and talking about fuckery and horse sodomy and goat buggery and, I think maybe, um, something about the degeneration of the entire fucking human race."

"He's going to tell us this is the biggest fucking debacle of his life," North said. "Hold on; I'm going to ask Colt if we get a bulk discount on the pitches."

"No, no, no," Shaw said. "He's going to tell us this is a classic example of community formation through social castigation."

Blowing water out of his nose, Hazard let himself watch Colt for a moment. His son was laughing as Ashley said something in his ear. Then Hazard turned and climbed to the seat again. He looked down at North and Shaw. He wondered if Somers was right and if he actually liked these two. He wondered how long he'd been underwater, if maybe there'd been some brain damage.

"Maybe it's more like public-pool-diarrhea-level humiliation," North suggested.

"No, this is definitely a dark night of the soul," Shaw said. "I can see him transmogrifying. Kind of like when you watch the Power Rangers—" He cut off with a squawk, glaring at North as he rubbed his arm.

"Both of you fuckwits shut up," Hazard said. He looked through the cyclone fencing. On the other side, Colt was grinning, Ashley's arm around his shoulder, while Foley counted out bills. For a moment, the water in Hazard's lashes, the high April sun, the clarity of the spring day—they gave everything a prismatic softness. The moment cohered into the pinch of wet fabric under his arms, the smell of the water, the trampled grass, the tang of rust, the laughter—good-natured laughter, for the most part, and a lot of good-natured smiles. And, of course, his son, who was happy and safe and shining.

Hazard scowled down at the knuckleheads. "And for your information, this isn't any of those things." He readied himself for the next pitch. "This is called being a dad."

FINAL ORDERS

Keep reading for a sneak preview of *Final Orders,* the last book in Hazard and Somerset: Arrows in the Hand.

CHAPTER ONE
MAY 14
THURSDAY
7:06 PM

"I AM HERE today because I care about our children."

Hazard snorted. He glanced over, hoping for some shared sentiment, and then scowled. He whispered, "Put away your phone."

His foster-son, Colt, hunched over the device and tapped the screen faster.

"As an American, I believe in the rights and dignity of every citizen."

The words pulled Hazard's attention back up to the podium. The speaker was a woman in her early forties, trim but obviously fighting for it, hair expensively bleached so that she almost looked like a natural blonde. She was wearing a dark suit; Hazard guessed she had a closetful of them at home, all of them described on the tag with phrases like "flattering to the figure" and "bold lines" and "boardroom-ready." Her name was Joyce Sturgis, and she'd contoured on her makeup so thickly that it looked like a peel-away.

Most of the audience, though, was gazing at her with respect bordering on worship. A couple of middle-aged white ladies to Hazard's right were clutching hands with an intensity that suggested cliff diving or the plunge of a roller coaster. The man directly in front of Hazard — older, white, with thick graying fur on his arms — wore a t-shirt that showed American-flag-themed boxing gloves and the words USA — CONSECUTIVE CHAMPION — TWO WORLD WARS. A heavyset Asian man in a rumpled suit had propped a sign against his chest that said WOULD JESUS READ YOUR BOOK?; he'd been waving it before one of the police officers in attendance made him put it down.

The mere fact that they needed police in attendance at a school board meeting should have been ridiculous. Had been ridiculous, in fact, when

Hazard had been home, talking it over with his husband. But only a few months before, a group of concerned parents had stormed a school board meeting and sent the board running—literally. And now, glancing across the room toward his husband, John-Henry Somerset, in his police chief's uniform, Hazard didn't think it was quite so ridiculous. Somers's face was set in hard lines as he scanned the crowd. Opposite him, Sam Yarmark was in uniform and providing additional security at the event; maybe it was the fluorescent lighting, or maybe Somers was having an effect as Yarmark's mentor, but Hazard had to admit that Yarmark no longer looked like a little wiener in that uniform.

People filled the high school gymnasium—standing room only—and the number of bodies, combined with a warm May evening, meant that the room was simmering. The smell of sweat mixed with wax from the floorboards. The spaces between Joyce's words were filled with the hum of the old speaker system and the restless squeak of soles on wood.

"But as a Christian—" Joyce didn't exactly pause, but she timed her breath right, and it stirred a murmur of approval from the crowd. "—I believe in Jesus Christ, and my faith and my responsibility to our children mean I have to be here today, even if I wish I didn't. I thank God for my family, who have chosen to support me in spite of the opposition we're facing from certain members of our community."

That last jab was doubtless directed at Hazard and others who had come to speak against Joyce tonight. The group included a wide range of people from Wahredua's communities, among them several of Hazard's friends: Dulac, Somers's former partner, and his boyfriend Darnell; Noah and Rebeca, Hazard's neighbors; Nico, Hazard's onetime ex and current administrative assistant; and Cora, Somers's ex-wife. Dulac's current partner, Detective Yolanda Palomo, had joined them too, although she stood a few feet off, an invisible line separating her from the friends.

"My daughter is a student at Wahredua High," Joyce said, indicating a girl near the podium. The girl was stout, and she had black, frizzy hair and a bad complexion. She'd taken a page from her mother's book; her makeup aimed for *Vogue*, but it had ended up closer to *Mad Magazine*. "And my husband and I are alumni." Her husband, seated next to the girl, had to be in his mid-forties. His face had something too pathetic to be called a beard, and he'd squeezed himself into a turquoise knit polo and cargo shorts— Hazard assumed that since the Pope wasn't in attendance, pants were optional. "It makes me sad to see how far this institution has fallen. I'm ashamed of what these men and women are doing to our community."

"Bitch," Dulac whispered.

Hazard glanced over. Darnell had a hand on Dulac's arm, but the detective ignored him. Something—anger?—pinched his face, and his hands were curled into fists so tightly that his knuckles blanched. Hazard was about to ask Dulac to be quiet, but then harsh breathing made him turn his head. Nico was pushing back shaggy hair. Sweat dotted his forehead, and under the coppery tone to his skin, he looked pale.

"Are you—" Hazard started to ask.

Nico cut him off with a violent shake of his head.

"Come on," Cora whispered. "I need some air."

After a moment, Nico nodded, and he stumbled along with her as they forced a path through the crowd. Cora cast a backward glance, and Hazard didn't need a cue card to know what that meant; Nico's panic attacks had been getting worse.

"She's a fucking bitch," Dulac whispered a little more loudly. The two women clutching hands turned to glare at him, and Hazard glared back until they looked away.

"She's full of it," Noah whispered. "She's just doing this for the attention."

Rebeca made a disagreeing noise. "I got into that 'concerned parents' group for a few days." She drew the air quotes with her fingers. "The one they have on Facebook. That was how long it took them to drill down into my profile and realize I was a crazy liberal. I don't think they're doing it for the attention, at least, not all of them. Some of those people are legit nuts."

"And that's a public health expert's opinion," Noah said with a grin.

"We have to face an ugly truth," Joyce said, her voice booming over the speakers with new volume. "And the truth is that the adults we have entrusted our children to are peddling pornography."

A ripple went through the crowd, and in its wake, an ugly murmur. The man in the CONSECUTIVE CHAMPIONS shirt leaned forward like he was at a dog fight.

"They are using that pornography to warp our children's minds. They are using it to groom them for sexual predators."

"Fucking bullshit," Dulac muttered. His mouth was white on one side where he was biting it. "I fucking love that book."

"This man is part of that. He's preparing to deliver our children up to pedophiles."

Another ugly shiver went through the throng, and Hazard felt it, saw it, something stirring and stretching—this crowd was about to become a mob. When Joyce turned to point behind her, everyone followed her finger.

291

Theo Stratford was around Hazard's age. He was a good-looking man, built wide across the shoulders, with strawberry-blond hair tied up in a bun as a concession to the formality of the evening. He had a heavy beard, and it accented his jaw and his cheekbones. He kept his face neutral, but he had one hand wrapped around a hardback book, and even from across the room Hazard could see the strain there.

"Tonight, I'm calling for the school board to request Mr. Stratford's resignation."

"I thought it was doctor," Noah murmured.

"And because we're fortunate to have the chief of police here, I am also asking him to do his duty as a sworn officer and arrest Mr. Stratford for distributing pornography to minors and for distribution of child pornography."

Behind Theo, his partner, Auggie, had his arms folded across his chest. He was short, his skin light brown, his dark hair cut and styled so fashionably that Hazard had once caught Nico taking a picture of it. He was annoyingly attractive and seemed to know it, and it only made things worse that he was, apparently, a decent human being. At that moment, granted, a decent human being who looked like he was contemplating murder.

"Mrs. Sturgis—" That was one of the school board members—Hazard couldn't remember her name. "—you have one minute remaining."

"I know what he's going to say when he gets up here," Joyce told the crowd. "He's going to tell you that this book and other books like it are about showing tolerance for people who are different for us. I'm all for tolerance. But this book, and the other pornography he's distributing, has no place in the hands of innocent children, let alone in a classroom. What he's going to tell you, about social-emotional learning and about supporting students and about diversity, it's what experts call a 'false flag' event. Like school shootings—"

"Mrs. Sturgis," one of the board members said sharply.

"—these aren't real problems. They're things that people, bad people, are using to scare you into giving up your rights as Americans."

"That's time, Mrs. Sturgis," the woman said.

"They're trying to scare you into giving up your rights as parents, your Second Amendment rights—"

"Mrs. Sturgis, that's time. You need to cede the floor."

"They're trying to scare you into giving up your God."

"Mrs. Sturgis!" The female school board member gestured to Yarmark, who started making his way through the crowd.

"And they're trying to scare you into giving up your children! I ask that the school board do the right thing tonight and cancel this author's visit, remove her books from our school, and ensure that appropriate legal action is taken against the men and women who have been grooming our children for pedophiles and sex traffickers!"

"Your time is up—"

"Thank you and goodnight!"

When Joyce stepped away from the podium, cheers surged up. The two women to Hazard's right raised their joined hands, shaking them in the air. The CONSECUTIVE CHAMPIONS guy clapped his hands overhead. The man in the rumpled suit held up his sign again. WOULD JESUS READ YOUR BOOK? Christ, Hazard thought. He wasn't even sure Jesus would read the Bible anymore.

As Joyce and her family cleared the area around the podium, Theo stepped forward, and Auggie took one of the seats behind him.

"This is fucking bullshit," Dulac said to no one in particular. "I'm going to say—fuck me. Is that Carmichael? And Keller?"

Hazard followed his gaze. Joyce and her husband were talking to another man and woman now. The man was Dusty Keller, one of Somers's first hires—the man had lasted less than a year on the force because he was a complete and utter asshat. The woman was Miranda Carmichael, one of the department's four detectives. She was in a t-shirt that said SAVE OUR CHILDREN, and she was nodding aggressively with every word that Joyce said.

"You've got to be fucking kidding me," Hazard said. He caught Palomo's face in profile and turned; her expression was blank as she watched her colleague—and former colleague—across the room.

"I'm going to say something," Dulac repeated, and he began to press his way through the crowd toward the podium.

Theo adjusted the mic. The speakers shrilled and quieted. Then Theo said, "I understand that tonight is a difficult night for many people, myself included."

A few jeers went up. CONSECUTIVE CHAMPIONS shouted, "Sit down!"

"My name is Theo Stratford, and I'm an English teacher at Wahredua High School. I'm also the teacher who coordinated Ms. Loretta Ames's visit; she's the author of some of the books we're discussing." He held up the hardback as evidence, but it was too far away for Hazard to read the title. "I believe that many of you are here because you are worried about your children and you want to keep them safe. I understand that; I have a daughter. I'd do anything in the world to keep her safe." He paused. He swallowed. When he continued, his voice was thick. "But ignorance is not the same thing as safety. Every day, children in our school struggle with issues represented in the books that are being challenged tonight. Every day, children struggle to feel accepted for who they are, to feel loved, to feel safe. They live with hate and ridicule and abuse. They face it at home. They come to school and face it from peers. They face it from some of their teachers. And for those children, these books are a lifeline. I'd ask you to consider: how can we ask children not to read about the very things that they are experiencing in their daily lives?"

The silence had a vibration like a strummed chord falling still. Then Keller shouted, "Pervert!"

"One more outburst like that," the female school board member said, "and we'll clear the room. Dr. Stratford?"

He nodded. "I'd like to read to you some excerpts from assignments—work done by students after reading Ms. Ames's book. I know I don't have much time, but I hope this will give you a sense of how meaningful this book is for the children we all care about." Held up a piece of paper. "This is from a sophomore: 'I never knew anybody else felt the way I did.' This is from another sophomore: 'I cried all night because I did the same thing to my cousin when he came out and I wish I hadn't.' This is from a senior: 'I didn't know. I really didn't know.' This is from a junior: 'I'm straight, but I'm going to join the gay student thing because of this book. Thank you for having us read it.' From a senior: 'I wish I'd read this book four years ago. I wouldn't have tried to kill myself.'"

The gravity of the words settled over the crowd. A few of the men shifted their weight and looked around. The women next to Hazard released their joined hands.

Behind Theo, a boy started to pace. The movement drew Hazard's attention; it had a familiar quality—ragged speed, uneven timing, the boy with his shoulders tight and his arms stiff at his sides. It was the adolescent male gearing up for a fight.

"Shit," Hazard said. "Colt?"

Colt made a noise. He was still bent over his phone.

"Colt, right now."

"What, jeez? Ash is being such a dick. I know he has his phone, but he's taking forever to answer because he's with Gwen, and—"

"I don't care about Ash or his girlfriend. I need you to—"

"She's not his girlfriend!"

"Colt, focus. Who's that?"

"Huh? Oh. Evan. Uh, Pawloski. Why? Is he—oh, damn!"

Hazard looked up in time to see Evan charge the podium.

Auggie must have spotted him out of the corner of his eye because he let out a warning cry and got to his feet. He was too slow to intercept Evan, but the shout alerted Theo, who turned just in time to get punched in the face. Theo's head rocked back, and he stumbled, hip-checking the podium. It rocked, and his papers fluttered down to the floor.

Evan pressed his advantage, swinging again, but Theo managed to get clear of the next punch, and then Auggie was there, shoving Evan back. The boy was shouting—the exact words were garbled, but "fucking queer" came through, as did "faggot."

"Order! Order!" The school board member was slapping the table. "Police!"

Somers was trying to get through the crowd. Yarmark was closer, but the press of bodies slowed him.

Dulac, however, was right there. He broke free from the crowd and jogged toward Auggie and Evan, who were still struggling. His movement seemed to trigger the rest of the crowd into action; Joyce's husband ran toward the scrum, and Dusty Keller was only a step behind him.

"Motherfucker," Hazard said. "John and Yarmark can't handle this shit on their own." He pushed Colt toward Noah. "Get him out of here."

Noah gave a tight, worried nod, and he and Rebeca began shepherding Colt toward the door. The crowd was dissolving—some of the people streaming toward the doors, more of them pressing in toward the fight. Hazard moved with the current for the first few paces. Then he began to shove, clearing a path.

"Police," shouted a voice next to him. Palomo pushed a red-faced, middle-aged white guy out of her way. She had her badge thrust out in front of her, and that, combined with the vigorous use of elbows, cleared a path for her.

Hazard and Palomo reached the fray at the same time as a fresh cluster of men, all of them bearded, all of them in camo.

"Get out of here," Palomo shouted. "Police! You will be placed under arrest—"

"Shut up, you cunt dyke," one of them said, swinging a lazy backhand.

Palomo did something—Hazard wasn't sure exactly what—and a moment later the big, bearded guy's camo ass was flat on the floor. He had a moment to appreciate the sight of his husband, in uniform, charging into the melee, grabbing Joyce's husband by the polo and dragging him off Dulac.

Then one of the camo boys turned on Hazard and took a swing—it had a mile of windup behind it, giving Hazard plenty of time to get clear. He set his feet and popped the son of a bitch in the face.

The fight ended quickly after that, as more officers poured into the gym and as the men in the fight lost their enthusiasm.

Hazard didn't realize how wrong things had gone until it was too late.

"All of them," Joyce was shouting from the side of the gym, being held back by her daughter. "You have to arrest all of them! They were all fighting!"

Hazard caught his husband's eye; Somers's chest was rising and falling quickly, and a flush rode under his golden skin. Somers set his jaw and gave a tiny nod.

"Fuck me," Hazard said. "This is why I didn't join the fucking PTO."

Then he turned and let Yarmark cuff him.

Acknowledgments

My deepest thanks go out to the following people (in reverse alphabetical order):

Wendy Wickett, for helping me fix Shaw's bun and the ushanka, for (I love it) the never-drink-liquids policy, and for giving me Aileen as the merry widow.

Jo Wegstein, for the tremendous amount of information and feedback she provided about everything supervisory, for helping me with my science stuff (as always—in this case, biology and physics), and for her keen assessment of Palomo and Dulac and the inequities in the early drafts.

Mark Wallace, for being willing to tell me what wasn't working when I needed to hear it, for fixing (among other things) all my capitalization errors, and for making me think more carefully about North and Shaw and their role in this book.

Dianne Thies, for help with TV show titles (you're never overthinking!), for her eternal vigilance (and patience) with hyphens (clock radio – Hazard would be so proud!), for solving the case of the missing Yarmark, and, of course, for bringing me back to the locker room.

Tray Stephenson, for catching a multitude of editorial sins, for encouraging me to think about the scenes that humanize Hazard, and his kind words about Shaw even when Shaw seemed even more bizarre than usual.

Nichole Reeder, for helping me swap Cora for Naomi, for pointing out that nobody knew they were Carson's aunt and uncle, and for giving me Huggies for Huggy's (among so many other things).

Cheryl Oakley, for her rigorous questioning of the plot (especially the events at the end, which make this a much stronger book), for asking me to revisit Benji and Naomi's dynamics, and for so many little things (like Hazard and Somers walking down the highway!).

Steve Leonard, for keeping track of Hazard's gun, for setting up North and Shaw as babysitters (there's a spinoff for another day!), and for being honest with me when he thought Hazard was being made fun of and when he went over the top.

Austin Gwin, for reminding me that it's deputy (instead of officer), for catching my typos, and for the wonderful cracked headlight cover, which is so much better than what I had in the previous version.

About the Author

For advanced access, exclusive content, limited-time promotions, and insider information, please sign up for my mailing list at **www.gregoryashe.com**.

94502381R00173